The Rain It Never Stops

Rick Lee

2QT Limited (Publishing)

First Edition 2014

2QT Limited (Publishing)
Lancaster LA2 8RE
www.2qt.co.uk

The author has his own website www.rick-lee.co.uk

Cover design and setting by Dale Rennard

Cover Image supplied by Varun Suresh

Printed in Great Britain by Lightning Source UK Ltd

This is a work of fiction and any resemblance to any person living or dead is purely coincidental.
The place names mentioned are real but have no connection with the events in this book

A CIP catalogue record for this title will be available from the National Library
ISBN 978-1-910077-12-2

'In war, truth is the first casualty.'

Aeschylus

Other titles by Rick Lee

(excerpts from the following titles can be found at the end of the book)

Daughter of The Rose (ISBN 9781908098474)

A Ripple of Lies (ISBN 9781908098771)

Some Dance to Forget (ISBN ISBN 9781908098948)

The White Rook (release 2015)

to funnel her down a short gully to where other members of the team could collect her.

Two hours later both bodies were lying on the tables in the hut, where they'd stay until the pathologist arrived. The police were already there and a mortuary van had been summoned. The rescue team sorted their gear and retired to the hotel bar, where the police officers were waiting. It was quiet. Nods and handshakes were exchanged between those who knew each other, which was most of them. They'd all been here before and being locals they'd little to say at the best of times. Jim ordered a round of Jennings and went over to talk to Hilts. As he was the leader of the rescue team, he knew she'd want a first hand report before she'd do anything else. She shifted on her seat so he could slide in beside her.

'You okay?' she asked.

He nodded and took a long sup at his ale.

'Aye. T'feller probably lasted longer. Probably the shock and cold as much as anything – both his legs were broken – one above the knee. There's a fair draft up them crags – even on a still day like today. Lass mebbe only a few minutes – head wound.'

'Any ideas?' she asked.

He looked into her dark eyes and shrugged.

'Could've been anything. One stumbled or fell – the other tried to save them – tried to go down to them, impossible to say, really. Trouble is – Wainright says he could do it – and it is safe, but … it only takes a second…'

He shrugged his shoulders again.

She looked down at her glass of milk.

'There are no IDs on them but I've sent Frank out with the car keys. I think he's already done the pub car park, so he's probably gone down to the triangle now.'

Jim Souter looked towards the door, but there was no sign

CHAPTER 1

Saturday 15th May 1982. Wasdale, Lake District, Cumbria.

The second body was harder to reach. It was lower down, caught in a dark cleft. A raven barked at them from a rocky spur above the dead woman. Ron threw a rock at the bird. It lifted off into the updraft with a diffident croak. Jim took the strain as Ron leaned backward and abseiled down to the woman in two short and three long leaps.

Even though he knew she'd be dead, it still unnerved him to see her sightless eyes staring across at Black Sail. Her blonde hair straggled from underneath her woolly hat and her left leg dangled uselessly. There wasn't much blood; most of it seemed to be matted on her jumper beneath her chin. He suspected a head wound, which would have made it a quick death. He reached out and felt for a pulse, but her neck was cold and there was nothing there.

He quickly tied himself on and called up to Jim, who came down to join him. This was exactly the position they'd worked on together in one of their more recent training courses and they soon gathered her unhelpful limbs into a cat's cradle of ropes and lowered her down to a larger ledge. From there they were able

When the room is quiet

The daylight almost gone

It seems there's something I should know

Well, I ought to leave

But the rain it never stops

And I've no particular place to go

'Ghosts' by Japan, released March 1982

of Frank yet.

'Were they kitted out?' she asked, as she put her hand on his arm.

'Aye – no complaints – I'd say they were fairly experienced. Boots were well worn in and dubbined, rucksacks with waterproofs, a flask and remains of sandwiches, fleeces – all the gear. Just unlucky I'd say.'

Detective Sergeant Hilda 'Hilts' Crake took a long look at her old school friend. He'd never been one to express his emotions, but she knew he 'were a deep one'.

'Thanks Jim,' she said.

He downed the rest of his pint and got up.

'I'll do the report tonight. You'll have it in the morning.'

She nodded and he made his way back to the crowd at the bar. She followed him with her eyes. When he reached the team, Ron Kepple put his arm on his friend's shoulder and looked over at her. He winked. She shook her head, drank her milk, and made for the door.

Outside DC Frank Rainor was trudging back across to the car park.

'VW campervan down at the triangle, Sarge,' he said, holding out a handbag.

'Sally Wallace from Chorley – couldn't see anything for him,' he added.

Hilda took the bag, walked over to one of the picnic tables, and emptied the contents. As Frank had said there was a bank card and cheque book bearing the woman's name; the usual clutter of stuff women carry about. A photograph of a couple of kids – oh God! Some poor sod in Chorley wasn't going to have nice job. A scuffed up timetable – 3WP period one Thursday etcetera. Teacher? Lots of upset kids. She had a kind face lying on the table in the hut – but maybe death had disguised her –

9

perhaps she'd been like Miss French with her spine-tingling eyes and that wicked thin smile.

She went back in to find Jim.

He was zipping up his fleece and ready to go.

'There's nothing in the vehicle about the chap,' she said.

He shrugged and looked round at the rest of the team, who all turned to look at her.

'We checked around, Hilts, nothing in the rucksacks,' said Will Cawthorne. 'Too late to go back now, but I'll get up there first thing if you like, lass.'

She nodded.

'I'm sorry – but yes, if you would. I'm supposed to be in charge until we get a new Inspector.'

'Yer allus was in charge, Hilts,' said Ron with a sly smile.

The others grinned agreement and returned to their drinks.

Hilda 'Hilts' Crake continued to stare at Jim. Did he really think he'd get a second chance? Two-timing bastard! She gave him the ghost of a 'Miss French' smile and walked back out.

The mortuary van had arrived and the bodies were being carried out of the climbing hut. Five minutes later they were driving back down the valley, the last of a glorious sunset sinking into the sea ahead of them.

* * * * *

Back at the police station she got the address from the VW's registration number and rang Chorley police station. They said they'd get back to her as soon as they'd been round. Hilda made her and Frank a cup of tea and they sat and waited. She'd phoned her mother and told her the story, saying she hoped to be back by eight. Within the hour her worst fears had been confirmed. Husband and wife, John and Sally Wallace, both teachers, two teenage kids spending the weekend with their gran – well known, experienced walkers and visitors to the Lakes. Nightmare. She thanked the Chorley officer and said she'd provide whatever assistance they could their end and put the phone down. She sat at her desk for what seemed an age. Frank came in and sat with her. Neither of them could think of anything to say – so eventually they went home.

As her van slid through the farmyard gate, her mother appeared at the door. Hilda got out and looked up at the stars. Venus blinked at her and Hilda gave her a sigh. Her mother had gone back in leaving the door open. Hilda walked across and entered the warmth of the kitchen. A tear crept from the corner of her eye. She shut the door.

Up on Stirrup Crag the roosting crows huddled into the clefts. In the starlight a silver ring glinted where it had come to rest.

* * * * *

Fletcher had never been to Leicestershire before and so far he couldn't see any reason to come again. Okay – so the local team had uncovered a connection between two women who'd gone missing in 1976 and given them a name – Fern Robinson – who had been a nurse and had access to and experience in administering drugs. The first victim to go missing – Helen Courtney – fitted the 'wicked stepmother' syndrome and her daughter Dawn remembered this Fern Robinson as being very kind and supportive to her when she'd been taken to the children's home where she worked. Unfortunately the father had killed himself within a few months of his wife's disappearance and the police had initially jumped to the conclusion that he'd been the guilty party.

The connection they'd made was with the disappearance of a ward sister called Pauline Brett from the general hospital. Fern

Robinson had worked in the same ward and other colleagues remembered that they hadn't got on – but they'd also admitted that Brett 'had it coming' – as she was a 'hard faced bitch', who was horrible to the kids.

The problem was that Pauline Brett had gone missing many months after Helen Courtney – which didn't add up. And in any case neither of the two unidentified bodies found in the killer's burial space could provide sufficient evidence to make a match with either of these two women.

Fletcher stood at the bar in The White Hart in Ashby de la Zouch and waited for the barmaid to get round to him. She didn't seem in any hurry, but Fletcher was quite enjoying the view. She was older than he was but she was making a better effort at making the best of what she'd got – although he doubted whether that was her real hair colour. Eventually she looked his way and gave him a knowing smile.

'You like what you see, mister?' she said as she came over.

'Better than the telly,' he murmured.

She smirked and put her hand on the beer pump revealing an array of rings, including an extra-large sparkler on her third finger.

'What would you like?' she said with a raised eyebrow.

He looked into her mascara-laden eyes.

'Well my second choice would be two pints of Tiger, please.'

She gave him a serious frown and took one of the two glasses he'd brought back to the bar.

'So is she your first choice then?' she asked nodding towards the young woman sitting in the far corner, staring out of the window.

Fletcher turned to look at his sergeant, Irene Garner. Since last November in Whitby and the brief yet excessive fling with the giant fisherman, she'd exchanged the Goth-style long black

12

hair and matching black clothes for a softer look. A long hank of dark brown hair hid her face – although the other side out of view was shaved nearly to the skin. The shiny brown leather jacket hid a pale blue top and her legs were crossed inside a short skirt – but she'd kept the Doc Martins. Her hand reached up with the cigarette and remained poised as her gaze turned towards Fletcher – followed by a cursory glance at the barmaid and a look of world weary disdain.

Fletcher took the two drinks back over to their table and eased himself into the chair with his back to the watching barmaid. Irene looked over his shoulder and swung round on the bench so that she was facing him, she put her hand round the pint glass. Her brown eyes kept looking beyond him for a few seconds before meeting his. A smile appeared and faded away as she leant back and took a long drag on her cigarette. Whatever she'd thought of saying was deleted. The two of them sat in silence.

'So what do you reckon?'

'Your chances?'

He shook his head.

'Finding Fern Robinson?'

He nodded.

'Better than fucking that fat tart.'

He looked down at his beer.

'Humour me, you arrogant bitch.'

She gave him a sly smile.

'Well, if Fern Robinson is our killer, and that's a big if – there's no evidence, only circumstantial connections. Even if we had her sitting in an interview room down the local cop shop, what would she say?'

'That yes she did work with Pauline Brett and no they didn't get on; that she was a mean-faced cow and treated the children in her care very badly. That yes she knew about Helen Courtney, but never met her, and yes she was another woman who ill-treated her stepdaughter – it's all on record.'

'But that's it. We know when the Courtney woman was abducted and the records at the home say that Robinson had two days leave. We don't know where she went and we don't know where she was when the other woman went missing. The photo on her records is worse than useless and you didn't think she looked anything like what you saw. The only strong clue is that she's disappeared … but then people disappear for all sorts of reasons. It's all conjecture – unsubstantiated.'

Fletcher sighed and sipped at his beer.

'And in any case …' continued Irene, 'her other victims were from elsewhere. The only thing we can be reasonably certain of is that she lived in Whitley Bay with Anna Kerr for three years and that she probably killed Caroline Soulby because Soulby killed her dog.'

He nodded and nothing else needed saying. Half an hour later they were heading north.

* * * * *

As it was a pleasant afternoon and no one was expecting them back, Irene suggested they didn't bother with the motorway and drove them up through the Peak District. Neither of them said very much and Fletcher eventually dozed off.

He came to with a start as Irene cursed and the car jolted to a stop.

Rubbing his eyes he stared out of the window at the stationary line of traffic in front of them.

'Where are we?' he muttered.

Irene sighed and shook her head.

'We're nearly at the M62,' she answered, indicating the blue sign in the distance.

He switched on the radio just in time to catch the travel news. There had been an accident on the motorway ahead and their route west was closed. The two of them groaned with frustration, but it was then that Fletcher saw the other sign, which is when everything started to go wrong.

* * * * *

Monday 17th May. Keswick.

Fletcher had been living with Laura Walshaw for over two years now and during that time they'd only had one really bad row and that was right at the beginning of their relationship. It was Todmorden which caused the problems, he had thought to himself.

Saturday afternoon he'd told Irene to take the turning to avoid the traffic jam, up through Littleborough with the intention of just passing through Todmorden on the way towards Burnley and cutting across to the M6 and home. But of course it hadn't turned out like that.

Fletcher had been telling a less than interested Irene about his adventures in Todmorden, when he suddenly shouted for her to pull in. Despite the fact this didn't seem like a good place to stop, she bumped the car up onto the kerb and watched as Fletcher tumbled out and flung his arms round a large black guy who seemed at first inclined to thump him one, but then realising who it was, returned the greeting with an equally warm hug and a dance. People stopped and stared before grumbling their way past the two men making an exhibition of themselves, most jumping to the predictable conclusion that the two men must have started early on the Golden Best. This didn't prove to

15

be far from the truth as the two of them, accompanied by a surly Irene, got started shortly afterwards.

The next few hours passed in a drunken haze, although Irene wisely took her leave of them after the first pint, deciding she'd rather go home than put up with a load of blokey reminiscence stuff.

So it wasn't until late on Sunday that Fletcher arrived back in Penrith, with a stonking hangover, to find that although he couldn't remember much of what had happened the previous night, Laura's sister, Jessica, on the other hand, who still lived in Todmorden, had been absolutely clear that she'd seen him cavorting with that hippie artist Cassie in the Golden Lion and was sure they'd gone off together.

It didn't matter what Fletcher said or how he pleaded with Laura to believe that nothing had happened. He spent the night in the spare bedroom and Laura had gone to work before he got up. Feeling sorry for himself and not wanting to face a sarcastic Irene, he phoned in sick and went back to bed.

Looking back on this sequence of events months later he wondered at how this seemingly desultory and unintentional path took him to that moment later that Monday afternoon in the café on Keswick High Street.

He'd eventually dragged himself out of bed and decided to go for a drive. He'd put his walking boots in the car with the intention of going for a blow on the tops. He couldn't recall why he'd decided to head to Keswick, but found himself waiting for a mug of tea and a bacon sandwich as he stared out at the passing tourists thronging the pavement.

The waitress appeared by his side, sandwich and mug in hand. He looked up at her expectantly, but she was gazing open mouthed through the window.

'Oh my God,' she whispered.

He followed her gaze and saw that, beyond a car parked half onto the pavement; two men were making their way through the doors of the Building Society opposite.

'That man's got a gun,' she said, as the mug and his bacon sandwich crashed to the floor.

Fletcher frowned at her.

'Are you sure?' he asked.

Her hands to her mouth, she nodded.

Fletcher stood up and held her by the arm.

'Have you got a phone?' he asked.

She looked at him as though he'd appeared from nowhere, but nodded again.

'Phone 999 and tell them what's happening,' he said and seeing her backing away he made for the door.

At this point a van pulled up in front of the café and a man jumped out and went quickly to the back door. Fletcher stepped out onto the street as the man came towards him carrying a tray of bread and pastries. Fletcher let him pass and without saying a word got calmly into the van and, as the engine was still running, he put it into reverse, turning the wheel hard left, and then slammed his foot down onto the pedal. The vehicle lurched backwards across the road and rammed into the side of what Fletcher had correctly assessed to be the getaway vehicle – the fact that the driver was wearing a balaclava was a strong clue. As this was the driver's side the man was trapped and the escape vehicle rendered inoperable. In the short gap between people registering what had happened and the screaming starting, Fletcher got out of the van and jogged across the road. People scattered, dropping bags and bumping into each other, which covered his approach. He stopped outside the shop to the right of the Building Society and flattened himself against the wall. The shop had a display of Lake District paraphernalia cluttering the pavement. Fletcher selected the thickest and knobbliest of walking sticks from a large plant pot and took a quick look through the window to see how the raid was going.

All he could see was people either on the floor or kneeling down. He crept along beneath the window level. As he reached the door, it burst open and another balaclava clad man charged out hugging a heavy bag. He jumped down the steps but froze in his tracks as he tried to take in the confusing image of a bread van humping his getaway car and his driver desperately trying to fight his way out through the crumpled passenger door. As his brain finally concluded that flight was the best option he turned to his right and hurtled off along the pavement.

Before Fletcher could decide whether to give chase or not, the other robber came backwards out of the swing door with his shot gun pointing back into the building. The man could only have had the slightest impression of someone to his right as Fletcher moved towards him. The next he knew was the stinging pain in his right leg, and losing his balance, he tumbled backwards down the steps. The gun was knocked out of his hands and exploded. Those people still nearby threw themselves to the ground. The man rolled across the pavement and tried to regain his feet. Fletcher leapt down the steps and delivered a vicious kick to the man's ribs. The villain yelled in pain, but scrabbled towards the gun, which was only a couple of yards away. As he reached out towards it, Fletcher brought his boot down on the man's outstretched hand and felt the sickening crunch of bones. The man screamed in agony and writhed about until Fletcher kicked him hard in the ribs again and winded him. At this point the getaway driver managed to wriggle out onto the pavement and attempted to get to his feet, only to be felled by a blow to his knee from the red faced maniac who'd felled his mate. He collapsed onto the pavement and the two robbers rolled around like a couple of stranded eels.

It was only later that Fletcher learnt that the bag carrier had been rugby tackled by a Workington prop forward and so all three of the gang ended up in hospital.

After the local uniforms pitched up, he went back across the road and had a hastily supplied replacement bacon sandwich and two mugs of tea. Despite all the stares and handshaking and plaudits that followed, his only thought was whether this would have any effect on Laura's mood. It did – but only slightly.

* * * * *

Not only did Fletcher's heroics fail to impress Laura, his superiors were also far from pleased. It didn't seem to matter that he'd stopped an armed robbery or that no member of the public was harmed, or that the three men had confessed to four other robberies. The Assistant Chief Constable informed him that numerous bystanders had thought that Fletcher's methods were excessively violent and whilst sympathising with those who thought Fletcher deserved a medal rather than a bollocking, he also pointed out that the destruction of two vehicles, which didn't belong to either of the two drivers, was unacceptable. Oddly enough Fletcher was too weary to argue and surprised his superiors with uncharacteristically apologetic responses. Anyway the bottom line was that an Inspector was needed for a potential murder inquiry in Whitehaven and that was where he was told to go. Laura suggested it might be a good idea for them to spend time apart for a while and so off he went.

On Tuesday morning when he set off, he decided to go over via Buttermere, but he shouldn't have bothered. It rained all the way and he didn't see a thing. It was still raining when he got to Whitehaven, and long afterwards when he recalled his experiences there he would declare that it had rained all the time. He never said it to anyone, but he knew that his old English teacher, Miss Elphinstone, would have pointed out that the rain was merely mirroring his own troubles, which continued to worsen every day.

He might have suspected this from his first meeting with Sergeant Hilda Crake, who made it clear from the outset that he wasn't welcome and that he knew nowt about folk in Cumberland. She was also reeling from the discovery of another body on her patch, the third in a week and already there seemed to be some disturbing connections between them.

* * * * *

At first there seemed little to link the climbing accident in Wasdale and the death of an old lady in her home outside Ennerdale Bridge. The pathologist was inclined to think that she'd probably had a heart attack. She was found lying in her bed, there was the possibility that she had been disturbed by a burglar, although apart from the fact the place had been ransacked, most of the items a burglar might have been after – the TV and some rather expensive jewellery – were untouched.

Her body wasn't found until the Monday after the Wasdale incident. It would have been later still if the postman hadn't knocked for her to sign for a parcel.

Hilda stood in the low-ceilinged room and surveyed the damage.

'What do you think, George?' she asked.

PC George Kelton had about a year to go and wasn't given to jumping to conclusions or saying much at the best of times. He filled the doorway and blocked out a considerable amount of the watery light trying to access the main room. He pursed his lips.

'Burglary gone wrong, lass,' he offered in his gruff voice. 'Mebbe she surprised them and they panicked. Ran away wi nowt. I expect it'll be some of them lads from Workington, who've been causing us trouble for months now. It'll not be long before we have a name or two.'

Hilda was inclined to agree with him, but something nagged at her that it was more complicated than that. The photographer had plenty of pictures of the room and its contents, so she bent down to study the contents of the drawer of an old writing desk. She knew from a brief glance at the books scattered all over the floor that this was an educated woman. She wasn't a local. Her immediate neighbours had told them she'd moved in about five years ago. They thought she'd been a professor at a University, but weren't sure which one. In a pile of letters which Hilda began to sift through she saw many of them included the coat of arms and title of Bristol University, so she made a note of one of the telephone numbers to follow up later.

'You know anything else about her, George?' she asked.

He shook his head.

'This place used to belong to the Skinners,' he said. 'When the old man died the young uns sold it off. No use to them. They've got a couple of farms up on the Solway.'

Hilda sighed. Normally if it was someone local he'd have been able to give her chapter and verse, genealogy going back a century or two.

It wasn't until later that further information began to justify her doubts.

* * * * *

The first thing was when the pathologist rang her up and told her to come over. Gilbert Eskett was another local not inclined to make hasty decisions.

'My first impression is that she had a heart attack and that hasn't changed,' he began.

21

Hilda knew better than to rush him. He pulled back the sheet to reveal the woman's body. Hilda had seen plenty of dead animals in her time and quite a few deceased old folk, so she wasn't particularly upset by the sight of another. Eskett pointed at the woman's right arm above the elbow.

Hilda looked at him.

'An injection?' she asked.

Eskett nodded.

'At first I wasn't particularly surprised by that, but now I've had the toxicology results back from the lab I'm not so sure.'

She waited.

'Digoxin,' he said. 'Just a bit too much.'

Hilda had a friend whose little boy had Digoxin regularly for a heart condition, so she knew how tiny the doses were he had to take.

'Given the condition of her heart it wouldn't surprise me if you find some in the house,' Eskett added, 'but I would be surprised if someone who took this drug regularly would be likely to overdose herself. She'd know very well how dangerous that would be.'

Hilda could see he hadn't finished.

'Unless of course it was deliberate.'

'You mean suicide … or murder?'

'Your job not mine I think,' he added and pulled the sheet back over the dead woman.

Hilda grunted and thanked him.

Back at the station there was a message from the old lady's nephew. He was on his way from London and was expecting to be here by late afternoon.

There was not much else Hilda could do but wait, but her sense of foreboding was increasing.

Mark Hardwicke was not the easiest person for Hilda Crake to take too. He was about her age, but there the similarities disappeared. He looked like he ought to be at a race meeting: camel hair coat, brogues, and when he took the trilby off, blonde floppy hair. Hilda didn't know many public school boys, but he looked like one to her. She'd gone to pick him up from the station and was surprised that the first conversation didn't include the usual weary comment about how far it was to West Cumbria, although he did comment on how lovely it looked in the spring sunlight.

For someone who had come to identify a body he didn't seem too grief-stricken, but this was to be one of many misunderstandings between them. They went straight to the mortuary and he stood quietly for a good few minutes before saying softly that this was his Aunt Sybil.

As they came out of the front door, she asked him what he was going to do next.

'Go to the house,' he answered.

She hesitated. Should she tell him what she'd just found out? Better wait until help arrived.

'I'm afraid that won't be possible today, sir. We're still examining it, although we will want you to take a look as soon as the scene of crime officers are finished. It'll be tomorrow morning I think.'

He looked at her with a steady gaze.

'Of course, Sergeant, I understand.'

'Do you want me to find you a room?' she asked.

He smiled again.

'No. I'm sure the hotel will be able to put me up.'

She nodded her understanding and watched him walk away.

Why hadn't he brought any luggage?

* * * * *

On arrival back at the station, the next piece of news was both shocking and embarrassing. On her desk was a message asking her to ring the coroner's office. She was put straight through to Alf Metcalfe himself.

'I can only assume, Sergeant Crake, that you've not read the pathologist's report on the Wasdale deaths?' he asked in his typically brusque manner.

Hilda could see the document half way down the pile on her desk and reached for it now.

'No I haven't, sir,' she said, as she saw to her horror the red comments near the top of the first sheet.

'Well, I think you should,' he added.

The red script could have been written in blood given the consequences that would surely follow such an oversight.

'I have it now, sir. I understand. Please accept my apologies. I will get back to you as soon as I can.'

She put the phone down and stared at the writing, muttering the words to herself as though she was hoping it might change their meaning.

'Cause of death was the neck injuries to both victims. All other injuries are post mortem.'

She ran her hand across her hair and pulled at her shirt collar. She could feel the redness burning on her face. She put her hand over her mouth as she read on.

'Time of death: Saturday morning – earlier than previously estimated.'

She stopped and looked out of the window.

'Oh God,' she said.

She read it all again and sighed. What was she to do?

'Hang on a minute,' she said to the room. 'Bloody pathologist! Why didn't he ring me?'

She picked up the phone, thought better of it and went downstairs to the main office.

'Wilma?' she asked the woman at the communications desk.

'Yeh, Sarge,' said the station's happiest person, but the smile faded as she took in the tenor of Hilda's voice and the redness of her face.

'Did the pathologist at Lancaster General try to get in touch with me?' asked Hilda.

Wilma frowned and reached for her record book.

'Er ... I don't think so, Sarge. Let me check.'

It didn't take long, but by the time Wilma confirmed her initial response, Hilda Crake was bursting for a fight. She turned on her heel and stormed out, leaving the room in a worried silence.

When she'd finished shouting at the arrogant bastard and he'd reluctantly agreed that he should have contacted her, she calmed down and asked him to get himself over to Whitehaven tomorrow at the latest and then she put the phone down. She took a deep breath and picked it up again. During the next ten minutes she called all the relevant people and ordered or persuaded them to attend a meeting the following morning, as well as ringing the ACC's office and putting him in the picture. She didn't like the tone of the silence at his end, but understood full well the likely outcome of her incompetence.

The following morning she assembled the team and told the pathologist to explain his findings. The officers listened in silence. When he had finished and asked if there were any questions, the looks were as sullen as gravestones.

Hilda made him suffer by summarising what he'd just said.

'So, what we originally thought was a tragic accident is now almost certainly a murder investigation unless the victims broke their own necks and then threw themselves off.'

The poor man nodded.

'And worse still, if they were already dead at eight o'clock in the morning they must have got up at five to be at the top of Stirrup Crag, which doesn't fit with what the guy says who collects the payments at the campsite, who saw the Wallace's camper van arrive at ten.'

'What have you got to say, Roy?' she asked, turning to the officer in charge of the SOCO team.

He coughed and cleared his throat.

'We'll have to go back up to the scene, Sergeant, but we've had another look at the clothes and equipment and ... to be honest, we should have picked up on the lack of wear and tear. Even if they'd taken the easiest route to the top of the crag, their boots and leggings would have shown more signs of mud and scuffing. We'd assumed the fact their uneaten sandwiches and the full flask wasn't significant, but of course now it would seem to make sense.'

She nodded and turned to another colleague.

'Okay Jenny, tell us the really bad news.'

DC Jenny Outhwaite ignored the looks from the assembled men and told them.

'The Wallaces were staying at Endmoor cottage, which belonged to Sybil Hardwicke. It's only about half a mile away from her house, but they're not visible from each other. Apparently they were frequent visitors there and often came with their children and other members of the family and friends. They were well known at the local pub and had a meal there Friday night. No one remembers seeing them set off Saturday morning, but a neighbour thinks the camper van had gone by nine o'clock when he went for the papers. There's no sign of a struggle at the cottage, and their clothes and belongings were still there.'

Hilda nodded at Gilbert Eskett and he told them about what might have happened to Sybil Hardwicke.

Hilda thanked him and waited for the hubbub to die down.

'Obviously we are not going to be left alone to deal with this. I understand that a DI from Penrith will arrive later this morning and there'll be other top brass turning up any minute. Until then we've to carry on with our enquiries at the cottage and in Wasdale. Frank, you get out there and talk to the campsite guy right now. Nothing to the press or anyone else, alright?'

She paused and looked at them all.

'I dare say I'm in for a bollocking and the rest of you shouldn't expect much sympathy from whoever turns up, so I suggest you give your boots a polish and straighten your ties. Just remember we know this place better than anyone else and we know all the usual suspects, so let's see if we can clear up our own mess before someone else does.'

Without waiting for any comments she walked out of the silent room.

When she'd gone there was a collective exhaling of breath followed by some quiet muttering as they went about their various jobs. They all now shared some of Hilda Crake's foreboding, understanding that such coincidences could only mean a lot more trouble than a climbing accident and an old lady having a heart attack.

CHAPTER 2

But Hilda Crake wasn't the first West Cumbrian to set eyes on Mick Fletcher.

As he took the right turn signposted to Whitehaven the rain was making a special effort to make him welcome by putting on a momentous display of road bouncing and gutter flooding. He slowed down and peered through the windscreen. Despite the horrendous downpour he could make out two dark clad figures trudging along the pavement. He pulled in and wound down the window an inch.

A hopeful boyish face appeared.

'Can you give us a lift, mister?' the lad asked, the rain dripping off his bum-fluff chin.

'Get in,' said Fletcher.

The door slammed shut and the car filled with that warm wet dog smell that Fletcher hated.

'Where are you going?' he asked.

'Anywhere in town,' said the boy.

'How about the police station?'

The boy gave an uneasy laugh. The girl with him stayed silent.

'Yeh. Yeh, that's great. Thanks.'

Fletcher glanced into the mirror to see a dark eye staring at him through a hank of bedraggled hair. The girl wasn't smiling.

He concentrated on the road.

'What are doing out in this?' he enquired.

The eye was still staring at him, but it was the boy who leant over and replied.

'It's my car,' he said. 'It just stopped. Don't know what's wrong with it.'

Fletcher nodded his understanding. The girl had moved and now he couldn't see her.

He thought of his stepdaughter Grace and smiled to himself. She was older now, but she'd no doubt done things like this.

He followed the boy's directions until he saw the police station and pulled in to the kerb. The boy thanked him and the two of them got out. He watched as they ran and jumped between the puddles. Putting the car in gear again he headed for the car park sign and in through the gate. He didn't remember smiling much after that for some time. What a mess.

* * * * *

Hilda had only been told his name, which meant nothing to her; even though it was less than a year ago that he'd been causing havoc just down the road in Barrow. Her first impression was to wonder how he got away with such a dishevelled appearance. Crumpled leather jacket, wet ruffled hair, lopsided grin and blue eyes.

He held out his hand.

'DI Mick Fletcher,' he said. 'Does it always rain like this here?'

She nodded and took his hand. It was cold.

'DS Crake, sir. Yes, especially for off-comers,' she added without a smile.

'No change there then,' he said as he walked over to the

boards she'd had hastily assembled earlier that morning. She reflected that he wouldn't get much information from them at the moment and sure enough his glance was cursory. He looked back at her.

'Any chance of a coffee?'

She nodded at a young officer near the door, who sloped out without a word.

'So what do you know?' he asked.

It was at this moment that Hilda realised she was wrong. His eyes weren't both blue. One was sea green. Startled by this, she was momentarily speechless. He seemed oblivious to her discomfort and stared relentlessly at her.

'Er ...' she stuttered, angry with herself for this lack of composure. 'Two bodies found on the fells in Wasdale. At first we thought it was an accident, but now it's got a whole lot more complicated. One old lady who probably died of a heart attack – maybe after disturbing a burglar ... sir.'

Both eyes continued to examine her. She looked away. PC Thompson reappeared with a mug of coffee, which he set down on the table in front of the Inspector and retreated from the room, but not before he'd clocked the frosty atmosphere.

'But?' asked Fletcher, as he sipped at the coffee.

She glared at him.

'But our local doctor has his doubts about that as well.'

He sighed. Why did people always get defensive when he was around? He hadn't asked for this. He hadn't shouted at anyone yet. Least of all this young DS. She was no Irene Garner that was for certain. She looked like she'd be happier in uniform. Dark suit, white shirt, black hair tied back from her face. Taller than him by an inch or two and well built. Farmer's daughter no doubt, although she had the look of that woman in Rochdale. What was her name? Diamond. Frances Diamond. But she'd had green eyes. This woman's eyes were dark, nearly black.

'Doubts?' he asked.

Hilda explained about the Digoxin. He considered this and then asked about the 'accident'. She explained what had happened and admitted her oversight. He didn't even raise an eyebrow, even though she knew her face was burning with shame.

'Um,' he said. 'Crake? Is that a local name?'

She frowned. 'Yes. My family have been here for generations. Used to be miners. That's all gone now. So we had to find something else to do ... sir.'

He grinned inwardly at the prickliness of this.

'I see.' He paused. 'First name?'

She frowned again.

'Hilda,' she said.

'Okay if I call you that?' he asked.

She shrugged her shoulders.

'It'll help later on,' he said. 'If I'm cross with you, it'll be Crake. Just so you'll know. But in front of your colleagues it'll be Sergeant. Okay?'

She shrugged her shoulders again.

He stood up.

'So let's bugger off before the brass arrives, eh. I find they always slow me down, don't you?'

She stared at him.

'Where do you want to go?' she asked.

'Which happened first?'

'The burglary I think.'

'Let's go then,' he said and headed for the door.

They'd only made it to the first corner when a large black Rover passed them.

Fletcher gave a dry laugh without any humour.

'That'll be them,' he murmured as he accelerated his car up

the hill.

* * * * *

Sybil Hardwicke's house wasn't grand but it was old. In this grey washed out day it looked very much at home in its surroundings: a weatherworn, traditional stone building nestling back into its own geology, which now supported a garden full of rhododendrons and a flourishing vegetable patch. Either this old lady had been a fit one or she'd had some help. A stand of firs protected it from the northwest winds, and there was a selection of other local trees providing plenty of seclusion.

Inside Fletcher picked his way through the chaos, bending down occasionally to look at a book or a photograph.

'Is this her?' he asked, holding up a picture of a group of people smiling at the camera.

Hilda came over and looked at it.

'The one in the middle,' she confirmed.

'Fairly recent?'

'I think so. Although we could ask her nephew.'

'Does he live here as well?'

'No. He lives down south somewhere. He arrived yesterday. Staying at the hotel in the village I think. Shall I go and see if he's there?'

'Good idea. Will the bar be open yet?'

She gave him a stern look.

'I expect so.'

They went in the car, even though it was only half a mile or so. They would have been soaked otherwise. Fletcher was glad he'd thrown all his walking gear in the boot. He was going to need it.

Mark Hardwicke was in the bar reading the Telegraph.

Hilda introduced them and got the drinks in. Fletcher

was not surprised to see she was on the orange juice, although Hardwicke had asked for a gin and tonic. Fletcher decided this was the place to stay. He sent Hilda off to sort it out, which only took her a couple of minutes, so Fletcher settled back in the armchair and listened to Mark Hardwicke's story.

His aunt had been a Professor of History at Bristol for nearly thirty years and had specialised in the study of the Roman occupation of Britain. She'd retired two years ago, but had owned the house for about five years, although she'd been coming to the area for a lot longer.

'On the trail of the Headless Dalmatian,' he added with a hearty laugh.

Fletcher and Hilda looked at each other in puzzlement.

'No. Not a dog, a Roman legionnaire. A mercenary. Posted from the sunny Adriatic to this midge infested backwater at the edge of the Empire.'

'Headless?' asked Fletcher.

'Yes. Apparently it was the indigenous population's way with their enemies. I understand they believed that you wouldn't be able to pass over to the next world without your head.' He laughed again.

'And why was she so interested in tracing this particular individual? I would have thought that was nigh on impossible?' mused Fletcher.

'Pretty well, I'd have thought so as well. But academics … they get a bee in their bonnet, and… ' he shrugged and drained his glass.

'Another?' he asked.

Fletcher nodded and offered his glass. Hilda shook her head. Hardwicke sauntered off towards the bar.

'Will I have to find my own way home … sir?' she asked.

Fletcher smiled.

'I get the impression you wouldn't approve of me driving you, would you?'

She glared at him.

'It's not just because I'm on duty. I don't drink anyway.'

Fletcher's smile faded.

'Good for you,' he said quietly.

Hardwicke returned with the drinks and settled back in his chair.

'It would be useful if you could accompany us back to the house in a bit,' said Fletcher. 'You might see something we have missed or you think significant.'

Hardwicke nodded agreement.

'Fine. Soon as you're ready.'

Fletcher's eyes narrowed.

'Just out of interest, sir, what do you do for a living?'

'Me? Oh, nothing so important or useful, I'm afraid. I buy and sell things. Mostly junk to people who don't know any better. Bit of a black sheep. Big disappointment to the family … except Aunt Sybil, of course.'

'Why was that?'

'Not sure really, I suppose I might have been the son she never had. She never married, but that's not to say she was a dry old spinster. Had quite a few flings in her time. Some quite famous people as well.'

He looked away.

Fletcher looked across at Hilda who returned his look without showing any emotion. Neither of them spoke.

Hardwicke didn't say anything for a few moments and Fletcher could tell there was something else. Something he was wondering whether he should share.

Instead he drained his glass and stood up.

'Can we go now?' he asked.

Fletcher agreed and the three of them walked back to the house as the rain had temporarily stopped.

As he stepped into the kitchen, Hardwicke stopped and took a deep breath.

'Did she suffer?' he asked.

Hilda looked at Fletcher and he nodded.

'I doubt it, sir,' she said. 'We think she had a heart attack. It could even have been in her sleep. She was found in her bed.'

Hardwicke turned to look at the sergeant, as if to check she was speaking the truth. She held his look.

'She's had a dickey heart for years,' he said. 'She took pills every day.'

'Yes sir. We found them and they were examined by the pathologist.'

He continued to look at her.

'But you're still not convinced, are you?' he asked.

Hilda shook her head.

'Was she a nervous person?' interrupted Fletcher.

Hardwicke looked at him and laughed.

'Certainly not,' he said. 'Hard as nails. Most of her students were terrified of her. Just ask John Wallace.'

Hilda's head jerked back towards him.

'John Wallace?'

Hardwicke looked at her with surprise.

'Yes. He was one of her students way back. He and Sally often rent the cottage along the lane. Aunt Sybil owned it along with all the land around here.'

Hilda looked at Fletcher, who frowned back at her.

'So you don't know about the accident?' Hilda asked.

'Accident?' asked Hardwicke.

Hilda looked at Fletcher hard, willing him to take over or help her out. He didn't.

She cleared her throat.

'Both Wallace and his wife died in a climbing accident last Saturday.'

Hardwicke was stunned.

'You mean?'

'I'm afraid so, sir, up on Stirrup Crag on Yewbarrow. We're not sure, but we think one of them fell and the other tried to save them.'

Hardwicke's eyes filled up.

'Both of them?'

'Yes, sir,' she said.

He walked back outside. The other two stayed where they were.

'You could have helped me out there, sir.'

Fletcher shook his head.

'You did fine, Hilda.'

Before she could say anything else, Hardwicke walked back into the room.

'So do you think the two things are connected?' he asked.

He looked from one to the other, but Hilda was determined not to say any more.

'We're still investigating, sir,' said Fletcher.

Hardwicke looked at them both, but said nothing.

'Perhaps you could take a look round now and see if there is anything that you think is missing or significant. It would be a great help,' Fletcher suggested.

For a second or two he thought Hardwicke might walk out, but then his shoulders relaxed and he looked around.

They followed him from room to room, watching him as he wandered here and there, occasionally bending down to pick something up or examine it where it lay. He spent some time looking through her jewellery collection and seemed to be looking for something specific, but only had one comment to make.

'Take it from me, Inspector. This is something I do know about. There's nothing really valuable here and in any case she was always giving stuff away. All you had to do was say you liked something and she'd insist you had it.'

Hilda showed him the photo they'd looked at earlier and he confirmed that the one in the middle was his aunt, although he wasn't sure who all the other people were.

'Lots of people came here you know,' he said, 'students, ex-students, colleagues, friends and family. She was always happy to share this place. She had a wide range of friendships, many of whom weren't academics or anything to do with her work.'

He pointed to a photograph on the wall.

'Look. That's her at Menwith Hill.'

Fletcher peered at the picture. Anti-nuclear protestors standing near a fence with banners and flags.

'She was at Greenham Common as well. She's been arrested on numerous occasions. I'm surprised you didn't know that?'

Hilda looked at her shoes. How bad was this going to get? When she looked up again she was relieved to see that Fletcher wasn't looking at her.

'So apart from the authorities, is there anyone else who might have meant her any harm?'

Hardwicke stood looking at another photograph. He shook his head, his eyes brimming with tears. He brushed them away fiercely.

'No. No one. Everyone loved and respected her. I don't think she had an enemy in the world,' he said, but realising what he'd previously declared, he continued, 'apart from the current government, of course.'

Neither Fletcher nor Hilda could think of anything to say

after that. They followed him out into the garden and waited as he walked round it. When he got back he'd regained some of his composure. They went back to the hotel.

Back in the bar he ordered a double whisky and Fletcher agreed to join him. Hilda said she thought she had better get back to the station to see if their superiors were still there. But before she went she had one last query.

'There was no sign of a forced entry, sir?'

Hardwicke gave a wry smile.

'She never locked a door in her life, sergeant. She said she thought it was unwelcoming. I dare say other people tried to tell her, like I did, that there were people in the world who took a different view to that, but she wouldn't listen.'

Hilda gave Fletcher one last look and then went off to phone for someone to come and get her.

Ten minutes later a car arrived. She introduced Frank to them. He passed on the message from the ACC; he was expecting a report from the Inspector by the end of the day. Fletcher made a face and told them to bugger off. So they did.

Even by Fletcher's standard he found Mark Hardwicke a difficult man to keep up with and by the next morning he couldn't remember much that he might have learnt, other than that the man was a born storyteller. It was nearly eleven o'clock when he got to the station and he wasn't pleased to see the milling crowd of extra reinforcements cluttering up every room and corridor. He made his way up the stairs to the incident room, but stopped at the top when he could hear the voice of Chief Superintendent Conley. He stood against the wall and gathered his breath. He'd only met the man once before and it hadn't changed his opinion of the majority of superior officers he'd met in his career. He listened as the pompous fart went on about hard slog and covering all the bases and other such bollocks, wondering if he could sneak back down and escape, when suddenly his ears pricked up.

'...introduce Detective Sergeant Simpson from the Rochdale Police who will explain some of the new developments in automated record keeping being introduced in his area.'

Fletcher nearly laughed out loud, but managed to control himself long enough to hear that his erstwhile colleague wasn't receiving any better a welcome from the locals than he had yesterday. He waited until the poor sod was into his second paragraph, before making his entrance. It didn't go down well.

Chief Superintendent Conroy was most displeased by Fletcher's cynicism and said so when he'd collared him after Simpson had finished. Fletcher dealt with him in his usual 'shut up and wait until he's finished, agree with everything he's said and then ignore it' routine.

Afterwards he took Simpson out for a coffee in a café on the promenade, or rather what was claiming to be the barrier built to prevent the sea encroaching onto the land. On this day it wasn't doing too well. The two of them had to dodge the waves that were storming the barricades and as it was still raining as if the sky had been irrevocably punctured, they were both dripping wet as Simpson forced the door shut behind them.

'Bloody hell, Fletch, what the fuck are we doing here?' he yelled.

Fletcher laughed and ordered two double espressos.

'Well, I don't know what you've done wrong this time, but it was going to Todmorden again did for me.'

'Running with them wild women, eh,' laughed Simpson.

'I may as well have done as far as Laura is concerned,' said Fletcher, with a grim face.

'How is the lovely Laura?'

'Still as lovely, but I've been exiled until further notice.'

'Uhuh,' said Simpson, suddenly a bit quiet.

'So what are you up to apart from trying to con us all with your computer wizardry?'

'Ay, there's the rub.' Simpson said.

'Shakespeare?'

'You're not the only one with a grammar school education, you know.'

'Ah. Not a lot of people know that.'

'No … and I'm getting seriously pissed off with the way anything new or inventive is treated with such suspicion.'

'Like this record keeping stuff you're on about?' Fletcher asked.

'Yeh. If we'd had even what I can do now three years ago we'd have caught the Ripper in a tenth of the time.'

'You mean only three victims?'

'Maybe, but certainly before he was anywhere near double figures.'

'So … what are you going to do?'

'Oz.'

'You've said that before.'

'Yeh but this time I mean it. Put my application in two months ago. Just have to pass the physical and I'm off.'

Fletcher laughed, but Simpson's face told a different story.

They went back to the station to find that his system had already come up with some very interesting information.

'Look at this, sir,' said Hilda, as she handed him a printout.

It took Fletcher some time to understand what he was looking at, but eventually he realised that it was Sybil Amelia Hardwicke's police record, which was impressive for a self-declared pacifist. The offences went back to before the war. She'd been arrested eighteen times, mainly for public order offences connected with various protest groups, including CND and left wing political activities. She'd been a member of the Communist Party until the late sixties and had been a regular at Greenham and other nuclear sites. This wasn't all. There was a long list of people who had similar records, including some MPs, who she'd been seen with or known to have collaborated with.

He looked at DS Simpson.

'I see what you mean, Sergeant.'

Simpson gave him a wry smile.

'I wasn't expecting to convert a barbarian like you, sir.'

Fletcher shot him a bright-eyed look.

'Am I in your bloody machine?'

Simpson gave him a big grin.

'Of course you are,' he said.

'And what about a certain young lady who has been running rings round me these last three years?'

Simpson went quiet.

'No. Not yet. But give it time, maybe a couple of years. When we start putting in other stuff: linking up with Somerset House, Social Services, health records and the rest...'

Fletcher shuddered at the thought of such an Orwellian future heading his way.

'So intuition and instincts consigned to the dustbin of history, eh?'

Simpson didn't laugh at this.

'Some things can't be replaced,' he said. 'I don't think they'll be retiring you just yet.'

Fletcher gave this some thought and scribbled on a piece of paper.

'So put these into your machine and see what it comes up with.'

Simpson looked at the list that Fletcher had just composed. He shook his head.

'You're ahead of the game as usual,' he murmured. 'I daren't even put some of these names in, and you know why. There's some stuff that's never going into any computer.'

Fletcher gave him a strange look.

'Okay. Well. See if you can make some connections between Professor Hardwicke and the two other victims.'

'Already done that,' smirked Simpson.

'So what are the connections?'

Simpson went over to his desk, picked up another sheet, and brought it to Fletcher.

'As I think you already know, John and Sally Wallace were students of hers, but so was another local. A woman called Alice Gill, who coincidentally died in a climbing accident in Wasdale two years ago.'

'And we know what we both think about coincidences don't we?' said Fletcher.

* * * * *

Hilda was surprised later on when Fletcher had asked to be taken to the scene of the 'accident' the following day. When she looked out the window at the grey sky, he'd told her that he wasn't going to be put off by a bit of rain and that he'd brought his gear.

She had to work hard to keep up with him as they set off up the east side of Yewbarrow; she realised he was no novice. She'd invited Jim Souter to tag along and she could tell he was impressed with the Inspector's gear. The two of them had quickly fallen into men talk and so she concentrated on keeping up with them.

As it turned out the sky had cleared a bit, and, although the way up was very boggy in places, they were soon at Dore Head looking down the scree into Mosedale. Above them, and to the right, the dark cliffs of Stirrup Crag loomed into the cloud.

'How far up were they?' asked Fletcher.

'Near the top,' said Jim.

He looked up at the mist as it floated about.

'Better put the anoraks back on, it looks nothing, but it'll soak you to the skin in minutes.'

The two police officers did as they were told.

'You been up there before?' asked Jim.

'No,' said Fletcher. 'But it's been on my list for some time.'

'Ay well,' said Jim. 'As I said to Hilts, Wainwright says it's doable and so it is … if you take your time. But those two aren't its only victims, so watch your step. It'll be greasy up there.'

Without another word he set off up the slope. Fletcher followed and Hilda brought up the rear. She had been here numerous times with her father, but that was long ago.

It didn't take them long, but as Jim had suspected the last thirty feet or so they were in thick mist. They reached the cairn and stopped to take a breather.

Jim pointed back down.

'I think they fell from about ten feet back down. If it had been like this it would have been easy to miss the track, but on that day it was clear. No way could they have got lost and I understand they were experienced fell walkers and had been this route before, so…'

'So?' repeated Fletcher.

'Well,' said Jim. 'They could have wanted to take a look down the crags. Take a photograph. One of them might have gone to pose at the edge. It would make an impressive picture with the Gable in the background … I don't know.'

Fletcher stared into the swirling mist and tried to imagine the view.

'One thing I am sure about though,' added Jim. 'It'd be bloody difficult to carry them up here. It took eight of us to get them down.'

Fletcher looked at Hilda.

'Not me, sir. Not a word,' she said looking daggers at her friend.

'No, Inspector, it wasn't Hilts, but word travels fast among us locals.'

Fletcher looked from one to the other.

'So how would anyone have got them up here?'

Jim looked at Hilda and then back to Fletcher.

'Only one way I can think off.'

Fletcher waited.

'Helicopter. It's the only answer.'

Fletcher waited to see if there was anymore.

Jim sighed.

'I've checked with the Coast Guard. Obviously it wasn't them, but they have to receive notice and give advice on all journeys which include crossing the fells.'

'And?' Fletcher asked, his patience wearing thin.

'No such flights recorded for that day at all.'

Fletcher shook his head and the wet dripped down his face.

'Just spit it out man,' he ordered, as he wiped his chin.

Jim Souter wasn't used to taking orders, but answered anyway.

'There were numerous flights to and from the power station, but all of them followed the coast. Mostly to the south.'

'So could they have been diverted?'

Jim nodded.

'Unlikely, but yes, it's possible.'

Fletcher stared at the cliff edge which hovered in and out of the clouds. He turned and looked over Jim's shoulder.

'Is it safe enough to take in the summit?' he asked.

Jim grinned.

'I thought you'd never ask.'

An hour and half later they were sitting outside the Wasdale Head Inn looking up at the flanks of the Yewbarrow. The rain clouds had gone and the river splashed and gurgled in its runnels. Only the top of the Scafell massif was still hiding under a few thinning wisps.

'Amazing,' said Fletcher.

Jim nodded and took a long pull on his Jennings.

'So tell me,' asked Fletcher. 'Who uses the helicopters from the power station?'

Jim shrugged and looked across at Hilda.

'Your call I think, Hilts,' he said.

Fletcher looked at her.

'We can ask, sir. But in my limited experience you'll need higher authority than yourself. I can tell you there's plenty of top nobs get flown in and out of there. Haven't the patience or time to come the scenic route like you … sir.'

He frowned at her. What did she mean by that?

'Top nobs?'

'BNFL Senior executives, MPs, ministers, business guests, foreign dignitaries, security people, those sorts of nobs. They're a law unto themselves – anything to do with Windscale,' she said, with a weary contempt.

'I see,' said Fletcher and his mind drifted back to the last days he had spent in Barrow, when 'nobs' like that made everything disappear. He thought about what Simpson had said yesterday. His heart sank.

He looked from one to the other. Neither of them flinched. He could tell they'd given up. Whatever had happened up there on the crags, they knew it would never be explained and they accepted it – were used to it. Why was that? Was it the same with the Professor?

He looked away. Beyond the church he could see the vast flank of Lingmell. He'd come down that way with Grace and her boyfriend one late afternoon earlier this year. There had been snow on the Pike and the three of them had spent a happy hour practising their ice axe arrest in one of the gullies. He heard Hilda and Jim get up without a word and make their way back into the bar. Hilts? What was that about? Apart from her sullenness he couldn't see any other resemblance to Steve McQueen in 'The Great Escape'.

He sat there for some time watching the clouds race across the fell sides and began to compose a plan.

* * * * *

Stanley Gill got back into his mud-caked Landrover and drove slowly back down the lake. The bright period wasn't going to last. He could see the heavy bank of clouds heading their way up from the estuary.

He'd not sat too close, but had caught a few words. Both Jim and Hilda had nodded at him at some point, but he was fairly sure the off-comer hadn't registered him. He'd found out that he was called Fletcher, which was bad enough – although he doubted he had any local connection – but his gran would have been very wary of a man with 'tyan ees'.

He drove home. There was nothing he could do. It would only get him into trouble. But as he drove past the lane leading to Sybil Hardwicke's place he slowed down. He knew there would be the possibility that some constable would be dozing in a car somewhere, but he had an excuse. He'd left some of his tools in her shed and the lawn would need mowing soon or it'd get out of hand. He sat there with the engine running. Her nephew was staying at the Inn. He put the Landrover into reverse and went back down into the village.

Half an hour later he pulled up outside the cottage. As he got out a young lad stepped out from behind the shed. Gill recognised him. It was young Colin, Ken Hodgson's lad. Still got some growing to do, but looking good in that uniform. Well, better than he ever looked on't farm.

'Oh, it's you,' he said.

'Ay lad. I was thinking the lawn needed seeing to.'

Colin Hodgson looked doubtful.

'I don't know about that, Mr Gill. I'll have to contact the station, talk to Sergeant Crake.'

'Well git on wi it then. I haven't all day and it'll be raining agin soon.'

Before the young constable could do anything, Gill set off towards the shed.

Inside the house Mark Hardwicke stood and watched this exchange through the window with a sad smile on his lips. He said nothing. Leave it to the locals seemed the best way forward. What he needed to look for could wait.

Colin Hodgson cursed and rushed back to his car.

Two minutes later he was back and shouting at Stanley Gill, as he dragged the mower out of the barn.

'Hey. Mr Gill,' shouted Colin. 'T'Sergeant says to wait on; she'll be here in half an hour.'

Gill looked at the young lad and then at Mark, who held up his hands in mock defeat and strolled off towards the terrace. Gill snorted and went back into the shed. Colin went over to see what Gill was doing, to find him searching through a stack of tools.

'I'm not sure,' began Colin.

'Ah, hush, lad,' said Gill 'They didn't come in here, did they?'

Colin Hodgson wasn't that ambitious, but even to his mind that sounded like Gill might know more than he was letting on.

'Them?' he asked.

Gill turned towards him and shielded his eyes against the sun, which had blinked out from behind a cloud.

'What?' he asked.

'You said 'them'. Did you see them?'

'See them. How could I? You think I was up in the middle of the night down here.'

Colin's heart began to beat faster. Was this how detectives caught murderers out?

'Who said it was the middle of the night?' he asked.

'Yer daft aypeth,' laughed Gill. 'It weren't me killed Sybil Hardwicke. Everyone knows it happened during the night. They'd hardly try to rob her while she was out and about. Anyone could have turned up.'

Colin thought hard. No one had said it was a murder enquiry yet. There'd been nothing in the papers. But he knew very well how word got about around here. He thought he'd better leave it alone. Let that new Inspector sort it out.

'Ay well. I think you should leave everything as it is for now,' he said.

Gill stood and looked at him, before spitting on the gravel.

'Gittin above tha station, young man. I'll be having words wi yer dad.'

He glared at the young constable, but the lad stood his ground.

Gill snorted again and stomped off. Colin heard the engine burst into life and with a crunch of gravel the old Landrover disappeared down the lane.

He looked across towards where the old lady's nephew had appeared at the door and walked over towards him. The man looked at him.

'I'm just going to sit here, if that's alright, Constable,' he said. 'It'll be raining soon enough and I'll be away back to the bar.'

Colin nodded at him and walked slowly back down to his car, wondering whether he should share his suspicions with Sergeant Crake.

Ten minutes later when she arrived he'd decided that he'd be better off keeping his ideas to himself. He was even more certain when he saw that she was accompanied by the Inspector.

'Afternoon, Colin,' said Hilda, but she was looking over towards the man sitting on the terrace. The Inspector stood beside her and looked at Colin.

'Sorry, Sarge, but Mr Gill has gone.'

'What did he want?' she asked.

'He said he ought to mow the lawn.'

'But you were suspicious?' asked Fletcher.

Colin looked at the Inspector as he felt the heat spread up his neck.

'Er … yes … no … sir,' he stuttered.

Fletcher laughed.

'Well, which is it, Constable?'

Colin looked at Hilda who offered little encouragement.

'Well, sir, it was just something he said.'

Fletcher waited. He knew that waiting was far more productive than asking more questions.

'He said 'they' and that they 'would have come during the night' … sir.'

Fletcher continued to stare.

'It's a fair supposition, Constable, and given the jungle drum system round here, I dare say he's not the only one to have heard that information.'

Colin looked at Hilda, but again there was no help.

'But you think something else?'

49

Colin was sweating. He feared for anyone caught in that gaze who'd done something really wrong.

'It's nothing, sir. Just something about the way he said 'them'.

'Like he'd seen them?'

'Uhuh.'

Fletcher didn't move.

'How long have you been a police officer, Colin?' he asked.

'Nearly two years now, sir.'

'Any arrests yet.'

'A few drunk and disorderlies, sir, and a couple of drunk driving.'

Fletcher waited again.

Hilda coughed. 'You did a good job on that arson case before Christmas, Colin. If it wasn't for you we'd have missed the stuff in the garage.'

Fletcher smiled.

'What was it, Constable? Just a feeling?'

Colin looked at his shoes.

'I suppose so, sir.'

'And Mr Gill?'

Colin looked back at him.

'Where's he live?'

Colin pointed up the fell side.

'Yon farm, sir.'

Fletcher looked where he was pointing.

'Ah,' he said. 'Let's go, shall we.'

Hilda nodded across at Mark Hardwicke.

Fletcher looked back at the house.

'If he knows there's something hidden, he only has to wait another day or two. Besides I don't think there is anything there. My instinct tells me this is one canny lady and any secrets will be far better hidden.'

Hilda couldn't argue with his thinking even though she didn't think Colin needed to come with them. Still, she wasn't in charge was she?

The three of them set off in the two cars. Fletcher's instinct told him what this young man seemed to have a nose for too. Coincidences. He'd seen the man at the Wasdale Head Inn and asked Hilda who he was. Stanley Gill — whose wife Alice had been one of Sybil Hardwicke's students, the one who had died in Piers Ghyll. Too many Gills, getting fishy, thought Fletcher, as their cars wound up the heavily rutted lane to the old farmhouse.

CHAPTER 3

Stanley Gill saw them coming. He looked at the photograph on the sideboard and went to put the kettle on.

He was standing in the doorway as the two cars slewed through the mud into his yard.

The three of them got out and headed towards him. He noticed with some pleasure that none of them had thought to put their boots on. But he didn't smile.

'Afternoon, Stanley,' said Hilda as she came up the steps.

'Tea?' he said.

'Ay,' she said.

He stepped back into the kitchen and over to the kettle, which was starting to whistle.

'You'll be Inspector Fletcher from Penrith?' he asked as he poured the water into a large blue teapot.

'Be more honest if I was to say Streatham,' said Fletcher.

Gill gave him a wry smile.

'Must have done summat really bad to end up in this neck o'the woods,' he said as he carried the teapot to the table.

'You've no idea how bad,' said Fletcher. 'Just assume the worst and double it.'

'Should I be scared?'

'Only if you've done something as bad.'

Gill gestured to them all to take a seat. Hilda declined and leant back against the sink. Colin sat down but looked as though he'd rather be back to the car, although he was taking in everything that happened.

Gill leant back in his chair.

'Well. Ethics?'

'Never set foot in the place,' said Fletcher.

Gill smiled. 'Very good, Inspector, not often you meet a policeman with a sense of humour.'

'Don't get too comfortable, it's only the gallows variety.'

'Well, as I was saying, to answer your rhetorical question about bad deeds. I think my Alice would say it depended on whether you feared Caesar or God.'

'Or neither?' asked Fletcher, wondering how they'd become involved in such an intellectual debate so quickly in this white-washed kitchen, halfway up the fell-side in the rain.

'Indeed,' acknowledged Gill. 'Which be thee?'

'A policeman's lot is not a happy one,' said Fletcher and paused. 'But in my experience one has more to fear from Caesar than God. He's more to lose and there are enemies always close to hand, so he tends to have about him men with a lean and hungry look.'

Gill smiled. 'Touché, Inspector. But I think you'll find my appearance is more to do with fighting wi tups and running on't fells rather than any desire to look the part.'

They both paused to regard the other.

Gill sighed and poured the tea. No one spoke again until they'd all had a drink. Round One was over. Round Two was even cagier.

'It's one of the things I miss, now Alice is gone,' he said.

'Alice?' asked Fletcher with a straight face.

'Don't make out you haven't been told,' said Gill, his eyes full of anger.

'I'd rather hear your version,' said Fletcher.

Gill glared at him. Fletcher stared back. Impasse.

Gill drank his tea with one gulp and with another quick glance at the photograph on the sideboard, began a clipped account of his wife's death.

'She died in Piers Ghyll. Do you know it?'

'I know where it is, I've walked up the path beside it, but I'm not a good enough climber to try and go up it.'

'She was,' said Gill. 'More than good enough.'

Fletcher waited as the man composed himself by staring through the window.

'She'd got it into her head that she'd find what she and Sybil Hardwicke had been looking for these last twenty years.'

'A headless Dalmatian?' asked Fletcher.

Gill gave him a stony look.

'Hardly. Ravens and worms can make a dead sheep disappear in a few weeks, so the chances of finding the remains of a Roman soldier from the second century AD are pretty remote.'

'So what, then?'

'I'm not sure. They played their cards close them two. Necessary if you didn't want the mockery of the ignorant.'

'Come on, you must have some idea,' said Fletcher.

Gill sighed again.

'I'm no historian. Can't read Latin for a start, but Sybil could and so could Alice.'

'Read what?' asked Fletcher.

'Classical history: Pliny, Julius Caesar, Agricola, Tacitus, Juvenal and other less well known writers. There's a room full of them upstairs if your Latin's up to it.'

Fletcher shook his head, remembering the stultifying

atmosphere of 'Herman' Goring's lessons.

'I know it's something to do with a Celtic tribe called the Rheged, who were allies of the Selgovae, a much bigger tribe in southern Scotland, and that it's also connected to the search for the lost legion, but it's the stuff of legends. I don't know that they were close, although that day Alice had that determined, bright eyed look she had when she was excited about something. I had work at a cottage over in Ennerdale, so I didn't go with her...'

He stopped. They waited. He got up and walked to the door. Silence filled the room. A dog started barking.

He spoke quietly without looking round.

'By nine o'clock I was getting a bit worried. She was with another very experienced climber, Gavin Wesker, and they both had head-torches in their rucksacks, but still I had a strange feeling. By the time I got there they'd brought her down. They took me to see her at the hut in Wasdale. I don't remember much after that. You're just as well asking Hilts. I wasn't really with it for a few months. Still...' His voice petered out.

The three officers waited, not catching each other's eye. Hilda took a handkerchief from her trouser pocket and wiped her nose. Fletcher stared at the photograph. Alice had short blonde hair and a slight smile. He realised that it was Great Gable in the background.

He stood up and went to take a closer look.

'It was taken from the top of Lingmell,' said Gill.

Fletcher turned to look at him.

'I thought so,' he said. 'I recognised the cairn.'

Gill came over to where he was standing and picked up the photograph.

'Ironic, I suppose. Must be right above where she fell.'

'Just a coincidence?' offered Fletcher.

'I don't believe in them ... and I don't think you do either,' said Gill as he put the photograph back in its place.

'No you're right, I don't. So what were you doing in Wasdale earlier?'

'Checking you out, seeing if you're doing a proper job.'

'Well that's very flattering. How are we doing?'

Gill looked across at Hilda.

'I'm assuming you know about Sally and John Wallace?'

Fletcher nodded.

'I saw a helicopter that day. I was up in the Forest, heading towards Seatallan; me and Fred Pearson were checking on his lambs. It came north east from Seascale to start with. We thought it might be the Coast Guard taking someone to Carlisle, but it wasn't them. It turned southeast as it crossed overhead and although we couldn't see it we could tell it was over Wasdale for a while and then we couldn't hear it any more. It was a day later I heard about the accident, so I assumed it had been called out to go to them. But now I know it was Jim Souter and his lads who got them off.'

Fletcher nodded his understanding.

'And now I know it was the same day Sybil was … died.'

Fletcher looked back across at Hilda.

'That's as succinct a summary as any of us could give, wouldn't you say Hilda?'

She nodded at them both.

'So Mr Gill, what's our next move do you think?'

Gill gathered up the cups and took them to the sink.

'I don't know, but like we said earlier, three deaths on the same day is a big coincidence. I don't know what the pathologists have found out, but I'd be surprised if all three of those deaths were accidental or natural.'

Fletcher could see he was close to wrapping up the discussion.

'Does that mean you know something we don't, Mr Gill?'

'I doubt it,' he replied. 'But you could find out who Sybil's visitor was the day before she was found dead. Black car arrived about this time in the afternoon and was still there when I went down to the pub, but it was gone when I came out.'

'Do you mean the hotel in the village?' asked Fletcher.

'Yeh, so you can check the times. Not sure how late it was – bit of a lock-in Thursday nights.'

He walked back across the room and opened a drawer in the sideboard and took out a scrap of paper and offered it to Fletcher.

'I remembered the number, so I wrote it down. Something about the car made me suspicious.'

Fletcher looked at the number.

'Thanks,' he said.

They looked at each other. Fletcher put out his hand and Gill took it in his. A big strong hand used to grabbing tups and wrestling them to the ground. Fletcher thought he'd rather have him on his side than the other.

'Is there anything else?' he asked.

'Ay. For what it's worth I don't believe Alice had an 'accident' either … but I can't prove that … yet. And before you ask me or Hilts, it wasn't Gavin. I'd trust him with my life on a climb and so would Alice. He's in bits, hasn't been near a rock-face since it happened. '

Fletcher's head was buzzing with further questions, but he needed time to think, so he shook the big hand and they left.

* * * * *

Back at the station Frank Rainor came to report that the man at the campsite couldn't say whether the man he saw getting out of the camper van was the same as the one in the photograph Frank showed him, but he hadn't see a woman. However, he did think there was another couple getting their boots on in the car park at the same time.

Fletcher shook his head.

'Can you follow that up, Frank?' he asked. The big man nodded and lumbered out.

Fletcher looked at Hilda.

'Well Hilda, what next?'

'I can try and get you into the power station if you want.'

'Is there no other way to find out? If it is someone from there then asking to see their records would be a bit of a giveaway.'

Hilda gave him a long stare.

'There is someone, a pilot. Normally he'd want top level documentation, but I'm assuming you don't want to go that route either, sir?'

Fletcher shook his head and grinned.

'Never been my chosen route, Hilda. See what you can do.'

She gave him another severe look.

'It'll be the weekend before I can see him.'

'Well that's when it'll have to be then.'

Fletcher looked at his watch.

'Tell you what, Hilda. Let's knock off early. I need to catch up with the junk-dealer. Couple of ideas I've got going round in my head … and in my experience lock-ins provide a very good source of local knowledge.'

Hilda nearly laughed at this pathetic excuse, but kept her counsel.

Fletcher headed for the door, but turned round with a smile on his face.

'Just one more question, Hilda. Why 'Hilts'? Can't imagine you're a baseball fan?'

She was unable to suppress a smile herself.

'Maybe I will see you in the bar tonight, sir. See if you can work it out.'

Fletcher laughed.

'Great. See you later.'

He was gone. Hilda continued to stare after him for a few minutes. She knew he was more determined than he let on. She'd had a phone call from a friend who worked with him in Barrow and he'd told her some alarming stories. How Fletcher had beaten up some young thug and set fire to a local gangster's night club, none of which was on the record. Anyway, she wasn't above bending the rules herself and agreeing to talk to Geoff Windsor was definitely out of order. But he owed her and she fancied him, so there, Inspector Clever Dick!

With that decided she abandoned the paperwork teetering off every side of her desk and headed for home, although the smile on her face was still there when her mother looked up from feeding the chickens to see her eldest daughter arriving home early for a change.

* * * * *

Fletcher found Mark Hardwicke in his aunt's study. He was standing by the bookshelves, taking one down after another and sighing with frustration.

'Are you looking for something in particular?' asked Fletcher.

He watched as Hardwicke flinched and then quickly composed himself. He didn't turn round.

'Guilty as charged, Inspector – except it's nothing in particular as you suggest. More hopeful than that.'

'Hopeful?'

Hardwicke turned towards him.

'As in 'hoping to come across a first edition' type of searching.'

Fletcher stared at him.

'Are there going to be other beneficiaries?' he asked.

Hardwicke shook his head and headed for the drinks cabinet, which Fletcher had been surprised to see earlier. There was plenty to choose from considering his aunt had been in her late sixties.

'Well. I dare say she will have left some of it to worthy causes. Amnesty. CND etcetera, but otherwise there's only me.'

'So what's the rush?'

'Oh, you know the usual. Bad habits. Large men in ill-fitting suits with limited compassion.'

Fletcher nodded.

'I see.'

He watched as Hardwicke poured himself a large scotch.

'You want one, Inspector?'

Before Fletcher could reply a shadow passed the window and a portly figure appeared in the doorway. As recognition dawned on Fletcher's face, Roger Aughton stepped over the threshold and put down a large case.

'Just in time I see, Mark. Entertaining the local constabulary, eh? Although I think you're wasting your time with this chap. Not to be trusted for one moment in my experience, and more than happy to take any lady friend from under your nose without a "by your leave".'

He smiled at the two of them and offered a hand in Fletcher's direction. Fletcher grinned and took the proffered hand in his.

'I see you two don't need an introduction,' said Hardwicke, reaching for another glass.

''Fraid not, old chap,' said Aughton as he removed his coat. 'Not that he's caught me out yet, you understand, but he does play an outrageously lucky hand of bridge, so don't think you can try that approach. We've a few mutual … er … friends as you might say, eh, Michael?'

Fletcher couldn't help but think of the time when Roger had sent him to pick up a 'friend' from the station at Hebden Bridge to find it was Louisa, which segued unhappily to Laura and their current contretemps. Less said about that the better, so he merely grumbled his acquiescence, whilst simultaneously warning bells began to ring. The last time Roger Aughton appeared out of nowhere he was acting as the herald for that slippery Special Branch bastard Adversane, and given the old lady's protest record, it seemed a bit two and two already.

Five minutes later the three of them were sitting in Sybil Hardwicke's comfortable armchairs, glasses to hand, whilst regarding each other with a mixture of studied calculation and curiosity.

'So what do you know, Michael?' asked Roger.

'Not a lot.'

Roger laughed. 'No change there then. As I said, Mark, he holds his cards close to his chest, but don't be surprised if he's keeping a naughty Jack up his sleeve.'

Fletcher merely smiled and waited.

'Nothing in the bloody papers, so thought I'd drop in to see if Mark needed any support. I'm up this way anyway for the Appleby Horse Fair amongst other punter fleecing activities,' said Roger.

Fletcher didn't doubt that they would be likely venues for Roger's wheeling and dealing, but he thought it more likely he was under orders from elsewhere.

'Um,' he said and took another mouthful of his whisky. Sybil Hardwicke certainly had good taste in malts.

'See, the thing is with Inspector Fletcher, Mark; he's got a very suspicious mind. Goes with the job I suppose.'

'So how is our 'mutual' friend, Mr Adversane?' asked Fletcher.

Roger managed a look of shocked outrage.

'Good grief, Michael. I'm not the man's errand boy.'

'Ay, but I suspect he had his spies watching the lady of this house,' said Fletcher.

Hardwicke gave no sign of understanding any of this, but then he hadn't said very much at all.

'Adversane?' he asked.

Roger pretended to bluster. 'Oh. Ignore him, Mark, dear boy. He's just an old school friend of mine, who Fletcher doesn't approve of, that's all.'

'So why would he want to spy on Aunt Sybil?' asked Hardwicke.

Fletcher raised his eyebrows at Roger, who continued with the flustered charade.

'Oh nothing really. You know Sybil was a bit of a troublemaker in her youth, weren't we all? But I'm sure it wouldn't be the sort of thing to interest Anthony.'

Fletcher sighed.

'Well, Roger, I'm afraid that's not the whole truth is it? She was still turning up on the protest marches and the odd sit-in. I think she was arrested for attacking an officer with her brolly only last autumn at some demo or other.'

Mark laughed at this.

'Hardly needed to be spied on though, Inspector, and I dare say the police weren't taking any prisoners themselves at the time.'

'No, maybe not, but she was under surveillance, that's for certain.'

Roger stopped blustering and got up to get a refill. The other two waited while he brought the bottle round. When he'd topped everyone up he went to stand looking out at the garden.

'So, you think her death wasn't accidental,' he asked quietly.

Fletcher took a sip.

'Doctor isn't sure. He thinks it's possible someone injected her with slightly too much of her heart medication. Possibly while she was asleep.'

'Asleep?' asked Roger.

'I doubt that,' said Hardwicke to Fletcher's surprise.

'Why's that, sir?' he asked.

'Well in the first place, she never seemed to need much sleep. Stayed up until after midnight and up by five most mornings. Plus she was a light sleeper. When I was younger I could never get back in from a late night binge without finding her waiting for me in the kitchen with the kettle on.'

Fletcher sighed. 'You see how it is, Roger. Gets more suspicious all the time. So who do you know who would go to the trouble of finding out someone's medication and then administering it in such a way that a doctor can't be certain whether she might have overdosed herself? Far too sophisticated for the average council house gang wouldn't you think?'

Roger turned to face him.

'But that doesn't mean it's any of Anthony's doing?'

'Ah, but it gets worse you see. Not only Aunt Sybil here, but her two friends as well.'

Mark gave him a puzzled look.

'You mean the Wallaces?' he asked. 'I thought that was a climbing accident.'

'That's what we were meant to think, but now it turns out that they may have been transported to the crags by helicopter … after they were murdered.'

'No…' murmured Hardwicke.

Roger gave Fletcher a stern look, but said nothing.

'So you see, gentlemen,' continued Fletcher, 'who has access to the sort of players, intelligence and equipment required to pull off operations such as that?'

The other two looked at each other, but neither of them could argue with him. No one spoke for a few minutes.

Roger finished his drink and set the glass down on a side table.

'Supposing it was true? What could Sybil and her friends have done or found out that required such an extreme response?' he asked.

'You tell me,' said Fletcher.

Again no one could think of an answer to that, so Roger did what he did best. He changed the subject.

'I don't know about you two chaps,' he announced, 'but I think it's time we headed down the lane to see what's for dinner.'

Fletcher and Hardwicke readily agreed with this suggestion and after Hardwicke had locked up, they strolled along together to the hotel.

They were fortunate in that the rain gods decided to give them a brief respite and even a few shafts of lemon coloured sunlight, which made the hedges and the spring flowers glisten and dance in the gentle breeze. As if they wished to emphasise the precision of this gift, a large black cloud doused the light as they stepped over the threshold into the darkened interior of the hotel lobby. If it was meant to create a mood changing effect it couldn't have been better engineered. The bar wasn't yet busy but the smells from the kitchen reinforced their appetites as they entered stage left.

As the other two headed for the window table Fletcher offered to get the first round in and went over to the bar, which was a decision he was never to forget.

Behind the bar was a young woman. At first Fletcher couldn't place her, but as she turned back from filling a couple of glasses from the optics and she looked in his direction he recalled the dark eye observing him from the back seat of his car. She frowned as she too searched her memory, but then her face brightened with a slight smile of recognition.

He smiled back. She finished serving the couple of men at the bar, before turning to Fletcher.

'Hello again,' he said.

'Hello yourself,' she said in a deeper voice than he was expecting.

'Drier in here, I think,' was all he could think of saying, feeling ridiculously gauche as he said it.

She nodded.

'What can I get you?' she asked.

Momentarily he couldn't think of what his two companions had asked for and turned to look in their direction. They weren't looking towards him and their heads were bowed close together in earnest conversation. He turned back to face the girl, who stood patiently waiting.

'Er … best make it a couple of malts and a pint of Jennings, please,' he said.

She nodded and turned away to the optics again. He watched her. Instead of the sodden mess he'd only glimpsed as she'd climbed into the back of his car, he now saw that her hair was a deep ruby brown which shimmered in the bright bar lights. As she turned away she pushed it back from her face so that it caught in a wave to one side of her head. She was wearing a plain black dress, which hung loosely on her slim body. He guessed she was maybe a bit younger than his stepdaughter, Grace, and the thought of looking at her in this way shook him. He looked away feeling guilty. When he glanced back he caught her eyes in the mirror – like the first time in the car. They held his look for a second too long, before she turned round with the two glasses and placed them on the bar. He picked them up and walked back to the two men, who stopped talking as he approached and accepted their drinks. Without a word he went back to the bar, took the drink she had placed there, handed over some money, and went back across the room. He took a gulp of his beer and placed it on the table, before making his way to the toilet. Throughout all this he didn't look at her again.

In the toilet he stared at himself in the mirror. What was going on? What could she see? A dishevelled man, needing a shave and a haircut, who was old enough to be her father; bloody ridiculous! He washed his face and ran his fingers through his hair.

'Stupid pillock,' he said and laughed at his reflection.

He stood up straight and adjusted his tie.

'Don't you think you're in enough trouble already, you daft sod?' he asked.

'Sorry?' said a voice from one of the cubicles.

Mick Fletcher saw that his reflection was blushing. He shook his head and blundered back out into the corridor. He stood there, gathering his breath. Running his hand over his forehead he realised he was sweating. Was he ill? Caught a chill in the rain? But he knew that wasn't true. He went back into the bar, making damn certain he didn't look in her direction.

Back at the table Roger and Hardwicke looked at him suspiciously as he pulled out a chair and sat facing them with his back to the bar. There was a ten pound note and some change on the table.

'Are you alright, Michael? Must be paying you too much.'

Fletcher looked at the money.

'Girl at the bar said you gave her a twenty and walked away.'

Fletcher reached out and took the money.

'Least you can do is to buy her a drink,' added Roger, with a laugh.

Fletcher looked up at him and put his hand up to his collar to loosen it. Roger frowned at him and looked over his shoulder at the girl. Before he could say anything Fletcher grunted, stood up and walked over to the bar, with the money in his hand.

There was no one waiting to be served, so the 'girl' was washing some glasses. Head down, hair falling to one side revealing a small mark on the back of her neck. Not a mark. A tattoo. Before he could focus on it, she brought her head up and, repeating the gesture she'd done earlier, swept her hair from one side to the other as she turned to face him. She looked at him. No smile. A serious face this time. Even troubled. Her eyes were dark, almost black like a bird's.

Again the look was penetrating. Disturbing.

'I'm sorry,' said Fletcher, holding out the money.

She stared at him, but didn't speak.

'My friends…' he gestured towards the two men. 'Stupid of me. Thank you.'

Now she did smile. Not a smirk of condescension, just a wry smile.

'Nah. Don't worry. Happens all the time,' she said.

He nodded, feeling more ridiculous the longer the exchange lasted.

'Can I get you a drink?' he asked.

She pushed a strand of hair from her eye. Her hand dropped from there to the collar of her dress.

'You don't need to do that.'

'No, please,' he heard himself say. 'What would you like?'

She shrugged.

'Okay, I'll have a coke. Thank you.'

Fletcher offered her the ten pound note. She took it and turned away to the till. It was a knot. A Celtic knot tattoo on her neck like that woman in Whitby, Carole Morgan, had on her scarred face, but much smaller. He could have sworn he heard his friend Cassie's voice in his head. A warning voice.

He flinched. She was facing him again with a frown on her face.

'Are you alright?' she asked as she offered him the change.

'Yeh … yeh,' he replied. 'Just tired, I think. Lot on my mind right now.'

She didn't say anything to that. The smile had gone, but the look remained.

He turned away unable to meet her gaze, walked back over to the table and sat down again. The two men continued with their conversation, but Fletcher couldn't tune in to them. It was as if his hearing wasn't working properly. His head was filled with a kaleidoscope of images and voices.

'You alright, Michael?'

Roger's voice came through the fog.

'Yeh … yeh, sure,' he said. 'Think I might be getting a cold or something. All this bloody rain, I expect.'

Roger gave him a doubtful look.

'Anyway, old thing, Mark was wondering whether we could stay in the house tonight? Is that possible, do you think?'

Fletcher looked from one to the other.

'Not my decision, but I'll give the station a ring if you like.'

'Would you? Most kind.'

Fletcher sighed and made his way out to the reception desk, making sure he didn't look in her direction.

The reception was empty. He rang the bell and waited.

As he looked out of the open front door, he could see a pale and loitering sun about to sink into a silver sea. He suddenly had a desperate longing for Laura. He turned back, reached across the desk, and picked up the phone. He dialled the number and waited as it rang. And rang. He placed it back on its receiver, just as the door opened and the girl from the bar appeared. She looked at his hand on the phone. He took it away. She looked at him.

'I need to make a phone call,' he said.

She nodded, but didn't move from the doorway.

'Police business,' he added.

'I know you're a policeman,' she said. 'You dropped us at the police station, remember.'

He grinned and indicated the phone.

'Go ahead,' she said and disappeared.

He made his call. Conroy had left for the day, but he'd already ordered most of the reinforcements back to their own stations and declared that the cases were now not to be considered suspicious deaths. Fletcher took this to mean there was no need to prevent Hardwicke from going to his aunt's house and replaced the phone. There was still no sign of a receptionist, so he tried Laura again, still no reply. He looked at the clock on the wall, nearly half seven. He looked back out towards the sunset. He'd missed it. No green flash. Just a silver sea and grey washed sky. He went back into the bar.

Roger and Hardwicke were studying the menu.

'No problem. You can get in when you want,' said Fletcher as he sat down. Another pint of Jennings had appeared on the table in front of him. No, it was the one he'd hardly touched. He took a deep gulp.

Hardwicke looked at him across the top of the menu.

'Does that mean that they think it's not suspicious?'

Fletcher pulled a face.

'Not my call, sir. Chief Superintendent Conroy is the man to talk to, but I expect he's heading for a Masonic knees up by now, its Thursday night after all.'

Roger laughed.

'Where d'you get that idea from, dear boy.'

'You. You old tart, who else,' said Fletcher, feeling some of the natural cynicism creeping back into his body.

Roger ignored that and announced he would try the venison and the other two concentrated on their own choices.

An hour and half later as they were fiddling with the cheese course the bar began to fill up, all locals, greeting each other with a range of gruff or laconic comments. Fletcher sat back and watched the gathering. Stanley Gill arrived and nodded in his direction before joining a group of older men with flat caps who were playing dominoes in a corner table.

Occasionally Fletcher would risk a glance over towards the bar, but the girl was now very busy. She'd been joined by an older woman who spent a lot of time joshing and chattering with the customers, but he rarely saw the girl engaged in such lively exchanges. She seemed to be content doing the job without a fuss. He did catch her sweeping her hair back in the way which fascinated him more than once.

The line came to him on one of those occasions in Miss Elphinstone's lilting tone: 'When you do dance, I wish you a wave of the sea.' Shakespeare, but he couldn't remember which play.

When it was his turn to buy another round he went to stand at the bar where the older woman seemed to be operating, but then had to suffer her inane banter. In this switched off manner, he was only vaguely aware of the arrival of noisy bunch of young men, who were making their way towards the bar. As Fletcher went to pick up his three glasses, a couple of them roughly pushed against him and nearly made him spill the drinks.

'Watch it, will you,' he said, as he put the glasses down again.

'Fuck off,' said one of the men and pushed him away.

'Don't do that,' said Fletcher quietly.

The young lad looked at him. He had curly black hair and bright blue eyes, too bright, thought Fletcher, and the pupils bigger than they ought to be.

'Or what?' said the lad, while his mate looked towards Fletcher as well.

'Or you'll upset me,' said Fletcher with a smile.

The lad looked at him in disbelief.

'Upset you, you fucking southern twat? Fuck off.'

'And I'd ask you to mind your language. There are ladies present,' said Fletcher.

The lad looked at the two ladies behind the bar.

'They're not fucking ladies, you daft bastard, and if you don't like it in here, fuck off somewhere else.'

With that he came up close to Fletcher and poked him in the chest. Fletcher caught his hand and with a practiced move twisted and swung the lad round and forced him against the bar. Even though this was quick the lad was quick as well. He kicked back at Fletcher's legs but Fletcher had moved to one side and used the lad's kicking momentum to push his head down hard onto the bar with a satisfying crunch of nasal bone splitting.

This all happened in a matter of seconds but the lad's mates quickly came to his aid, surrounding Fletcher. There was a quick glint of steel in one of the gang's hand. Fletcher let go of his attacker and backed away.

The bar had gone silent.

'You fucking bastard. You've broken my fucking nose!' said the lad, blood streaming through his fingers and down his shirt.

'Hey,' said the bar lady, coming towards them. 'Stop that right now … or I'll call the police.'

Before anyone else could do anything, Fletcher pulled out his warrant card and showed it to assembled crowd.

'Already here, madam,' he said. 'But I might have to ask you

71

to get reinforcements if Little Boy Blue here doesn't back off and leave.'

The 'boy' in question roared and made to lunge at Fletcher, but another member of the gang, a much bigger lad, grabbed him and pulled him back. The bar lady retreated towards the door to the reception.

'You're fucking dead you, copper!' rasped the lad, struggling to free himself from his mate's grasp.

'Don't be daft, Tex,' said another, the one with the knife, which had now disappeared. 'He can't stay in here forever, we'll sort him later.'

Tex freed himself and stepped towards Fletcher.

'You'd better make yourself scarce, copper, or you'll wish you'd never come here.'

Fletcher stood his ground.

'Actually, young man, I quite like it here, so I suggest you leave and then everyone can get on with their evening.'

Tex glared at him.

'If you leave now then I won't waste my time looking you up in our mugs' record book and coming to find you. 'Disturbing the peace', 'using foul language in a public place', 'assaulting a police officer,' 'consumption of Class A drugs' would get us started and that's assuming I'm not arresting your friend here for 'possession of a dangerous weapon'.'

The room went even quieter.

Two of the gang looked round at the assembled audience.

'Come on Tex, let's go,' one of them whispered.

'Shut the fuck up,' shouted Tex.

He eyeballed Fletcher.

'You're dead, copper.'

With that he turned on his heel, and not bothering to stop the blood still dripping from his nose, he pushed his way past his gang and barged into a couple of unwary customers who were just arriving.

'Hey, watch where you're going,' said one of them. But his friend, gauging the situation more quickly, pulled him out of the way. The rest of the gang followed, one or two of them knocking a few tables and chairs over as they went.

The room gradually came back to life. Whispered conversations got louder and people returned to where they'd been sitting. No one spoke to Fletcher. He realised he was shaking. A glass of brandy appeared on the bar in front of him. He looked up at the woman.

'Thanks,' he said and downed it in one gulp.

'Ay, well,' she said with a serious expression, thought of saying something else, but changed her mind. With one final look she went back along the bar to where someone was waiting. As she walked away, Fletcher followed her until she came level with the girl. She was standing with her arms round her chest with a blank look on her face. As he made eye-contact she held it for a second and then looked away, before moving towards another customer who had come to the bar.

Picking up the two drinks he walked back to his companions. Neither of them spoke as he placed the drinks in front of them and returned to the bar to collect his own.

On returning he sat down and took a sip of his beer. Roger was the first to speak.

'Well, Michael, what can I say?'

'I'm sorry about that,' said Fletcher, before he could go on.

'Well … I must say that was … astonishing,' said Roger. 'I'd heard that you had a violent streak, but … well, astonishing.'

'Not sure where it comes from really,' mumbled Fletcher. 'Anyway I'll try to keep my head down now. Don't want to have to sleep on Aunt Sybil's sofa, do I?'

Hardwicke seemed lost for words, but any intention Fletcher had of making that the end of the evening's surprises was dashed as the approaching noise outside rose to a crescendo.

CHAPTER 4

As the noise died away, not long after Fletcher had realised that it was the roar of a battalion of motorbikes, he was surprised to see that, apart from Roger and himself, the rest of the bar seemed singularly unperturbed.

Roger took his hands from his ears and gave Fletcher a worried look.

'It's alright,' explained Hardwicke with a grin. 'It isn't the same gang coming back with reinforcements.'

'No?' asked Roger, not entirely convinced.

'No,' said Fletcher, as the penny dropped. 'It's Steve McQueen's stunt double and her chapter.'

Sure enough the door opened and ten or twelve figures appeared all dressed in black, removing their helmets and shaking out their long hair. Most of them were men, but there were two women as well. One of the women was tall with a shock of bright red hair, laughing and pushing a much smaller man towards the bar.

'You lost, Boakie,' she was saying as she slapped him on the back. He continued on to the bar and leant against it with a sheepish smile on his face.

The rest of them commandeered a couple of tables near the

door and unzipped themselves out of leather jackets and placed helmets carefully on window ledges and a convenient side table. They'd obviously been here before and apart from a few smiles and the odd comment the rest of the clientele ignored them.

The other woman with long black hair came and stood in front of Fletcher's table.

'I should have worked it out earlier,' said Fletcher with a shake of the head.

Hilda grinned at him.

'Yeh well, you wouldn't believe the trouble I've had convincing the brass that it's okay for me to do this.'

'Oh, I can believe it,' said Fletcher.

Roger stood up and offered his hand.

'If you're a colleague of Michael's, I'm sure you're used to his lack of manners, young lady. Roger Aughton. I'm an old friend of his and Mark here.'

Hilda removed her glove.

'Hilda Crake. It's alright, sir. I've only known him for a couple of days. I've met worse.'

She nodded at Mark.

'You'll probably get a visit tomorrow, sir. All three deaths have now been declared not suspicious, although there will still have to be a coroner's court. I think they're both scheduled for Tuesday morning.'

'Tuesday?' asked Fletcher. 'That's a bit quick.'

Hilda raised her eyebrows.

'Ours is not to reason why, Inspector,' she said.

Roger laughed.

'I doubt the phrase is in Michael's lexicon.'

Fletcher was already shaking his head.

'Normally at least two to three weeks in my experience and that's when it's completely straightforward,' he said.

'Often much longer here,' said Hilda.

The four of them gave this some thought.

'Does that mean I can go ahead and organise her funeral?' asked Hardwicke.

'Yes, sir,' said Hilda. 'In fact I was asked to let you know.'

The small man called Boakie tapped her on her shoulder.

'Drink's over here, Hilts,' he said with a less than friendly glance at the three men.

'I'd better go,' she said. 'We're going over Hard Knott Pass tonight, a break in the rain and a full moon I'm told.'

"Rather you than me," thought Fletcher remembering the tortuous route, which he'd only managed once.

'See you in the morning, sir,' she said and went back to her friends.

Fletcher watched them for a few moments. Strange how people's personalities changed when they were in different company. The suspicious reticence he'd come to expect from Hilda was nowhere to be seen with these rough and ready bikers. She was obviously one of them and he didn't doubt that one of those noisy monsters parked outside would be hers. He just knew she'd be no one's pillion rider. He turned back to his companions.

'…be a full church,' Hardwicke was saying. 'She always said she wanted it to be at St Mary's.'

Roger looked at Fletcher.

'What are you thinking, Michael? Dark thoughts I suspect.'

Fletcher looked back across at the bikers, where the red haired girl was making them laugh. He'd seen that most of them were drinking coke or juice although there was the odd half pint.

'Not sure, Roger,' he said. 'Seems to me that someone wants Sybil and her two friends safe in the ground and out of the way as soon as possible.'

'I'm afraid it'll be more final than that, Inspector. Aunt Sybil has always been adamant about being cremated, ever since she came back from Nepal.'

Fletcher nodded. He was of the same opinion himself, although it was a more recent decision than that. Seeing all those oddly preserved bodies in that pine clearing had unnerved him and then the two in those 'fairy glens'. The thought of being buried alive was beyond thinking about.

'She also said where she'd prefer her ashes to be thrown, although I'm not sure whether it's allowed…'

The other two waited, but he bit his lip.

Roger sighed.

'Well, what we don't know we can't blab about, eh, Michael?'

Fletcher nodded, but he'd already worked it out. He smiled at Hardwicke.

'Nothing to do with us, Mark, do what you know she wanted.'

Hardwicke looked like he might blurt it out, but didn't get the chance. The bikers were leaving. Boakie had gathered up all the glasses onto a tray and was taking them back to the bar. Hilda accompanied him with a couple of glasses. Fletcher followed her with his eyes. She looked great in the leathers and her hair down, full of confidence.

But as he watched he saw her go along the bar towards where the girl was serving someone. Hilda said something and leant across towards her. The girl didn't take her hands off the glass or the pump she was pulling, but leant sideways so that Hilda could peck her on the cheek. Fletcher frowned. He watched as the two of them had a brief conversation, before Hilda came away, waved at them, and walked out the door after the rest of her friends.

Sisters? The girl behind the bar was a good six inches shorter. Definitely not a farmer's daughter, much lighter build. Different colour hair, but the eyes? Yes! The eyes were the same, black ball black. So? Different fathers?

Roger was tugging at his jacket.

'You with us, Michael?'

'Not quite. Just doing some sums,' he lied.

'So what answers have you come up with?'

He turned to face them.

'Well … if you want my opinion?'

They waited.

'As I said earlier, it smells like Special Branch to me. Your friend Adversane. Give him a ring if you want?'

Roger flapped the suggestion aside.

'Mark was wondering if it was anything to do with the rumours.'

'What rumours?' asked Fletcher.

'Michael doesn't read the papers, do you?' said Roger.

'I spend too much of my time listening to villains telling lies than to waste any more of my life reading stories made up by the professional liars.'

'He's talking about the war,' said Roger.

'War? What war?' asked Fletcher, genuinely puzzled.

'The Falklands War, of course.'

Fletcher stared at him.

'Aunt Sybil was no friend of the government. Especially this one,' said Hardwicke.

Fletcher waited. He wasn't surprised given the track record he'd seen.

Mark glanced at Roger who nodded his encouragement.

'I was talking to her only a few days ago. Just after the Belgrano was sunk.'

Fletcher had a vague memory of seeing this on the news somewhere, but he still couldn't see any connection.

'What was she saying?' he asked.

'That it was against international law.'

'How do you mean? It's a war. 'All is fair in' etcetera,' he said, looking down at his empty glass.

'Ah, but there are rules,' said Roger. 'Geneva Convention, UN agreement, Exclusion zones.'

'Um,' said Fletcher, standing up and reaching for their glasses. 'Same again?'

They both nodded. He walked over to the bar. This time he went to stand where the girl was working. She looked across at him as she served someone else. He had to wait while she served another customer before it was his turn. All the while he tried not to stare at her, but each glance confirmed for him, that if she and Hilda were sisters, then it was definitely not the same parents. Different bone structures, hair colour, size and gestures. Hilda was strong and deliberate in her movements, probably as much to do with spending all that time in a male work environment and with male friends. Whereas this girl was slight, languid and, Fletcher guessed, a solitary person.

She stood in front of him.

'Same again?' she asked.

He nodded. She took his glass and put it up to the pump. She didn't look at him. It was as if she'd never met him before. Her head was down concentrating on the beer.

'So, how do you know Hilda?' he asked.

At first he thought she wasn't going to answer him, but then she finished pouring the beer and placed it on the bar in front of him.

'She's my big sister,' she said and turned away towards the optics.

Fletcher waited. She placed the two glasses in front of him. He held out a note.

'Not easy to tell that,' he commented.

She opened the till and retrieved the change.

'Different fathers, different natures, different lives,' she said and offered him the money. There was one ring on her left hand little finger. A small black stone set on a plain silver band. Her nails were painted black and there were scratches on the back of the hand holding out the money. Despite this he could see the hands were elegant, what his big sister would have called pianist's hands.

'But the same colour eyes,' said Fletcher, without thinking.

Those eyes hardened towards him and her dark eyebrows rose imperceptibly.

'How observant of you,' she said with a slightly sarcastic tone. 'Hilda said you were odd.'

'Odd?' he asked.

'Your eyes,' she answered and walked away towards another customer.

He picked up the glasses and walked back to the table, but as he sat down he glanced across at her. She was looking at him as she about to pull another pint and unconsciously did that 'wave' gesture with her hair, before she looked down. He felt a shiver down his back and turned away without responding.

He realised that Roger was talking to him again.

'What do you think Michael?'

'What?'

'About Thatcher?'

'What about her?' Fletcher asked.

'Do you trust her?'

Fletcher looked at Roger as if he was stupid.

'Why should I trust her? She's a politician,' he said as though no one could think anything different.

'Aunt Sybil said Thatcher saw the war as a stroke of luck. An opportunity to distract the Sun readers from the fact that they hadn't got a job,' said Hardwicke.

'And so Thatcher's sent someone to bump her off?' Fletcher asked with a smirk.

Hardwicke gave him a strange look.

'Do you remember Watergate?' he asked.

'In the States? Nixon, you mean?' asked Fletcher.

'So you know what a whistle-blower is?' Hardwicke asked

Fletcher nodded.

'Well, Aunt Sybil was in touch with … some people. People who know about that sort of stuff. I was here – a year or so ago at her house. They were making all sorts of accusations, saying they knew what was really going on. Can't remember the details, got too drunk in the end. Most of it was about the nuclear power station. You know, the cases of leukaemia, that the sea glows green in the dark, loads of 'things' washed up…'

'Things?' asked Fletcher.

'Sea creatures with horrible growths, gross deformities, more heads than normal,' said Hardwicke.

Fletcher shuddered at the thought.

'But what's that got to do with the war or Thatcher?' he asked.

'Well, a lot of those people are also against the war, I think. They think it's a set-up.'

Fletcher looked puzzled.

'How so? The Argies started it didn't they?'

'Yeh, but it seems that the Belgrano was sailing away from the Exclusion Zone when it was sunk.'

'Who says?'

'Well, there's some confusion, although Thatcher is saying it's not true and that it was a threat to our forces down there.'

Fletcher snorted with frustration.

82

'Well there's bugger all we can do about it. Don't hold your breath waiting for her or anyone else to tell you the truth ...' Fletcher faltered as he caught the look on Roger's face.

'But don't you see, Michael? If Sybil had found out something and she was going to 'blow the whistle', then that would be a reason to silence her.'

Fletcher looked from one to the other.

'I've two problems with that, gentlemen. One, how would an old lady – okay, a well-connected, intelligent, respected academic – get that sort of information? And two, who would pay her any attention?'

Roger looked at Hardwicke, but the latter shrugged his shoulders.

'All I'm saying is that she knew people who might be able to get that information ... but I don't know how or what she could have done with it,' said Roger.

Fletcher shook his head.

'Exactly, I mean there are some journalists out there who might want to embarrass the government, but there's ways of stopping them.'

Fletcher looked meaningfully at Roger, knowing that he knew the cases that he had been involved in, but was unable to talk about.

Roger nodded at him as though he knew what he was thinking.

'I'm afraid that Michael's right, Mark.'

The three of them paused and had a drink.

'Mind you,' said Fletcher. 'Coroner's court on Tuesday is damn fast, unbelievable in fact. Perhaps that might be a chance to get some answers. You two could go, ask a few awkward questions. And maybe tomorrow I'll find out more.'

The other two looked at him.

'But … to be honest this has all the hallmarks of a Special Branch stitch-up. I bet there are D-notices flying everywhere. I'll probably be told I'm no longer needed here and that's me out of the equation. No access to files or the people involved. Shut down. Been there, had the stitches.'

After that they changed the subject. A few of Roger's risqué stories and he and Mark were off back to the house. Fletcher sat on his own for a bit, occasionally looking over at Hilda's sister, but he'd lost interest really. She paid him no attention whatsoever.

He tried phoning Laura again. Still no reply. Where the hell was she?

He was on the point of heading for some late night TV, knowing full well he'd find it hard to get to sleep, when a gang of the few remaining customers came through the reception area and headed into the lounge. Stanley Gill was one of the last in this group and he beckoned to Fletcher.

'Not hitting the sack yet are you, Inspector. I hear you're a card-player? There are a couple of games about to start in the lounge. Drinks still being served. Why don't you join us? I'll introduce you to some of the local villains.'

Fletcher sighed.

'Why not?' he said. 'It's likely to be my last night here anyway.'

He followed Gill into the room and was soon thirty quid down and only two games in. If that had been the worst that had happened everything would have been okay. In fact, he reflected much later that night, it was the sort of bad decision he often seemed to make … particularly when he was 'in enough trouble already'.

It wasn't the cards – although Laura's Aunt Magda might have something to say about that, because after a couple more hands his luck – or his concentration – changed for the better.

An hour later he was winning well over seventy quid and he was getting a few dirty looks.

Suddenly from behind him a voice told them that if they wanted any more to drink it was now because 'I'm off to bed and you needn't think you can help yourself.'

He knew it was Hilda's sister, but decided against turning round to look at her. Some of the assembled company got up and approached the lounge bar. He peeped at his cards again, a full house, Jacks over sevens.

'I tell you what lads,' he said, 'as it's probably my last night here and I've skinned you something rotten. I'll get this last one.'

At first there was no response, but then Stanley laughed.

'Well, there's a turn up for the books, a copper – a Londoner, mind – buying a round.'

'Ay,' said the bald bloke sitting opposite Fletcher, 'and I can't spot his bloody tricks, and it's not for want of trying. He's either a jammy bastard or the best cardsharp I've ever played with.'

'Cardsharp!' said Fletcher, placing his hand face down on the table. 'You should meet my wife.'

This got a laugh, but he hadn't finished.

'On second thoughts, there's a pot of over sixty quid already on this table and I reckon Kojak here is going to take me all the way … up to a ton, I should think. Here's the deal. I could buy everyone a drink or someone could come and take my hand … and they can get the round in.'

The bar was silent and then the whispering started. Fletcher watched the man opposite. He didn't flinch, but his pupils dilated. Fletcher knew he couldn't have Kings or Queens, Three Aces were a possibility, but not likely. Running flush? Four of a kind? Impossible. The whispering stopped.

'I'll take it,' said a quiet voice. Fletcher turned to see a small, weather-beaten man coming towards him.

'Don't be daft, Gav,' said another voice. 'He's reeling yer in.'

'Pretending to be generous, but needing to get out of a hole,' said another.

The man stood next to Fletcher, who with a wink at 'Kojak', got up, leaving the cards face down on the table. The man called Gav sat down, but didn't even look or touch the cards.

Kojak flinched now, but there was a smile on his face.

'Whose call is it?' asked Gav.

'Mine,' said Kojak.

Gav still didn't look at the cards, just stared at his opponent. A few voices called out, some encouraging him, some telling him to pull out while he still had time.

'May as well do as the man said,' said Kojak placing two twenties on the table.

Gav stared at the money and then turned over the cards one at a time. The crowd gasped - lots of 'bloody hells' and' jammy bastards'.

Kojak held the moment for as long as he could. After all it was going to be talked about for a long time. He slowly turned his cards over. One, two, three aces. One King ... and the fourth Jack.

There was a brief hiatus as they took it in before the room erupted. Men shouting and cheering. The drinks flowed. Gavin and Fletcher were slapped repeatedly on the back or had their hands roughly shaken, but the same was also meted out to Kojak, who was actually called Harry. He came over to shake Fletcher's hand.

'Are you as lucky in love?' he said.

'No complaints so far,' said Fletcher with a grin.

Harry shook his head. 'As I said: 'jammy bastard' – just not fair. Not fair at all.'

The crowd made a savage inroad into Gavin's hundred

pounds and by the time most people were leaving it was well after two o'clock. Hilda's sister had disappeared long ago after telling everyone to keep the noise down and the last one out to turn off the lights please.

In the end there were only four people left. Fletcher, Gavin, Stanley, and a big guy called Ron. They sat at one of the card tables, final double malts going down slow.

As he'd surmised, Gavin was the climber who'd been with Stanley's wife, Alice, when she died. Ron was another member of the rescue team. Eventually the conversation turned to the Wallaces.

'So what do you think happened?' asked Fletcher.

Gavin and Stanley looked at Ron, who put up his hands in mock surrender.

'Hey, I don't know. Honestly,' he said.

They waited. He took a sip of his whisky.

'It was me and Jim got them down alright, but heck, how could we know what had really happened? They looked like they'd fallen, one after the other probably. Who's to say?'

'But could they have been dropped from a helicopter?' asked Fletcher.

Ron shrugged his shoulders. 'I dunno. It's possible. But why?'

Fletcher didn't think it was worth sharing the discussion he'd had earlier with Roger and Hardwicke.

But Stanley had his own theory.

'I saw the helicopter that day. I think it's possible … and we all know they were anti-nuclear protestors. Sybil and the Wallaces. I think it could have been summat to do wi that.'

Gavin nodded his agreement, but the conversation stalled after that. Fletcher didn't think he'd mention the coroner's court.

Stanley sighed and downed the last of his whisky.

'I'd better be off. Working over in Buttermere tomorrow. Bit of plumbing. Scrabbling about in sink cupboards, so I need to sleep some of this off.'

He got up and went to place his glass on the bar top. Ron followed suit and the two of them left.

Gavin looked deep into his whisky. Fletcher felt there was something he wanted to say. He waited.

'Not the only person to have an unlikely accident round here,' he said eventually without looking up.

Fletcher hesitated, not sure whether to reveal what Stanley had told him about Alice, but realised he wasn't likely to get another chance.

'You mean Alice?' he asked.

Gavin looked at him.

'You want to talk about it?' said Fletcher.

Gavin walked over to the bar and plucked one of the bottles off the back shelf, brought it over and poured them both another large dram.

'I've talked about it plenty enough, but it still doesn't make sense.'

Fletcher waited, realising it was better not to interrupt.

'We were in Piers Ghyll. High up, beyond the elbow, coming back down.'

Fletcher nodded his understanding.

'It's not too bad, some awkward pitches, but nothing beyond Alice or me. Most of it, we didn't even rope up.'

He paused. Fletcher took a sip of his whisky.

'There's huge chock stone just round t'corner. It's quite an exposed climb coming up, but coming down it's a quick abseil. I went first and she followed, but as she got to me she was calling out. Saying she'd seen something in one of the cracks off to the left above the chock. She untied herself and set off back up.'

Gavin took another sip. Fletcher could see that his hand was shaking.

'It was getting dark. I warned her to be careful, but she'd gone. She was a quick neat climber. It's maybe a hard v.diff. Something she'd solo without any trouble. Only the exposure to worry about and she was nerveless.'

He looked at Fletcher to see if he was following. Fletcher nodded. Gavin took a deep breath.

'I could hear her, but once she was above the chock I couldn't see her. She was gone a good few minutes. At first I could hear her on the rocks, but then it went quiet. I was starting to worry, but then she called out. I couldn't tell what she said. Then...'

He stopped again, looked at Fletcher, and took a big gulp of whisky, making himself gasp. Fletcher looked away; he knew the man was going to cry.

He heard him fight back a sob.

'She fell past me, hit a large boulder, and ended up in the water.'

Again Gavin had to steel himself.

'I went down to her. Calling out her name. I reached her. She was still alive. She could see me. She spoke to me.'

Fletcher could hardly bear it.

'What did she say?' he asked.

'She said ... she said ... "It's him. He's there. We've found ..." and then she passed out.'

Fletcher stared at him.

'Who? Who was there?'

Gavin cried now, his shoulders shuddering with emotion, tears dripping off his face. Fletcher reached out and held his hand. It gripped him back fiercely.

Slowly the man managed to regain control. He rubbed his face across his sleeve, wiping gobs of snot and wet away. Fletcher found a handkerchief and offered it to him. He took it, wiped his chin, and blew his nose. A sad smile appeared on his face.

'Sorry, I mean, thanks,' he said.

Fletcher said nothing.

'I wasn't sure. All I heard was some rocks falling. At the time I thought they'd been loosened by Alice, but now…'

'What?' asked Fletcher.

'Well, at the time, all I could think of was getting her out of the water, keeping her warm – you know all the standard stuff. I wrapped her in all the clothes I'd got, covered her with my survival bag, left some water and ran all the way down.'

Fletcher couldn't help but think of Laura and how he would have felt in that situation. He shivered.

'She was still alive when we got back. She opened her eyes and smiled at me. The other guys got her onto a stretcher. We were back down within the hour. I've never known them move so fast. All the time I ran beside them, kept talking to her, shouting at her. Sometimes her eyes were open, but when we got her into the hut she'd gone. Jim tried everything. The doctor arrived, gave her an injection, but we'd lost her.'

He cried again.

'She said one other thing to me. It was just after we'd got back up to her. She said "It's him. He's safe. He's not…'

Fletcher waited to see if there was anymore. He glanced at the clock. Five past three. He looked towards the window. Outside there was a ghostly brilliance, the full moon that Hilda had promised.

'I've not been back there,' said Gavin. 'But I will do … soon. Now I think I know who she was talking about.'

Fletcher looked at him.

'Who?'

Gavin shook his head.

90

'I'm not going to tell you yet. I need someone to come with me who I can trust, who won't tell me I'm being stupid ... which rules our Rob or Jim or any of the others. I thought of Stanley, but I can't do that to him. I think he's come to terms with it. He's accepted it. Moved on.'

Fletcher felt dubious about that, but said nothing.

'Will you do that?' asked Gavin, gripping his arm again.

Fletcher nodded, but hesitated.

'I'm no climber,' he said. 'I know what you climbers call a 'hard v.diff.' I'll need to be roped up.'

'No problem,' said Gavin, 'but you will do it, won't you?'

Fletcher looked into his eyes.

'Yeh. When?'

'Next week? Thursday maybe. I'm owed time off, but I need time to prepare myself.'

'Okay,' said Fletcher, 'Thursday.'

Gavin looked at his watch.

'Bloody hell, I'll be in trouble. Sheila will be ringing the police.'

He stood up, downed the last of his drink, and grabbed his jacket.

Fletcher stood up as well.

'Have you far to go? You're not going to drive are you?'

Gavin shook his head.

'No. We're off the lane going up to Stanley's. Quarter of hour on foot.'

As he made for the door, Fletcher called out to him.

'Why me?'

Gavin stood with his back to him.

'You hardly know me...' added Fletcher.

Gavin turned towards him. His face was serious but his eyes glittered in the shadows.

'It's something climbers have to be good at. Knowing who you can trust...'

Fletcher frowned, although he knew what Gavin meant. He felt the same about certain colleagues, Irene, Sadie, Frank Worthington ... it wasn't a long list.

Gavin gave a hoarse laugh, 'And you're lucky ... damn lucky.'

One more look and he was gone. The door swung to, creaking in the gathering silence.

Fletcher put the glasses on the bar and turned off the lights. The whole of the entrance and the garden was lit up by the moonlight. He stood and stared for a while and then turned to go towards the stairs.

His heart missed a beat.

Half way up, crouched like a pixie was a dark figure, arms round her knees, her face white in the moonlight, with two black holes for eyes. Eyes that stared straight at him.

It was her.

'Good grief,' he whispered. 'What are you doing? Frightened the life out of me.'

'You're good,' she said and stood up. It was like watching a cat stretch.

'What d'you mean?' he asked.

'A good listener.'

He took a step towards her.

'Practice I suppose,' he said. 'Comes with the job.'

'Nah, I think you're a natural,' she said, taking a step backward up the stairs as she reached out to hold the bannister rail.

'So, were you spying on us?' he asked.

'I wasn't,' she replied. 'I couldn't hear any voices, but I could see the light was still on so I came down to turn it off. Didn't want to interrupt ... or stop him.'

Fletcher couldn't think of anything else to say, but didn't

want to get any closer.

'That's a real sad story,' she added.

'It is,' Fletcher agreed.

Their eyes met. At this moment he would have denied it, but later on he would admit to himself that it was *the* moment.

'I'm going back to bed now,' she said and turned away.

Fletcher couldn't stop himself.

'Me too,' he said.

She turned back to him and pushed her hair back from her face, but she didn't say anything, just looked at him.

'What's your name?' he asked.

She kept looking at him for what seemed an age, her face a white oval in the gloom.

'Sorcha,' she said and without another word climbed up the stairs and disappeared.

Fletcher stood there for a long time until he realised he was shivering … even though it wasn't cold.

Eventually he followed her upstairs and lay on his bed with the lunar light flooding the room. It was a long time before he slept.

* * * * *

Fletcher didn't remember setting the alarm, but came awake abruptly when it went off. His dream evaporated before he could catch it, but he knew it was bad. He was covered in sweat.

He took a quick shower and picked up the phone. Still no answer at Laura's. He was getting worried. If, as he expected, he'd be told that he was no longer needed, he'd get straight in his car and go home as soon as he could.

Downstairs he had a quick cup of coffee and two pieces of toast. Surprisingly, thinking about how much he must have drunk, he didn't feel too bad.

There was no sign of Sorcha. He asked the woman on reception as casually as he could if she would be around later. The woman gave him a suspicious look.

'I'd be surprised if I saw her before midday. She only does evenings. Shall I give her a message?'

'No, it's alright. It doesn't matter,' he said and handed over his key. 'I might be back on Monday, so can you keep the room?'

The woman nodded. She obviously knew he wasn't paying for it. He headed for his car. What an idiot? What would the woman think? What would Sorcha think?

He got in the car and drove to the station, wondering all the while how she spelled her name and where it came from. Nothing like 'Hilda'.

Hilda was there waiting for him.

He could tell the station had returned to its normal pedestrian mode and found her at her desk slowly demolishing the mountain of paperwork she'd been putting off for over a week.

'How was the moonlight trip?' he asked.

She looked up and grinned.

'Fantastic,' she said, but the smile disappeared as she remembered what else had happened.

'Mind you, we nearly had a nasty accident just after Whahouse Bridge.'

'What were you doing? Dragging your knee on the tarmac,' he asked, thinking of what those guys did in the TT races.

She gave him a stern look.

'We don't do any of that fancy stuff,' she said.

Fletcher slapped his own wrist. She ignored him.

'Gerry was in the lead, slowed down to take the bend after the bridge and nearly came off, ended up in the hedge.'

'Blow-out?' asked Fletcher.

'No. He swears there was someone running across the road.'

Fletcher waited, suppressing any comments about drink or bravado.

'We all stopped, looked round, shouted out … Boakie even went down under the bridge. Nothing.'

'So what do you think?' asked Fletcher.

Hilda hesitated.

'If you laugh at me I'll … I'll…' she laughed, as she saw his hands go up.

'I won't laugh,' he said. 'I wouldn't dare.'

She checked to see if he was serious, decided he was, and took a breath.

'Well. Whahouse is known for its ghosts … that's all. Anyway once we'd checked Gerry was okay to go on, we carried on up to the top of the pass, over Wrynose and back round the coast road, I was in bed by twelve. What about you?'

'I was led astray I'm afraid. That Stanley Gill, he's a bad influence. Me and cards in a saloon bar. Always ends in a gunfight. Bodies all over the place.'

She made a face.

'Did they take all your money off you?'

'Not exactly, but I'll leave it to the survivors to tell you their version.'

'Uhuh,' she said, uncertain what that might be. Not the truth that's for certain.

Fletcher looked at the boards which were still covered with photos and diagrams of Sybil Hardwicke's house.

'So … game over, eh?' he asked.

Hilda looked across at them.

'Think so. Conroy wants to speak to you … as soon as you get in,' she said.

'Ay well. I'm not here yet. I'll get you a coffee.'

'Oh, and Frank checked that black car that Stanley saw outside Mrs Hardwicke's house last Thursday.'

'Don't tell me … stolen?' asked Fletcher.

She nodded.

'Same day. From outside a big hotel in Leeds. Belongs to a local councillor.'

They both grinned at the cheek of it. He made to go, but then turned to add,

'Interesting chap, that Gavin … what's his other name again?'

'You mean Alice's friend?'

He nodded.

'Wesker.'

'He's asked me to go up the Ghyll with him,' he said, wondering how Hilda would respond to that.

She looked up from her papers. Her eyes widened and a frown wrinkled her forehead.

'Did he?'

Fletcher nodded.

'You are honoured,' she said. 'He's not climbed since, never mind up the Ghyll.'

Fletcher could see what she was thinking.

'I don't think it's my climbing skills which picked me out. Struggled on Jack's Rake me. But he thinks I'm lucky.'

'Um. Well if some of the tall tales I hear about when you were in Barrow are anything to go by, he's probably right.'

Fletcher thought of a few ripostes to that, but decided it was better to go and get the coffee.

On returning he asked for Conroy's number and picked up the phone. He had to wait to be put through, before doing the regulation 'Yes sir, No sir,' routine and put the phone down nicely.

'So, Sergeant, I'm on my bike. Up to Carlisle for a talking to and home in time for tea.'

Hilda nodded.

'Well,' she said. 'I will miss your sparkling repartee and perhaps next time we're heading for the Agricultural Arms I'll give you a ring.'

'Now, how did you know that's my favourite pub?' he asked.

'Background information, care of DS Garner, sir.'

Fletcher laughed.

'Treachery,' he said. 'Women. Can't trust them.'

Hilda was on her feet and came towards him.

'I wasn't sure how we were going to get on, but as I said to your friend, I've suffered worse.'

Fletcher took her hand and shook it.

'Well, can't say fairer than that, Sergeant. Wish me luck. By my reckoning I'm for Scottie land next.'

Without more ado the pair of them parted and Fletcher set off towards Cockermouth and beyond. It was only as he was stuck at the junction at the main road, that he had a sudden thought.

He pulled in by the next pub and went in to use the phone.

It rang for some time, until it was picked up and he heard a voice he'd sorely missed.

'Laura?' he said.

There was a pause. He could hear her breathing. Was she going to put the phone down?

'Took you long enough,' she said.

He breathed again.

CHAPTER 5

Fletcher pulled into the car park at Carlisle police headquarters and sat in the car for a few moments. He knew he ought to be composing explanations for not following procedures, embarrassing his superiors by making sarcastic comments about record keeping not being the only way to solve crimes and his less than polite approach to criminals.

But instead he was thinking about the women in his life. When he'd finally figured out that Laura had gone to Newcastle to stay with Grace, he'd managed to negotiate a bit of a truce, which involved him in getting himself to Geordie HQ in time for a walk on the beach, followed by a Chinese restaurant and something called the Wooden Doll for community singing afterwards. No mention of extra time or penalties, but he thought that probably depended on the full time result. One thing he knew though, he was three nil down, and even if away scores counted double, it was going to be a tough match.

However this hadn't stopped him from making a detour via the hotel at Ennerdale Bridge. What was he doing for fuck's sake? He'd gone in and pretended he'd left his wash bag in his room. The woman on reception picked up the phone. The person on the other end told her that the room had been cleaned over an hour ago and that they hadn't seen any wash bag.

He shook his head at her, but before he could think of some other excuse to be there, Sorcha came down the stairs and walked out through the open door. It was as if he was invisible. No glance in his direction. No recognition. Like she was sleepwalking. He apologised to the receptionist and followed her out, knowing the woman was watching him. He didn't care, but he was too late, Sorcha had disappeared. He got in the car and set off.

There she was walking along the road. He pulled in. She came level and he wound down the window.

'Hi,' he said.

She stared at him.

'What do you want?' she asked.

'Er ... nothing,' he said. 'Just wondering if you were going my way?'

She looked along the road.

'Well, I wasn't going anywhere really,' she replied. 'Where are you going?'

'Carlisle,' he said.

'Ooh. Big city. Lucky you.'

'Not really,' he said. 'Heading for a bollocking. I've upset the Chief Superintendent.'

She gave that some thought.

'You going through Cockermouth?'

He nodded.

She walked round to other side of the car and got in.

'May as well,' she said. 'Nowt else to do.'

He didn't ask.

He drove for a few miles before he could think of anything to say. She didn't seem to have any need to talk.

'So what's there to do in Cockermouth?' he asked.

She gave him a sour look.

'Nowt.'

He waited.

'There's nothing happens round here … ever,' she added.

Fletcher didn't think of mentioning the recent deaths or his contretemps with the young thugs last night, but he could see her point of view. They hadn't passed a single car.

'You could move away.'

'I've tried that,' she said.

'No good?'

'Manchester. Sex and drugs and rock'n'roll. Lads who think they're God's gift. Older blokes squeezing your bum … but in the end, no different than here.'

This was the longest speech he'd heard her say. It was full of weary bitterness. He recognised it, but never felt it. Life had always moved fast for him. Even if it was often not in the direction he thought he wanted to go.

They were coming into the middle of the town.

'Pull in there,' she said, pointing at a gap in the roadside parking.

After she got out she turned and leant down to thank him.

'Are you coming back on Monday?' she asked.

'No idea,' he said. 'Why?'

'Nothing.'

Her hair fell across her face and she pushed it back. It didn't seem to bother or irritate her.

'Well. It was good to see you put that arrogant bastard in his place.'

'Who? Tex?'

'Tex!' she said with a spit of venom. 'His real name is Gordon.'

She laughed and Fletcher grinned at her, but the laugh died.

'Well. Maybe see you Monday,' she said.

He watched her walk away. An unhurried saunter. No looking back. A thin, pale green T-shirt, frayed blue jeans, and an old leather jacket. He watched until she stopped at a shop window and then went in.

As he drove away he caught a glimpse of her through the shop window. She looked back at him as she stood at a clothes rack.

He kept going but if he'd been brave enough he'd have pulled in and gone back. Bought her anything she wanted. Gone for a meal. A walk. Anything to be with her. Hear her voice. Watch her hands. Touch her hair. Look in her eyes.

Now he looked out of the window. Cars glistening in the sunshine as it fought its way through the clouds. He felt his body was drained of energy. The thought of listening to Conroy droning on was unbearable.

He'd no idea how long he sat there and jumped when someone knocked on his window. He looked out. Lots of braid and a peaked cap; he wound down the window. An ACC, by his pips, confronted him.

'You can't park here,' the man said, pointing at the sign, which clearly said his name and rank.

Later, Fletcher was astonished with himself. He'd not been unpleasant at all. He'd apologised and moved his car to the other end of the car park.

Upstairs he listened to the long list of complaints and transgressions that had offended the big man. He didn't take most of it in, but focussed on the man's moustache, which had a life of its own. In the end Fletcher decided it was a furry caterpillar that was struggling to escape the sticky phlegm coming out of the man's mouth. It was this that alerted him to the fact that, as well as his face getting redder and redder, Conroy's voice was getting louder and hoarser. Fletcher tuned back in to catch the final words.

'Are you listening to me, Inspector?' shouted Conroy.

Fletcher wanted to say 'Of course not you, stupid tosser!', but found that he was saying: 'Of course, sir. Sorry, sir.'

Flummoxed by this unrecognisably contrite Fletcher, the Chief Superintendent was lost for words.

'Is that it, sir, are you finished?' asked Fletcher brightly and smiled at his superior.

Instead of having a heart attack, Conroy settled for bellowing at him.

'Yes, I have. Now bugger off back to Penrith. God knows how Aske puts up with you. Goodbye and good riddance.'

Fletcher didn't give him any time to add to this tirade, but walked out of the room and down the stairs as fast as he could. He was nearly out through the door, when a woman's voice rose above the hubbub in the entrance hall.

'DI Fletcher,' she gasped as she caught up with him.

He stopped, aware of all the eyes and ears turned towards them. The woman gathered her breath.

'Message for you, sir,' she said, holding out a slip of paper. He recognised her now. She was the poor sod who'd somehow managed to become Conroy's secretary. She'd shown him in earlier on.

He smiled at her and took the paper. Rather than read it there in front of the now attentive crowd, he thanked her and continued out into the rain, which went from shower setting to complete downpour as he ran across the car park, getting confused and having to track back until he saw his car. Fumbling his keys, he dropped them and was utterly soaked by the time he managed to open the door and get in.

He turned on the radio and sat looking out at the rain, which now happily eased off and went to occasional spitting as he sank into wet dog mode. The radio was providing him with the useful information that it was going to rain heavily today.

The paper was still in his hand and some of the ink had run, but he groaned when he took in what it said.

'Michael. I understand you're on your way to Newcastle. I will be in The Angel at Corbridge for lunch. I'm paying. Be there. L.'

There were two L's in Fletcher's life. He never quite knew which one was in charge, but he did know he couldn't ignore either of them. But still, if Louisa Cunninghame-Knox was paying for his lunch, who was he to argue? He sighed at the level of sartorial criticism he would have to face before he got to eat the lunch, and started the car.

* * * * *

Of course this meant even more voices in his head as he got himself onto the trucker's death track otherwise known as the A69. He managed to survive all the way until the Greenhead turning, when he was relieved to transfer to the B road, which followed the course of Hadrian's Wall. Grace had told him about this route since she'd moved to Newcastle. She was now in her second year at Durham, but she and her boyfriend Quill had found the cathedral city a bit claustrophobic and preferred the rougher edginess of the Geordie capital, which Fletcher sort of understood, although now they'd settled in Tynemouth he felt they were dangerously close to Anna Kerr in Whitley Bay. His past was always hanging around waiting to spin him back into the web of fate or 'wyrd' as Cassie would say.

He turned the radio off and opened the window a touch. He knew he was making a good fist of the wet retriever impression, but there was nothing he could do about it. He realised that the weather was improving as he headed east and cursed the Pennines. Eventually the voices died away as he drove along the relatively empty road, catching occasional glimpses of the wall itself.

He'd never felt the need to go and clamber about the old stones, although he approved of the purpose. He wondered whether he would be sent to 'Scottie land'. He'd been as far as Louisa's house on the Tweed and that was only just over the border. Did they do things differently in the Scottish Police force? Would he be able to understand a word they said? He had enough trouble with English northerners as it was. Rochdale, Todmorden, Penrith, Barrow, they all spoke different languages, for God's sake.

So what did Louisa want? And how did she know he was on his way to Newcastle? Obvious really, he supposed. Female communication systems. He wondered whether Louisa might have known Sybil Hardwicke. He'd decided Mark was probably a public school boy and in any case he knew Roger, so chances were she'd know the family if nothing else. It was often the case, ever since he'd met her in Rochdale, that not only did she know everyone, but that she'd been to school with them or knew someone else who had been. She was the one who nearly helped him find the "Snow White Killer", telling him about her classmate, Caroline Soulby, the final victim, but they still hadn't manage to track "Rose White" down.

He got to the junction with the A68 and turned south towards Corbridge. He didn't know the place but expected the Angel to be fairly central and well-known. He looked at the car clock. Half twelve. On his left was a pub, The Wheatsheaf. He quickly made up his mind and pulled into the car park. Getting his bag out of the back he strode into the pub, ordered a pint, and made for the toilet. Ten minutes later he was back in the car, with dry clothes and directions to the Angel.

Five to one he opened the door of the restaurant and saw the familiar blonde hair behind the back of high stall in the far corner of the room. He walked over and subjected himself to her blue-eyed inspection.

'Only just in time Michael. Glad to see to you've had time to change. I was expecting a wet spaniel. Still it is time you got rid of that dreadful coat and acquired a pair of modern shoes.'

He bent to kiss her proffered cheek.

'Whilst you are always the embodiment of haute couture, Louisa,' he said. Was that blouse silk? It was up to her neck and held at the throat by a silver brooch with a blue stone. Although she still had her hair immaculately coiffured in the Lauren Bacall style, there was no chance of it falling across her face. He caught the whiff of her perfume as he'd kissed her cheek. Unmistakeable, but so delicate, he'd never found out what it was.

She ignored the compliment and pointed at the menu.

'There's plenty of red meat on offer, Michael. I'm having the Dover sole. I've ordered you something suitable to drink.'

She sipped at a tall glass containing what Fletcher assumed would be an expensive Chablis. Even as he considered this, a glass of red arrived at his elbow. A young waitress gave him the once over and raised her eyebrows.

'Give my gentleman friend a minute of two, my dear,' said Louisa.

The waitress went away.

Fletcher quickly selected his meal and offered his glass towards Louisa. The chink sounded round the empty dining room.

He gestured behind him.

'Booked them all, did you?' he asked.

She gave him a shrewd look.

'There are many advantages to being rich, Michael, and getting what you want, how you want it, is one of them, but in this case it's you who is the true beneficiary.'

'Very kind I'm sure. Couldn't be more different than last night.'

Louisa's eyes were cold.

'I have little interest in your public bar proclivities, Michael, as you well know, so I'd rather you keep the comparison to yourself.'

'Uhuh. So why have I been summoned?' he asked.

'I think you know already,' she said. 'I may not like the way you dress or behave, but I know you're not stupid. Well, not as far as criminal activities are concerned.'

'Am I about to get a yellow card?' he asked.

Louisa frowned.

'I shouldn't underestimate the danger that you're in, Michael. In this particular game, you and I are definitely second eleven.'

'I can't believe that you've been demoted, Louisa, but I think you know I'm about to be surplus to requirements. Maybe have to play in a pub team instead.'

'This is a wearisome metaphor,' Louisa said with a sigh.

The waitress arrived with their food.

'Let's eat,' she said. So they did.

* * * * *

Afterwards they'd retired to a smaller room, studded with red leather armchairs. The maître d' followed them through and enquired about digestifs. They both declined, but ordered coffee.

'To business,' said Louisa. 'No more pussy-footing around.'

Fletcher knew he wasn't expected to speak.

'I'm here as Anthony's emissary.'

Fletcher nodded, biting back on some point-scoring quote from Julius Caesar.

'He says, and I quote, "Tell your untamed attack dog, that it's not the wolves he should worry about. It's the bulldogs who are roaming free at the moment and they don't take kindly to any interference".'

'I thought we'd abandoned the metaphors,' he asked.

Louisa mouthed touché.

'He also said that the shopkeeper's daughter has a long memory and was keeping score. She's determined to stay in business and if that means she'll have to find another supplier for the corned beef, then so be it.'

Fletcher sighed.

'Alright, I'd already got the message. I can spot a Special Branch shut down when I see one.'

Louisa shook her head.

'No Michael. This time it's the real spooks. Northwoods.'

That he didn't understand.

'MI5, GCHQ,' she explained. 'Or worse.'

'Worse?'

'Think public school headmaster's room. Think about a junior boy who thought he could give away school secrets. Bring in matron, who has a long held grudge against this boy.'

Fletcher couldn't imagine any of this, but he knew what it meant.

'You mean someone's done something they really don't want other people to know about?'

Louisa agreed with her eyes.

'And someone needs to be eliminated?'

Again the slightest dilation in her eyes.

'More than one?'

Her eyes widened.

He held up three fingers.

Louisa flexed her left hand and brought up the two smallest fingers on her right hand. Seven!

'Almost a cull,' said Fletcher.

Louisa nodded at the waitress as she placed their coffee cups down carefully. She waited until the girl had gone and the door was pulled to.

'The thing is, Michael. It doesn't matter how many it needs to be. There's no turning back now … as the lady has already declared.'

Fletcher took a sip of his coffee. A bit too acrid for his taste. He added a sugar lump.

'So, gob shut and walk away?' he asked.

Louisa wrinkled her nose at the common tone, but nodded again.

'You've been fortunate, Michael, and clever,' she said. 'Some people don't like that. They'd like it if you were to go too far. Don't give them the excuse.'

Fletcher took another sip of coffee and relaxed back in his seat. He wondered if there was anything else.

But there wasn't.

Louisa didn't go in for chit-chat and so five minutes later he watched as her Jaguar slowly crunched out of the forecourt and accelerated up the hill out of town. She wasn't driving. A tall young man in a light grey suit had appeared from nowhere as though she'd hung him up in the cloakroom. Fletcher wasn't introduced as she'd kissed him goodbye.

He stared up the road as the gravel resettled itself and the branches of the road-side trees stopped swaying. He realised that she hadn't mentioned Laura at all and yet how else would she have known where he was going? Was that good or bad news? He knew she'd always side with Laura. Some bond made between them the first time they'd met at Roger's. Something to do with Laura's Aunt Magda's Tarot reading.

He got in his car and set off along the same road. No hope

of keeping up with her. He had to at least look like he wasn't breaking the speed limit. In any case he was in no hurry. He needed to plan some sort of defensive strategy, which would somehow get the game cancelled at least. Before the community singing if he could manage it.

As it turned out he was happy to accept defeat. It wasn't a disaster. Not a six nil hammering.

He arrived at Grace's flat about half past three. Laura answered the door. One-nil. Quickest goal in history. She'd had all her long waves and curls cut off! And replaced by a shiny dark helmet. Fletcher was dumbstruck. She raised her eyebrows and gave him a wry smile.

'You need to be very careful what you say next, Mick Fletcher,' she said, which was just what he was thinking.

'Amazing!' was the best and most honest answer he could come up with.

First warning, no yellow card, but it could have been a straight red.

They went through into the kitchen.

'You can kiss me, you know,' she said.

'Sorry,' he muttered. 'Not sure I was allowed.'

'Don't play games, Mick,' she said and pulled him towards her.

An hour later she sat up in bed and sighed.

'I've missed you, Mick Fletcher. You bastard.'

He lay on his back, gathering his breath.

'Me too,' he managed. 'I mean, I missed you too.'

She said nothing. They lay there pondering their next words.

'It was Grace's idea,' she said.

He turned to look at her, unsure of what she might mean.

She ran her fingers through her hair.

'The haircut, dummy,' she said and got out of the bed and

109

walked over to the mirror.

He watched as she finger combed her hair back into the shape it was supposed to be.

'What do you really think?' she asked, looking at him through the mirror.

'I … well … it was a bit of a shock, but now I'm getting used to it, I think I like it. Makes you look younger.'

She turned to stare at him. Totally naked, hands on shapely hips, legs apart and breasts still glistening with sweat after their recent exertion. God, she was beautiful. An Amazon.

'Mick Fletcher,' she said quietly. 'Tell me the truth. Did you get that from Grace?'

He shook his head.

'Well, I think so too, so you'd better watch your step.'

He gave her a puzzled look.

'I mean you need a haircut and a shave, before we go and buy you a decent shirt and a new jacket. So get into the shower and get a move on, we're booked for dinner at seven thirty.'

* * * * *

The next couple of hours were a bit of a whirlwind of shops and changing rooms, which normally Fletcher would have hated, but his distaste for shopping was mollified by noticing how many admiring glances Laura was getting from both men and women.

Finally they were dropped in Chinatown and did a circuit before arriving at the restaurant she'd chosen, where to his further surprise they found Grace and Quill propping up the bar waiting for them.

The evening got better as it went on. The meal was great. The company was great. Lots of laughter and stories and the community singing was a huge success.

This was the part of the event Fletcher had been dreading

and he was still full of trepidation as the taxi pulled up outside a modern-looking pub. The Wooden Doll. He never found out where the name had come from, but the experience was memorable.

Inside it was crowded and they were lucky to find a table with four chairs. The music had begun and Fletcher sighed with relief when he realised that there was a stage and a band already installed. Laura squeezed his hand.

'It's alright, Mick, you don't have to sing,' she said and laughed.

After a couple of numbers the band was augmented with a volunteer from the audience and this turned out to be the accepted procedure.

Except at about ten thirty, something extraordinary happened.

Over the other side of the room there was a group of people gathered round a couple of tables. They didn't seem any different from most of the other locals and Fletcher hadn't taken much notice of them, although on reflection he had noted that Grace kept looking across at them.

It was from the middle of this group that a thin faced man, maybe ten years older than Fletcher, got to his feet after the band had just completed another loudly applauded number. Without any introduction he began to sing. The audience all turned towards the voice.

And what a voice. At first a slight wavering, but once into the second line he was away. He sang three songs, unaccompanied, one after the other with no words or explanation in between. The band didn't lift a finger. The songs were all Geordie anthems. Even Fletcher had heard some of them before. 'Cushie Butterfield, 'The Lampton Worm', and finally, 'The Keel Row'. In most other situations Fletcher guessed any Geordie audience would have joined in, but here they wanted to listen to this one voice, which was so astonishingly powerful and full of emotion. By the time he sat down, many of the audience were in tears, but that didn't prevent them from all standing up and cheering and shouting for more.

He did one more: 'Byker Hill and Walker Shore,' which reduced Fletcher to tears.

Afterwards as they walked back to the flat, Fletcher asked what they knew about him, but Grace said she didn't even know his name and that they'd been lucky that night.

'More often than not he's there, but he doesn't always sing and everyone knows not to try and make him,' she told Fletcher.

It was sometime before Fletcher got to sleep that night. He'd not had much to drink and his mind was buzzing. Laura had been 'Amazon-like' in her fierce love making, which was fantastic, of course, but afterwards he found himself gazing at the ceiling, listening to her steady breathing and trying to stop the images of Sorcha from invading his mind.

How could this be? Here he was lying next to woman he loved. A woman, despite everything, who seemed to love him as well – passionately, if the last hour was anything to go by. By comparison Sorcha was a non-starter. She was a miserable twenty-something, who seemed to have grown a hard carapace of world weary cynicism. How could that be attractive?

He turned over as carefully as he could and slipped out of the bed. He went to stand by the window and peeped through the gap in the curtains. Another moonlit night.

Without waking Laura, he managed to get dressed and let himself out of the flat. At first he thought he'd just walk the streets, but another idea wormed its way through his worried thoughts. He felt in his coat pocket and found his keys.

Ten minutes later he'd parked on the promenade at Whitley

Bay near the spot where he and Irene had waited for Anna to come back from her walk on the beach the previous autumn. There was no-one in sight. The beach stretched away into the night, a vast sheen of wet sand like a rippled mirror. He could make out the waves in the distance gently flopping one after another. The tide must have recently gone out.

He went down the steps and started across the sand. It was only when he'd walked twenty steps or so, that he realised the sand was really wet. He looked down at his new shoes. That was definitely a yellow card. He bent down and took them off. Socks as well. There was a rock protruding from the sand. He looked round. Not a soul to be seen. He placed them neatly on the rock, rolled up his trousers and carried on.

He continued on down until he was at the edge of the water. He gave the waves a doubtful look, but that childish desire to walk through the ripples overpowered his fear of the cold. Which was as well as the water was icy. But his body quickly adjusted and he soon forgot about the cold. He paddled a few steps and stopped to watch the seabirds swooping low across the water, as he realised it was getting light. In front of him some little brown birds were scurrying about pecking at the sand. Eventually the cold did come back and he came out of the water and began walking back to where he'd left his shoes. Except of course he couldn't remember where they were. He studied the bank and saw a figure moving slowly along the promenade. A dog gambolled down the slope and ran hither and thither. He thought he recognised one of the buildings on the promenade and headed for that.

He climbed up a few steps and looked for his car. It was more than two hundred yards away. He tried walking on the gravel path, but gave up and went back down onto the beach. That way he was pretty certain to find his shoes.

He found the rock, but the shoes and socks had gone. He looked around in disbelief. The person he'd seen had disappeared. There was one other person in sight, but they were hundreds of yards away. He went up the steps and picked his way across the gravel to his car. The only time he'd driven a car in bare feet before was last summer, when he and Laura had been to St Tropez.

He drove back to the flat and parked the car. He opened the door quietly and crept in. He'd got as far as the bedroom door, when a quiet voice came from the kitchen doorway.

'Where on earth have you been?' said Laura.

He sheepishly went to her and put his arms around her.

'Oh! She's warm!' said Miss Elphinstone's voice. 'A Winter's Tale.'

'Couldn't sleep. Been for a walk on the beach,' he explained.

She hugged him close and kissed him full on the lips.

'Work or me?' she asked as she pulled away.

'Both,' he lied.

She took him into the bedroom and they got back into bed. She didn't seem to have noticed yet that he had no socks or shoes on.

'Tell me,' she said.

'Work or you?' he asked.

'I can sort out anything to do with me,' she replied, indicating with her hand under the blanket how this was probably going to be achieved. He closed his eyes and enjoyed the moment. But then she gave him a quick squeeze and took her hand away.

'So tell me what happened in Whitehaven.'

He lay back and groaned.

He gave her a concise report, one that both DS Garner and Chief Inspector Worthington, now retired, would have been pleased with. He told her about the three deaths, about the apparent connections and then the shut-down.

'So that's it then?' she asked.

'I'm afraid so … and as I expect you know I've been warned off by Adversane again.'

She looked at him

'Louisa?'

He nodded.

Her look was sustained for a good few seconds before she looked away.

'So you're not going back?' she asked.

'Only for the coroner's court,' he lied … again.

'When's that?' she asked.

'Tuesday,' he said.

She looked back at him sharply. 'Tuesday? That's a bit quick isn't it?'

He nodded.

'To paraphrase Louisa, "When you're that powerful, you can have what you want, how you want it, and when you want it." But,' he said, 'I'll have to go back Monday to help with the documentation. The Chief Superintendent has taken away all the extra men and so the DS is on her own.'

Laura's eyes bored into him.

'On *her* own?' she asked.

He shook his head.

'Laura. She's not my type. She's a biker and … she's got long black greasy hair … and more importantly she doesn't fancy me at all.'

Laura's serious face broke into a grin.

'Well I think that might be the cue for me to sort out any problems you might have with us.'

The resulting squealing, yelling and grunting must surely have woken and embarrassed Grace and Quill, but nothing was said an hour or so later, when they assembled for breakfast.

* * * * *

The rest of the weekend passed off happily enough. Saturday was a washout. The rain seemed to have followed Fletcher over the hills. The four of them played bridge in the evening after a fish supper. Sunday they went for a walk in the afternoon and Grace and Quill went to the cinema in the evening. Fletcher and Laura were in bed by nine and he slept like a dead seal.

Laura didn't sleep so well. He'd eventually confessed to losing his shoes, but she knew there was something else he wasn't telling her. Maybe it was something he couldn't tell her, like with those other cases. But he didn't seem that bothered about this case. Normally that was the sort of thing that really got him angry, but this was different. There was a sort of sadness in him. Like something was hurting him. She was worried and decided she would have to do something about it, but what?

In the end, she slept, but her last thoughts were of contacting Louisa. Not something she liked doing. She was never sure of her. There was an arrogant ruthless edge to the woman that frightened her. She'd seen it the first time they'd played bridge and although she seemed to be protective towards Mick, she suspected that was more to do with what he knew about her indiscretions than any affection for him. What she did know was that if Louisa wanted Mick, she'd take him.

* * * * *

Her concern was increased the following morning, when Mick told her over breakfast that he wouldn't be back until Thursday night as he'd promised to go for a climb with a man called Gavin. She'd believed him when he told her about how the woman had died and that this was also a bit of an unresolved case, although

116

Mick seemed doubtful whether anything could be done about that either.

'Are you alright climbing with this bloke?' she asked.

'Oh, yeh,' said Fletcher, 'he's going to bring ropes and all the gear and he's in the mountain rescue team, so I couldn't be in better hands.'

'So why you?' she asked.

He shrugged his shoulders.

'Well, mainly because I'm not one of his friends. He says he wants to show me something up the Ghyll which he thinks his friends would just laugh at.'

Laura frowned.

'Meaning what?'

'I'm not sure. He seems convinced that it wasn't an accident. Something to do with what they were looking for.'

'What were they looking for?'

'Don't laugh,' he said. 'A headless Dalmatian.'

She did laugh.

'Not a dog. A Roman soldier,' said Fletcher, but he wasn't able to stop himself smiling at the terrible pun.

Laura laughed again.

'As in 'ancient' Roman soldier?' she asked.

'Uhuh,' said Fletcher. 'Apparently that was what they were all looking for. Sybil Hardwicke and the Wallaces as well.'

'And you believe all that?' she asked.

'Well, not the headless ghost bit, although it is historically possible, the Romans did conscript mercenaries, and there were supposed to be Dalmatian legionaries at Hard Knott Fort, which is only over the hill from Scafell. Apparently Sybil and Alice had found some contemporary writing which tells this particular story.'

Laura looked at him

'Is that all?'

Fletcher gave her a sly grin.

'No. He reckons I'm a lucky bastard as well.'

Laura laughed.

'Can't argue with that,' she said, but gave him a serious look.

'You'd better be careful, Mick Fletcher. One day your luck may run out.'

He couldn't think of anything to say to that, but the burden of his lies sagged that bit heavier as he kissed her goodbye and set off.

Laura was going back to work on Tuesday, but she'd already made her mind up to head further north today, if Louisa was at home.

A brief phone call before Fletcher was even the other side of Newcastle confirmed this possibility and as he drove onto the A69, she was aiming for the A1.

CHAPTER 6

As Fletcher and Laura headed in different directions, a third person, who also had strong feelings about Fletcher's 'luck', was leaving the M6 at junction 36. He was heading towards the same locality as Fletcher, but had no intention of meeting him or even being seen by him.

In any case he thought it highly unlikely that the irritating little man would recognise him. The only time they'd nearly met was at Louisa's house near Rochdale three years ago. He remembered seeing him in the entrance hall goading Louisa's then husband, George Hetherington. This was on the one occasion when Louisa's respectable façade was nearly pierced. He'd known that she'd developed this penchant for younger men whilst she was still not that old herself. She didn't marry them. That would have been ridiculous. Even if she was a penniless aristocrat, she knew how to find men with money who would provide her with the level of comfort she considered hers by right. This didn't include being faithful to them.

And in Rochdale the young man who Louisa had seduced just happened to be embroiled with a young woman who he needed to eliminate. He'd been astonished to see her again walking along the street with his brother's child. But he'd not refused the opportunity to remove the lingering threat to everything he'd managed to achieve. And the young teacher had nearly taken the rap for it. Fletcher had tried his best, but in the end it was Louisa who had provided Jack Knight with his alibi, on condition of course, that no one would ever find out where he'd been that fateful night.

He looked out of the window. It had started to rain as they came north of Manchester, but that seemed nothing compared to the downpour they were now surging through. His driver had slowed a little since they'd left the motorway and they still had a long way to go.

He looked back at the file that he'd had assembled.

DI Michael Fletcher was an interesting adversary. He'd managed to almost balance out the indiscretions, flagrant breaches of procedure and suspensions with an impressive list of arrests and commendations. After his near brush with himself in Rochdale, Fletcher had been involved in two other incidents which had involved him with the security services. There had been the near catastrophic nuclear disaster averted in Todmorden and then the successful removal of a number of undesirables following his 'flamboyant' interventions in Barrow. On both occasions he seemed to have accepted the instruction to keep quiet afterwards and he knew that Special Branch regarded him as a useful battering bull in a china shop to help them uncover suspected terrorist plots and tackle unsavoury gangsters with little regard for lawful methods. He suspected Adversane probably liked him for other more salacious reasons, but he wasn't bothered by that. He also knew that Louisa had taken it upon herself to become the detective's protector and guardian angel. He didn't fear her, but he remembered her well enough from their shared childhood to know that the pompous, elegant hauteur hid a guile and ruthless cunning of which he was very wary.

He looked out of the window again and the rain was still coming down. He saw the sign for Barrow slide away to the left as they began to climb upwards towards the clouds. He could have commissioned a helicopter for this journey, but there had been enough trouble caused by the incompetence of the elimination squad. He needed to make sure the business was completed and all loose ends securely tied up. He was still smarting from the harsh words he'd had to endure from the Minister himself. His only consolation being the absolute certainty that the weasel-faced buffoon would not survive the next cabinet cull and would have to take the blame for any of the problems they'd encountered.

He knew that Fletcher had been taken off the case and that he'd surprisingly seemed to have accepted the dismissal and gone home. He wasn't so sure about this. Fletcher didn't strike him as the sort of person to give up so easily, especially as the evidence had been so obviously tampered with. Fletcher's record was liberally sprinkled with examples of lone wolf activity, and being told to leave it alone seemed only to encourage and inflame his determination. He wouldn't be at all surprised to find that he was back on the case by the time he got there.

He closed Fletcher's file and picked up another, which he'd already read through several times. It detailed every error-strewn twist and turn in unpicking the connections and unlikely contacts in Sybil Amelia Hardwicke's little coterie of madcap conspirators. How the woman had inspired such devotion was beyond him. Even with their dying breath, not one of them had confessed to even knowing her. The Wallaces they'd known about for a long time. Phone tapping and surveillance had made that relatively easy, although the couple were careful never to say anything on the phone. Alice Gill had been a beguiling diversion which proved to be just that – a diversionary tactic of Hardwicke's to confuse and distract those assigned to investigate her. It had worked beautifully. Special Branch had wasted a considerable amount of time and resources tracking them here, there and everywhere as the younger woman went from one archive to another all over the country. They'd even pored over all their correspondences, trying to detect some arcane code that they must be using. All of it a charade. Brilliant.

It had been down to his moles in GCHQ to spot the real traitor. As usual it had been sex that had been used to undo the young man's loyalty. In the file on his lap the man was still only referred to by his MI5 codename, Salvador. Ironically this had been chosen before the Argentines had made their move. Despite the fact or because he'd been to Eton himself, he knew the weakness that many of these public school boys had for the forbidden fruit of homosexual entanglements. In this case it was almost laughable the way he'd been so openly enticed. This had nearly worked. He'd not hid the relationship, knowing full well he was being watched, but the very openness had made the watchers less suspicious. They'd initially paid no attention to his much cooler relationship with an older woman who had taken up residence in the same block of flats where he lived. In fact they didn't seem to have a relationship at all other than the polite exchange of greetings on the stairs or in the lift.

It was one of his team of investigators who happened to spot the connection. Elizabeth Kirby had studied at Bristol University, which in itself meant little, she was a Geology graduate, but she'd also been to Menwith Hill. Just the once, but they'd found a photograph, a long shot, but undeniably Sybil Hardwicke and Kirby talking together outside a tent. Further investigation found a series of other connections through which the two of them had communicated. Kirby didn't need to exert much pressure on the poor boy. When he confessed he'd shown them the photograph she'd slipped under his door. Not only highly explicit and identifiably himself, but a truly obscene image. Even he had been shocked by its sadistic nature … and he was a sadist himself. Except of course he preferred to hurt women not silly boys. It still wasn't clear how much any of the individuals concerned knew what they were part of, but that would come out in due time.

He closed the file.

Now it was crucial that anybody else who knew anything, which could expose the lies it had been necessary to tell, needed to be eliminated. If that included DI Fletcher then so be it.

He looked out of the window again.

The rain was interminable. He couldn't see anything other than the hillsides sliding past. Ferns and stone. It reminded him of his father's estate. He shuddered with distaste.

* * * * *

Fletcher went first to Ennerdale Bridge, where his plan encountered its first setback.

There was a large coach taking up most of the car park, emblazoned with the owner's name, and proudly declaring its Yorkshire origin. The entrance hall was milling with men in suits, although there were a few token women, also in suits. Fletcher went up to the desk and eventually attracted the attention of the flushed and overwrought receptionist.

'Oh!' she said, looking at him, as though he was someone she remembered, but couldn't place. Fletcher helped her out.

'Detective Inspector Fletcher,' he said. 'Can I have my key please?'

'Er … well … no,' she said, frowning at him.

He looked at her.

'It's been cancelled,' she said.

'Who by?' he asked.

She shook her head.

'Not sure, sir,' I didn't take the call; you'll have to ask Mrs Carmichael.'

Fletcher looked round. He assumed she meant the woman in the bar.

He though he caught a glimpse of her in the lounge, so without saying anything else to the receptionist he set off in pursuit.

It didn't do him any good. He caught up with her, but she gave him short shrift. The police station had contacted her and told her the room wasn't needed anymore. The bank managers had been booked for months and so she gave one of them his room. She didn't have enough anyway. Her problem had been solved by Stanley Gill who had offered a couple of the holiday cottages he looked after and here he was now strolling into the entrance hall. He came over to talk to Fletcher. The woman took the opportunity and disappeared.

'Looks like a convention of penguins, wouldn't you say?' he asked.

Fletcher nodded.

'I don't know about that, but one of them's pinched my room,' he replied.

'I thought you'd gone back to Penrith?' said Gill.

'Who told you that?

'Hilts,' said Gill.

'Um, well … here I am in the flesh,' said Fletcher with a grimace.

The two of them looked at the swarming managers. Neither of them had ever seen a bank manager who smiled, but this lot were one big happy crowd. Maybe they were going to compare putdowns or sob stories. Whatever it was they were far too giddy and carefree. Some of them weren't even wearing ties!

'She said the cases were closed. Coroner's court tomorrow,' said Gill.

Fletcher looked at him.

'Does that seem odd to you?' he asked.

Gill returned his look and considered the question.

'Are you saying things are being hushed up?' he asked quietly.

Fletcher held his gaze.

'You didn't hear that from me. I'm not here remember, I've gone back to Penrith.'

Gill's eyes narrowed.

'So you won't be interested in a holiday cottage?'

'Not officially, no,' replied Fletcher.

Gill got the message. He told him to ring him later, when he'd sorted his four penguins.

Fletcher nodded his understanding and walked back out to his car. Two minutes later he watched Gill carrying a couple of suitcases and accompanied by four of the managers, two older men and two of the younger women. Fletcher smirked to himself. He could see what was happening there. Gill winked at him and opened the back of his old minibus. The two male mangers made great show of opening doors and helping the two young women climb aboard. Sickening.

With another grin in his direction, Gill closed the back door and got into the driving seat and away they went.

Fletcher stayed in his car for some time longer. He doubted whether he'd see Sorcha at this time of day, it wasn't even eleven o'clock yet. After giving it some thought he got back out again and went into the reception and asked to use the phone. He got a doubtful look from the still flustered receptionist, but he told her it was police business.

He rang the police station and asked for Hilda.

When she eventually came on the phone, he could tell she was as equally flustered.

'Headless chickens?' he asked.

'You better believe it!' she said. 'The bloody top brass is all in a lather. Wanting everything yesterday, although funnily enough they're not at all interested in anything you might have written down. Not that you did, of course.'

'It works for me,' he said.

'Aye,' she said, 'and I expect there's a trail of abandoned sergeants all over the country having to account for you.'

'Afraid so,' he replied. 'Anyway, how about if I buy you a nice coffee at that café on the sea front?'

There was a pause.

'You mean you're here?'

'Bad penny me. Been said before,' he answered.

'But…'

'That as well. Half an hour or I'll tell them about the three pints you had before you went on that midnight ride the other night.'

He put the phone down before she had time to yell at him and went back to his car. He hadn't liked doing that, but he needed to know what was going on. Any doubts he had about the shut-down were now confirmed, but what was it all about? He'd bought a paper, which told him that the Royal Marines had landed on Falklands soil on Saturday night and the fighting was well underway. He'd seen the Sun headline as well … and on the back pages that QPR had held Tottenham to a draw in the cup final. So it wasn't all bad news.

Something told him it must be to do with the war as Roger had suggested, but he couldn't see how Sybil Hardwicke and the Wallaces could possibly be such a threat that they needed to be killed ... and where was Adversane? This is when the smooth bastard usually turned up, which is why he'd not wanted to go to the station. He turned the key and started the engine, just as some of the penguins came outside. Instead of their regulation suits they'd all been transformed into bright orange or yellow parakeets. Outward bound course standard issue of 'we're not going to lose you stupid townies' gear. He felt like mowing them down, but instead drove slowly past them and onwards to the seaside.

* * * * *

By quarter to twelve Fletcher had finished his coffee and was beginning to think Hilda wasn't coming, but here she was striding towards him across the promenade. The door burst open and she came straight over to his table. She was out of breath, but still managed to glower at him.

'I've got quarter of an hour maximum ... sir,' she said through gritted teeth.

Fletcher signalled to the café owner and tried his best smile out on Hilda. It didn't work.

'I tell you what, Hilda,' he said. 'As I'm not here officially, shall we drop the 'sir'. 'You bastard' is the more usual form of address I get from a number of women I know.'

Hilda gave him a prolonged glare, but finally burst out laughing.

Fletcher wasn't sure whether this was better or worse. He waited until she'd composed herself.

'I've never met so many jumped-up farts in my life,' she said eventually. 'Station is bloody crawling with them. Not that they're getting much out of our lads, mind. They can do dumb insolence as well as anyone.'

Fletcher thought back to one or two of the monosyllabic

127

responses he'd got from some of her colleagues and nodded his appreciation.

'So? Does one of these men in black go by the name 'Adversane'?' he asked.

She shook her head, but waited until the café owner placed two more cups of coffee in front of them. He gave Hilda an enquiring look, but she just smiled at him.

'Not that I've met,' she answered when he'd gone, 'but then most of them don't tell us their names … and it's all 'Henry' and 'Charles' between themselves.'

She'd tried out her best impersonation of their posh voices, but knew she'd failed.

Fletcher looked out of the window at the sea. Once again it was trying its level best to get across the wall. Not that you could see very much through the rain-streaked glass.

'So what are they asking for?' he asked.

'Everything, filling boxes with it. Carting them off to their van. We've all had to sign official secrets documents saying we won't say anything to anybody about the three deaths or the subsequent investigation.'

'Uhuh,' said Fletcher.

'I read one of them all the way through,' she said with a shudder. 'Frightening.'

'You better believe it as well,' he said quietly. 'I've seen one of their enforcers at work. Cold hearted doesn't get anywhere near.'

'So who are they?' she asked.

'Normally I'd say Special Branch, but I'm reliably informed that these people are 'worse'. MI5, I think.'

Hilda shook her head.

'Is this because of the war?' she asked.

He nodded.

'Listen. Is there any way we can communicate which they're not likely to know about?'

She gave this some thought.

'Where are you staying?'

'Ah. Well. As you probably know my room at the inn has been taken by a bloody Yorkshire bank manager no less.'

Hilda frowned.

'What? At the hotel?'

'All geared up for a falling off a rock face somewhere this morning.'

'Um, so where are you staying?'

'Not sure yet, unless your mate Stanley can help me,' he answered.

She shook her head. He wasn't sure that was because Stanley wasn't her mate or not.

'But you could still go to the bar, couldn't you,' she asked.

He nodded, not daring to guess what she might be about to say.

She looked round and then leant towards him.

'You remember the girl behind the bar? Miserable looking. Doesn't say much.'

He nodded trying to stop his heart from going into overdrive.

'Well, she's my half-sister. Long story. Don't bother.'

He nodded, but declined to tell her that he already knew this. Hilda continued.

'She's called Sorcha. Her dad was Irish. Waste of space. Buggered off when she was still a baby.'

Fletcher tried to seem only mildly interested.

'You could leave messages with her and she would ring my mother. Just say you want to talk to me and then I can ring you at wherever Stanley puts you up or at the hotel. I'll speak to him,' she said.

He nodded his understanding.

She looked at her watch.

'I'd better be going.'

She stood up. He stayed where he was.

'Two other things,' she said.

He listened.

'My friend? The one who works at the power station.'

He nodded.

'There was an emergency callout on Saturday morning when the Wallaces died. He didn't go on it. A pilot arrived from somewhere else. My contact saw them putting some crates on it with a forklift. Nothing put in the callout records. He checked. It's his job. His boss told him not to worry about it. But the helicopter was out for four hours. Hardly any fuel left. Could have been to Lancaster and back or Barrow. Never happened before, although there are plenty of trips involving VIPs they're told not to talk about anyway, so he didn't think anything of it until I asked him.'

Fletcher waited.

'And?' he asked.

She leant forward onto the table.

'The parcel?'

'What parcel?'

'The one the postman needed signing for, the day he found Sybil Hardwicke.'

'Well? Where is it?'

'He doesn't know and it wasn't there when we got there.'

'What did he do with it?'

'He says he was so shaken he just left it on the hall table.'

'Did he see anyone else?'

She shook her head.

'He didn't think about it until later. He came in this morning.

Only told me, because he thought he would get into trouble. I told him not to worry, not to talk to anyone. '

'Well done,' said Fletcher.

'I don't think anyone else knows about it ... yet,' she added.

'Perhaps I ought to talk to him?'

She took a pen out of her jacket and wrote an address down on a piece of paper.

'Don't frighten him, he's a good friend of mine,' she added.

He gave her a look of mock disbelief.

'Yeh, you do,' she said. 'It's your eyes. You remind me of a sheepdog my dad had.'

Fletcher looked askance.

She turned to go, but stopped at the door.

'He had to put it down in the end. It were a sheep worrier. No use to him, like.'

One final grimace and she was gone. He stared into space. What was it Cassie had said to him, when she was painting his portrait? 'It's the way you stare at everyone and everything. People feel threatened. Your anger's like a fire burning you up. You're a bad angel. An outsider. An avenger.'

He shook his head, as though that might free him of his demons, but they wouldn't go, especially the voice telling him it was fate. That Sorcha was someone he had to ... what? Deal with?

He looked at the piece of paper.

The café owner appeared in front of him.

'Anything else?' he asked picking up the coffee cups.

'Not too late for a bacon sandwich, is it?' asked Fletcher.

The man grinned.

'It's never too late for a bacon sandwich. How do you want it done?'

Fletcher grinned back.

'Burnt,' he said. 'Oh, and do you have a map of the town handy?'

'Coming up,' said the man.

He came back a few moments later with a tatty, much thumbed street map and Fletcher quickly found the address he was looking for.

Quarter of an hour later he was on his way. He figured by the time he got there the postman might be getting home from his round.

Sure enough he found the van outside the door and the man standing in his kitchen with a mug of tea in his hand.

Fletcher explained who he was and how it wasn't going any further than him.

The man gave him a doubtful look.

Fletcher reassured him by telling him that he was off the case as well, but trying to cover his and Hilda's backs.

'Aye, well,' the postman said. 'Copshop was heaving with off-comers this morning,' he said. 'If she hadn't appeared from nowhere, I'd have been off. That time in the morning I thought there'd be hardly anyone around. I'd called at her house earlier and her mother had said she'd gone in first thing, like.'

Fletcher nodded.

'Men in black?'

'Ay,' said the postman.

'Less you know the better,' said Fletcher. 'Trust me.'

'I know nothing,' said the postman and pulled a face.

Fletcher wasn't sure what that meant, but carried on.

'The parcel?'

The postman leaned against the sink.

'I knocked and went in, like I always did,' he said. 'Called out, put the parcel down on the table in the hall.'

He looked away, eyes welling up.

Fletcher thought he'd help him out.

'So you went upstairs and found her, came back down and went for help?'

The man nodded, took a large grubby handkerchief out of his pocket, and wiped his nose.

'It was awful. Seeing her like that. In the bed. I thought she was asleep, but she were cold. Stone cold.'

Fletcher gave him time to recover.

'So where did you go for help?' he asked.

'The hotel in the village. I knew it would be open. No use going to the phone box. Gets vandalised regular. I'd seen the glass was broken again that morning.'

'So you phoned from there?'

He shook his head.

'I could hardly speak. Joan did it.'

'The receptionist?'

'No, the owner.'

'And then what?'

'We waited at the hotel.'

'So you didn't see the parcel again?'

He shook his head.

'Any idea what might have been in it?

The man shrugged his shoulders.

'Papers. Documents. She said she still did some marking.'

'Has anyone else asked you about it?'

The man gave him a worried look.

'No. Why?' he asked.

Fletcher was thinking.

'So what should you have done with it? In normal circumstances?' asked Fletcher.

The man frowned.

'You mean if there's no one to sign for a parcel?'

133

Fletcher nodded.

The man sighed.

'Well, I'd leave a note and take it back to the office. Maybe I'd try again the next day, depending on who it was and whether I thought they'd be there eventually. But after ten days it would go back to the main sorting office and if there was a sender's address it would be returned.'

'Was there a sender's address?'

The postman put his mug down on the sink and closed his eyes. Fletcher waited.

'I think it was one of those she got from the University,' he said as he opened his eyes.

'University?'

'Aye. Bristol. She was a professor there I think. They had the University's badge on them.'

Fletcher held his breath.

'Was there a name?' he said quietly.

The man closed his eyes again.

'Can't see it,' he said, frowning hard, 'but they didn't tend to have a name.'

Fletcher waited to see if there was anymore, but that was all he was going to get.

'I tell you what though,' he said as he made to leave. 'My best advice to you if you get asked is to say you left it on the table and you assumed the police had got it.'

The man nodded his understanding.

Fletcher went to the door, but then turned towards him.

'Was there anyone else at the hotel when you went for help?'

The man thought about it.

'No. I don't think so. Viv the receptionist hadn't turned up. Joan was in a bit of a flap. She'd even asked Sorcha to get up, but I didn't see her and then Viv arrived. She'd had trouble with her car.'

Fletcher shook his head and went.

In the car he headed back to Ennerdale Bridge. The rain had come on heavy again and was bouncing off the tarmac. A mile or so short he pulled into a National Park picnic site.

What was he going to ask Sorcha? Why would she take the parcel? How could she know it was there? As the postman had hinted, it's possible she didn't even get up. No one had said there was any connection between her and Sybil Hardwicke. Why should there be? Yet, she must have known who she was. Must have met her. It didn't make sense. Fletcher's unlikely coincidence detector was twitching. Who else could have taken it? No-one stepped forward.

He put the car into gear, his heart galloping faster and faster.

* * * * *

The black Daimler pulled up at the security gates outside the nuclear power station. This wasn't the main entrance, but the car and its occupants were expected. The security guards caused them little delay.

Five minutes later the car stopped outside an office block and the driver got out and opened the rear door for his passenger.

James Torqill Ferris climbed out of the car, releasing his tall, angular body into the rain sodden air. His driver covered his brief journey from car to the entrance of the building with a large black umbrella. Ferris had no real need for the Barbour full length coat, but he always wore it if he was going anywhere north of London. He had been born and brought up in the Scottish borders, but he rarely visited, apart from the odd trip to make sure that the estate was being properly managed.

He'd had enough of rain, trees, and Gothic monstrosities and all that false aristocracy. His family were descended from cattle thieves, had fought the Douglas and the Percy for generations. He had no pride in any of that, although he knew their duplicitous blood ran strong in his veins.

He'd not come here out of any sense of national or even political fervour. He merely enjoyed the exercise of power, of seeing people about him who were unctuous and afraid. The threesome approaching him now was exhibiting a fine demonstration of these two qualities. He knew who they were, but wasn't about to be impressed or show anything other than a cold politeness. They were only the people in charge of this monstrous energy supply, the workings of which didn't interest him in the slightest. More importantly they worked at the most reliable security organisation in the vicinity.

'Worked' probably wasn't the right word, he reflected as they introduced themselves as Head of Resources, Transport Manager, and Head of Security. He followed them upstairs to a comfortably furnished function room, where they'd assembled the documents he'd asked for. Security rotas, timetables, personnel reports on possible security risks, local agitators and journalists – the usual things.

He glanced at the summaries and lists of names, but saw nothing to worry him. His main concern had been the local coroner, who had been both belligerent and unhelpful, until they'd found out about his drinking and the affair he was having with a local solicitor's wife. Bringing this to his attention had persuaded him to take a short break on health grounds and a stand-in had been quickly brought up from Manchester. He was a younger man from a half decent school intent on reaching the higher echelons and so was more than happy to reconsider the evidence. That evidence had been now crucially changed by exerting similar pressure on the two pathologists, although the local one had to be intimidated by a senior member of his profession, before he would admit that he couldn't be absolutely certain that the Digoxin dose couldn't have been self-administered. The man at Lancaster had changed his mind in the first place, so could hardly now insist the coroner accept his second prognosis. In any case the recent arrival of some of his extended family from Pakistan made him far more inclined not to upset the government officials who had visited him at home.

As there were no other witnesses, the coroner's decision would have to be 'death by natural causes or accident'. Either way it would be all over and done with by Tuesday dinnertime.

Ferris dismissed the three stooges and waited for the arrival of the Assistant Chief Constable. He'd read the man's file earlier. He'd come up through the ranks and was now probably two levels above his competence, so had notched up a few black marks along the way. Sufficient for Ferris to be able to ensure his cooperation at any rate, as his informants had told him that the man would do anything to maintain and improve his position.

There was a knock at the door and the man appeared.

All that gold braid and the silly hat. The things that some men aspire to, thought Ferris. He listened with half an ear to the man's rambling report. God, how did he get to this level?

He stopped him in mid-sentence.

'Yes, Assistant Chief Constable, I appreciate your thoroughness, but I have only one concern.'

The ACC frowned. He wasn't used to being interrupted, not realising that the majority of his inferiors rarely listened to him and ignored most things he asked them to do.

'Yes?' he asked, uncertain what this concern might be.

'DI Fletcher? What has happened to him?'

ACC Gough smiled. This wasn't a problem.

'Gone back to Penrith, with flea in his ear. No need to worry about him.'

Ferris wasn't used to being addressed in this off-hand manner and so took the opportunity to demonstrate the stupid man's ignorance.

'If by Penrith, you mean his stepdaughter's flat in Tynemouth ... I'd suggest you need to spend a bit of your spare time studying an atlas of the United Kingdom. By my estimation they are at least eighty miles apart.'

Gough stared at the tall man in front of him. He'd heard that he could be witheringly critical, but that comment was impertinent. However he was astonished to hear this information. He had been told personally by Conroy that he'd seen the obnoxious man off on Friday afternoon. He told Ferris this.

'That's as maybe,' came the reply. 'Unfortunately we lost contact after he'd set off this morning. An unusually poor piece of operational behaviour which has, of course, seen the two officers concerned severely reprimanded. However as they lost him somewhere near Carlisle and he hasn't arrived for work in Penrith, I think we can assume he's headed this way.'

ACC Gough considered his options. What he wanted to do was punch this arrogant toffee-nosed bastard in the face, but given that was likely to terminate his career, he decided to offer to find the errant detective.

'I'll get straight on to it,' he said. 'If he's on my patch I'll find him soon enough.'

Ferris gave him a blank stare.

'Actually my men are already searching, so it would be unhelpful if your officers got in their way. I would prefer it if you just made sure none of your people would provide him with any support or information. Once my men have found him, we will deal with him. He's no longer your problem.'

Gough was now confused. Was he being dismissed? He

dithered.

Ferris both loathed and enjoyed dithering. Loathed it because it was one of the surest signs of weakness in a man and enjoyed it because it confirmed his sense of control.

'To be clear, Assistant Chief Constable, I would like it if you personally saw to it that there was no communication between Fletcher and the detective sergeant at Whitehaven, who I believe is called Crake, Hilda Crake. You may not be aware of it, but DI Fletcher has a reputation of adopting and grooming young female officers into his irregular way of working.'

Gough stared at him in disbelief. He'd never even heard of or met the woman.

'It may seem a minor task to you, but I must insist you carry this out immediately and personally.'

Gough was rooted to the spot. Who did this bastard think he was?

As if Ferris could read his mind, which given the man's expression wasn't that hard, he barked at him.

'When I say 'immediately', I expect people to disappear.'

Gough hesitated for two seconds too long, but he did disappear.

Ferris walked to the window and looked out at the cooling towers and beyond at a cold grey line which he took to be the sea. The ghost of a smile passed over his lips, but was replaced by the tightening of his face to make it even more chiselled than usual.

What should he do when Fletcher was found? There had been an unnecessarily high body count already. He would prefer not to have to kill him. In truth he wished he could persuade the man to work for him. His record showed little sign of dithering. However his record also spoke of high moral rectitude, which Ferris regarded as one of the worst of human weaknesses. He picked up the phone and summoned his driver upstairs. Apart from the legitimate use of police resources and MI5 operatives, he occasionally resorted to his own personal enforcement agent.

He'd met Stephane Lottin in Kinshasha. The details were still hazy, because he'd contracted some terrible jungle fever. Ferris had managed to avoid being captured by the rebels by hiding in the garden of the Embassy and making a run for it as it and many of the other embassies were attacked and ransacked. Lottin nearly killed him. He was on the run from the French legionnaires. He and a couple of others had come across a group of government soldiers who'd made off with a huge stash of diamonds. There had been a gun battle, during which all the Zairian soldiers had been killed. It was only when they were searching the bodies that they discovered the bag. Just an ordinary soldier's kit bag. Unfortunately the diamonds were too much of temptation. The legionnaires fell out and killed each other. Lottin only managed to escape because he'd been knocked out by a glancing blow to the head and the others thought he was dead.

Armed with only his jungle knife he made his way back to the capital and came across Ferris trying to get to the airport. He jumped him thinking he was a soldier, but quickly realised the man was carrying the best sort of diplomatic immunity. A British passport. The two of them were picked up by the victorious Franco-Belgian forces and Ferris was able to provide him with a new identity. Since then he'd taken the name Stephen Jarvis and had carried out numerous unrecorded activities for Ferris. He'd been in the Legion for eight years and had acquired a lethal, yet inconspicuous, expertise in making problems and people disappear.

Now he entered the room with that feline stealth that Ferris so admired and came over to the window to await his instructions.

140

Ferris reached inside his jacket pocket, produced a photograph of Fletcher, and gave it to Stephane.

'I need you to find this man and follow him,' he said.

Stephane nodded and pocketed the picture.

Ferris gave him the address of the hotel and suggested he start there. He wasn't to kill him yet, but it might be necessary in the next few days, so his whereabouts was important. Stephane asked whether he should take the car and Ferris told him he'd arranged for him to have use of one of the power station vans. Without another word he left as silently as he'd arrived.

Ferris looked out the window. The rain had become heavier. But this time tomorrow, everything should be cut and dried. Apparently the Hardwicke woman had wanted to be cremated. How very helpful of her. Hippie nonsense.

CHAPTER 7

The next shift in Fletcher's fortunes was down to good luck. If he'd not heard the sirens and seen the police cars hurtling along the lanes towards him, he'd have been waiting at the entrance to the car park and they would have spotted him. As it was he ducked down and waited until the three cars had gone past. It was only because he'd pulled right in off the road and was hidden by the toilet block, that they didn't see him.

It was obvious where they were going, so he couldn't go back to the hotel now. What was he going to do? All thoughts about Sorcha went out of his head as he tried to figure out how to avoid being found and removed from all possibility of further investigation. Perhaps he could get to Stanley Gill's place and persuade him to find him a hideaway. He'd set up a communication channel with Hilda and he thought neither of them were going to give him away. But this was getting complicated.

He reached over to the back seat and felt inside his rucksack for the large scale map of the area which he'd brought with him. After just a few minutes he could see that the only way he could get round to Gill's house was to risk going back to Cleator Moor to cross the River Ehen before following a long minor road detour all the way round to the lake and back in again. Almost

360 degrees round the village. But once he was over the river he'd be on roads they were unlikely to think he would take. He folded up the map and wound the window down. He couldn't hear any sirens. For a moment he hesitated. But he didn't dither.

Five minutes and he was across the bridge, into Cleator Moor, and almost immediately right onto the little road signed to Kirkland. It was when he'd eventually turned south again and came to a hamlet called Croasdale that he had a thought; he saw a telephone box, which wasn't vandalised. He parked across the road.

Fortunately he had enough change. A female voice answered, Viv, the receptionist.

He asked if a Mr Hardwicke happened to be in the bar.

'I think I just saw him going in there,' she answered. 'Who shall I say is calling, sir.'

'His solicitor,' he replied. 'It is rather urgent.'

'I'll see if I can get him, sir. Please wait a moment.'

She put the phone down, so that Fletcher could hear voices. He couldn't hear what they were saying, but he'd put money on that he could hear Conroy's timbre.

'Hello, Mark Hardwicke, here. Is that you, Sedgeley?'

'Pretend it is,' said Fletcher. 'It's Roger's private dick.'

There was a brief moment when he thought he'd blown it or Hardwicke hadn't understood, but then the public school training kicked in.

'Of course, Sedgers, old boy,' he said. 'Guess who's turned up? That old rogue Aughton. Always was one to smell out a house sale. What can I do for you?'

'Are the police there?' asked Fletcher.

'Absolutely, old chap. Seven or eight of them beetling about. Bit of a flap on, I think.'

'Anyone we know?'

'Yes, I think so. How can I help?'

'Have they been to the house?'

'Came to find us there, but they're all here now.'

'Good,' said Fletcher. 'I'm going to beg a favour.'

'Fire away old chap, always up for a little excitement, don't you know.'

Considering the situation, Fletcher had to admire the man's sang-froid.

'You remember that sofa? I was wondering if it was still available.'

'Absolutely old chap, not a problem. Come for it any time.'

'Thanks Mark. Don't know when. I'll wait for the dust to settle.'

'That's fine,' said Hardwicke.

'Bye,' said Fletcher and put the phone down.

He got back in his car and looked at the map again. His main problem now was to get rid of the car.

He studied the map.

Ten minutes later he arrived at the Bowness car park about half way up the northern side of Ennerdale Water. He parked in the far corner behind a shed. The sun had come out and he could see the tops. He knew from studying the map that the high fells on the right as he looked up the valley were Pillar and Scoat Fell. He could just make out the triangular peak of Steeple against the skyline. Laura and he had done the Mosedale Horseshoe from Wasdale last summer. He remembered a brilliant blue sky day, only marred by twisting his ankle scree-running on the steep descent from Dore Head.

He got out of the car and took his rucksack out of the boot. Five minutes later he'd changed into his walking gear and stuffed his other clothes into the rucksack. He locked the car and set off down to the lake.

It was a gentle stroll with amazing views. If he survived all this, he'd bring Laura here and go for a long walk. It didn't take long before he was at the weir on the western end of the lake. He stopped to listen to the silence.

Not silence, water forcing its way across the weir, a couple of cheepy chaffinches bobbing about, and bees bustling insistently on some tall raggedy foxgloves. Did the bees get fizzy on the digitalis? He shook his head. Why so many questions? A cry from a buzzard lazily circling on the warm updrafts high above, it didn't question the nature of this facility; it just floated higher and higher on a soft invisible corkscrew. There were clouds and they were scudding, but not too grey … yet.

He watched as a pale butterfly fussed around some drab harebells near where he sat on a warm boulder. As he studied it he saw that its wings were marbled with dark veins and that the pale blue invisibly blurred into pale yellow. He could see the long thin proboscis prodding into the centre of the flower. He'd no idea what type it was and realised that other than cabbage white and red admiral he didn't know the names of any other butterfly.

Did it matter?

The un-named creature fluttered away giddily, indifferent to his ignorance.

He looked up the lake.

It shimmered in the fading sunlight: areas of blue and grey and silver alternating into the distance.

He realised he was prevaricating. No. Procrastinating. Hamlet's tragic flaw but not usually his, in fact normally people thought he was quite the opposite. The bull in the china shop. It was an odd phrase. Must be imaginary, surely … but a perfect image. You could see the anger, the glaring eyes, the wrinkled neck muscles, the ticks of frustration, the tail whipping delicate porcelain into the air, a casual twitch of the shoulder knocking over thousands of pounds worth of Meissen, a sudden rush, head down, crushing tables and cupboards into splinters and the Wedgewood powdered into smithereens. You could hear the crashing and crunching of wood and pottery, the snorting and the uneven clatter of hooves. You could even smell the animal heat and imagine the tearing and crushing impact of that hot body if you were unfortunate enough to be a trapped customer or the terrified owner.

Was that him?

He shook his head and laughed at himself.

No. He was better than that. Not just a hunk of brute force, flying thoughtlessly into action. Angry? Yes … and why not? People were being killed because others didn't want their dirty secrets to come out. He had been hounded out of the scene, because he dared to ask the wrong … no, the right questions.

He reached inside his rucksack and took out the map again. He traced the zigzag road for half a mile to where there was a footpath off to the right, which by-passed the village and came out onto the lane that would bring him to Sybil's house.

He stood up.

'But that's not the problem, is it, Michael?' he said to himself, using Louisa's knowing tone.

He set off along the lane, into the deep shade of the fir trees standing heavy and thick on both sides. A tunnel of green. His thoughts glided to the disquiet lurking in the murky recesses of his mind. The curtain of silken hair hiding most of her face, one ebony eye staring at him, not smiling, staring into his inner being. The glimmer of a world-weary smile. Why was this happening to him?

He strode on. Knowing that he must go, even though his heart shivered at the prospect.

* * * * *

Fletcher had disappeared.

Ferris put the phone down. He didn't like it. Didn't like it one bit. Damn the man.

Stephane had just confirmed what Ferris had been told by a gruff Chief Superintendent called Conroy. At least this man didn't prevaricate. Although Ferris was annoyed that Gough had ignored his instructions and delegated the task he'd specifically been told to carry out personally. Ferris would see to it that the man suffered for this. But no one had seen Fletcher or his car. They'd been to the hotel and Hardwicke's house. Searched them both. Conroy had questioned all the officers at Whitehaven who had any dealings with the man, but only received some sullen shrugs and the occasional 'good riddance' from one or two. DI Fletcher was not universally liked and was regarded with outright suspicion by many. He hadn't followed procedures or completed any paperwork. If the DS, Hilda Crake, had seen him today she was a damn good liar.

Ferris was convinced the man had done his job properly, but not convinced that Fletcher had given up. He told Stephane to keep on looking, whilst he made some phone calls. Following this he rang Conroy back and gave him the names and numbers of Fletcher's Penrith colleagues, as well as the man's woman friend and her daughter.

It didn't take long. Most denied any knowledge of his whereabouts, whilst the woman, Laura Wilshaw, was still on her way home from Newcastle.

He wasn't the sort to pace the floor or to send himself into the fray. He rather preferred the image of a spider, twitching its web of spun entrapment. He stared out of the window at the thin line of sea.

Think worst case scenario.

Suppose Fletcher had got wind of the search. Perhaps even now he was watching from some hideaway. Where would that be? Who might protect him? Harbour him?

He thought he understood the man. He'd hide where he'd think the searchers would least suspect. In a place they'd think he wouldn't dare reappear. Conroy had said they'd searched the hotel and Hardwicke's house. But supposing he'd been watching them do that? And now he'd have gone back. Sitting with a glass of whisky in that bloody old woman's parlour.

He picked up the portable phone and pressed the button.

Nothing but static. Stephane must be out of signal. Damn hills.

He stood there for a few moments weighing up the odds.

No dithering. He strode quickly to the door, walked down to the ground floor and out to the Daimler. A swift half of Jennings in the late afternoon seemed the appropriate response, although it was some time since he'd had that dubious pleasure. Before setting off he checked the glove compartment for his gun.

* * * * *

Fletcher came out from the heavy, pine-laden tunnel onto the open lane. Directly ahead was the sign announcing the name of the village, to his right the stile and the path beyond, which led to Sybil Hardwicke's house. He looked again along the road to the village. He could see the slate roof of the church on the left, must be about half a mile. He went over to the fence. Here was another older stile and half hidden by a hedge of late blossoming blackthorn was an old sign, which simply said 'To the church'.

He stood and considered his options. There was every chance his erstwhile colleagues were still hanging around at the hotel and the house, but perhaps the church was somewhere he could wait until dark. An approaching car made up his mind. He slipped over the stile and hid behind the trees. The path was overgrown but obviously still in use and the hedges were high, preventing anyone from seeing him from the road. Even better the clouds were now obscuring the afternoon sun and looking ominously heavier. He hurried along the path swishing the long grass and occasional nettles away.

Within half an hour he could see over the wall into the graveyard. At the end of the wall there was a metal gate – the type where you had to push it one way and then bring it back in front of yourself – if you weren't too fat. A kissing gate? He thought of Roger and grinned to himself. He imagined Mark Hardwicke sharing their conversation and the old rogue giggling in delight at the ruse he'd suggested.

A few yards further and he was pushing open the sturdy wooden door and stepping into the hushed space. As his eyes adjusted to the gloom he took in the rows of pews leading to a curved chancel with the organ prominently visible on the left. The remaining light was filtering through the stained glass making a smudgy coloured stain on the whitewashed wall. He realised that although he had been unaware of noises outside, they had now gone. Hushed was the right word. He took off his rucksack and eased himself into a pew.

In the ensuing silence he pondered his situation. Very John Buchan he thought. Here he was on the run, a confirmed non-believer from childhood, seeking shelter; no not just shelter, but sanctuary from the forces of evil! 'How melodramatic!' he smiled to himself. Still there was no denying the sense of seclusion and the illusion of safety.

This brief escape lasted for a few minutes during which his thoughts reverted to his guilty secret – a sweep of her hand and a wave of hair – only for this tentative balloon to be exploded by the arrival through a side door of a Brunhilde-esque figure singing at the top of her stentorian voice. She was halfway towards the organ, managing an awkward and not particularly venerating bow in the general direction of the altar as she went, when she sensed she wasn't alone. She stopped in her tracks and peered down the aisle.

'I'm so sorry,' she boomed. 'Didn't see you there. A thousand apologies.'

Fletcher was too astounded to respond, so she pointed towards the organ.

'Forgot my damn glasses … again. Oops, sorry, totally out of order.'

She hesitated when she didn't get any response and gestured towards her glasses, which Fletcher could now see perched on the music rack over the open keyboard. He found his voice.

'Don't mind me, madam,' he said, as he got to his feet and picked up his rucksack. 'I'm not a believer and I've heard far worse. Just pausing for a rest after a day out on the fells.'

'And you're very welcome,' said the woman, as she retrieved her errant spectacles.

'Where have you been to today? Grand day for it.'

Fletcher stood his ground as she marched up the aisle towards him.

'Aye,' he said. 'I've come over from Wasdale via the Pillar and Steeple.'

'A wonderful walk that is too,' she said.

As she came up close he found himself looking up. Must be six foot two at least. Medium length fair hair held back by an incongruous Alice band. Hint of a moustache and arms like Popeye. Fletcher couldn't stop the image of a vicar looking like Olive Oil. He smiled.

'So,' she said, still too loud and only a handshake away. 'If you were hoping for a bed for the night in the village, you'll be out of luck, the hotel is booked up … unless my eyes deceive me and you are a bank manager?'

He shook his head and laughed.

'Your eyes are in perfect good order, madam. Absolutely no possibility of that.'

'Well, in that case and to make up for my bursting in on your moment of non-denominational reflection, how about a nice cup of tea and a chunk of home-made cake?'

'Sounds good to me,' he replied.

'Margaret Cavendish-Fielden, although I only answer to Mags,' she said offering a large hand, which Fletcher took apprehensively. He was right. It was a bone crushing handshake, but at least the wincing gave him time to come up with an alias.

'Mick Garner,' he offered, inwardly smirking at the outrage this would cause the genuine owner of the surname. She gave him a suspicious look, so he doubted she believed him.

'Walk this way,' she said and set off at a pace Fletcher thought most people would call galloping.

Five minutes later he was sitting at a well-scrubbed oak table big enough to cater for a family of twelve in a kitchen as big as the whole ground floor of the house he'd been brought up in.

Mags busied herself with a large teapot and farmer size mugs, before disappearing into what Fletcher assumed would be a larder like his Aunty Emily's. In fact apart from his aunt being much thinner, there was a large resemblance to her here, large being the pertinent word.

'I don't think you'll even get a meal tonight either,' she bellowed from off-stage, before reappearing with an enormous cake tin.

Fletcher shook his head as the lid was removed to reveal two-thirds of the biggest fruit cake he'd ever seen.

'Still, with the hotel being so busy, I'm already catering for five extra tonight, so you're very welcome, we've nearly as many beds as they have anyway. It's only casserole, mind, so it's a take it or leave it offer.'

Fletcher knew he'd not managed to offer much in the way of response to this on-going tirade of questions which didn't seem to require answers, so he merely nodded.

'That'll be six then,' she said and pulled the kettle off its hob.

He waited as the teapot was given a fierce swirl and the milk jug was offered.

When the cake was cut and the tea poured, she strode over to the old Aga and opened the door revealing the glowing coals inside.

'Coming on nicely, thank you very much, old girl,' she said and closed the door again.

'Inherited her from the previous incumbent,' she said and stood admiring it whilst she wiped her hands on a large tea towel.

Fletcher knew that Laura would have made approving comments, but was quite enjoying not having to say very much. So he was completely taken aback with her next statement.

'You may not be a believer, but I hadn't got you down as a dissembler … Inspector,' she said, her large eyes boring into his.

Fletcher returned the look.

'Ah,' he breathed. 'Cover blown, eh?'

She pulled out a chair and sat down.

'It's alright, as you might expect, I am on the side of the angels.'

He smiled.

'And why would you think that I am?'

'Word gets around in a small community, Inspector, and the word is that you're at odds with the official position.'

Fletcher gave her a searching look.

'Meaning?' he asked.

She put both of her large hands round the mug in front of her and looked down at them.

'I knew Sybil Hardwicke,' she said in the quietest voice he'd heard her use. 'She was my friend. I told her about the house, when old Jeb Skinner died. We'd been here for about ten years by then and she'd been to stay with us on numerous occasions.'

She looked up. She had pale green eyes flecked with brown and darker fragments. Fletcher waited.

'I'd known her brother from Oxford, we had a brief affair before I met Godfrey and we were at his wedding. I'm Mark's godmother.'

'He didn't mention you?' said Fletcher.

'No. Well ... we've had a bit of a falling out. I'm afraid our attitudes towards money and the lending thereof differ wildly. He owes us a substantial sum and I'm not entirely sure we will see any of it even with what Sybil has no doubt unwisely left him.'

This merely confirmed Fletcher's suspicions. He recalled the guilty way Mark had turned round when he'd first met him at the house.

'However, I've offered an olive branch this evening; he's one of the dinner guests.'

Fletcher nodded.

'And is one of the others Roger Aughton?'

She laughed.

'You don't need to be a detective to work that out. He's the one who gave you the strongest commendation.'

Fletcher smiled at this.

'And the other three ... let me guess.'

She raised her eyebrows, but waited.

'Stanley Gill and a man called Gavin and his wife, Sheila?'

153

She gave him a look of surprise.

'Very good, inspector, didn't take you long to figure out the whole gang.'

Fletcher nodded.

'The Wallaces as well?' he asked.

She stood up, pulled out a large checked handkerchief from her shirt pocket and blew her nose.

'Yes,' she managed. 'It's evil. Downright evil,' she said through gritted teeth.

'Um,' said Fletcher. 'I'm not sure about that, but then I'm not sure how big the secret is that they wish to be kept that way.'

Mags gave a snort of exasperation.

'Well, we know who's in charge don't we? That bloody corner shop madam.'

Fletcher raised his eyebrows at the anger.

'I'd always thought vicar's wives would be true blue church and country,' he said.

'Not this one, Inspector, although Godfrey often fits the bill despite the ear-grinding he gets afterwards. I'm from a very old and very rich family, but that's before I went up to Oxford and was given an education by the Hardwickes, Crossman, and their like. Sybil's father was a Quaker and a friend of the Rowntrees and the Pease family, so the family had a long tradition of pacifist, socialist and philanthropic activism … as well as a healthy disregard for 'proper behaviour'. My mother was horrified … which made it even better.'

She gave a sad laugh.

The two of them sat in silence for a few moments. Mags seemed lost in a past reverie, whilst Fletcher was making some more up-to-date calculations. He'd noticed the VW camper van on the drive next to a much newer Landrover. But more importantly how was he going to get to talk to Sorcha? He needed to know what was in that parcel. He ignored the siren voice asking if there was anything else he wanted to discuss.

So it was that he jumped as Mags got to her feet and slapped her hands together.

'Stop maudlin, Margaret, there's a table to lay, potatoes to peel and vegetables to prepare.'

She looked at Fletcher.

'What's your metier, Inspector?'

'Er – potato peeling, ma'am,' he answered getting to his feet and looking round for the little blighters.

'On the floor in the larder, bottom right,' she answered, pointing at the doorway.

'Knife in the drawer there and you'll find a bucket under the sink. You need to do the lot. Stanley comes with a remarkable appetite when he's invited out.'

Two minutes later he was sitting on a stool, head down, peeling spuds into a large galvanised bucket. It reminded him of the cubs. Even the thought of it brought back the slow, burning sensation in his left foot. A spark had jumped unseen from the campfire and settled in his thick sock beneath the buckle of his sandal. The round scar was still there. The foot twitched at the memory.

Mags kept up a torrent of chatter about Sybil and marches and being arrested and the all night parties. He was only half listening, as he continued to try to figure out a way of getting to Sorcha. He knew anything he said would be treated with a query, so he knew it had to be as near the truth as he dare. He sensed a pause in the tirade and looked up.

She was sitting at the table chopping onions, tears dribbling down her face. She laughed and put the knife down so she could go and wash her hands in the sink.

'It's the only thing that works … Sybil taught me that. It's the

155

unction from the onions on your skin not the fumes.' This made her cry even more. She wiped her face with a towel.

'Pull yourself together woman,' she said fiercely.

Fletcher took his chance.

'Did you know that the postman left a parcel for Sybil the morning he found her?'

She hesitated over the onions and looked up.

'No ... I didn't. What was in it?'

'Aha ... that's the point, we don't know. It's disappeared.'

He told her what Hilda and the postman had said. She nodded her understanding.

'Any ideas?' he asked.

'About what was in it or what happened to it?'

'Either.'

She gathered up the onions and put them into a large frying pan.

'Well, like the postman said, she still took on marking, but it's not really the right time of year. She only deals with postgrads now...'

She faltered, realising she was using the incorrect tense.

'But...' She put the pan on the stove and gave it a good shake.

Fletcher picked up another potato and resolutely began to peel it without looking at her.

'But ... if it's anything to do with why she was killed, then it might have been something from Elizabeth.'

'Elizabeth?' he asked.

Mags looked at him and hesitated.

'The less I tell you the better, but shall we say someone who had her fingers in lots of murky pies.'

Why did everybody turn to metaphor when they were talking about the secret services? Fletcher wondered.

'Would this particular pie be called Northfields?' he asked.

156

She gave him another stern look.

'Not just a pretty face,' she replied.

He laughed.

'Never has been,' he said.

They eyed each other. Fletcher took another plunge.

'But I have a suspect who might be the only one with an opportunity, although I have no idea about her motive.'

Mags frowned and stood looking at him, resting her hands on the table.

'She?'

He looked down at the potatoes and took what he hoped was a silent breath.

'Um, as Holmes would have said, "if every other possibility has been eliminated then no matter how unlikely or inexplicable" etcetera…'

He kept his head down.

'Well come on, man. Out with it!' she exclaimed.

'The young woman behind the bar…'

'You mean Sorcha?'

'I think that's her name…'

Mags waited, her face blank, giving nothing away.

'Apparently, she was asked to get up, because the receptionist was late and the landlady needed some help. The postman said he didn't see her, but there was no one else around at the time. It was early … before eight.'

Mags turned and pulled up a chair.

'Now there's a thing…' she said.

Fletcher waited.

'Guess who was the first person through that door to tell us what had happened?'

Fletcher pursed his lips.

'I remember at the time how surprised I was to see her up

so early. Unheard of. She was in floods of tears, poor thing. Took me ages to get her to tell me, then I started. I couldn't believe it. Went down and found the place crawling with police and ambulances. Wasn't allowed anywhere near ... and I haven't been since.' She paused. 'And I'm not sure how I would deal with it. The place would seem so empty without Sybil.'

Fletcher watched as she stared at the vegetables in front of her as though they were something she'd never seen before or knew what to do with.

'So ... Sorcha?' he asked.

Mags came to and stared at him.

'Well ... did you know she was Hilda Crake's sister?'

He nodded.

'Only half-sister mind; couldn't be more different. Hilda's a good woman. She's well respected round here.'

Fletcher picked up another potato.

'But, Sorcha's a ... a ... shall we say 'damaged goods'. What my mother would call a waif and stray.'

'But why would she take the parcel?' asked Fletcher.

'Um ... I don't know, but...' Again she hesitated.

Fletcher didn't push it. Reached down for another potato. Only a couple left after this one.

'The thing is you'd need to know Sybil. She was ... how can I put it? Special? Definitely, but if you met her, you'd think she was just someone's granny. Except her eyes, not as unusual as yours, but you knew straight away when she caught you with a look. Small shiny beads, bright with a burning intelligence, but more than that, a knowingness. A way of looking that went straight through to your core. Not menacing, but you knew you couldn't fool her or get away with a half-truth ... and then her voice. She could speak loud enough when she wanted to; say in a lecture theatre or at a meeting or across a crowd. But equally she could hold an audience spellbound with a whisper. Especially if she was telling a story.'

'Like the headless Dalmatian legionnaire?' asked Fletcher looking up with a grin.

Mags laughed.

'Oh yes. But that wasn't her only ghost story. That's how she taught her students history. "Voices from the past", she called them.'

'In Latin?'

'But of course, or old French, or Anglo-Saxon or Gaelic, even Old Norse. She knew all the old sagas off by heart.'

Fletcher felt he was beginning to understand the woman for the first time. No longer just a victim, but someone people loved and admired.

'So how did she deal with Sorcha?' he couldn't help asking.

Mags frowned and shook her head.

'Sorcha is hard work, but Sybil found a way in. I don't know how. She never talked to me about her, but would smile at her name or whisper 'surra-ka', which is how it's pronounced in Gaelic, or quote Dostoevsky - "The darker the night, the brighter the stars, the deeper the grief, the closer is God!"'

Fletcher knew he'd have to wait.

'I don't know what went on between them. Alice called her the sorceress's apprentice. Alice was a bit jealous of Sorcha. I think she thought she was the chosen apprentice ... that she'd somehow earned it, whilst Sorcha ... she did nothing. Except, of course, she can sing like an angel.'

Fletcher looked up. He'd run out of potatoes.

'Really?'

'Oh, yes,' said Mags. 'I don't think she had much in the way of training, although I know Sybil offered to pay for it. She even managed to persuade her to go the music school in Manchester, but she didn't last more than a couple of weeks. She couldn't cope with the other students. Said they were arrogant.'

Fletcher stood up with his bucket.

Mags reached out for it and gave the contents a cursory inspection.

'You've done that before, Inspector,' she said without any mockery.

He nodded.

'I do have one or two skills. But please. Less of the 'inspector', Mick will do.'

'Ah, Michael, the warrior angel, conqueror of Satan,' she said.

He sighed.

'I prefer Mick,' he said.

'Anyway,' she continued, 'the short answer is I don't know why Sorcha would have taken the parcel. Unless Sybil had told her she was expecting it. Sorcha wouldn't get out of bed that early for anyone else I know.'

'Um … well, it could be a crucial piece of evidence, but I can't…'

'Oh I see. That's not a problem. I'll lay the table for seven, although I doubt she'll be keen, but I'll ring up and ask.'

'Discreetly,' added Fletcher as she set off towards the door.

'But, of course,' she replied. 'Trust in me.'

She was gone. He'd done it. But whether he'd deceived her he wasn't sure.

He tipped the bucket of potatoes into the sink and gave them a quick wash, before looking round for a suitable container. He'd just selected a large pan when Mags returned.

'That'll do fine,' she said taking hold of the pan and filling it with water.

Fletcher let her take over.

'And the answer is yes. No hesitation whatsoever. You must have some special power. Like Sybil.'

He turned away to avoid her seeing his response to that.

'And Sybil would have loved it. She was always one for a mystery and I have a feeling you would have found her a beguiling host. She may have been well over sixty, but she still had the occasional affair. Men and women.'

He looked back to see what she was meaning and met her steady gaze.

'Well, we'll have to see,' he said. 'There may be a simple solution we haven't thought of.'

Mags put the pan on the stove.

'The only other thing you need to know about Sorcha is that she's a promiscuous little vixen with a long history of violent behaviour. Thrown out of primary school for biting another child so badly he needed stitches. She had lots of trouble at secondary school, including assaulting a male teacher and putting him in hospital. Arrested on numerous occasions outside pubs or late night parties. I know all this because I'm a local JP. If it wasn't for her sister, she'd have been in prison by now.'

Fletcher listened to all this with mounting disquiet.

'But there's little love lost there. I think Hilda only does it for their mother.'

Fletcher waited to see if there was any more.

Mags gave him a final stare and then clapped her hands.

'Wine, Michael? I don't suppose you've any in that rucksack?'

He grinned.

'So off to the cellar with you,' she said and pointed towards another door he'd not noticed.

'The light switch is on the right hand side. Look out for the ghouls and the rats and bring us back a crate of whatever you fancy. I'm off to get changed.'

161

Before he could say anything she'd bustled out of the room and disappeared, although before he'd taken a step he could hear her lusty singing voice once more echoing round the old house.

He crossed the kitchen and opened the door. Darkened steps descended into the gloom. He switched on the light, but not before memories of another descent into a labyrinth of underground tunnels made him shudder.

But this was simply a large cellar with an extensive array of bottles. He spent a happy quarter of an hour choosing a selection. He was no expert but there were plenty of names he recognised, and many more he didn't.

When he reappeared upstairs, he was surprised to see that Mags had changed from the no-nonsense shirt and trousers she had been wearing into a flowing bright yellow full length dress.

'Don't stare, Michael,' she said, but did a twirl like a six year old.

'I detested my mother, but I did inherit her wardrobe, so I take every opportunity to get them out. This is a one-off Coco Chanel, so only admiring comments allowed.'

Fletcher laughed.

'You look fabulous,' he said.

'Correct response and now get them bottles uncorked,' she bellowed, as she swept out of the room again.

Fletcher found a corkscrew and set to.

It was only as he was selecting glasses from the cupboard that he stopped to think what might happen next.

It hadn't occurred to him that Sorcha might have a history like that and he still had no idea why she would have taken the parcel, but something told him it was no accident and that this evening could take some more unexpected turns.

He placed the glasses on the table and wondered where the cutlery might be kept.

He didn't hear anything and so nearly jumped out of his skin when he turned and saw a figure standing in the doorway.

CHAPTER 8

Laura had arrived at Louisa's house later that morning. It was nearly a year ago that she and Fletcher had been to the reception after Louisa had married John Knox. She remembered a glittering affair which ran on well into the following morning. She also remembered the feelings of awkwardness and being out of place amongst a gathering of such rich and confident people.

Some of this returned as she drove up the long avenue towards the house. But she'd forgotten how magnificent it looked until she came through the trees and saw the castellations and the grey stone façade. The sun momentarily caught the windows and almost blinded her with its myriad reflections. She slewed the car across the gravel and came to a halt. There was no one in sight.

She got out of the car and stood looking up at the stone effigies on the roof. Other than here she'd only ever seen such things at Alnwick Castle, but knew they were designed to perform the same task, trying to convince attackers that the building was heavily garrisoned.

A raven croaked that peculiar gulped bottle sound at her from beside one of these figures and launched itself into the air. She watched as it flapped lethargically away towards where she knew the river bordered the gardens. Other than that there wasn't a sound. She closed the car door and began to walk across the gravel. Her new shoes crunched on the grey stones which glinted with black sparkles.

The windows which had temporarily blinded her were now opaque rectangles staring blankly at her as she approached. She stopped and looked back across the drive. It felt like she was being watched, but there was no one there. The fir trees stood like sentinels with their backs to her, shielding her from the rest of the world. She suddenly felt very small and alone.

She hesitated. Perhaps it was a bad idea to come. Louisa hadn't been exactly welcoming, had sounded cold and matter of fact on the phone.

She turned back towards the house and urged herself forward. A furrow of determination formed on her forehead and she began to climb the steps towards the massive glossy black front doors.

Without knowing why, she sensed something behind her and turned with mounting trepidation. The hairs on the back of her bare arms tingled as she focussed on the dog not thirty yards away. It wasn't moving, but the hair on its thick neck stood erect like a rigid fur collar. She was frozen to the spot. All the visceral memory of that attack one morning on her way to school came hurtling back. The blacksmith's dog leaping out and biting her leg. She began to shake and backed towards the door. A hand rested on her shoulder and she jumped in terror. She spun round to see a small dapper man in a tweed jacket and tie. His smile evaporated as he recognised her fear.

'It's alright, Laura,' he said and took her by the elbow. 'He won't hurt you.'

When she looked back at the dog, he was slowly coming across the gravel towards them, but its tail was wagging and she could see that, unlike the dog of her nightmare, this one was old and arthritic. It gave a low growl and stopped to scratch its belly with a hind paw.

John Knox took her through the door and closed it behind him. She realised her teeth were chattering and she was still shivering with fear. She allowed herself to be led into a long corridor which took them to a large sunlit room with a view of the Tweed beyond. Standing by the window was the familiar figure of Louisa Cunninghame, holding a phone to her ear.

She waved a greeting before turning towards the window and continued to talk in a low voice. Her husband guided Laura to a huge armchair and told her he'd fetch her a drink. She accepted tea.

Louisa stood in front of her and offered her hand.

'I'm sorry about that, Laura,' she said. 'Damn accountants. Always fussing about a few groats.'

Without further comment, she went to sit in a high-backed armchair. Laura watched that sinuous walk and posture; how she crossed her legs and smoothed her skirt and adjusted an invisible stray hair.

'I assume John is being mother and preventing the staff from carrying out their jobs, whilst getting in the way of preparations for lunch. You will stay, of course,' she stated.

Laura nodded, realising it wasn't a question. She had stopped shivering and was desperately trying to regain some composure. If Louisa saw any of her fear, she didn't acknowledge it.

For a few seconds neither of them spoke. Laura found this unnerving, as she was aware that Louisa was giving her an inspection like Miss Hepworth used to do at her High School. In her case this was generally followed by a sigh of disappointment and a stern recommendation to do something about an item of errant clothing or appearance. Louisa's response was therefore a complete surprise.

'I love the new hairstyle, Laura. It really suits you. I wish I was brave enough to take such a risk.'

Laura gave her a startled look, before checking if there had been any patronising tone in her voice. It had seemed genuine, but still it confounded her.

'No. I mean it. You look stunning,' said Louisa, and to Laura's further surprise, she got up and came towards her. Before Laura could back away, Louisa reached out and stroked her hair and cupped the heaviness of it at the base of her neck. It was such an overtly intimate and unexpected a gesture that Laura didn't have time to flinch. Instead and to her further astonishment she found it intensely arousing. She closed her eyes and allowed the caress to continue. She felt Louisa's fingers follow the curve of her hair against her cheek and was bereft as it disappeared. She opened her eyes to find Louisa's blue gaze upon her.

Without any comment or further touch Louisa backed away and folded her body back into the chair. They sat in silence looking at each other. The one retrieving her haughty demeanour, whilst the other readjusted her legs like a nervous interviewee.

The moment was broken as John Knox came into the room carrying a tray and the promised tea.

The rest of the morning and lunch passed without further ado and it wasn't until the two women were ensconced in a couple of chairs in the large, plant filled conservatory that the serious conversation began.

'Has Michael gone back to Whitehaven?' asked Louisa.

Laura nodded.

'He promised to be back by Friday,' she added.

'Aha,' said Louisa, using that distinctive Scottish word of understanding, but not wishing to give anything else away.

Laura waited.

167

Louisa took her time before placing the elegant china cup back on its saucer. Her eyes transfixed Laura.

'I don't want to frighten you, Laura … but he is in great danger.'

'Why? Who?' asked Laura, without thinking.

Louisa made a severe face and carefully stroked her hair.

'The 'why' is the usual. Pursuing injustice and not knowing when to put the mouse down.'

Laura nodded and gave her a wan smile.

'The 'who', however, on this occasion, is far more worrying. It's not Special Branch he's upsetting, but people far more edgy and much more ruthless. I don't know the full story and I doubt I ever will, but something has happened and these people are determined to keep it under wraps … and they will do anything … and I mean anything to keep it like that.'

Laura considered this for a few moments.

'So what can I do?' she asked.

Louisa's look was fierce.

'Nothing,' she said.

'Nothing?'

Louisa stood up and made her way towards a plant with huge red flowers.

'You know … better than me … how stubborn he can be, so I'm calling in some favours. A couple of people who are players in these sorts of games, you can think of them as guardian angels. Hopefully he'll run out of steam. The ruthless ones are covering their tracks and leaving little to find … and they're very good at that. The main problem for them will be resolved within the week. Ashes can tell no secrets.'

Laura couldn't begin to understand what all this meant, but knew she wasn't expected to make any comment. She stayed still and watched as Louisa dead-headed the decaying flowers one by one.

If Louisa had been going to say any more, Laura would never know. The door opened and a young man entered with a hesitant manner. Louisa looked at him and he nodded with his eyes. She dismissed him without a word.

Laura thought that was it, but to her final astonishment, Louisa turned to a mahogany side table, opened a little drawer, and took out a new pack of cards.

She came back to where Laura was sitting, quickly unwrapped the pack, and placed it on the table.

Laura knew what she wanted and watched as she fanned out the cards. Louisa didn't hesitate, but fingered a card from the left hand arc. She held it up to look at it, before flipping it round between her mauve painted nails and showed it to Laura. The King of Spades.

Without pause, Aunt Magda's voice sounded in Laura's head. She read the card.

'A dark-haired man, ambitious, successful, and authoritative.'

Louisa nodded and sighed. Little else was said. Five minutes later Laura was wending her way down the long drive with the caress of Louisa's final kiss resting lightly on her cheek, the faint aroma of her perfume lingering in the air.

But her lingering memory from this strange encounter was the sight of those dark red flowers falling to the grey slate floor. Dying petals, settling where they fell … vivid, crumpled, and torn.

✻ ✻ ✻ ✻ ✻

Ferris spent only an hour in the village going to the house and the hotel. There was no sign of Fletcher and the only person who might have been suspected of harbouring him, that old tart, Aughton, had left before Ferris had arrived. Further enquiries indicated he'd set off for Appleby and though they'd considered the possibility of Fletcher hiding in the back of the dealer's van, and had it stopped by traffic officers; there was no sign of him. Widening the search to include nearby houses seemed too much even for Ferris. It would only arouse anxiety and suspicion amongst the locals and if the press got a whiff of it, they'd make the situation even worse.

He found Stephane chatting to a young woman behind the bar in the hotel. Stephane had a predilection for young girls, but Ferris suspected that this one was too old for him and that he was just seeing if she knew anything.

He gave him a surreptitious signal and waited in the car outside.

Stephane arrived two minutes later and slipped into the passenger seat.

'Anything?' asked Ferris.

Stephane shook his head.

'I think he's gone,' he said quietly.

Ferris stared through the windscreen.

'I'm not so sure.'

Stephane shrugged and waited.

'What about the DS?' asked Ferris.

Again Stephane shrugged.

'Do you want me to check her out?'

Ferris gave it some thought. He hated being outplayed, but the policeman seemed to have gone to ground. There seemed little point in causing any more trouble.

'No. Let's leave it. There's the possibility he'll turn up at the inquest. It's the only time he could interfere with things and after that it'll be too late.'

Stephane nodded his agreement.

They both sat silently for a few moments.

'Time for a little R & R, I think,' said Ferris and started the car.

*   *   *   *   *

Fletcher stared at her.

She stared back.

'You made me jump,' he said.

'Guilty conscience, I expect,' she said.

He frowned at her. Could she suspect how he felt about her?

'Is Mags around?' she said.

'Yeh. She was here a minute ago. Don't know where she's gone. Be back soon, I think.'

Sorcha stayed in the doorway and continued staring at him.

'What are you doing here?' she asked.

Fletcher shuffled his feet like a naughty schoolboy.

'Er ... not sure really. I've been for a walk ... ended up in the church ... met Mags. Got invited for dinner.'

Sorcha continued to stare, her eyes boring into him. His heart skipped a beat as she brushed the hair back from her face.

'They're looking for you, you know?' she said.

'Who?' he asked.

'The police ... and some other men.'

'What other men?'

'Not police, I think. One of them was chatting me up half an hour ago. Good looking bloke with a foreign accent. Might have been French or sommat,' she said.

Fletcher waited.

She took a step into the room. He backed away and went round the other side of the table, pulled out a chair and sat down, trying hard to control his thumping heart.

'How did you know he was looking for me?' he asked.

She stood and looked at him.

'He asked what all the fuss was about. So I told him.'

'So he didn't mention me?'

'No ... but then he asked why they were still searching everywhere if it wasn't a murder investigation.'

'What did you say to that?'

'I said I didn't know.'

Fletcher looked at her. She stared back. He couldn't tell what was going on behind those inky eyes and what Mags had told him had confused him.

'So are they still there?'

She shook her head.

'No, I saw him get into a big black car. There was another man in the driving seat. After a few minutes they drove away.'

'Was the other man a policeman?'

She shook her head making her hair fall across her left eye.

'I don't think so. He looked more like a lawyer or something. Dark suit.'

'Men in black,' muttered Fletcher.

They stayed silent for what seemed an eternity but it was probably only a few seconds.

'Why are you hiding?' she asked.

'Me? I'm not hiding,' he said.

She gave him a hard look.

'You don't believe it was just a heart attack, do you?' she said.

He looked back at her.

'Why do say that?'

'I just know,' she said.

He paused

'What do you think?'

She came over towards him now and stood the other side of the table. He could smell her. Not a perfume, only body heat and newly washed hair. He wasn't sure. But it nearly overpowered him. He closed his eyes for a second.

She was still there when he opened them again, a slight frown on her forehead. She brushed the hair away.

'She wouldn't do that,' she said.

'You mean take an overdose?'

She nodded.

'She was too ... too ... full of life...'

She looked away and bit her lip.

He waited.

Another long second or two passed.

She leant forward onto the table and looked straight at him.

'Someone killed her and it wasn't a burglar. Someone who was frightened of her.'

'"Frightened?"Who would be scared of an old lady like her?'

Sorcha's eyes blazed.

'She may have been old, but she was...'

He could see her searching for the right words, but her eyes were filling up.

'Clever?' he offered.

She rubbed her hand across her face, denying the tears their interruption.

'More than clever!' she blurted out. 'She was ... she had ... power! That's it, she was strong! Not a weak old lady. People were afraid of her sometimes. She could see right into your head. Knew what you were thinking before you knew yourself...'

She stopped and turned away, her hand going up to her face. He heard a suppressed sob and saw her thin body shudder. He wanted to reach out and hold her.

She looked back at him, hair across her face. A fierce, angry face.

'I loved her,' she said.

Fletcher could think of nothing to say or do. He looked her in the eyes. She fought back the tears.

Mags came into the room and stopped in her tracks, halted by the crackling tension in the air. But she quickly gathered her wits and strode towards Sorcha. She put her arms around her and kissed her hair. Fletcher groaned inwardly, instantly consumed with agonising jealousy.

Mags pushed Sorcha away and held her at arm's length.

'Sorcha, my dear, you're here already. How did you manage that? What have you said to Joan?'

Sorcha laughed. A wicked laugh.

'I told her I was feeling bad. I gave her my mad look. She gave in.'

She laughed again and gave Fletcher a reprise of her 'mad look'. It was scary. He pretended to be terrified. They all three laughed.

'Michael,' said Mags. 'Pour the two of us a glass of that Chianti. I've a feeling this is going to be a long night. We need sustenance.'

Fletcher reached out for the bottle and gave Sorcha an enquiring glance.

She gave him a thin smile.

'I don't drink,' she said.

He raised his eyebrows.

'Not since I was last up in front of the judge,' she said, indicating Mags. 'She told me it was prison next time.'

He looked from one to the other.

'The assault victim withdrew his accusation, although I suspect Hilda's discussion with him regarding what might happen if he didn't might have been the main reason … anyway, we don't want to talk about that tonight,' said Mags.

Sorcha shook her head and went over to the sink to pour

herself a glass of water.

Fletcher offered a glass to Mags, who put it to her nose and sniffed.

'Ah … "a beaker full of the warm south, full of the true, the blushful Hippocrene, with beaded bubbles winking at the brim…"'

Fletcher held his glass aloft.

'Here's to poets!' he said.

'…and soothsayers…' said Mags as she took a sip, which turned into a gulp as an insistent rapping at the kitchen door startled her.

The door was pushed open. 'Not a moment too soon, eh, Hardwicke, dear boy,' cried Roger Aughton as he strode into the room, carrying a supermarket bag clinking with bottles. Both men were soaking wet, hair plastered to their skulls and their coats dripping onto the slate floor.

Five minutes later the three men were sitting at the table, slurping at the Chianti, two coats still making puddles beneath the hooks in the hall, whilst Mags clattered plates and Sorcha leant against the wall. She was to one side of Fletcher almost over his shoulder, so he couldn't see her without turning round, but he could sense her presence, hear her breathing, and smell the sweet fragrance of her hair. She didn't contribute much to the conversation, but then very few people did once Roger was in full flow.

He told them how Mark and he had made a big fuss leaving the house and being stopped by the police only ten miles away; how they'd enjoyed half an hour at the cattle market in Cockermouth then returned along the back roads into the village and left their car behind the cricket hut, before tramping through the fields to the vicarage.

But that was only a precursor to some other adventure they'd had together in Kerry involving the acquisition of a few hundred Sweet Afton from the back of some van or other.

This storytelling only stopped when Gavin, Sheila, and Stanley arrived. The meal was served and the wine flowed. Godfrey, the vicar, appeared halfway through the first course and Fletcher was relieved to see that he was nothing like Olive Oil. He was a small, sharp-witted chap who held his own when the stories turned to the risqué. Fletcher could see that although they'd look a bit odd dancing together, he understood why Mags would have fallen for him and how his strong Yorkshire accent would have so offended her mother.

* * * * *

Fletcher couldn't remember much else or how he'd managed to end up in a large bed in a high-ceilinged room, so he found it difficult to work out whether the person speaking so urgently to him and tugging at his arm was in a dream or not. This was instantly rectified by the glass of cold water thrown into his face. He gasped and blinked, trying to struggle up. A cool hand covered his mouth just before the cursing could begin.

The next thing he knew he was looking into a pair of vaguely familiar eyes and his brain scrabbled to understand what was happening.

'Shush,' said the voice and he nodded his understanding. The hand was taken away.

'We have to go now,' she said.

He tried to sit up, but hadn't realised how near he was to the edge of the bed. Before he could get any grip, he'd tumbled out onto the floor and lay there trying to gather his breath and cope with the banging in his head.

A hand reached out and helped him back onto the bed so he could sit up.

Sorcha held out a glass. There was no light other than the full moon shining through the window.

He suddenly realised he was completely naked and quickly covered himself with his free hand.

Her serious face, half lit by the moon, collapsed into a girlish giggle.

'I've seen worse than that,' she laughed, and was immediately serious again.

'Where have we to go?' he asked.

'Bristol,' she said.

He nodded.

'Elizabeth Kirby?'

She stared at him.

'Yes,' she said.

* * * * *

Five minutes later he was dressed and they crept downstairs and out through the unlocked kitchen door. Someone was snoring so loudly that the two of them could have been wearing armour and not been heard.

Outside Sorcha headed for the VW campervan. She had the key in her hand and opened the driver's door.

'Have you got a licence?' asked Fletcher.

'Since I was seventeen,' she said. 'And before you ask, it's clean. I can't afford a car, but you're in no state to drive.'

He couldn't argue with that or the fact that he couldn't believe he was going to spend who knows how many hours in her company … and he hadn't even had to invent a reason.

He soon relaxed when it became obvious that she was a careful and skilful driver. She also knew the roads, so they avoided the coast road and drove up and over what she called Corney Fell. This took them away from the street and house lights and soon they were floating along with the moon lighting up all the fells. It was breath-taking. Like flying.

Coming down to the Duddon they sank back into the cloud and the rain set in. It didn't ease up until he was awoken by the sound of gravel and the squeak of the old van's handbrake. Outside he could see a brightly lit café and that the sky was brightening over to his left. He hadn't managed to stay awake for long after they'd reached the M6 and they'd hardly spoken a word to each other before that.

Sorcha got out of the van and he trailed after her into the café. She ordered two breakfasts and Fletcher went to the toilet.

The mirror didn't lie and was disinclined to offer any compliments. He washed his face and cleaned his teeth with his fingers. His eyes were red-ringed and he looked like he'd slept in a ditch. He headed back out.

Sorcha was sitting at a side table looking out at the weak morning sun shining on the wet grass.

'Where are we?' asked Fletcher.

'Just south of Whitchurch on the A49,' she said, turning to face him. She didn't look any different, just as captivatingly beautiful as ever. The benefits of not drinking he told himself.

'How are you feeling?' she asked.

'Better than I did when you woke me up,' he replied.

She had no more to say and their breakfast had arrived. They ate in silence. They were the only people in the café and the owner was busy getting ready for the morning rush. There wasn't even a radio.

After Fletcher had gone to order another couple of coffees, he sat down again and looked across at her.

'Why are you doing this?' he asked.

She stared at him.

'I want to know who killed Sybil,' she said.

178

Fletcher looked back at her, but she returned his questioning gaze. He leant forward and clasped his hands together on the table.

'Does that mean you know why she was killed?'

She looked away out the window. She didn't speak until the woman brought their drinks and returned to the kitchen.

'Not really … except what Sybil told me.'

Fletcher didn't push her.

She looked back at him.

'She said that someone had told her a secret. "A terrible act has been committed in our name…" was what she actually said.'

'But you've no idea what that might be?'

She shook her head and pushed her hair back.

Fletcher took a sip of his drink and leant back in his chair.

'So where are we going?' he asked.

'I tried ringing Elizabeth, but she isn't answering.'

'Can you tell me who she is?'

Sorcha shook her head again.

'Not really. I've only seen her twice and I've never talked to her.'

Fletcher sighed.

'"It's better for everyone", is what Sybil used to say. "The less you know the less you can give away",' she said.

'So do you know where this Elizabeth lives?'

She nodded and produced a piece of paper. It was an address in Clifton, The Paragon. Fletcher didn't know Bristol at all, so it didn't mean anything to him, although the name was strange. A paragon: something or someone beyond comparison?

'But you think she might know something?'

Sorcha shrugged her thin shoulders.

'I don't know anyone else.'

Fletcher couldn't think of any other questions, so they drank

179

their coffee. He paid and they set off.

It soon became obvious to Fletcher that Sorcha knew this road well. She wasn't looking at a map and she knew exactly where to turn.

As she navigated an awkward junction in a busy market town called Ludlow, he questioned this.

'Of course I do. I used to drive Sybil this way regularly.'

'You mean to Bristol?'

'Often, but sometimes we'd go to her family's cottage near Hereford.'

'But you never went to see this Elizabeth?'

'Not me. Sybil still has a house in Clifton. She'd go to see Elizabeth on her own.'

Fletcher was becoming more and more aware how secretive this woman's life had been. Was this out of necessity or some paranoid fear?

He kept quiet for some time pondering his dealings with Special Branch and other secret agencies. He knew he didn't have a full picture. His only real contact was with Anthony Adversane and he'd hardly call him a friend. In any case he was singularly absent from this case. What did that mean? If, as Louisa had warned him, he was upsetting MI5 or 'Northfields', whatever that was, then maybe he was in a more dangerous situation than before. He couldn't imagine anyone more ruthless or two-faced than Adversane. What hold did Louisa have over him?

'Not far now,' said Sorcha as they took a sign saying the M5.

Again they managed a whole hour without conversation before she was guiding the camper van down the slip way onto the motorway. Another hour later she was weaving her way through city streets and finally pulled up outside a terrace house in Clifton.

She sat staring out of the window. Fletcher waited. It was a wide quiet street with trees in a line between the two lanes. He glanced across at Sorcha. Tears were dribbling softly down her face. Outside it was raining. Not heavy, but a desultory drizzle. Fletcher felt unbearably sad.

Suddenly he felt her hand on his. He didn't dare look, but stayed still; as still as he'd tried to be when he was watching the herons in the woodland pool near his Aunty Emily's. He listened to her quiet sobs and felt her cool hand on his. There was nothing he could think to say. He turned his hand over and held hers gently. She squeezed his hand hard and suddenly she was leaning over and putting her arms around his neck. He held her tight and let her cry and cry. He'd never known such desperate grief. He felt helpless and yet didn't want it to end.

After she'd stopped sobbing and shuddering, she untangled herself and pulled away.

'I'm sorry,' she said.

'Don't be,' he replied, offering her his handkerchief.

Eventually they got out of the car and walked down the street. When she stopped and produced a key and put it in the lock, he looked at the number of available parking spaces in front of the door. She turned back towards him

'Standard procedure for Sybil I'm afraid. We always sat and watched for a few minutes. See who was around.'

Feeling a mixture of being stupid and being incongruously betrayed, Fletcher followed her up the stairs to a green door on the first floor. Here again Sorcha had a key, but instead put her ear to the door and listened. When she had done this for a moment or two she tried the handle. It opened without a sound and the smell hit them.

Fletcher put his hand over his mouth and Sorcha backed away with a look of horror.

'Stay there,' he said, before taking a deep breath and closing the door behind him.

It didn't take long and he was careful not to touch anything with his bare hands. The flat was large but had only four rooms. He knew instantly where the body was from the sound of the flies. He peered into the kitchen where all the buzzing was coming from.

It was a cat. Or what was left of it. The flies fizzed angrily as he opened the door, but settled again when he made no effort to take their prize from them. A quick look round the other rooms told him there were no human remains, but he couldn't tell whether this was only ordinary professorial untidiness or whether it had been searched. He went back to the door.

Sorcha was still leaning against the wall, hands to her mouth, her eyes searching his.

'It's only a cat,' he said.

Sorcha nodded her understanding. Fletcher pulled the door to and went over to her.

'One question, was Sybil a tidy person?'

Sorcha made a face.

'Lots of books and papers all over the place? On the floor, tables, and chairs?' he asked.

She nodded.

'But no food, otherwise the cat might have managed,' he said.

'Do you want to look? See if there's anything I've missed?' he asked, glancing down the stairwell.

She nodded. 'I'll try.'

He opened the door and she stepped in, his handkerchief over her nose and mouth. He waited with the door closed. She avoided the kitchen without being told and quickly glanced into the other three rooms. She only hesitated for a few seconds in the large sitting room scouring the walls and the furniture covered with books as Fletcher had asked.

She came back and they left the flat, closing the door quietly behind them. Two minutes later they were back in the van. She drove them round three or four corners and parked up again. She turned off the engine and they sat in silence for a few moments.

'Someone has been in there,' she whispered.

'How do you know?'

'The pictures weren't straight. Sybil couldn't bear that. She was always putting them right in other people's houses, especially in the vicarage … but the books…' she shrugged.

Fletcher gave this some thought, although he knew what this meant.

'A professional searcher,' he said. 'Someone who knew what they looking for and could make it look like they hadn't been there. Someone who knew that the owner was already dead.'

They both stared through the windscreen. Fletcher didn't know what was going through Sorcha's head.

'It wasn't her cat,' she said. 'Cicero died two years ago.'

Fletcher smiled at her. She managed a sad one back.

'She said she couldn't bear another animal death … but it didn't stop her talking to him.'

'The cat or the Roman?' asked Fletcher.

'Both of them.'

Across the road was a small brightly painted café. He pointed at it.

'Coffee?'

She agreed and they left the van where it was and crossed the road.

The man behind the counter was a cheerful little guy with a multi-coloured hat perched above his smiley brown eyes.

'Wassup, man,' he asked.

'Dead cat,' said Fletcher.

The smile disappeared.

'Sorry,' said the man. 'You tek a seat now, an I'll bring ya a nice cuppa o' my best coffee.'

They sat down near the window. A very large black man looked up from his paper and gave them a reassuring smile.

'Trubble allus comes when ya nat lookin,' he said quietly.

Fletcher nodded his thanks and sat down opposite Sorcha.

The coffee duly came and it was strong and black. They took their time.

'Do you know where this other street is?' he asked.

She shook her head.

'No. But Sybil always went on foot and if Elizabeth wasn't in, she'd be back in ten minutes or so.'

Fletcher looked over at the man who was cleaning cups and singing in a low voice.

'Hey, do you know where The Paragon is?' he asked.

'No problem, mister,' he said and came over to their table.

'Ya go outta here an tek the first right an ya is on York Gardens. Ya goes alang there and up onto tha crescent. Down to the end and it's facing ya. It's real easy.'

'Thanks,' said Fletcher. He got up and gave him a fiver. He went towards the counter, but Fletcher called after him.

'No, man, that's okay. Thanks for the help.'

'You're a prince, ma friend,' said the café owner and gave them another beaming smile.

The two of them set off in the direction he'd told them. They were there in ten minutes.

The sign told them it was a cul-de-sac and they quickly realised the houses were only on the left hand side. They found the number they wanted and looked up at the two storey building. Each of the houses had an unusual round entrance which stuck out towards the pavement. Fletcher found the bell and pressed the middle.

He suspected they were both expecting the worst, but the two of them were surprised when the door was opened and a young man stared out at them.

Fletcher flashed his card and said they were looking for Elizabeth Kirby.

The man looked worried.

'Why? Has something happened to her?' he asked.

'Not that we know,' replied Fletcher. 'Do you know where she is?'

The man hesitated, before pulling the door wide.

'You'd better come in,' he said.

Inside it was brightly lit, the sun streaming through big windows. He took them through to a large kitchen with a view over trees and a deep valley. Fletcher thought he could see water below.

'I'm Charles, her son,' said the young man. 'Why are you looking for her?'

Fletcher looked round the room. It was tidy and clean. Modern fittings, plenty of new shiny pans. Bright colourful crockery.

'Well, sir. I believe your mother was a friend of a lady called Sybil Hardwicke?'

Charles Kirby stared at him.

'Yes ... I heard she'd died. A heart attack wasn't it?'

'Uhuh...' said Fletcher.

'Except it wasn't,' muttered Sorcha.

Fletcher gave her a look. She made a face.

Kirby looked from one to the other.

'What does she mean?' he asked Fletcher.

'Yeh, this is Sorcha, she was a friend of Miss Hardwicke as well ... but the official opinion is that it was a heart attack.'

He looked at the clock on the wall.

'In fact the inquest is about to start in an hour or so.'

Kirby again looked from one to the other.

'So why do you need to talk to my mother?' he asked.

Fletcher sighed.

'A few loose ends, sir, that's all. We think your mother may have answers to a few outstanding questions.'

Kirby gave him a penetrating stare, before shrugging his shoulders and turning towards the window. Fletcher looked at Sorcha and put his fingers to his lips. She scowled at him.

'I don't know where she is, Inspector,' said the young man without looking round.

Fletcher waited to see if there was anymore. There didn't seem to be.

'Is it usual for your mother not to let you know where she is?' he asked.

Kirby turned towards him and nodded.

'There's nothing 'usual' about my mother, Inspector. She disappears for weeks on end without saying a word and then I get a call or a card from Naples, or a Scottish island, or a tent in the Negreb. She's not at all predictable, especially now she doesn't have to lecture or run tutorials.'

'So when did you last see her or talk to her.'

Kirby considered this and then reached into the pocket of a jacket that was hanging on the back of a chair. He consulted a small diary.

'Friday the fourteenth,' he said and closed the book and returned it to its pocket. 'I've no idea where she was, although it sounded like she was on a train. I was at work, so we didn't talk for long. Private conversations are frowned upon, I'm afraid.'

'You work in a bank?' asked Fletcher, trying for a lightness of tone, but his speculative mind was far ahead.

Kirby gave him another stern look and shook his head.

'Insurance, actually,' he replied, but Fletcher wasn't convinced.

'And you've not heard anything since?' he asked.

'Only a postcard,' replied Kirby, pointing at a pin board next to the fridge.

Fletcher reached towards it.

'May I?' he asked.

Kirby nodded.

'Not much help is it. The card's probably one she's had since last year and the postmark says Leeds.'

Fletcher looked at a picture of a long empty beach and a blue sky. He guessed Greece, but when he turned it over it claimed to be the Isle of Lewis.

'The message is her gnomic style … that is something you can count on…' Kirby said, with what nearly became a smile, but it quickly faded.

Fletcher looked at the message. It was in Latin.

'I expect you can read it, sir? Can you translate?'

Again, the faintest of smiles.

'I don't need to do that. She's been saying it to me since I was a child.'

Fletcher smiled back, but couldn't disguise his impatience.

'An tanquam ultima…' Kirby began

'…omnes actus vitae,' finished Sorcha.

Fletcher looked at them both and waited.

'I shouldn't read too much into it, if I were you,' said Kirby, who was now looking at Sorcha with a puzzled frown.

'Well, would someone like to enlighten the ignorant, please,' asked Fletcher.

Kirby demurred towards Sorcha, who didn't smile, but did offer the translation.

187

'Do every act of your life as if it were your last,' she mumbled.

Fletcher sighed and pinned the card back to the board.

'But you reckon this isn't a warning, just a family saying?'

Kirby nodded.

'Although I doubt my father would agree. She said he always thought there was something better round the corner. So they didn't last past my seventh birthday. He left us to find someone who was less … cynical.'

Fletcher went to look out at the garden. It was well kept. Lots of flowers.

'So … you don't know where she is and you're not worried and she won't be with your father.'

Kirby nodded.

'Unless she's dead,' he answered after a few seconds.

'Um … so any ideas where she might have gone, friends, other relatives, holiday cottages...'

Again Kirby was shaking his head.

'She has more friends than Rabbit,' he said, 'but no other relatives I'm afraid. I could put together a list, but it would be long and if she were with someone they're not necessarily going to admit to it.'

Fletcher snorted with exasperation.

'Well, Mr Kirby, thank you for your cooperation and help. If she does turn up or contact you will you ask her to get in touch with one of my colleagues?'

He gave him Irene Garner's name and number and he and Sorcha saw themselves out.

They retraced their steps to find the van, but when they got there, Fletcher walked past and through the open door of a pub across the road.

He ordered himself a pint and asked Sorcha what she wanted. She asked for a glass of water.

188

'Cul-de-sac,' he sighed. 'Francoise Dorleac and 'wot's his name'.'

Sorcha gave him a puzzled look.

'It's a film by Polanski. She was the sister of Catherine Deneuve and the bloke is ... little bald bloke ... he was the blind forger in the Great Escape ... you know?'

She was still shaking her head.

'No ... but I think I know where Elizabeth might be.'

He stopped in mid-drink.

'So are you going to keep that a secret?'

She sipped her water.

'The words on the card. They're on the wall in one of the rooms in that cottage I told you about near Hereford.'

'Ah,' said Fletcher.

He didn't know whether to listen to his exasperation or the growing sense of resignation or to the boyish excitement of further adventure with this girl with the deep dark eyes.

CHAPTER 9

The morning of the inquest into the death of Sybil Amelia Hardwicke went exactly as James Ferris had planned it.

The inquest itself was a brief affair, during which the stand-in pathologist gave his medical opinion and Chief Superintendent Conroy gave his report. The acting coroner was in no doubt that the woman died of a heart attack and there was no evidence that this was caused by anything other than that she had suffered from a chronic heart condition for most of her life – in other words 'death from natural causes'. In the surprising and regrettable absence of any member of the family, the coroner was only able to say that it should be recorded that he offered them his condolences.

The whole affair was over in less than half an hour.

* * * * *

It wasn't that Mark Hardwicke had not wanted to be there, along with his friends Roger Aughton, Margaret and Godfrey Fielden-Cavendish. Despite the amount of alcohol consumed the previous night they were all up, breakfasted and ready to set off at ten fifteen, giving themselves more than enough time to be there for eleven o'clock.

Except of course they hadn't factored in the possibility that Wath Bridge over the Ehen would be closed for urgent repairs that same morning. As the workmen hadn't arrived until about half nine and erected their barrier and diversion signs, there was no warning from any of the locals about this.

Mags and Godfrey had been mildly disconcerted to find that Fletcher had elected to borrow Mags's old camper van, but had assumed he'd gone on ahead. Roger confirmed that this sort of behaviour was 'de rigeur' for the cantankerous detective, but never-the-less Godfrey thought it a bit of a liberty.

They arrived at the back of the disgruntled queue of traffic, as the drivers tried to make up their minds which of the two alternative routes they would take. Some were happy to follow the diversion sign sending them south towards Egremont, whilst many of the locals preferred to turn round and head for the minor roads to the north. However this meant they caused more delay by doing a series of three, five, and seven point turns in the narrow bottleneck. Arriving at the back of this commotion, Godfrey acted with commendable speed, using the four wheel drive facility of his landrover and taking advantage of a nearby field gateway to turn round in double-quick time.

Five minutes later they were back through the village and steaming up the road towards Kirkland, which is where the second obstruction materialised. As they came round a corner a lorry appeared to have skidded and overturned right in front of them, blocking the lane entirely. Godfrey skilfully brought the landrover to an exemplary emergency stop one would expect from an ex-RAF driver. Obviously, their immediate thoughts were for the poor driver, but they were relieved to see the man wriggling his way out of his window like a gunner getting out of

191

his tank.

He was most apologetic, but the fact was they were stuck. Even with Godfrey's local connections it was good hour before a couple of tractors were able to haul the lorry back onto its wheels and they could continue their journey. By the time they arrived, the courtroom was locked and the building was deserted.

Not knowing what to do, Roger suggested the hotel bar opposite and they followed him across the road. Mark Hardwicke couldn't believe what was happening, whilst Godfrey was ringing everyone he knew to try to get some information, which proved to be exasperatingly unsuccessful. It was only after the arrival of a wary looking DS Hilda Crake that they found out what had happened.

She told them the verdict and claimed she knew nothing about the diversion at the bridge. In fact a quick call to the station revealed that the bridge had been declared safe after all and traffic was now using it again. No one at County Hall could explain why the bridge had been closed and no one knew anything about any concern for its viability. The public works department had not dispatched any of its workmen to the bridge either.

Both she and the infuriated band of Sybil's nephew and his friends were made even more suspicious when they heard that the lorry the local farmers had spent half a morning up-righting did not belong to the driver either. He had subsequently disappeared and they later heard it had been stolen that morning from outside a haulage firm in Cockermouth.

'It's a set-up,' declared Mags. 'Godfrey, get onto that chap you know at the local rag. Somebody must have been sent to the inquest.'

It was all to no avail. No one ever knew any more than they knew right there and then.

A junior reporter had been dispatched to the inquest and had duly reported the facts which didn't even make the next edition. Although Sybil had lived in the area for five years, that didn't make her 'a local'. Her exploits as a CND activist and her academic renown were of no interest to a community whose painfully reduced employment prospects were almost entirely dependent on the nuclear industry. There were obituaries in the Guardian and the Telegraph, but these highlighted her academic achievements rather than her activism.

In any case all the newspapers were full of the sinking of HMS Antelope and other events in the South Atlantic. No one was bothered with some old woman who'd had a heart attack and died in her bed.

* * * * *

James Ferris settled comfortably into the black leather seat of the Daimler as Stephane eased it down the slip road onto the M6 and accelerated into the outside lane. Ferris had communicated the successful completion of the operation to his superior and received the usual cursory thanks from the man who he knew he'd succeed one day … an event which this little caper had moved a few steps closer.

Stephane had already arranged for an appropriate reward for them both on the way south, although Ferris was still worrying about Fletcher. He'd been informed about his arrival in Bristol, but the fools had managed to lose the detective again in the lanes west of Gloucester. He had ordered that they check out the most likely next stop on his journey, but was concerned to hear that Fletcher was accompanied by a young woman who had been seen in Sybil Hardwicke's company on more than one occasion. As yet they had no identification, but he knew it was only a matter of time.

If the irritating man wasn't going to listen to the warnings he'd sent out, then eventually he'd pay the price for his interference, however much it might upset that pompous ass Adversane. Yet another fool promoted above his level of competence.

He closed his eyes and began to imagine the delicious pleasure he'd planned for himself. The photographs Stephane had shown him had already conjured up a range of possibilities and the woman had been highly recommended by a fellow connoisseur.

* * * * *

It was only as they were safely off the M5 that Fletcher suddenly remembered the parcel. He'd taken over the driving duty, but was following Sorcha's curt directions. She'd not said anything else since they'd left Bristol and seemed to be turning something over and over behind a threatening frown which wasn't that far removed from what she'd called her 'mad' look.

Fletcher followed the instruction to turn right onto a minor road and spotted a board advertising a road-side caff. Sure enough it was tucked into a lay-by a few miles further on and seemed to have seen off the lunchtime crowd. He pulled in and parked up. Sorcha stared resolutely through the front windscreen. Any thoughts of questioning her about the parcel scuttled to the back of his head.

He got out of the car and walked back to the caff. The woman was cheerfully tidying up, but was happy to produce a couple of mugs of tea and two bacon sandwiches with practised ease.

'Busy day?' asked Fletcher.

'Can't complain,' she replied.

Fletcher stared back down the road. A newish Vauxhall Cavalier slowed down, but then the driver appeared to change his mind and it accelerated past. He knew instantly that it was the car that had followed them off the M5. With that sort of engine, it should have overtaken the geriatric VW within a couple of miles. So someone was on their tail. He knew that Special Branch would use a series of cars to track a suspect who they didn't want to alert, so he suspected that wouldn't be the only one.

'Are you going far?' asked the woman, as she placed the sandwiches wrapped in paper napkins on the shelf in front of him next to the mugs of steaming tea.

Thinking quickly he came up with the first place he could think of.

'Rochdale,' he said.

He paid and walked back to the VW. The woman watched him. Funny couple? Maybe she's his daughter? Rochdale? She shook her head. Not her problem.

Sorcha got out as he approached and took one of the mugs from the little tray the woman had given him. She looked him in the eye.

'Did you see it?' she asked.

'The Cavalier?' he asked.

'I don't know what sort of car it was. The dark blue one?'

He nodded.

'Yeh, it followed us off the motorway.'

'It was in Sybil's road as well,' she said.

Fletcher looked at her.

'It's how it always was with Sybil,' she added. 'She would just smile and wave at them.'

Fletcher considered this as another car pulled in at the other end of the lay-by. Two men in suits got out and approached the van. They didn't look towards them, but Sorcha shook her head at Fletcher.

'Don't think so,' she said.

Fletcher looked at the men and back at her. She shrugged

and climbed back into the VW. She didn't say any more and only ate half of her sandwich, before offering the rest to him.

Back on the road he set off the way they'd been going, but at the first village she told him to take a right and they went down what looked like a farm track. He looked across at her, but she was staring straight ahead.

Half an hour later, after going through a farmyard and across what he was pretty certain must have been a private estate with mature trees and open grassland between them, they bumped out onto a minor road. At one point he had glimpsed a stately house down an avenue of other giant trees.

'Diversionary tactic number three,' murmured Sorcha.

He laughed.

'What happened to one and two?' he asked.

'Didn't think we needed them,' she said.

He slowed down to follow a tractor grumbling along the lane with a trailer piled high with straw bales.

So how many are there?'

'At least twelve, I think.'

'What was that place we went through back there?'

'Sybil said it was Uncle Beaver's family's house, but it belongs to some old rock star now.'

'Anyone I'd know?'

'She never said.'

'And you wouldn't have asked', thought Fletcher to himself. Her surliness was beginning to annoy him. It reminded him of a younger Grace ... and that made him even more uncomfortable.

The tractor swung left into a farmyard and he speeded up again. By now it was mid-afternoon and ahead of him he could see clouds building up, obscuring the sun. The lane wound this way and that through high hedges, with occasional glimpses into fields to right and left, but very few houses. Despite this she didn't give him many changes of direction until he could see a church spire and red roofs ahead as they came up an incline.

'In the village there's a pub on your right. The car park is round the back to the left.'

He did as he was told. She got out of the van and pulled out her rucksack from the seat behind.

In the bar she left him and went to the loo. He ordered a pint for himself of something he'd never heard of and a glass of water for 'Sulky Sue'.

The place was empty, the barman an indifferent young man with little to say. Fletcher took the drinks into a corner and waited.

It was so long he was considering going to check she hadn't disappeared, but at that moment the door opened and she came back into the room. She'd washed her hair and tied it back in a loose ponytail; changed her t-shirt and jeans for a blue dress. But more surprising still, she managed a weak smile. His desire was instantly re-awakened.

'I'm sorry,' she said as she sat down and reached across to kiss him on the cheek.

He was so startled he felt himself blush.

'What for?' he mumbled.

'Being a miserable cow,' she said.

He made a face.

'It's following that route, taking the diversionary tactics … brings it…'

She began to cry. Not loud, just a few tear tracks running down her freshly washed face. She wiped them away and cursed herself.

He didn't know what to do. His face was still recovering from the touch of her lips and brushing of her hair.

'I don't know how many times we did this. To her it was all

an adventure. She made it seem like we were in a film. She was someone called Hannay and I was the girlfriend played by Faye Dunaway.'

Fletcher shook his head, but he knew instantly that the old girl had meant Buchan's hero in the 'The Thirty-Nine Steps'. More melodrama.

'This pub was where we hid out until it got dark. Once we even stayed overnight.'

He remembered what Mags had said, "But she still had the occasional affair. Men or women." He looked at Sorcha. She was staring into the distance in a trance of remembering.

He coughed to bring her back. She turned her black gaze his way.

'So is that what we're doing,' he asked, looking out of the window. 'Waiting till it's dark.'

Outside it was as if the weather was trying to help. There was no sun. The clouds hung heavy in the sky and a street light over the road was spluttering into life. It was only half past three.

When he looked back at her, her eyes were on him. In the semi-darkness of the corner they'd taken on a luminous quality as the irises merged with her pupils. He felt trapped, cornered, transfixed.

'Are you afraid of the dark?' she asked.

He shook himself out of that menacing stare.

'Not particularly,' he said. 'Depends what I'm doing.'

She continued to stare.

'And what are you doing?'

He wanted to break away, head for the safety of the bar, order another drink, but he couldn't move. He said the only thing he could think to break her hold.

'What did you do with the parcel?' he asked.

There was not a moment's hesitation.

'I thought you'd never ask,' she answered and sat back in the seat.

He raised his eyebrows trying to regain some measure of control.

'Why don't you get us both another drink,' she murmured.

He stood up.

'Water?'

She shook her head.

'Double vodka,' she said with a sly look.

Before he could question this, she laughed and looked round.

'We're a long way from Mags's patch and I'm not driving,' she said, her eyes now dancing with laughter.

He went over to the bar. What was she like? Mesmerising.

The barman looked across at her. She had her back to him. He pulled on the pump.

'You her dad then?' he asked.

Fletcher frowned and shook his head.

'Uncle?' smirked the barman as he placed the pint on the bar.

Fletcher shook his head again.

The barman caught the look on his face.

'Only asking,' he said and put a glass up to the vodka optic.

Fletcher placed a tenner on the bar.

'I shouldn't jump to conclusions, if I was you,' he said. 'Some people might take offence.'

The barman shrugged his shoulder and picked up the money.

Fletcher waited for his change.

The barman turned and leant across the bar.

'I'm not trying to offend you, squire,' he said. 'Merely warn you. She ain't what she seems.'

Fletcher gave him a frown and walked away.

He placed the drink in front of Sorcha. She grinned at him.

'What are you grinning at?' he asked.

'Boy at the bar? Says I'm a slag?'

'No, but he did say, "you ain't what you seem",' said Fletcher, wondering what her reaction might be.

She made a resigned face.

'That might be because I told him I didn't fuck little boys,' she said.

Fletcher looked over her shoulder. The 'little boy' was serving two blokes who'd just come in. When he looked back at her she was putting her empty glass down. Her face was close to the 'mad' look.

'Let's go before I kill the little shit,' she said and stood up, grabbed her bag and stormed out.

Fletcher took a gulp of his pint and followed her, but not without turning to see the barman smirking at him with a finger in the air winding an imaginary string around it. The two men were looking in his direction as well, grinning in a way only yokels can. He resisted the urge to go over and knock the smiles off their fat faces.

She was waiting beside the van. He got in and she joined him in the cab.

He sat looking through the windscreen.

'I couldn't believe what the postman was saying. Still can't,' she began.

Fletcher didn't dare look at her.

'I went along the back lane. I could tell it was true the minute I got near. I could tell she wasn't there.'

There was a long silence. The rain had started and was now rattling on the van roof.

'I went in. Up the stairs...'

He couldn't hear any tears, but there had been an intake of breath. He still didn't look at her, but could sense her warm body near his, the scent of her hair filling his head.

'She was lying on the bed. Her eyes were open. Staring at me. But there was no smile.'

Another long moment passed.

'There was always a smile.'

Now the tears came.

He let them fall unhindered. Even though he wanted to hold her, comfort her.

He felt her hand on his.

He held it gently.

She left it there.

He could feel the warmth of her touch and the cool thinness of a ring. Had she just put it on in the pub? He was sure she hadn't been wearing it before.

Her voice broke through his questions.

'I couldn't touch her. I wish I had, but I knew she was dead.'

After a few more seconds she unfolded her fingers from his.

'I went back down to the hall and saw the parcel. I knew somehow it was connected to why she was dead … so I took it.'

It was only now that Fletcher could look at her.

She reached inside the rucksack on her lap, pulled out a brown parcel, and offered it to him.

He took it. It was quite a large package, but floppy and quite heavy. It was torn open and he could see that it was full of papers. A quick glance told him they were essays. He fingered through the first few: different handwriting with titles like, 'The Edge of the Roman Empire' and, 'Rheged – the Lost Tribe.'

'There's nothing special,' she said. 'We'll have to give them back.'

He looked across at her. She didn't meet his gaze.

'Do you want me to do it?' he asked.

She nodded.

A car pulled up alongside and three young men got out. The one on their side looked at them sternly before following his mates into the pub.

Fletcher leaned behind and put the parcel on the floor.

'Where to now?' he asked.

'Out to the main road and carry on straight across.'

He followed her instructions and they were soon away from the lights of the village. Dark hedges obscured most of the scenery. The rain was still heavy and he splashed through increasingly bigger puddles on the poorly maintained country road.

This turned out to be the sort of road they followed for the next few hours. There were occasional small hamlets with dimly lit windows or slivers of yellow light coming through closely pulled to curtains. They only met a couple of other vehicles, which slowed down to negotiate the narrow road.

Fletcher had no idea where they were going and couldn't even work out which direction they were heading now that a gloomy dank darkness had fallen.

They didn't converse. He merely followed her monotone instructions.

At last he could see the lights of a larger village ahead. They came to a bigger road. He waited as a stream of lorries and cars passed in front of them. Sorcha nodded him across towards the houses. They drove into the village centre. There were a couple of brightly lit shops and a pub, as well as a number of houses clustered beneath the street lights.

Sorcha pointed towards a lane off to the right.

They climbed a steep hill with short drives off either side leading to bungalows. The lane came to a dead end with a big gate barring the way.

'Turn round and park near that tree,' she said.

Having completed the manoeuvre, he turned off the engine and the lights.

'Donald Pleasance,' he muttered to himself.

He felt rather than could see her frowning at him.

'Cul-de-sac,' he explained.

She shook her head and continued to stare out down the dimly lit road.

The rain peppered the roof. They could see it bouncing off the road. There was no one in sight.

'The cottage is through that gate and up a path onto the Common. It'll be muddy tonight, but I don't think they'll know about this way in,' she said in a whisper.

Without saying anything they waited until the sound of the rain lessened. She found her jeans and pulled them on over the dress.

They got out of the car and locked the door. Fletcher followed her as she went through a little gate to the side and began climbing the steep bank overhung with dripping trees. The overflowing undergrowth on either side meant they were both wet through within a few yards, but she continued climbing.

It took about twenty minutes. The first few hundred yards were a steady climb through the thick claustrophobic wood, but eventually they came out of the trees and the ground levelled out. It was a cinder path, like an old railway line, but wider, winding its way between big bushes on either side. It was rutted and full of puddles. Fletcher could feel the water penetrating his totally unsuitable shoes.

A white shape appeared to his left. There was a quiet whinny of annoyance and he watched as the shape snorted and moved off behind a bush. He'd never been comfortable with horses and in the dark he was even less confident. Sorcha plodded on without a word. He hurried to catch up.

Another white shape flickered into view. But this was a building; a long low cottage hidden by heavily leafed trees. There was the sweet smell of apple blossom and he felt the burn of a nettle sting on his hand.

She stopped and held him by his arm. He realised he was breathing heavily. She waited, listening, as his breathing subsided to be replaced by a strained wariness. The rain had stopped and all he could hear was the odd rustling from the bushes and the occasional hoot of an owl.

Sorcha let go of his arm and moved towards the cottage. In the middle of a hedge there was gap and he watched as she climbed over a simple stile. He reached out for the post and felt his way over.

They were in a large garden. There was grass underfoot and what he took to be a small vegetable plot to one side. Sorcha was making her way towards the blurred shape of a door on the left of the building. As she reached it she beckoned to him to follow. She bent down and felt beneath a large stone to one side.

A minute later they were inside the cottage. It had that musty smell of being closed up for some time. She didn't turn on any lights but made her way with the confidence of familiarity. They went along a narrow corridor into a rough stone-floored space with a large door, coats on a line of hooks and a tidy row of boots and wellingtons. The windows were tiny.

Sorcha continued through into a low-ceilinged kitchen. She went unerringly to a cupboard in the corner and he heard the click of a switch. No lights came on, but she came back towards him and pushed him aside so she could reach the cooker. There was a rustle of fingers on a shelf and then the flare of a match. Nothing happened as she fumbled with the control until the match sputtered and died. Cursing, she went back to the cupboard and this time bent down and disappeared. There were some more curses and the sound of a struggle, before she re-appeared. This time the second match blossomed into the orange and blue glow of a gas ring. A kettle was found and filled with water. She rummaged in cupboards and opened a fridge.

Fletcher was directed to a larder and with the aid of a torch found some pasta, tins of beans and tomatoes. There were a couple of onions in a basket and soon two pans were busy.

It took a good hour before they'd sated their appetites. Now they sat in another room with the heavy curtains closed, drinking a rather expensive bottle of Italian red, as the small fire she'd lit made their shadows flicker on the wall.

Suddenly she got up and made for a door he'd not been through yet. She turned and explained.

'I'm just checking the bedrooms,' she said and was gone.

He stayed where he was and stared into the flames. At first he couldn't hear a thing, but then there were foot-falls and a couple of bumps above his head. The noises stopped and a couple of minutes later she reappeared.

'I think someone's been here,' she said. 'Come and look.'

He followed her up a tiny, narrow staircase and found himself in a warren of little doors and rooms, many of them with sloping roofs. He noticed that most of the rooms had single beds or bunks, but in the one Sorcha wanted him to inspect, there was only one bed and it was rumpled and the blanket thrown to one side. On a small cupboard there was a book, face down, a glass on its side and a plate.

Sorcha opened the wardrobe to reveal a pair of shoes, a couple of dresses, and some underwear.

'They're not Sybil's, she said. 'But it's her room.'

He looked round. There was only one small picture on the wall. In the light of the torch he couldn't make it out. Apart from the book on the cupboard there were no others.

As if she could read his mind, she told him the books were all in another room she'd not shown him yet.

They returned downstairs. He poured some more wine.

'What do you think?' he asked.

She stared at the fire for some time.

'I think someone's been sleeping in her bed,' she eventually murmured.

'Is that so unusual?'

She nodded.

'It's not that she would have objected, but I think people respected her privacy. I think that's only the second or third time I've been in that room myself.'

He shivered. They were both wearing things she'd found them while they cooked the food. Their own clothes were hanging, wet through, on some racks in the kitchen.

'It wasn't as if anyone was ever up before her and taking her cups of tea. She was always the first one up in the morning.'

He took a sip of his wine.

'I think it must have been Elizabeth,' she said.

'Why?' he asked.

'The picture on the wall in that bedroom is the saying on her postcard.'

He nodded his understanding.

They sat in silence for a few minutes listening to the fire settling in its grate.

He looked up to find those big dark orbs staring at him.

'Are you married?'

He couldn't prevent his eyebrows from rising, but shook his head.

'But you do have a woman, don't you?' she said.

He smiled.

'I don't think she'd like the way you've put it, but I have a …

girlfriend. Yes.'

'Girlfriend,' she laughed. 'You're too old to have a 'girlfriend'. How old are you anyway?'

'Old enough,' he said, feeling stupid.

'For what? To be my dad?'

He blushed and looked away.

'I'm sorry,' she said. 'What's she called?'

'Laura.'

'Do you love her?'

Startled by this directness, he looked up at her. She was leaning forward towards him, her gaze intent and penetrating. She was only the second person to ask him this question. One he'd resolutely not asked himself, although, he realised, he knew full well the answer to it.

He nodded.

She leant back, didn't laugh. Her face was sombre and half hidden from the firelight.

'What is she like?'

He paused uncertain where this interrogation was going.

'She's tall, short dark hair, beautiful eyes...' he managed.

She shook her head.

'Men,' she laughed softly. 'I ask you what she's like and you tell me what she looks like. I meant what sort of a person is she?'

He stared at her, momentarily stuck for words, but then they started to come...

'Direct, loving, fierce, scary...'

'Does she know you're with me?'

Her look was stern, her thoughts hidden.

He shook his head.

She took a big swig of her drink.

'You know what?' she said.

He waited, apprehension filling every artery.

'We're wasting our time here,' she said. 'I reckon whoever it is has found Elizabeth and killed her as well or she's hiding somewhere else.'

'Maybe you're right,' he said.

'Anyway I'm going to go to bed now.'

She drained her glass and stood up. She stepped forward so that she was within arm's reach.

'I'm going to sleep in the room next to Sybil's.'

She leant forward and kissed him on the cheek. He didn't respond. She gave him a shrug and walked to the door.

'You can sleep where you like.'

With a final unreadable smile, she was gone.

He sat there for a long time staring into the fire. An army of faces questioned his thoughts. He denied them all. Her face swam before him, her hair over her eye. Her hand came up and pushed it back. She smiled. Her unreadable smile. He put his head in hands and shuddered.

* * * * *

He must have fallen asleep. He awoke in a cold sweat. The fire was out, but there were lights moving outside. He got up and peered through the crack in the curtain. Up the slope beyond the cottage, he could see torch lights and the dipped lights of a car at a gate. Thin figures like the aliens at the end of 'Close Encounters' passed back and forth as they came walking slowly down.

A hand gripped his elbow. It was Sorcha. She dragged him towards the window. The cold night air seeped in as she pulled up the bottom sash. She jumped through and urged him to follow. He fell and hurt his knee. She handed him a pair of boots. They were too big and she dragged him on before he'd time to tie the laces. They were stumbling across the garden to the stile, over it, and onto the cinder track. They were running through the puddles. He fell again. She stopped and pulled him up again. His hand was covered in nettle stings. There was the sudden hefty galloping of hooves and snorting. He felt the rush of their weight displacing the air as they trampled past and headed towards the men with their torches.

They ran down through the wood, he slithered and tripped, catching his arms against branches. They reached the gate and tumbled through. The camper van was still there. Sorcha put the key in the lock and they got in. It started first time and they roared down the cul-de-sac as she struggled to find second gear.

Out on the road she turned left onto a bigger road and accelerated up a steep hill. The old van fought her all the way but as Fletcher saw the dark red slivers in the sky over to his right, they reached the top and looked down onto a brightly lit town filling the bowl of land in front of them.

Sorcha hurried the van down the winding slope and in the town turned this way and that until they arrived at a looming grey church. She parked in a corner and pointed towards a café across the road.

Inside they ordered coffee.

Fletcher sat looking out of the window.

What was happening? It was as if the world he knew had disintegrated and he'd re-awaken in some dystopian future world full of thought police and runaways.

Sorcha gave him a weak smile.

'Diversion number ten,' she said.

'"If in doubt head for a church", was another one of Sybil's sayings ... although, of course, she was an atheist,' she added.

They sat in the café while the early morning workers began to populate the town centre.

Later she took him into the big church, which was in fact a cathedral, and showed him the Mappa Mundi. For no obvious reason he thought of Laura and went looking for a phone box.

'Hello,' he said. 'It's me.'

The silence at the other end was terrifying.

'Where are you?'

'Outside Hereford cathedral,' he said. He could see Sorcha sitting on a bench watching the crowds go by.

There was another long pause.

'What the hell are you doing there?'

'Long story. Not easy to tell.'

He heard her sigh.

'Laura, I love you,' he said.

After few seconds she put the phone down.

He didn't know what to do so he went back out into the street. It began to rain.

*****

Stephane Lottin was used to violence. Much of it he'd meted out himself, although he'd seen many others doing it as well. He'd watched people die and heard them die. He'd felt the soft spurt of blood from a severed artery splatter on his face and his hands. He'd felt the last struggles as he held someone tight. He'd seen the effects of guns and mortars and explosions. He'd killed in anger and he'd killed in cold blood. He knew that he was likely to die a violent death himself, although he didn't fear it. To begin with he'd done it to survive, and now he did it for money, but he'd never enjoyed any of it.

James Ferris on the other hand took his only pleasure from the slow suffering of others. Stephane had met other people like him, but none so pitiless.

They'd stopped at a road-side motel. The two women arrived separately. Stephane took the young girl to his room. He didn't hurt her. It wasn't part of sex for him. It didn't take long and he paid her well. He called for a taxi and she was gone.

He walked back up to his room and sat in the chair beside the bed. He didn't read or switch on the television, just stared into space. He could do this for hours if necessary and he would have found it difficult to recall any thoughts. The desert had taught him this quietness. The still long hours of the night with the stars cast like a shawl above him, or the howling of the sandstorm coming and going. Neither bothered him or awed him. He'd learnt to merely exist.

Eventually the phone rang. He didn't answer it, but made his way to the other room. He never knew what to expect, sometimes only a body, sometimes a blood bath. This time the woman wasn't dead and she was still in her dress. He helped her down the stairs and into the car he'd stolen earlier. She was crying, and shivering, and whimpering like a dog. He took her to the nearest hospital and helped her to the door. She staggered and fell. He left her there and drove back to the motel.

Ferris was waiting for him. Stephane knew immediately that something had gone wrong. Ferris followed him downstairs and they sped away in their car. They were south of Birmingham before Ferris spoke, only a few taut words.

'The detective and the girl must be eliminated, Stephane.'

Stephane nodded his understanding. The policeman was nothing, but the girl had aroused him. He dismissed the image and accelerated past a slow-moving lorry.

CHAPTER 10

It was late afternoon when they arrived back in Ennerdale.

There had been very little conversation, as if the swishing of the continuous rain and drizzle had suffocated their ability to communicate. Not that Fletcher could think of anything to say anyway. He'd always thought of himself as a strong person, who had dealt with life's vicissitudes as best he could. But then he recalled his previous period of exile from Laura and this time there was no going back to Courtney and Cassie in Todmorden, given that was the cause of this second 'banishment' – a word which provoked him to mutter long forgotten lines, "The damned use that word in hell - howlings attend it."

Sorcha glanced in his direction. He shook his head and gave her a sad smile.

'It's nothing,' he said. 'My old English teacher had a way of making you remember all sorts of stuff.'

Sorcha sighed and shook her head, although she didn't share any of her own schoolgirl experiences. Fletcher remembered what Mags had told him and thought it best not to pursue that line of enquiry.

The rain and the silence filled the space and the time.

There was no let-up when they crossed the bridge after Cleator Moor. Neither of them noticed the pile of discarded road signs lying in a brown puddle near the wall and there was no one in sight as they pulled up into the vicarage courtyard.

Sorcha turned off the engine and they both sat staring out at the flourishing trees, their bright green leaves gaily lapping up the avalanche from the leaden skies.

It seemed an age, but was probably only a minute or so before the vicarage door opened and Mags stood looking out at them.

The two car thieves gave each other a wary glance. Fletcher formulated a couple of warning sentences, but was unable to articulate them. Sorcha took the keys out of the ignition and opened the door. Even in the few steps from the van to the warmth of the vicarage entrance hall, they were both drenched and stood like a couple of sulky dogs in the darkness, until Mags ordered them to remove their coats and shoes and get themselves into the kitchen.

Five minutes later they were both tucking greedily into some hot onion soup and freshly baked bread. Mags had busied herself with providing this and hadn't made any attempt to interrogate them so far.

'Tea,' she said, placing two steaming mugs in front of them and sat down with her own. Her eyes announced they could start their confession as soon as they liked, but they both suspected their stories were poor and unlikely to arouse much sympathy or understanding.

'You may as well tell me your version, Michael,' she said, eventually. 'I've listened to too many of Sorcha's threadbare reports to expect much information from her.'

Sorcha glared at her, but couldn't hold Mags's gaze.

'We went in search of Elizabeth,' he began.

Mags gave Sorcha a knowing look, but she was hidden behind

her wet hair, her elbow on the table supporting her hang-dog head.

'But she wasn't there,' concluded Mags.

Fletcher shook his head.

'But her son was there, saying she often disappeared for weeks on end,' he said.

Mags looked at him with a blank face. Fletcher wondered what he'd said, until a switch clicked on somewhere deep inside his brain.

'She hasn't got a son, has she?' he asked in a whisper.

'That's cruel,' replied Mags.

'What?' he asked.

She picked up his bowl and stood up.

'Elizabeth had a son, but he died in an accident. Riding his motorbike too fast. Must be more than ten years ago now.'

Sorcha came out from her hiding place.

'That's sick,' she said.

Mags took her bowl as well and stepped over to the sink. She gave them a quick swish in the soapy water and turned to face them both.

'I expect they were waiting for you?'

Fletcher nodded. Were they all involved in this cat and mouse behaviour?

'Followed us back towards the cottage, but Sorcha used the 'diversionary tactics' to lose them.'

'Didn't stop them catching up with us though, did it?' added Sorcha.

'So what did you find out?' Mags asked.

'Nothing,' admitted Fletcher. 'Other than they seemed to think it was important to follow us everywhere. I expect they're out there now. Watching. And waiting.'

Mags agreed.

The three of them said nothing for a few moments, each of them calculating their own little sums and projections.

'So what happened at the inquest?' asked Fletcher.

Mags snorted.

'They blocked the roads with invented bridge repairs and a stolen lorry. The courtroom door was locked by the time we got there. Hilda told us that it was, 'death by natural causes'. All done and dusted. The funeral is next Wednesday.'

Fletcher sighed and leaned back in his chair. It was only this that reminded him he was wearing someone else's clothes. He stood up.

'I think I left my rucksack upstairs,' he said, and indicated the dreadful woollen jumper he was sporting. 'Need to get out of these 'borrowed robes',' he added.

'They're where you left them,' said Mags and watched him make his way out of the kitchen.

He was half way up the stairs when he could hear her talking quietly to Sorcha. He didn't hear any replies.

* * * * *

Later when he came back down and found that Sorcha had gone, he asked after Mark and Roger.

'They've gone back to London,' explained Mags. 'Mark said he had arrangements to make and needed to talk to his solicitor. Roger has gone with him for moral support.'

Fletcher was restless. He stalked around the kitchen until he came to rest at the window. It was still raining, although there was a bright patch over the church.

'I think it's over, Michael,' said Mags in an empty, quiet voice.

He turned to look at her. His eyes were fierce and for once she looked away.

'Bastards!'

Mags managed a smile.

'Unfortunately I think you'll find that the people you're referring to probably have as lengthy, eminent and carefully recorded heritage as myself. Going right back to the original 'bastard', who brought them over here.'

He couldn't help but smile at that and thought of Louisa.

'Can I make a phone call?' he asked.

'Of course, but not from here, if you don't want them to listen into it.'

Fletcher smiled again.

'Where would you suggest?'

She gave this some thought.

'Well, I hesitate to suggest it, because it's not somewhere I'd feel comfortable, but I dare say you've been in worse places.'

He waited.

'Just across the river where it was blocked, turn left and carry on. It's a pub on the right facing a church. The Brook.'

'Bit of a dive?'

Mags shook her head.

'More likely that you won't understand a word they say.'

Fletcher nodded his understanding.

'I'd take you there but I've got a Mother's Union meeting in half an hour and I don't think my farmers' wives would take kindly to finding that I'd neglected them to go to the Brook Inn for a pint with an off-comer.'

'Point taken,' said Fletcher, although he was relieved that he could get out of this overheated kitchen and do something positive.

She handed him the van keys and suggested he park it a hundred yards up the road from the pub.

'It may be old, but it's got a lot of memories bound up in its old carcass,' she added.

216

Glad to escape. Fletcher fired up the old 'carcass' and trundled down the lane.

He drove past the pub and parked down a small side road. The rain had paused for breath, although the damp air heralded a restart any minute.

He pulled up his cagoule hood and walked slowly along towards the pub. The street lights were not doing much of a job and the lights in the pub windows were less than inviting, but he pushed at the door and scrabbled through the unlit entrance porch.

At first he could hardly see anything. It was as if they'd only grudgingly accepted the invention of electricity and were still worried they might use it all up. He focussed on the bar and the few figures around it. Some faces turned towards him, whilst others maintained their hunched stances, unwilling to even show any curiosity.

There was no music, no dart-players, no pool table; not even a gang of four old gimmers clacking dominoes in a corner. Fletcher thought he'd probably not even interrupted any conversations. The faces that turned towards him held no expression, merely a resigned glumness which filled the heavy space. Clothing and appearances were muted, so that he felt he'd stepped back into some silent movie picturing a Dickensian world.

The floor was uneven slate slabs and he nearly stumbled as he took the few steps towards the bar. No one moved or spoke.

He reached the counter and looked at the hand pumps. There was nothing he recognised and only one pump had a label on it anyway.

'A pint, please,' he said, not certain as to whether they'd understood him or would respond.

The man behind the bar had watched him approach with the regulation blank face. His shirt collar was skewed and had not seen a washing machine for some time. As he unfurled his folded arms to reveal heavily tattooed forearms, Fletcher watched his wrinkled face break into what might pass for a smile.

'Jennin's?' he asked in a voice smelling of Capstan Full Strength.

Fletcher nodded and looked to his left.

A little man regarded him with a single eye. The other was covered with a tattered, pink, plastic eye-patch. Again a smile appeared, this time revealing a galley load of broken teeth.

Fletcher smiled back.

'Evening,' he said.

The little man winked with his single eye and touched his cap.

'Nin,' he said.

Fletcher turned back to see a tattooed arm placing a froth topped glass on the bar in front of him.

He looked at the barman, who grunted an unintelligible sound at him. Fletcher offered him a fiver.

When the man gave him the change, Fletcher asked if he could use the phone. The man grunted again and indicated a darkened doorway over to the right. Fletcher took a big gulp of his beer, which tasted surprisingly good, and made his way over to the doorway. Through it he found himself in a short dark corridor which ended in a half open door, revealing cracked urinals.

On the wall was a phone balanced on a rickety ledge. He picked it up and dialled the number, relieved to think that he didn't need to see the numbers to do this.

His first call was unsuccessful. It was only half six and sometimes Laura stayed late on a Wednesday, so he wasn't too surprised. He tried the other number, which was answered.

He had to wait, but eventually he could hear the husky tone.

'Yes, Michael.'

'I thought you might like to know I'm still alive,' he said.

There was a pause. A sigh.

'I warned you Michael. They're not playing anymore. You're upsetting some seriously nasty people.'

'But not your friend Anthony?' he sneered.

'I told you that,' she replied.

'So do you know who?'

This time there was a longer pause.

'It wouldn't help you to know any names, Michael. In fact it would be much better if you didn't know.'

'So you do know?'

'Look,' she said. 'Get yourself back to Laura and forget everything you've seen and heard. It's the only safe option … for both of you…'

Fletcher considered this.

'You mean they would harm her?'

'They wouldn't hesitate, if they thought it was the only way to stop you.'

There was another longer pause between them. He could imagine her standing by one of the huge windows, blue dress, the sheen of her hair in the moonlight, manicured hand holding the phone, silver and diamonds glittering, a glass of wine on a small side table.

'Michael?'

'All right, I give in. Tell them I'm giving up. But tomorrow I'm going climbing with a friend. Friday I'll be going home.'

Another pause and the line went dead.

He placed the phone back on its rest and thought of making the first call again, but decided against it. He went back into the bar.

Nothing had changed. No one looked across at him. He went

back to his drink and took another gulp. There was something strangely restful about not having to communicate or make small talk. This crowd were experts. He was there for another five minutes or so and the only sound came from the cat snoring on a chair near the window.

He put down his empty glass and made for the door. No one said goodbye or turned to see him go. He turned at the doorway and looked back. A set of hunched shoulders ignored him. The barman was leaning against the wall, his arms folded, staring at him. He left.

Outside the streetlights had not got any stronger. The road shone dully in the orange light. He walked along to where he'd parked the van. Despite the total lack of activity in the bar, he was overcome with a strong sense of foreboding. He turned the corner. The van was where he'd parked it and there was no one to be seen. He went to open the door. There was the slightest of scrunches on the gravel behind him. Enough to make him instinctively duck. The metal pipe crashed into the side of the windscreen. He heard it crack. He turned and punched hard. His aim was true. He felt the crunch of ribs and the body hunch up. There was a gasp and his attacker faltered back. Fletcher's kick caught him below the knee and he went down with a yelp of pain. But that was it.

There were seven or eight of them. He was dragged past the van and further down the cul-de-sac. Two of them held his arms while the others rained blows and kicks at him. He tried to stay on his feet but eventually his arms were released and he was down. He covered his head with one arm and put the other between his legs. But they had stopped.

He peered out at the legs around him. They backed away and he looked up. As they parted he could see another pair of legs. Skinny legs. Jeans. Black leather jacket. Wicked smirk on his pockmarked face. Tex.

'Not so clever now, copper?' he said.

Fletcher eased himself onto one elbow and wiped the blood out of his eyes. He couldn't tell where it was coming from, but there was plenty of it. The worst pain was coming from his left side. Please not broken ribs. Again.

'Don't suppose we could settle this amicably with a bit of arm wrestling,' he suggested with a grimace. He doubted whether he could even stand up.

'No chance,' said Tex as he sauntered over. 'I prefer to watch people being beaten up rather than do it myself. Although in your case, I'm looking forward to making a mess of your ugly face.' He stopped a good few feet from Fletcher. Certainly too far for him to hope to reach the little monster with a desperate lunge. He glanced left and right. He was right, eight against one.

Tex reached into his jacket pocket and pulled out a knife. Fletcher's favourite. A Stanley.

'I hope you've tightened the screw on that,' he managed with a gasp. 'Could give yourself a nasty cut with one of them.'

Tex laughed.

'Don't worry copper. I've had plenty of practice.'

He stood up and nodded at one of his gang. Fletcher was too slow. The kick caught him in the kidneys and he yelled in agony as he arched his back. The next kick clunked into his chin and he rolled up against the wall. Fear gripped his insides as he braced himself, trying to ignore the pain in his side.

But nothing happened.

He peered back towards where Tex had been standing. He was still there, but looking to his right. Fletcher realised that someone was speaking and that the gang was slowly moving away from him.

'… suggest you run home to mummy before I blow your

stupid spotty face off.'

Fletcher couldn't see who was speaking and his brain was desperately trying to place the voice.

Tex had recovered some of his bravado.

'You wouldn't dare use that here,' he said.

'You want to bet,' said the voice.

'You fucking old gimmer! I'm not frightened of you. It's probably not even loaded.'

There was a slight pause during which the gang seemed to gain some self-belief, but then this was quite literally blown away.

The noise in that small gap between the two terraced houses either side was completely deafening. Fletcher screamed in terror, but quickly realised he wasn't the only one.

When the yelling stopped, he could see that virtually the whole gang was lying huddled on the floor. At first he feared they might all be dead, but then they started to flinch and twitch. Soon they were all struggling to their feet and scuttling away towards the back alleys either side, whimpering like scolded dogs as they went.

Only Tex was left lying on the floor. He sat up and stared at his arm. He took his hand away from where he was holding it and a spurt of dark blood leapt into the air. He screamed in terror and grabbed it again.

At this point a figure stepped forward past the van and Fletcher could see the shotgun held in his hands. The barrel was still pointing at Tex. It was Stanley Gill.

Fletcher groaned and tried to get up, but only succeeded in nearly passing out with the pain. He lay on his side as he watched Gill walk up to the lad moaning on the floor. Gill leant down and slapped him hard across the face. Tex gasped and stared up at his attacker.

Gill broke the shotgun and laid it on the gravel. From round his neck he took his scarf and roughly grabbed Tex's arm.

'Lie still, you daft little sod. I'm tying me best scarf round yer arm to stop yer from bleeding to death.'

Tex did as he was told, but had passed out before Gill had finished.

There was a scuffling in one of the corners and Gill looked up.

'Jack Baxter. Git yersen along to t'Brook and git them to ring fer t'ambulance!'

A pale faced youth appeared from the shadows, hesitated, and then ran off.

Gill turned towards where Fletcher lay and sighed.

'Me fether tolt me to niver play wi matches nay knives, eh, Inspector?'

Fletcher smiled at him and fainted.

* * * * *

He came round in the ambulance, the sound of the siren poking him into consciousness. Across the aisle he could see Tex lying still with his eyes closed. An ambulance woman was fiddling with a blood bag swaying around on a metal pole. The tubes flopped about but they were already connected to Tex's arm. The woman must have sensed his eyes on her and turned to look at him.

'Evening,' she said and gave him a stern look.

'Is he alive?' Fletcher asked.

She looked back at Tex.

'Ay. He'll live. What about you?'

'I've been better.'

He tried to lean up, but the pain in his side reminded him what he'd just been through.

'I'd lie still if I was you,' she said leaning towards him. He did as he was told.

When he opened his eyes again she was looking at him. He smiled at her and she smiled back.

'Stanley said you're a police officer?'

He nodded.

He could tell she was about to say something else, but thought better of it.

'I know,' he said. 'But they're only kids.'

She shrugged her shoulders.

'Well, he'll not be causing anyone any trouble for a bit.'

Fletcher looked across at the silent Tex.

'You know him?'

She shrugged again.

'Ay I know him … or rather I know his mother. Poor cow. She deserves better than him.'

Fletcher thought it better not to enquire any further and closed his eyes again.

* * * * *

Three hours later, he was sitting up in the hospital bed waiting for a doctor to arrive. He'd been for an X-ray and surprisingly there was nothing broken, although his side still hurt like hell.

The door opened and Mags stood looking at him.

'I'm sorry, Michael, my stupid fault. I should have come with you.'

Fletcher grinned at the thought of that, but knew laughter was out of the question.

'No problem,' he said. 'Although it was a good job you sent Stanley after me, otherwise I might have had to put the whole gang in hospital.'

She shook her head at this, but before she could say anything else a young woman in a white coat came into the room.

Fletcher realised he must be getting old, because this doctor looked only a bit older than Sorcha. She took a brisk look at the record sheet hanging on the bottom of his bed and gave him a weary smile.

'Well, Mr Fletcher. I think we're going to let you go. One of your colleagues has been on the phone to say you'd probably walk out anyway, even if I tried to stop you. As it is I think you're okay, nothing broken, although you'll not be chasing any villains for a week or so. I'll get someone to give you some painkillers and then you can go.'

Fletcher gave his best cockney grin. It didn't work. She looked at Mags and the two of them shared that 'what can you do?' look.

'If I was you I'd take a few days off,' she said as she reached the door.

Fletcher was already trying to get off the bed. He gasped with pain, but still managed to give her a wave.

Mags helped him up and led him out to the car.

* * * * *

The vicarage rose up out of the rain filled darkness, with only the porch light illuminating a rectangle on the gravel drive. In the kitchen the Aga was filling the room with its friendly warmth and a pan now began to bubble merrily on the hob. Fletcher sat nursing a gin and tonic while Mags banged about making something to eat. They hadn't said much to each other since leaving the hospital.

'I think I ought to use your phone this time,' he said.

Mags nodded and pointed towards the hallway. He got to his feet with a grunt, but the pain was lessening now he'd taken the painkillers.

He limped out to the hall and picked up the phone.

It rang for some time and he was about to replace it when

there was a click and the sound of her breathing.

'Laura? Please don't put the phone down,' he said.

There was silence at the other end, but she did as he asked.

'I've been in a bit of a tussle with some local lads, so I won't be doing anything much for a few days.'

Not a word.

'I'm staying at the local vicarage, so hopefully I'll be stopped from getting into any more trouble.'

He waited.

'Are you hurt?' she asked.

He winced as he sat down.

'Nothing a few days rest won't cure. Nothing broken.'

He could hear her sigh.

'I miss you,' he said.

This time there was a longer pause. He waited with baited breath.

'And I miss you … you bastard…'

What could he say? So he didn't.

'So when will you be coming home?' she asked quietly.

'At the weekend. I promise,' he said.

'Don't make promises, Mick. I'll believe it when I see you.'

There was another short pause and the phone went dead.

He put the phone down and went slowly back into the kitchen. Mags placed a bowl of soup on the table and gave him a questioning look.

'Could have been worse,' he said.

* * * * *

He couldn't remember the rest of the evening or getting himself into bed, but he woke in a darkened room with a start. He flinched and felt his side. Still sore, but not as bad as he'd expected.

He went to the loo and peered through the small window onto the churchyard below. The whole scene was grey. A fine drizzle blurred everything. He went back to his room and found some clothes then went down stairs.

The kitchen was empty but warm. On the table were cereal packets and a loaf of bread sitting next to an array of marmalades and jam. He helped himself and was nearly finished when the outside door opened and Mags came stomping in with some shopping.

'Right, Michael. You're due a visit from a colleague to talk to you about last night's little escapade and this evening I've booked Gavin and Sheila to come for a few rounds of bridge. Otherwise you've to rest. Understood?'

He nodded meekly, but was pleased to hear about the second half of the day's entertainment.

'Hilda?' he asked.

'Not sure,' said Mags as she began to sort the shopping. 'I think she might be interviewing that young thug instead. He'd better hope it's not me on the panel when he's well enough.'

Fletcher stared at his piece of toast.

'I'd be interested to know if the lad was just out for revenge or maybe he'd been offered a little contract.'

'Revenge?' asked Mags.

He told her about the incident in the pub last week.

'Um,' she said. 'From the little I know of him, I don't think he'd need much encouragement … but I dare say Hilda will be asking the right sort of questions.'

It was Fletcher's turn to shrug.

Mags gave him a glare.

'She's good at her job, Michael, and you interfering wouldn't help, would it?'

He acquiesced.

Neither of them could think of anything else to say and left it at that.

* * * * *

It was half ten when there was a knock at the door and DC Frank Rainor sidled into the sitting room where Fletcher had been sent 'to read a book or something and get out from under Mags's feet'.

'Morning, sir,' said Frank.

Fletcher had heard Mags instructing him to remove 'that old coat and leave it to drip in the hall'. He also heard him accepting a cup of tea, so Fletcher was hopeful he might receive the same.

'Take a seat, Sergeant,' he said and watched as the man hesitantly selected one of the old settees that were gathered round the roaring fire in the stone fireplace. It was obvious the man was ill at ease and would much rather have been giving the young thug a hard time than being sent on this errand.

'Short straw, eh, Frank?' asked Fletcher with a grin.

Frank gave him a doubtful look and then a watery smile.

But before he could agree to this, Mags came in with a tray of tea and scones. She quickly bustled back out again, but leaving them in no doubt that crumbs would not be tolerated.

The two of them sat like a couple of fourth years in the headmaster's study, not sure whether they'd earned the spread and hoping the other would open the batting. Fletcher put him out of his misery and asked if he'd like to take his statement. Frank sighed with relief and got out his notepad and pen.

It didn't take long and Fletcher told him that he wouldn't be pressing charges. Frank raised an eyebrow at that, but wrote it down anyway.

'Anyway, off the record Frank, what I really want to know is if the little git had been put up to it or not. Perhaps a softly, softly

228

approach might work?'

Frank shook his head and said he'd ask Sergeant Crake.

Interview over, he was up and gone.

Fletcher sat and stared at the rain. There was nothing more he could do, even if the little runt gave them a name, which he doubted. His mind wandered to Sorcha. Where was she? With this thought in mind he dozed off. Mags looked in, tutted at the crumbs, but took the tray away. He missed the sun coming out and the rainbow spanning the churchyard. The rain returned and he slept on.

* * * * *

Sorcha knew nothing of Fletcher's contretemps, as she'd had a longstanding appointment to keep. She'd left the vicarage the previous evening and, after getting a change of clothes and packing some others, she'd hitched a lift into Carlisle in time to get to the motorway services by early evening.

By six o'clock she was sitting near the door of the drivers' cafe. She'd had time to apply a bit of make-up and give her hair a brush, but wished she'd managed a shower. She didn't have to wait long. The intervening door opened and Ciaran tapped her on the shoulder. She followed him out to his truck. He stopped in the gap between his lorry and the one parked next to it and dragged her into the shadows. Without a word he pushed her back against the cab and kissed her hard on the lips. His hands urgently explored the curves and hollows of her body. She didn't resist, but, eyes shut, gave herself up to him. On other occasions this had led to ferocious coupling, either against the side of the truck or on the gravel, but the rain and the moment were different this time. They parted, kissed again, before climbing into the cab. Ciaran turned the ignition and the huge lorry roared into life. Five minutes later they were on their way south.

She stared though the spray.

'Anything?' he asked.

She shook her head.

'Any trouble with yer man?'

Again she shook her head, but couldn't stop a smile appearing on her face. But it was gone by the time Ciaran glanced across.

'He's okay,' she said.

Ciaran glanced across again and put his hand on her thigh. She smiled at him and stroked his cheek.

A slower lorry ahead of him distracted him for a while as he moved out to overtake. They were starting to go up the long climb to Shap summit. She let him concentrate going through the gears. It was nearly seven when he pulled into the lorry park in Kendal and the two of them held each other again.

As the ambulance was taking Fletcher to hospital in Whitehaven, they were making love in the room Ciaran had booked for the night. Later after a quick shower, they ran down the high street jumping the puddles until they reached the venue, up the stairs and into the smoke-filled club.

Mags was right about Sorcha's voice, but would surely not approve of her wasting it, even damaging it, singing with a rock band for an audience high on drugs and alcohol and mid-week ennui. Afterwards they ended up at a party which went on until dawn. They found a room to continue what they'd started and sneaked in sheepishly for breakfast provided by a completely unaware landlady, who treated them like a honeymoon couple, doling out extra bacon and eggs to feed their famished bodies.

It was only as they sat in the cab where Ciaran had parked along from Lancaster station that they had another brief conversation about the policeman and what he might be on to.

'I think he's going to give up,' she said.

'Scared?' asked Ciaran, without a hint of sarcasm. He knew

enough about the enemy not to dismiss them.

'No. Realistic,' she replied, before hesitating. She was aware of Ciaran's eyes upon her, his suspicion aroused. She forced herself to look into them.

'I think he knows people.'

'People?'

She nodded.

'You mean Special Branch?'

She nodded again.

'But someone else as well. I think he's been warned off.'

Ciaran watched as a car waited to get past his lorry obstructing the narrow road.

'I'd better go,' he said.

She reached across and kissed him. He held her close. Their dark heads leant together for a final few seconds. A last kiss and she was climbing down out of the cab. He watched her walk away. She turned. He waved. The lorry lurched forward and rumbled down the road. She watched until it disappeared, before crossing towards the station, oblivious to the torrential rain bouncing off the station forecourt, whilst others huddled in the entrance hall or ran to escape the downpour.

On the train she stared sightlessly at the passing scenery and considered the layers of deception through which she slip slided every day of her life. Sybil had been the one person she was able to share that turmoil with and now she was dead. Sorcha couldn't even cry. Her face and heart hardened with each window-smeared mile as the sullen train trundled across the estuaries and round the hidden mass of Black Combe.

She was back in time to do the Thursday evening lock-in. She was even more blank-faced than usual towards the lecherous looks and pathetic banter of the men in the bar, pulling pints like a robot, as though she was just an extension of the till. But this didn't stop her from selecting one of the overnight guests and inviting him to her room at the end of the evening. She'd long ago learned that random sex was the most effective way of exhausting her anger and self-hatred. He couldn't believe his luck, even though he found himself outside her door an hour later wondering what he'd done wrong. The following morning's bruises would prove it wasn't a dream, but he didn't feel like bragging about the experience. He knew it was none of his doing and that somehow he'd been used. Nevertheless he knew he'd not forget the girl with the jet black eyes, though he didn't even learn her name.

* * * * *

Earlier that same morning another man sat upright in the dark corridor on the fifth floor of a huge white-faced government building in Westminster. There was a brass plaque on the wall next to the main doors downstairs, but it gave no indication as to the nature of the activities that went on above the heads of the passing tourists and government officials.

He had been there for over half an hour. There had been no other people in the corridor, no one getting out of the lift, or opening one of the shiny mahogany doors, and no sound issuing from behind them. The carpet was dark red and thick. The windows at the end looked out towards the river, which flowed past at its stately pace. There was no sound from the traffic outside.

During the whole time he had been sitting there, he neither moved nor made a sound. His eyes were open but they were focussed far beyond the corridor or the wall opposite. The only clues that he wasn't a waxwork were the occasional slow blink of his eyes and a brief muscular spasm in his left wrist.

Stephane Lottin was in the desert. The horizon was a blur

between white and blue. There was nothing else. He wasn't waiting. Merely existing in space and time.

The door to his left opened and James Ferris appeared. Lottin stood up. Ferris closed the door. He walked across to the window. Lottin stayed where he was.

'I understand our little plan failed to achieve its intention, Stephane?'

Lottin didn't move. Rhetoric was wasted on him.

Ferris turned to face him.

'I believe the original sentence was "Who will rid me of this troublesome priest?"'

English historical references were also lost on Lottin, although he understood the meaning, but still he didn't move.

'Strange how the church has lost its power yet can still harbour one's enemies...'

Lottin now looked at Ferris.

'I believe our friend is going for a scramble tomorrow and accidents do happen...'

There was silence between them. Lottin could sense the other man's tension. Anger can cause a man to lose control and take risks. He was not that sort of a man. He understood the task. The reasons were of no interest to him. He would take no pleasure in the activity, but it would provide some measure of contentment as a consequence. He judged that it was time to go. So he went.

Ferris stood there for a few minutes after he'd gone. His face hardly altered, barely a flicker of distaste. He opened the door and went back into the room.

* * * * *

Fletcher slept until late in the afternoon.

After a bath and a change of clothes he presented himself in the kitchen. He was able to help with some of the preparation for the meal and welcomed the dinner guests, Gavin and Sheila, with a smile and glass of wine.

Following the meal they repaired to the drawing room where the cards awaited and they played an enjoyable clutch of hands. Mags made a resolute, if adventurous partner, and they won two rubbers to one.

He and Gavin talked briefly about tomorrow's delayed expedition and the more experienced man was at pains to reassure Fletcher that it was a short walk in and a steady climb with only one easy pitch at the end. Fletcher knew very well that a 'hard v.diff.' would be anything but easy for him in his current state, but was determined to fulfil the promise he'd made the man.

As they were saying goodnight at the door, he thought briefly and longingly of going along for the Thursday night lock-in, but a quick glance at Mags told him this was not going to happen. So he accepted a brandy and took himself to bed.

Sleep did not come easy and he recalled that time in Todmorden, after Laura had thrown him out and he ended up wandering the hills on his own. So he slept uneasily, fitfully and was racked with incomprehensible dreams.

CHAPTER 11

Friday 28th May

The back page of the Guardian that morning brought the disappointing news that Spurs had scrambled victory in the FA Cup replay with an early penalty from Hoddle, even though QPR had been the better team throughout. Fletcher ignored the front page news concerning the latest action in the Falklands War and abandoned the paper in a rumpled heap on the kitchen table.

Bending to get his boots on reminded him that his side still ached. He went back upstairs and took a couple more pills. While he was there he saw Gavin's landrover pull up in the yard. He heard Mags calling him and made his way down, not without some trepidation.

This hadn't left him by the time the two of them were striding along the path out of Wasdale Head, with both Great Gable and Lingmell still shrouded in mist. But at least it wasn't raining.

'I think we're in luck,' said Gavin, indicating the movement of the clouds amongst the gullies and pinnacles up on Gable. Fletcher knew that hiding somewhere up there was the Needle and Great Gully, but he couldn't see them yet.

'And we're not going that high,' his companion added.

Fletcher knew he was being reassured, but he also knew his heart was already fluttering at the thought of the climbing. He forced himself onwards to keep up with the younger man.

The first part of the walk was easy going as they followed the beck, but after half an hour or so they began to climb up to the right towards the Ghyll. Here Fletcher was soon left behind. Gavin waited for him at the point where you could look straight up into the deep cleft. They stopped a while and listened to the waterfall and the calls of the crows on the cliffs. Suddenly Gavin pointed upwards.

'Look!' he cried. 'Peregrines.'

Fletcher looked up and saw the two birds, diving and soaring in the updraft.

They continued on. The clouds weren't so high here, as they huddled out of the prevailing wind. They could see as far as the elbow of the Ghyll, where it turned a sharp left. Fletcher knew that this was where they were heading and hoped that the cloud would have risen sufficiently. He didn't have much time to think about this as Gavin kept up a steady pace, even though it became steeper with every step.

Eventually they stopped to rest again. His side throbbed with a dull ache. They had now reached the gully and the going was going to get much harder. Fletcher looked up at the sheer grey walls, which disappeared into the lofty crags above, higher on the right and hidden in the swirling white cloud.

They went on.

Fletcher must have lost awareness, putting one foot in front of the other and was brought up short as he reached to pull himself up a short rock face. Gavin had stopped and Fletcher nearly reached for his boot. The two of them stood on the top of a little ridge with a waterfall tumbling down a twenty-foot drop to their right. A stonechat stuttered from one rock to another chiding them with its pebbly call.

Other than the sound of the water and the bird, the silence was immense. It was as if the steep sides of the enclosing walls were wreathed in soundless white cloaks, compressing the space, making the stillness more solid ... until above them they heard the trickle of stones. Neither of them was surprised by this. Gullies like this were constantly on the move. Gravity and the elements ensured a continuous river of stone.

Gavin pointed up to where a lone mountain ash clung to the steep rock face.

'We'll be able to see the chock stone from there,' he said.

Fletcher's chest gave a shudder and he forced himself to grin.

'Bring it on,' he said.

Gavin smiled back and set off again. Fletcher sighed and reached out for the first handhold.

It was another forty minutes before they reached the elbow and Gavin waited while Fletcher hauled himself up the last few feet.

Above them the clouds were still writhing about the pillars of rock on both sides. They were now so close some of the white wraiths were floating past them as they looked up into the chaos of the upper section of the climb. Fletcher didn't suffer from vertigo, but he quickly focussed on the smooth bulge of the giant boulder blocking the whole Ghyll not thirty feet above them. This was the climb and he could see immediately that the way on the left looked terrifyingly vertical whilst there looked like reassuringly wide ledges on the right. This was where Gavin now headed.

What looked like wide ledges from thirty feet away became more daunting as they got nearer. The ledges were ten to fifteen feet apart and sloped unhelpfully away from the rock face. Gavin stopped at the lowest one and took off his rucksack. He retrieved

237

his rope and other climbing gear and began to sort it out.

'We can leave your rucksack here,' he said. 'We'll abseil back down again.'

Fletcher was relieved to take his bag off and placed in into a cleft in the rock by his feet. He sat down and found some chocolate and his flask, while he watched Gavin putting on his harness and attaching the slings and karabiners to his belt. Fletcher had done some climbing and attended a few courses. He wasn't a novice, but he knew this was going to be tough. The rock was smooth and the handholds looked few and far between.

Gavin had a drink and looked up at the wall.

'There are two cruxes,' he said.

He pointed upwards.

'You see that flange of rock there?' he asked.

Fletcher looked where he was pointing. It didn't look like much to him from here.

'Once you've got your hands on that, you're nearly half way up,' said Gavin.

Fletcher gave him a doubtful look and nodded.

'Don't tell me anymore,' he said.

Gavin turned and smiled.

'You'll be fine.'

He spent the next few minutes reminding Fletcher of the calls and tying him on. But eventually the two of them were quiet. A crow floated past beneath them without a croak.

Gavin pointed down to a small pool, which hovered over one of the waterfalls below.

'That's where Alice ended up,' he said.

Fletcher looked at the ledge. If she'd not stopped there she'd have fallen another twenty feet onto the jagged rocks below. He tried not to imagine it.

He looked up. If she'd fallen from the top of the boulder, that must be twenty-five feet at least. Amazing she was still alive after that. He looked back at Gavin.

His eyes had filled up, but he roughly brushed the tears aside. If his nerve had been weakened, Fletcher couldn't see it. But he knew what climbers said. Concentrate on climbing not falling.

'Let's go,' Gavin said, as if he'd tuned into Fletcher's thinking, and turned to face the wall.

Fletcher watched as his companion climbed the first pitch. Even though he knew Gavin was a skilled climber, he was still impressed by the smooth and unhurried way he climbed. He reached the flange of rock in ten or twelve seemingly effortless moves. Here he leant out and fumbled in a cleft towards his left until he found a suitable hole. In a few moments he'd put in the nut and attached the karabiner. Seconds later he was hanging off it to test the hold and then began climbing again. Within a few feet he disappeared. Fletcher looked round into the emptiness. He hated that. Overhangs.

There wasn't any word for a good few minutes. Fletcher was starting to worry. His chest felt tight and his breathing shallow.

'Okay,' shouted Gavin. 'I'm tied on. Climb when you're ready.'

Fletcher tried to control his breathing, but knew the sooner he got on with it, the better he'd be. He reached up to the first hold and pulled.

The next ten minutes were some of the scariest moments of his whole life. As he'd surmised the hand-holds were thin. He'd only managed three moves before his foot slipped and the rope tightened hard. It hurt, but it was damn reassuring.

'It's okay. I've got you,' floated down from above. Fletcher recognised that laconic tone that climbers used. He shook his head and forced himself upwards. As he'd also suspected the worst bit was above the flange. At one point, two moves above that, he had one foot on the thin ridge of the flange, his other foot above on a knife edge crack, his left hand finger-tipped into a tiny fold and his right hand scrabbling for purchase, but finding none and he still couldn't see Gavin. The rope was taut above him and his chest begged for release.

'There's a great push up above your knee.'

Fletcher looked to his left. He could see the tiny three-inch ledge Gavin was referring to, but it was a good foot above his knee. How was he going to do that? His right hand fluttered helplessly over the smooth rock. He could feel the panic rising like a flood consuming his chest and limbs. Alice's resting place blurred into view between his feet. He closed his eyes. He felt the rope give a bit. He opened his eyes, his cheek rough against the rock face. To his right he saw a vertical strip protruding from the rock face. He reached out and felt the reassuring half-inch hold. He pulled to his right and his left foot slowly rose up until he managed to get it onto the ledge. One breath and he pushed with all his strength.

The next three moves were a blur. Gavin's foot came into view. Two more pushes he was clinging on next to him. Gavin's face was one big smile.

'Nice move,' he said and indicated the enormous stone settee to his right. Fletcher settled into it and closed his eyes.

'Woo …' was all he could say.

When he opened them again, Gavin was still smiling and offering him a piece of chocolate.

'Well done,' he added. 'You're not bad. Not bad at all.'

Fletcher made a face and looked about him.

They were slightly to one side at the top of the great boulder. Below him the rest of it disappeared and he couldn't see his rucksack or the ledge where Alice had landed. Above him the Ghyll continued in further vertical cliffs and waterfalls, giant steps, up into the clouds. Either side the cliffs rose like cathedral pillars into white nothingness.

Gavin had unhooked himself and was climbing over the sharp edged chunks of rocks backed up behind the chock stone. He'd crossed over to the other side and was now looking back at the wall above Fletcher.

Fletcher turned to look above himself and in that moment he saw it.

A flash of tawny and white fur.

There it was again writhing its way amongst the boulders.

Gavin shouted.

'Did you see that?' he yelled.

Fletcher yelled back.

'It's going upwards,' he called back as he watched the sinuous humps of its body appearing and disappearing between the rocks. It was a stoat. He was sure.

'Stoat,' he shouted.

Gavin was making his way back across to him, but now Fletcher turned and looked to where he'd first seen the creature. Above and to his right somewhere? A thin, dark crack?

He got up and scrabbled upwards to it. Gavin shouted after him.

'Be careful, Mick.'

Fletcher reached the crack. It was wider now he was up close. He realised that the big slab he'd just crawled across had fallen quite recently from where it must have hidden this cleft. He reached inside and felt nothing. There was a bigger fissure behind. Flattening himself against the rock he squeezed himself though and behind, into a black hole.

Something told him that the hole was big. A cave? He could hear Gavin scuffling about behind him.

'Fletch? Where are you?'

'Here,' he replied and heard his voice echo cavernously.

He looked back the way he'd come and could see Gavin through the thinnest of gaps peering at him.

'I see you. Don't move. I'll get my torch,' said Gavin, and he disappeared.

It seemed a long time and Fletcher wanted to get more comfortable, but he sensed the emptiness of the space in front of him and didn't dare move.

Gavin reappeared and managed to reach far enough for Fletcher to stretch back and fumble for the torch.

At first he only managed to blind himself by switching it on into his face. But then he was able to point it into the darkness.

'What can you see?' shouted Gavin.

Fletcher stared at the size of the opening in front of him. He knew there were a few other natural caves in the Lake District, but he didn't think there was any the size of this.

He could see a wall to his right and further along to the left, but the floor receded away from him like a room cut in the rock. Above an uneven roof descended away from him. Towards the back of the cave the torchlight was lost in the engulfing darkness. He flinched as he felt Gavin slide in beside him. The pair of them stared in shocked silence at what they'd discovered.

'This is it,' whispered Gavin.

Fletcher frowned into the shadows.

'What do you mean?'

'This is what Alice found.'

Fletcher turned to Gavin.

'You mean this is the Dalmatian's hiding place?' he asked.

'Maybe?'

'Do you think it's manmade?' asked Fletcher.

'Don't know, I can't see any signs of it,' replied Gavin indicating the walls.

242

The two of them took a few hesitant steps across the floor and both instinctively looked back to see if they could still see the entrance. It was faint but they could both see the thin shaft of faint light marking their way out.

Fletcher shone the light back into the body of the cave again. At first he'd thought the floor was level but now saw that over to the left the torchlight picked out uneven shapes at the side. As the light swung across this jumble something blinked back at him.

His first thought was that it was something alive, like a rat or the stoat, but going back he saw that it wasn't the blink of an eye, but something else. Something that wasn't alive. He heard the intake of Gavin's breath next to him.

They moved slowly over to where the dull gleam beckoned them.

What they saw next would stay with them forever.

There, huddled into a hollow in the rock formation, were the unmistakeable shapes of human remains. Most noticeably, a brown skull, face down beside a long femur. They went closer.

There was something that looked like a pot, half buried in the gravelly earth and by the side of that was the object that had glinted at them. At first Fletcher thought it might be a cross, but then realised there was a longer shape in the earth next to it. It was a sword.

He shook his head.

He wasn't sure, but pretty certain that anything from Roman times would be dust by now. He bent down and felt Gavin follow suit. On closer inspection he could tell that the sword shape was just that, a rusty shape in the gravel. The dust of a metal blade leaving a telltale outline like a negative. But the hilt was made of sterner stuff. Gold?

Gavin pointed at the collection of bones. Amongst them were

other objects that glinted dully. He reached down and touched one of them, pulled it out and held it up in the torchlight. It was a bracelet. He gently fingered the dust away and the dull glinting grew stronger and was pocked with other colours. Jewels. Catching the light like Christmas baubles.

He held it up and the two of them looked at each other in wonder. Without speaking they carefully picked out other things and laid them on the floor.

To one side Fletcher found a horde of dark glistening oval beads and gathered them up in his hands.

'Black pearls from the River Irt,' whispered Gavin.

'What?' asked Fletcher in disbelief.

'Really. I've seen them before,' added Gavin.

Fletcher rolled them around in his hand. Cool and smooth. The black stone in the ring on Sorcha's finger scuttled through his thoughts.

Gavin stood up. I'll go and get my rucksack,' he said, and moved carefully over to the light of the entrance. 'You gather everything together and we'll go back down.'

Fletcher could hardly take his eyes of the treasure already clumped together on the floor beside him. He nodded.

On his own once the scuffling had stopped he used the torch to look round. Back above the entrance hole he could see something that looked like steps in the wall. He went over and sure enough there was evidence of man-made endeavour. He held the torch up and saw that they led behind a turret of rock near the ceiling. The steps were easier than climbing and soon he could see that there was another entrance in the crook of the ceiling. It wasn't as big as the other one and he needed to lie flat to struggle out into the daylight.

The first thing he realised was that it had started to rain again. Just a light pattering, but he knew it would quickly make the rock into a nightmare of greasy footfalls.

He was about to call out to Gavin, when he heard another sound. He ducked down back into his cockpit and listened.

There was a voice. Not Gavin's. Not Stanley Gill, a foreign accent, it was a man speaking quietly.

'Where is your companion?' he was asking.

He couldn't hear what Gavin said in reply, but knew he'd be unlikely to give him away.

'I watched you climbing together,' the man said.

Again there must have been a reply, but Fletcher couldn't hear it.

His mind was racing. Who could it be? Sorcha's words reverberated in his head. 'One of them was chatting me up half an hour ago. Good-looking bloke with a foreign accent, might have been French or sommat…'

He made a decision and carefully eased his way out of the hole and peered over the edge.

Below him stood a man in a grey cagoule and a black ski-hat. On the ground in front of him Gavin was lying on his back groaning. The man knelt next to him and punched him the face.

'Where is he?' he asked.

Fletcher scrambled out from his hiding place and looked down at the stranger.

The man looked up, smiled, and released his hold on Gavin, who groaned and lay still.

'Ah. Inspector,' said the man.

'You won't get away with this,' said Fletcher.

The man smiled again and produced a gun from his pocket.

'I think I will, Inspector.'

'A bullet wound will need some explaining,' said Fletcher and moved slightly nearer the rock face.

'I'm sure we can come up with a plausible explanation.'

'Such as?' asked Fletcher as he spied a loose rock by his foot.

'Oh I don't know. You and your friend having an argument perhaps.'

Fletcher shifted his weight and glanced at the rock.

'Why would we bring a gun up here?' he asked.

'Frightened of the wolves?' said the man with a quiet laugh.

Fletcher laughed back.

'We killed the last one five hundred years ago. Didn't you know?'

The man raised his gun. Fletcher ducked down and kicked the rock over the edge at the same time.

The explosion wasn't as loud as Fletcher had expected, but it still reverberated round the curtain of rocks. He scrambled back into the hole and almost fell down the steps dropping the torch on the way. He heard it clunk on the floor and roll over into the heap of bones.

He scrabbled towards it and held his breath. Not a sound. But he knew it wouldn't be long before the man found the way in. He looked round. What could he use? He picked up the femur, fighting back the revulsion he felt rising in his throat. It didn't feel as heavy as he expected but it didn't disintegrate into dust like most of the rest of the bones seemed to have done. He hefted it in his right hand and stood up. A sparkle caught his eye over in the pile of treasure. He bent down again and retrieved the bracelet. It fitted snugly round his fist. He had never used a knuckleduster, but this would do.

He turned at the sound of boot on rock near the lower entrance. He looked around. Did the man have a torch? He couldn't see anything and turned his off. He reckoned he'd stand a better chance knowing the space in the dark. But then he had another idea. He bent down and readjusted the skull so that it was upright and placed the lit torch inside it.

Quickly he tiptoed across to the entrance and looked back at his handiwork. It might give him a couple of seconds. The daylight flickered as the man came through the gap. Fletcher's plan worked. Although he entered in a rush, the sight of the light shining through the skull's eye sockets stopped him in his tracks. Fletcher hit him as hard as he could on his back. The femur splintered and disintegrated. The man staggered forward, but turned as Fletcher followed up with a shoulder charge. Skill defeated intent. The man bent and rolled Fletcher over his shoulder, and sent him tumbling heavily into the bones. Before he could recover the man was on top of him. Fletcher's flailing arms were no use. The man simply batted them aside and then slapped him hard across the face, even though blood was pouring from a gash on his head and splattering into Fletcher's face.

Before Fletcher could do anything else, the man grabbed him by the neck in a strangulation hold and stared down at his victim. Fletcher was gasping for breath, and his struggles were weakening. The man grunted and flicked blood from his forehead. He didn't speak, but Fletcher could feel him gathering his strength.

At which point there was a huge explosion and the man's face disappeared in a splattering of blood and flesh and bone and brains. Fletcher couldn't see, but could feel warm matter and liquid all over his face. He felt the weight of the man's body sinking on top of him. He pushed him away and rubbed at his eyes. Dimly he could see the cave. The man's weight slipped to one side and Fletcher rolled away. He was covered in warm stuff. The torch was still on and lit a scene of such terrible carnage that Fletcher gagged and nearly threw up. He staggered to his knees and looked away from the mess of human flesh in front of him. What had happened? The cave had stopped reverberating and was now filling with a gruesome, claustrophobic silence.

He scrabbled for the torch. The skull had disintegrated. He turned and shone it round the cave. He thought he heard the sounds of rocks tumbling outside, but then nothing. He thought of calling out, but decided not to. He crawled towards the daylight on all fours and stumbled down to where Gavin lay still. He touched his face.

'Gavin,' he whispered. The eyelids fluttered open and a look of terror filled his face as he peered at the blood-spattered face in front of him. Fletcher held his hand.

'He's dead Gavin. We're okay,' he said.

Gavin looked at him again and managed a weak nod, then he groaned and his eyes rolled.

'Where are you hurt?' asked Fletcher.

Gavin mumbled something, which sounded like 'egg' and then Fletcher noticed the awkward position of his left leg. He reached down and felt down his side until he got below his knee. Gavin jolted awake with a scream of agony, before groaning back into unconsciousness.

Fletcher couldn't think how the man could have broken Gavin's leg, but he knew that getting him off was going to be impossible on his own.

He retrieved Gavin's bag. Inside he found a survival bag and a large first aid kit. He'd done some basic first aid training and knew he needed to keep Gavin as warm and dry as possible. He was going to have to leave him and he was more likely to die of hypothermia and shock than the injury itself. He fumbled though the kit and found some glucose tablets and put them in his pocket. Next he found a bandage and pulled out Gavin's walking stick. Even though he'd been outside for only a few minutes he was soaked and the blood and mess had worked its way down his jacket.

Every now and then he looked around, up and down the

Ghyll, but there was no one in sight. He felt he was being watched and there must be someone else there. He couldn't understand what had happened; he just wanted to help his friend.

Whilst Gavin was unconscious it was easier to tie the stick to his leg although the first move made him groan. Fletcher tied the bandage as tight as he could.

He wondered what else he could do. He covered him in every bit of clothing he could find and laid the bivvy bag on top using a couple of heavy stones to hold it down.

He grabbed the coil of rope. At least he wouldn't have to climb down the chock stone … if he could remember how to abseil.

Thinking of this, he decided now was the moment to give Gavin the glucose and hope it would bring him round. It did. Enough for Gavin to tell him haltingly what to do. Fletcher tried to reassure him that he would be as fast as possible, but Gavin's head sank into the warmth of his fleece and so taking one more look at the other man's body, Fletcher left him.

The descent was a tale of slipping and sliding and falling and he couldn't run until he was back down by the beck, but he made good time, and staggered breathless into the Wasdale Head car park not forty minutes later. When he'd recovered his breath and the assembled crowd had got over the shock of seeing a man covered in blood and brains, the rescue team were called and five climbers left their drinks and ran off along the path.

It took them over two hours to bring Gavin down, but as the ambulance sped away, Hilda was able to convince Fletcher that Gavin wasn't going to die. It was only then he told her about the cave and the other man. She gave him a long hard stare.

'Why didn't you say before?' she asked.

'Well, he's not going anywhere and I thought it best if we dealt with Gavin first.'

She gave this some thought.

'Do you know who he is?'

'No … but I think I know someone who might recognise what's left of him.'

She gave him another look.

'But it'll not be easy.'

He told her.

* * * * *

It was late in the afternoon after the forensic guys had been dragged up the gully and done some preliminary investigation, that the body was brought down and taken to the mortuary. Cause of death was fairly obvious as the man's neck and head were blown apart. Fletcher went back to the vicarage and then on to the hospital. Gavin was sitting up, but was a bit dopey from the painkillers. A doctor had told him it was clean break and he would be able to climb again.

Hilda took Sorcha to the mortuary and she coolly identified what was left of the man's face as the guy in the bar, but he had no identification of any sort on him. The gun was taken away to be examined.

Fletcher went back to the vicarage exhausted and was in bed by nine o'clock.

* * * * *

Sat 29th May.

The following morning's events were even more unbelievable.

The first Fletcher knew about anything was when he got a phone call from Hilda.

'The body's gone,' she said.

'Which body?'

'The one in the mortuary. The gunman.'

'How?'

'Well. I don't know, do I?' she answered.

'Was there a guard?'

'Of course not! Who steals bodies?'

Fletcher cursed.

'People who don't want them found of course!' he yelled and slammed the phone down.

Mags looked at him. He explained. She shook her head in further disbelief.

The next thing was even more incredible. Fletcher had asked to go up to the cave with the forensic crew again. It was a lot easier when they got to the boulder because the rescue team had put up a ladder. The two replacement guards gave him a surly look.

Fletcher hesitated at the entrance and took a deep breath.

He knew the forensic crew had left a battery of lights inside and so he was not expecting the darkness he now descended into. He went back for a torch.

'Maybe a lead's come away,' said one of the crew as he fiddled with his bags.

Fletcher went back down with his torch.

As he came into the space he could see the lights and the batteries as they'd left them last night. None of them were working. But as he shone his torch around the cave he realised there was nothing for them to illuminate. He gasped.

No bones. No skull … and no treasure.

He stood in the silent space and gaped.

A couple of the forensic team came in after him to find him just standing there.

'Where's it all gone?' he asked.

They stared at him. He told them about the treasure and the

bones. They looked at him and then at each other. The man was obviously in shock.

The three of them looked all over the cave. They went back out to the guards and questioned them. They denied seeing anyone or falling asleep.

The forensic team and Fletcher went back down. He rang Hilda from the pub.

She arrived twenty minutes later.

He could tell no one believed him, although he was having a strong sense of déjà vu.

'What do you mean this has happened to you before?' demanded Hilda.

He told her about the gothic mansion near Penrith where everything had disappeared in an enormous fire. Hilda was dubious.

'But there wasn't a fire in the cave.'

He nodded his agreement.

He had a mouthful of beer.

'I'll tell you another thing,' he said.

Hilda frowned.

'The forensic team took lots of photographs, yeh?' he said.

She nodded.

'I bet you next month's salary they don't come out.'

She stared at him and shook her head.

* * * * *

But he was wrong. They were fine. Gruesome images of the body, but no skull or crossed bones. No treasure. All gone.

Accusations were made and strongly denied.

The photographer and the guards were adamant and disgruntled, glaring at Fletcher, not understanding why he should keep telling his ridiculous story.

Eventually everyone had to agree that whatever had been in the cave was no longer there and they had no proof there ever had been anything, which meant that everyone then began to question Fletcher and Gavin's assertions. But by then Fletcher knew it was hopeless. He agreed to be interviewed again next week. He got Mags to take him to the bus station and got the slow bus home.

CHAPTER 12

To say he wasn't welcomed with open arms was an understatement. In the first place, Laura wasn't there when he arrived at the house. He let himself in and made something to eat, put his washing in the machine and wandered about the house, which felt empty and desolate.

In the end he rang the building society and was told Laura had just left. Ten minutes later he heard her key in the lock.

Her first response was frosty.

'When did you get back?' she asked.

'About an hour ago.'

She went to put the kettle on. No kiss. No hug. No smile.

She stood looking out of the kitchen window. Fletcher wanted to hold her, kiss her, and feel her warm body pressed against his, but wisely bided his time. He was still amazed by her short hair, which had been persuaded not to curl somehow. He waited.

'So is that it? Are you back home now?' she asked without turning round.

He sighed.

'I think so. Not sure. Haven't been to see the DCI yet,' he muttered.

'Are you going to tell me what happened?' she asked as the kettle began to whistle.

He waited while she poured the hot water into the teapot. She leant back against the sink and glowered at him. Her brown eyes were filled with distrust.

He stood by the door and looked at his shoes.

'Well it's a long story and I can't believe some of it myself,' he began.

He was right. It was long and meandering and in places plain ridiculous, but he struggled on. Laura only interrupted him a couple of times. He omitted any reference to Sorcha, yet knew it would come back to bite him.

Eventually he told her what had happened up the Ghyll, which left her shaking her head in weary disbelief. He gave up and sat down. Tired beyond measure, he put his head in his hands and groaned.

He didn't hear her approach, but felt her hand on his neck. She kissed his head and they embraced awkwardly. Without speaking she led him into the front room. They kissed and embraced, their bodies trembling with emotion. Tears were kissed away. The embrace became a fight. They tore each other's clothes apart and coupled like beasts on the carpet, kicking at the furniture if it got in the way. Tears and gasps. Grunting and yelling.

Afterwards they lay exhausted, their glistening bodies entwined, chests heaving and loins soaking into the carpet.

The doorbell rang.

They froze in horror, listening acutely. Both terrified to hear the scratching of Grace's key in the lock. Silence. The bell rang again. Fletcher got up and peered through the net curtain.

It was Irene standing with her arms folded, looking back down the drive, where Laura's car was parked.

Fletcher whispered to Laura, who, cursing, grabbed her clothes and hurried upstairs. He pulled on his pants and his shirt, only to discover it was torn. He threw it behind the settee and closing the door behind him, made for the front door.

Irene turned as he appeared and looked at his naked chest and bare feet.

She grinned.

'Ah, sorry, sir,' she said, 'but…'

'But what, Sergeant?'

She hesitated, unable to meet his fierce eyes.

'I met Elizabeth Kirby. She wants to speak to you.'

Fletcher stared at her.

'What?'

Irene made a decision.

'Dog and Gun in an hour … sir?'

It was his turn to hesitate.

'Er … yeh … good idea, Sergeant.'

She smiled and beat a retreat. He stood watching her disappearing figure, feeling both embarrassed and confused.

So Elizabeth Kirby wasn't dead? But what could she tell him? Why had she contacted Irene? Did that mean the man pretending to be her son was on her side? Was he ever going to be able to walk away from this? He shut the door and traipsed upstairs.

Laura came out of the shower to find him sitting on the corner of the bed. He was still in his trousers and was staring into space.

'So it's not over?' said Laura, drying her hair.

Fletcher shook his head.

'I don't know,' was all he could manage.

She sat on the bed next to him and put her arm round him.

'There's something I haven't told you,' she said.

He looked at her with a worried face.

256

'I went to see Louisa,' she said.

'Louisa?'

'Yes. I went to her house on the Tweed.'

Fletcher stared at her open mouthed.

'She told me to tell you to walk away. She said you were upsetting some very bad people and that she couldn't help you anymore.'

He didn't know what to say.

She stood up and went to sit at the dressing table. She began to brush her hair, looking at him through mirror.

He watched her, lust rousing him with every stroke of her hand.

'But I know you can't stop,' she said.

He stood up and undid his trousers. She turned and faced him.

Later at the pub, she sat next to him as Irene told them how she'd met Elizabeth Kirby.

'She rang me at the Fox and Hounds ...' she began, 'which was bizarre enough. She said she'd meet me at Preston station on Friday morning.'

'But how did you know who she was?' asked Fletcher

'I didn't, but she said she had vital information to give to you.'

'Couldn't she tell you on the phone?' he asked.

'I didn't get chance to ask her that, she finished the call.'

Fletcher sighed.

'So you went to meet her?'

Irene nodded.

'But you don't know what she looks like?'

'And I still don't,' said Irene.

Fletcher and Laura shared a look.

'What do you mean?'

'Well,' said Irene, as she took a sip of her pint. 'I was standing on the platform wondering how I would recognise her, when I felt a hand on my shoulder. Before I could turn to look, she said, "Don't turn around. It's better that you don't see me." So I didn't.'

'And then what?' asked an increasingly impatient Fletcher.

'She said she wanted me to arrange a meeting with you.'

'Where? When?'

Irene placed a small piece of folded paper on the table. Fletcher felt this was getting ridiculous, but he unfolded the paper and read it, before showing it to Laura. All it said was Detective Story RX SatE16/17.

'What's this mean?' asked Fetcher showing it to Laura.

'I've checked,' said Irene. 'Detective Story is a play. It's on at the Royal Exchange in Manchester tonight.'

'A play?' asked Fletcher.' I've never heard of it.'

'Neither have I, but that's where she wants to meet you,' said Irene. 'I assume she's thinking there will be someone with you.'

She looked at Laura, who stared back at her. Fletcher looked from one to the other.

'You don't have to do this,' said Fletcher to Laura.

She paused looking straight at Irene.

'What do you think, Irene?'

Irene shrugged her shoulders.

'How often does he take you out?' she laughed. 'If you get a move on you could get a meal in before it starts.'

This made them all laugh, although Fletcher didn't like it.

Two hours later the pair of them were sitting in the Exchange restaurant. The place wasn't especially busy and they got a table without any fuss.

Laura had found a programme seller and was reading the cast list. She didn't know any of the actors, but the play seemed

258

to have good reviews and when she read the storyline, she remembered she'd seen a film version long ago with a young Kirk Douglas.

None of this impressed Fletcher, who whinged on about proper plays like Hamlet and Caucasian Chalk Circle. The food didn't impress him either.

'Bloody lettuce and a few beans, rabbit food,' he muttered. Laura laughed and made a rabbit teeth face at him. He grinned back.

They found their seats and watched as the auditorium filled up. Fletcher was surprised that, by the time of the first bell, the theatre was nearly full. The audience was noisy and there were lots of latecomers making earlier arrivals stand to let them through. This happened two or three times to Fletcher and Laura as they were at the end of a row. Laura nodded to the empty seat on the row behind.

'That'll be her seat I expect,' she said.

Fletcher was beginning to think the whole thing was the most ridiculous charade and merely shrugged his shoulders.

The seat was still empty as the lights went down and the first characters burst onto the stage.

Despite his initial scepticism Fletcher was gradually drawn into the story and forgot to keep checking on the empty seat, so he was surprised to see it was still empty as the first half finished. They went in search of their pre-ordered drinks and stood amongst the throng as everyone drank and chatted. Most people seemed to be enjoying the play and were commenting on individual actors. Fletcher and Laura didn't have much to say and were wondering whether this was going to be a no show. As the interval bell rang, Laura set off to the toilet. As Fletcher watched her walk away, he felt a pang of guilt mixed with desire. He turned and searched the crowd. He'd no idea what this mysterious woman might look like.

As the second bell rang he saw Laura reappear outside the toilet. A man in a grey coat with a black collar stood in front of her. He had white hair and a beard. Fletcher began to push his way through the crowd, against the flow of those heading back into the auditorium. By the time he reached Laura the man had gone.

'Are you alright?' he asked.

Laura gave him a bemused look.

'I think so.'

'What did that man want?'

'He gave me this card and told us to come soon.'

She handed Fletcher a coloured card, which was an advert for a restaurant. On the back was a small map and telephone number. Someone had written RX on the map, so that Fletcher could see the restaurant was only a few hundred yards away.

They looked at each other.

'In for a penny,' said Laura.

Fletcher nodded and they made their way out into the brightly lit streets. The rain had been heavy, leaving large puddles, which people were jumping over or walking around.

It only took them three or four minutes to reach a huge square with monumental buildings on three sides. To their left they could see the sign for the restaurant. When they reached it they saw that the entrance was down a flight of steps into the basement. They looked at each other again and Fletcher led the way.

Pushing through heavy curtains inside the door they found themselves in a carpeted area with lots of mirrors and dim lights. Many of the tables were occupied and a few people looked at them suspiciously. Most of them were men, with black hair and dark faces. A man with a red hat and a moustache beckoned them in and they were taken between the tables to a door at the back. Moustache man knocked on the door and the white haired man, who had accosted Laura, quickly opened it. They were ushered inside.

Facing them was a woman sat at a table set for four, partially hidden from Fletcher by a lampshade hanging down over the table. His first impression was dictated by the red nails and the misshapen fingers of her left hand in which she held a lit cigarette. She stood up as they came in and Fletcher found himself looking at a thinner, taller version of Louisa, but she had grey streaked, dark hair cut very short like a man's. Her lips were the same startling scarlet as her finger nails.

She offered her hand while the white haired man pulled out a chair for Laura to sit. Fletcher took the cool hand in his and sat in the other chair. The man poured some wine into two glasses and quietly stood to one side. Nothing was said, but everyone's eyes flitted from one to another.

'Even if you were followed, they won't get in here,' said the woman, as she returned to her seat. She had that confident Home Counties accent which always rankled with Fletcher. 'And there are at least two other ways out, so don't worry.'

Fletcher waited. He wasn't going to play this silly game.

The woman gave him a brief smile.

'I won't trouble you with explanations or questions, Inspector. The less you know about me the better.'

He looked beyond her to see Laura looking at him. Her face was blank. He looked back into the woman's pale face. She held the cigarette to her lips, but then continued to speak.

'Sybil died because of me. I sent her the proof of what Thatcher has done in our name in the Falklands ... out of sheer vindictiveness and contrary to the Geneva Convention and human dignity.'

261

Fletcher flinched as she leant across and gripped his arm.

'Sorcha has the only evidence, but even if she understands the full import of it, she has learnt to trust no one. You must convince her to pass it to someone who will be able to bring it into the light of scrutiny without endangering their own lives.'

The grip on his arm intensified. He glanced over to where Laura was staring at them. 'It's in your hands now,' said the woman.

'Are you Elizabeth Kirby?' he asked.

She withdrew her hand and stubbed out her unfinished cigarette.

'I'm sure you have a lot of questions, Inspector, but there's nothing else you can usefully know.'

Fletcher didn't move.

'Why should I do what you want?' he said in a growl, which made Laura's eyes go wide.

The woman was obviously not used to being thwarted. She gave him a disparaging look.

'I have been assured you are a seeker after justice, Inspector.'

He said nothing. He hoped other people didn't think he was as pompous as that. She looked at him. Her blank face slowly creased into a cynical smile.

'I was also told you were 'difficult' and 'bloody-minded'.'

'Guilty as charged,' said Fletcher and met her gaze.

'Do you read the papers, Inspector?'

'Only the sport. In fact, only the QPR results to be honest.'

She gave him another blank stare.

'What about SPQR?'

'Dead and gone,' he answered, thinking of the Dalmatian's treasure.

'But the principles therein?' she asked.

'I've come to the conclusion that people with principles can

262

rarely be trusted,' he said. Especially those who use terms like 'therein', he thought.

The woman sighed and took another cigarette out of the packet on the table and clicked her lighter until it worked. She put the cigarette to her lips and took a long pull, sending smoke through her nostrils into the air above her. All the while she kept her eyes on Fletcher. He could see the lines on her face. She was older than Louisa, but she had that underlying arrogance of the aristocratic class. Was she like Mags? Fighting a battle against her class, taking revenge for the impositions of childhood.

'So you're telling me you don't know anything about the war being currently waged by the British government?'

'Not much,' he said.

'So the murder of hundreds of young soldiers in cold blood means nothing to you?'

Fletcher leaned forward.

'It's war isn't it? That's what happens. Thousands of young men … and women … die. There's little I can do about it. '

'But there is this time, Inspector; you're probably the only person who can persuade Sorcha to give up those documents.'

'Me? Why me? I hardly know her,' he said, shuffling uncomfortably in his seat, knowing Laura's eyes were on him.

The woman looked at Laura and then back at Fletcher.

'I don't think that's true, do you?'

This time he did look at Laura. Her face was a mask.

'I've spent time in her company that's true, but I'm old enough to be her father. There's nothing between us. I went with her because I thought I might find out who had killed Sybil Hardwicke. We didn't and I've been told to give it up. In fact it's been made very clear to me that I should steer clear … for my own safety and those who I care about.'

Again she looked at Laura.

'But you know that Sybil and Sally and John were killed by M16.'

Fletcher paused again.

'I don't know that for certain ... and if they were there's nothing I can do about it either ... on my own.'

She leaned back in her seat.

'What if I were to tell you that there is a way you could help expose this government's lies and bring the perpetrators to justice?'

'How?' he asked.

'If you can get the documents ... I can pass them to someone who can take them on.'

Fletcher looked back at Laura. She gave him a look of concentration and then shrugged her shoulders. He looked back at the woman.

'Who?'

She shook her head.

'I can't tell you that. Not before he's seen the documents.'

Fletcher paused again.

'So you want me to trust you?'

She nodded.

'Why should I?'

She sighed again.

'I can't make you. But if you don't, they will get away with it.'

Stalemate. The two of them stared at each other. For the first time Fletcher realised her eyes were like Sorcha's. Black and hollow. He looked away.

'Okay. I'll think about it,' he said.

Kirby stood up and offered her hand again. In her outstretched fingers was a card.

'Thank you,' she said. 'If she gives you the documents, ring this number and say 'the brighter the stars', nothing else. We'll come and find you. If she doesn't, then...'

Fletcher nodded, but inside he was groaning at the whole cloak and dagger business.

The man stood up as well.

'Gregor will show the way out,' she said, and she stood with her arms folded as they were ushered out of a different door. Two minutes later they found themselves out into a dark back alley.

'Go down to the end and turn left. You'll see the theatre from there,' said the man as he disappeared back into the building. The door closed with a scrunch of metal and they heard bolts and bars dropping into place. At the end of the alleyway they stepped back out into the bright lights. The rain had stopped, but the roads shone and the air was cold and damp.

'I need a drink,' said Fletcher.

They didn't know where they were going but guessed the direction of the station. They soon found a busy, noisy bar. Fletcher pushed to the front and got them a couple of drinks. There were no seats so they stood in the crush.

'What next?' asked Laura.

Fletcher hesitated.

'It's as I thought. Sorcha took a parcel that was left for the Sybil Hardwicke and she's hiding some documents, which reveal something the government's done in the Falklands. God knows what,' he added. 'Although I think that means she's in a lot of danger.'

Laura took a sip of her drink and glanced about them.

'So, will you go back and find her?'

He couldn't look at her.

'I expect I will, but I don't know that she'll admit to what she's done.'

'Can't you tell someone else?' asked Laura.

Fletcher shook his head.

'Like who?' he asked.

Laura had no answer to that. They emptied their glasses and set out in search of the station.

* * * * *

On the train home, they had little to say. Laura eventually huddled down against Fletcher's shoulder and closed her eyes. He watched the darkened fields rushing past occasionally interrupted by the flashing images of brightly lit houses. People going about their Saturday night living: evening meals, watching the telly, parties, arguments, family gatherings, all oblivious to Fletcher's dilemmas. And, he thought, disinterested in them as well.

He regarded his reflection flittering in the window. The play had set out the beginnings of a moral dilemma for the detective hero, whilst here was Fletcher, alone and uncertain. He could pass it on to a superior officer, but he had little faith in them and in any case what would he tell them? Some mad woman playing at spies telling him to chase after a disturbed young woman, who may have damning evidence against a gung-ho government, but unlikely to back him up with an appearance. Even someone as disinterested as he, when it came to the morals of the political classes, could tell that the war was a vote winner, appealing to the masses with its Argie-bashing warmongering.

But he also knew that it was his fascination with Sorcha, which was his real dilemma. This was reinforced as Laura groaned and snuggled further into his side. Did she already suspect him?

He turned these worries over and over with little hope of resolution. Eventually the train pulled into the station and he woke Laura. An hour later he was lying wide-awake as she slept by his side. It was nearly dawn when sleep overtook him.

* * * * *

After a desultory Sunday, during which they were unable to go
for a walk, because the weather was so awful, Fletcher was up
early on Monday morning. He and Laura had agreed that he
would go back for his interview with Hilda and stay on for Sybil
Hardwicke's funeral on Wednesday. If he was able to talk to
Sorcha and persuade her to give up the documents, then so be it,
but if not it was over and Fletcher would be back the same
afternoon.

Their parting was awkward. Fletcher thought she probably
suspected that he was having an affair with Sorcha, but couldn't
bear it to be true. Neither could he. When he turned to wave at
her as the car arrived to pick him up, she'd gone inside.

First thing, he went to see DCI Aske in Penrith. As he walked
through the station, eyes followed him and he knew many of
them weren't friendly. Aske was waiting for him, his office door
open. He went in.

He knew Aske rated him and stood up for him, but he could
see the man was reaching the end of his patience.

'Take a seat, Inspector,' he said. Fletcher preferred to stand.
Aske sighed and closed the file in front of him. He stood up.

'Let's go for a drive,' he said.

They went in Aske's car. He drove them out of town, south
onto the A6, over the bridge and right after the village, by which
time Fletcher knew where they were going.

Aske parked the car in the lay-by and the two men walked
through the gate and up onto the circular ridge of Mayburgh
Henge: all this without a word being spoken. This was the site of
Fletcher's first day working in Penrith two years ago, coming to
see the body of a dead prostitute, which had been thrown over

the fence onto the motorway embankment.

They stood and listened to the wind in the trees and the muted roar of the motorway. A small herd of sheep eyed them from the other side, decided they weren't a threat, and continued munching.

'I've stuck up for you, Fletcher,' said Aske, without looking at him.

'I know,' said Fletcher.

'But I think you've gone too far this time. My phone hasn't stopped ringing since you went solo a week ago.'

Fletcher didn't think Aske was expecting a reply so kept his mouth shut. Incongruously a heron flapped slowly into the ancient arena and settled next to the large pool, which had gathered around the central stone. It had only just folded its wings, when it noticed them and immediately took off again. No sign of panic, merely realising its mistake and correcting it.

'A bit like you, eh, Fletcher?' observed Aske.

Fletcher gave a wry smile, which was returned.

'You mean like not belonging here and doing my own thing,' he asked.

'Something like that, yeh.'

They began to walk slowly round the embankment.

'You're going back to Whitehaven today to be interviewed? Is that right?'

Fletcher nodded.

'Conroy's going to be there,' said Aske.

'Lucky old me,' said Fletcher with a grimace.

'He's not a bad apple, Fletcher. Old fashioned, but straight as a die.'

Fletcher sighed. Was there a real reason for this off the record chat? He let him walk on.

'They're going to send me to Scottie-land, aren't they?' he

asked.

Aske stopped and looked back at him.

'I've no idea, Fletcher, but you're finished here. There is nothing more I can do.'

There didn't seem much point in any further conversation, so they walked back to the car and Aske drove him to the station. He sanctioned the use of a pool car until Thursday. Fletcher looked at his desk and decided the only thing he wanted was the picture of Laura, Grace and himself, which he stuffed in his case. Irene was nowhere to be seen and for that he was thankful. That could wait. Ten minutes later he was on the A66 to Keswick.

He arrived in Whitehaven just after ten. Hilda had seen him in the car park and came down to meet him. She took him straight through to one of the interview rooms and ordered some coffee.

'Chief Superintendent Conroy is going to sit in, sir. Nothing I can do.'

'Don't worry, Hilda. I'll cope,' he said with a smile.

'I don't doubt it,' said Hilda, 'but try not to upset him. It's the rest of us who'll suffer.'

Before he could reply the door opened and in strode the corpulent figure of the Chief Superintendent. Neither of them was sitting so they remained where they were.

'All right, sergeant, you carry on. I'm only here to make sure none of us get into any further bother.'

This was said without even looking at Fletcher. He picked up a chair and placed it where he could see both of them and straightened his jacket. The chair made an anguished squeak as he placed his heavy frame on its tired legs.

The other two sat facing each other and the interview began.

The story was still a mixture of the bizarre and the ridiculous and the unbelievable.

After Hilda had listened to him answering all the questions

as succinctly as he could, she turned to Conroy and asked him if he had any further questions.

Conroy had been staring at Fletcher for most of the session and his gaze didn't falter.

'I don't know where you're going to be sent, Inspector, but I pity the poor sods who will have the misfortune to have you thrust into their midst. Ye Gods, man! The damnest pack of lies I've ever heard. Murder and mayhem!'

He stood up and towered over Fletcher, his face in danger of reddening into purple.

Fletcher bit his tongue several times on a series of counters to this accusation, but 'marf shut' seemed the best option right now.

Conroy gave him time, but eventually turned on his heel and stormed out.

Hilda let out a huge sigh of relief.

'Drink, sergeant?' asked Fletcher.

She shook her head.

'He wants this typed up and in his hand within the half hour,' she said.

'In that case, said Fletcher. 'I'll love you and leave you. I'm going to the pub. I'll be staying until after the funeral. How's Gavin by the way?'

'On crutches, but at home. Don't you go winding him up, mind.'

Fletcher shook his head.

'I'll send you a postcard.'

Hilda watched him go and looked down at her notes. How was she going to make these scribbles make sense?

* * * * *

Fletcher had long ago stopped expecting things to make sense. He drove out to Ennerdale. The sun was shining through the clouds and it felt like summer at last. There were daffodils in the churchyard and bluebells under the trees. He nearly whistled.

He'd intended to go straight to the pub, but as he drove past the vicarage gates he saw Mags's camper van in the entrance to the drive. He braked hard and pulled in. She saw him at the last moment and stopped the other side of the road.

They both got out and embraced in the middle of the road.

'My goodness, Michael, what a terrible experience you have had,' she said. 'I'm just taking a cake to Gavin. Do you want to come?'

He did, and leaving his car in her drive, he got into her campervan and they went up the lane to Gavin's house. He wanted to ask about Sorcha, but thought he'd wait and see. She might be in the bar tonight after all.

Gavin was in good spirits and insisted on getting up on his crutches and wincing his way around the kitchen. Sheila had given up trying to look after him and had gone back to work.

'So how did the interview go?' he asked, when they were all furnished with coffee and plates for the cake.

'Like clockwork,' said Fletcher through a mouth full of crumbs.

'Meaning?' asked Gavin.

'They asked the questions. I gave them all the right answers or 'don't know',' he replied. 'They're no wiser than they were before, but it's all written down now, so they can catch me out later if I try to say something different.'

'And are you going to say something different?' asked Mags.

'You never know. Let's hope Gavin's account fits with mine.'

Gavin sighed.

'Well, I was unconscious most of the time, so I doubt it.'

'Ay well, seeing as I was still wearing most of the guy's face when I got down to the pub, it's a bit difficult to believe that I could have shot him.'

Mags went a lighter shade of pale.

'And thanks by the way,' said Fletcher. 'I wouldn't have even got up there without you.'

'No,' said Gavin, 'it was you who saved my life. So I think we're quits.'

Mags stared at them both with a puzzled frown.

He could see the doubt in her eyes. She wasn't the only one and Fletcher knew that most people thought he'd shot the man.

They were all silent for a few moments.

'So what do you think? Did we really see what I think we saw?' asked Gavin.

Fletcher stood up and said he had to get something from his bag. The other two watched him go with worried faces.

He was gone only a few minutes and returned with his anorak. As they watched he felt in the pockets and pulled out a piece of mangled metal. It was the bracelet. He didn't remember making contact with the man's face, but it was still in one piece. He put it on the table.

Gavin and Mags stared at it, then at Fletcher and then at each other, but before they could say anything, he reached into another pocket and pulled out a fistful of black pearls that he tumbled onto the tablecloth. The other two gasped.

'But …' was all Gavin could manage as he reached out and picked up one of the pearls.

'Michael? Why haven't you…?' was as far as Mags could get before she couldn't stop herself from following suit.

'To be honest I'd forgotten I had them … and then when I found them at home, I'd had time to think about things, and … I'm not sure really. It's difficult to explain. Something that

272

happened to me before...'

His voice trailed off, as he fumbled with the bracelet and managed to bend it back into some sort of shape.

The three of them sat for a long time contemplating what lay in front of them.

'So what should I do now?' asked Fletcher.

Gavin and Mags looked at each and nodded.

'Sally and John's children,' said Mags.

'And Stanley,' added Gavin.

Fletcher looked from one to the other.

'Seems right to me. Will you give them to them?'

'You can give them yourself; they'll be here tomorrow for the funeral on Wednesday.'

Fletcher looked at Mags.

'Will you look after them for me until then?'

She nodded and gathered the clutch of glinting jewels together.

Gavin found a bag and watched them from the kitchen door as they got into the van and went back down the road.

Mags insisted on showing Fletcher she was putting the treasure into the vicarage's elderly safe. He was pretty certain that any of the old safebreakers he knew would have no trouble getting into it, but he was glad the stuff was no longer in his pockets.

Mags insisted he stayed at the vicarage and he took his bag up to the room he'd had before.

By this time he was desperate to go and see if Sorcha was in the pub and made some excuse, which he was sure Mags didn't believe.

* * * * *

Five minutes later he walked into the bar.

Sorcha was standing behind it gazing into space. There was no one else there.

She jumped when he spoke her name from the doorway. A fearful look crossed her face, before she replaced it with her first choice nonchalant weariness.

'What are you doing here?' she asked.

Before he could answer her hand came up and swept her hair to one side. Any doubts he might have had, anything he'd told himself to forget, disappeared with that simple gesture.

Her features hardened as he fought to produce some kind of response.

'Well,' she said. 'I expect you'll want a drink at least.'

He nodded and stepped across to the bar.

'I need to speak to you,' he said.

'Why?' she asked as she pulled him a pint.

'The parcel,' he blurted out.

She gave him a stern look.

'I gave it to you.'

'Yeh, but you took something out, didn't you?'

She looked away.

Fletcher reached across the bar and held her arm.

She looked at his hand and he let it fall away.

'You're in great danger. There are people who will kill you to get it,' he said, looking around to check no one was there.

'Not if I don't tell them where it is,' she said quietly.

Fletcher didn't know whether to be more scared that what Elizabeth had said was true or not.

He looked around as a group of walkers came into the bar, laughing, and joking with each other.

'I can't talk to you now, I've just started work,' she said and walked towards the foursome, they had stopped at the bar.

Fletcher watched as she smiled and took their orders, before he made a decision and marched off to the reception.

Five minutes later he was back with Joan the owner, who was looking cross, but worried at the same time. She went behind the bar and spoke quietly to Sorcha, who gave Fletcher a surly look. But Joan continued with what she needed to say. Eventually with a resigned look on her face, Sorcha wiped her hands on a towel and came out from behind the bar.

'That's great,' she said. 'She only employs me because Mags begged her to. Now she has the perfect excuse to sack me. "Helping police with their enquiries!"'

She walked to the foot of the stairs.

'I'm going to get a change of clothes,' she said.

This puzzled him, but five minutes later she came back down with a rucksack over her shoulder and marched out the front door and stood waiting next to his car.

He followed her.

'I'm sorry. I'll make it right, when we get back. Promise.'

Sorcha got into the car and adopted her sullen, not speaking, face.

He got in and drove out of the car park. A mile down the road he pulled into the National Trust car park and turned off the engine.

'Where is it?' he asked.

She gave him a vicious look.

'Do you think I'm going to give it up just like that?'

Fletcher shook his head.

'I met Elizabeth Kirby on Saturday night in Manchester. She assured me it would be passed to someone who would do what Sybil would have wanted.'

Sorcha stared at him.

'How do I know you're telling the truth?'

'You don't. You'll have to trust me.'

She continued to stare at him.

'What colour nails?' she asked.

His eyes went big. 'Scarlet. Like her lips.'

'And her right hand?'

'Fine, but her left has only two fingers and a thumb … which is the one she holds her cigarette with.'

Sorcha held his gaze for a long time, before looking away.

'Okay. You drive,' she said. 'I'll tell you where to go.'

From that moment until they got to their destination, she didn't speak, except to give him curt instructions.

He'd never even heard of Fleetwood, never mind been there.

'Down at heel' didn't convey the sense of desperate poverty he'd passed through before they finally stopped on the seafront. A container ship was bellowing black smoke into the late afternoon sky. They got out of the car and crossed the road to watch as it slowly backed out into the heaving water. Fletcher was amazed how the hulk was navigated out into what he later understood was a narrow deep water channel between the two markers out there in the thrashing waves. Sorcha seemed equally absorbed and ignored him if he looked at her or said anything.

But as soon as the ship was churning the waves out beyond the pier, she turned and walked back across the road towards a large hotel standing back from the esplanade. He followed.

Outside the entrance hall she stood and waited for him.

'What are we doing here?' he asked.

'We're staying the night,' she said.

He stared at her in disbelief.

'It's what you want isn't it?' she asked as she pushed through the heavy doors.

He chased after her, but she was already at the reception desk. The woman sitting there looked up and smiled at them both.

Fletcher was completely thrown.

'Can I help?' the woman asked.

'Er … yes … two single rooms for tonight, please,' he said.

She hesitated and looked at them both.

'He's my dad,' said Sorcha.

The woman was still doubtful, but looked down at the book in front of her.

Five minutes later in the dingy room he'd been reluctantly allocated, Fletcher was standing looking out at the sea. The sun had disappeared behind a bank of menacing grey clouds.

Sorcha had been given a room on a higher floor. The woman had obviously thought she'd at least make it difficult for them.

The phone rang. He picked it up.

'Are you coming up to me or shall I come down to you?' she asked.

He agreed to go to her room. Like in a dream. What was he doing?

He stood like a lemon outside the door. He could hear voices getting louder on the stairs. He'd never felt so guilty in his entire life. The door opened and he slipped in.

Any feeling of relief was quickly dispelled as Sorcha sashayed back across the room in her bra and knickers. Her jeans and boots lay scattered on the floor. She sat on the bed and took a sip from the glass of what he surmised was vodka and coke. She leant back and grinned at him.

'Are you scared, Inspector?' she asked with a smirk on her face.

He stayed where he was.

'Why are you doing this?' he asked.

'Like I said, it's what you want.'

He shook his head.

'No.'

She sat up and hugged her knees. She was too thin, he thought. Her bones jutted out at the shoulders.

'Yes it is, ever since that night in the bar. You were so goggle-eyed you forgot your change. I knew then and so did you.'

'But why here?' he stuttered.

'Ah well. That's because the other thing you want is in a safe in the bank round the corner … and it shut at half past three. Long before we got here.'

Fletcher considered this.

'But why here? In this Godforsaken place?'

She laughed.

'You've just watched why here, chugging out to sea, stupid!'

She took another swig of her drink.

He walked over to the window and there wallowing in the heavy sea was the ship heading towards the bank of cloud, which had surprisingly begun to thin and allow a watery yellow sun to struggle through.

'Where's it going?' he asked.

'Larne.'

'Larne? Where's that?'

'Northern Ireland, dummy,' she laughed again.

He turned to look at her.

She was walking towards him, but now a blue dress was hanging off those sharp boned shoulders.

He closed his eyes.

CHAPTER 13

Not only had Fletcher never been to Fleetwood, he'd not been to Blackpool either, so he didn't know what to expect as the green and white tram clattered along the sea front, although he did recognise the Tower when it came in sight. Sorcha was in the most animated mood he'd ever seen. She kept giggling to herself and her eyes were shining in a way that convinced him she'd consumed something else as well as the vodka. He'd not said anything so far.

Back in the room, when he'd opened his eyes, she was standing so close he flinched, but there was nowhere to go. She looked into his eyes. Up this close he could see that her irises were actually a dark brown, but the pupils were dilated like those round black pearls. He could feel her breath on his cheek and see the lipstick glistening on her lips.

Her thin arms came up and entwined themselves around his neck. He reached out to hold her waist meaning to push her away, but her face came closer and she kissed him, on the lips. Neither of them closed their eyes.

At first he didn't respond, but knew he couldn't resist. His right arm went round her waist and his left reached up and, after so much longing, stroked her hair from her face. He returned

279

her kiss. It was only for a few seconds, but time slid sideways.

She unlocked her lips, withdrew her arms, and pushed herself gently away.

Still no words were spoken. He was helpless, unsure of what to do. She backed away, turned, and went back to the bed, bent down and pulled out a pair of blue high-heeled shoes from her bag.

Standing up, she gave him a shy smile.

'Let's go and have some fun,' she said and held out her hand.

Now, as they descended from the top deck of the tram and alighted on the pavement, she held his hand again and led him into one of the brightly lit funfairs, one of the endless chain of tawdry gaudiness tottering along the landward side of the promenade.

He never bothered much with seaside fun palaces in his youth, although he remembered the running battles along the seafront at Brighton. He grinned to himself. How they'd trashed that place.

Sorcha virtually ran from one machine or game to another as though she needed to have a go on all of them in one night. He followed her like a dog, supplying her with coins and getting more and more change from grinning youths with Elvis quiffs in brightly painted kiosks. They whooshed around on the dodgems, two young guys bashing into him, before they tried to force Sorcha into a corner. But she was too expert for them and left them crunched into each other. She got out and ran screaming in delight onto the next thing. A huge up and down, round and round helter-skelter of terror.

Eventually she relented and allowed Fletcher to ask someone the whereabouts of a decent restaurant. If the one they ended up in was their idea of decent, he couldn't imagine the worst they could have sent them to.

He didn't mind Chinese, but it wasn't the best. Sorcha didn't care. She ate like she'd been starved for a month. Bowl after bowl came and was cleared until she was sated, she leant back in the chair and felt her bloated belly, made a face and pretended to be a fat Buddha.

By now it was dark. Except, of course, it wasn't. Everything was lit up. They wandered back to the front and she found space for a choc-ice.

They crossed between a couple of trundling trams, which both blared at them, and went to lean against the railing and look out across the beach.

'Where's the sea?' asked Fletcher, peering into the gloom.

'Halfway to Ireland,' she replied. 'It's still got a bit to go, won't be back until tomorrow morning.'

He looked at her. She was biting her ice-cream, but there was a serious look on her face.

'What next?' he asked, not daring to think what might happen if they went back to the hotel.

'Music,' she said. 'What do you like?'

He couldn't remember seeing any possible venues, although they'd passed plenty of pubs.

'Small Faces, the Who, Temptations ... ska.'

'What about folk?'

'Painful. Diddley-do.'

'You're right,' she said, and despite wearing such ridiculous high heels, she began to run along the prom. Feeling equally silly he followed.

She skipped across the road and dived down a narrow alley. Halfway along she skittered to a stop and tumbled down some hidden steps into yet another dark basement. At the bottom was a giant, bald, toad-in-a-hole. She leapt upon on him and screamed as he held her aloft like a rag doll.

Fletcher stood at the top of the steps with a bemused look on his face. The subterranean giant gently put Sorcha down and glared up at the stranger.

'It's alright, Bingo,' she yelled, 'he's with me.'

The man still glowered up at him, but finally allowed an ugly smile to grow on his face. It wasn't pretty, but Fletcher thought it meant he could descend.

The big man had rapped on the door, which now opened to exhale the sound of a band in full roar inside. Fletcher reached the bottom step and found the man's face in front of his.

'You be careful, copper. If she comes to any harm, you'll wish you never met her.'

Fletcher knew only a nod was acceptable, so he nodded.

The man allowed him to squeeze past into the noise.

The club was tiny, but there were probably over a hundred people crowded into the low-ceilinged space. The sound was deafening. The fight to the bar was a giant, elbow- bruising scrum. The band was lit by a whirlwind of changing colours, which spilled out onto the audience, many of who were writhing about to the thumping rhythm. The man at the front of the stage was shouting into a mike, while the lead guitar player was stomping back and forth like a huge praying mantis with long thin black legs and arms swinging like a pendulum, like Pete Townsend, but somehow more menacing, if that was possible.

Sorcha had disappeared before Fletcher had squeezed past the doorman. He looked everywhere but couldn't see her. Assuming she would be sticking to her starter, he managed to get to the bar and ordered a double vodka and a bottle of beer for himself. The prices were extortionate.

He allowed himself to be taken back out by the undertow of successful customers, whilst the oncoming wave of the thirsty strove to reach the bar. He still couldn't see Sorcha, but managed to steer himself into a backwater at the far side of the room. There was a shelf running along the wall, already stocked with an array of half empty glasses and bottles. He made a space and parked her vodka.

The number ended and the noise lessened, although the bass player seemed reluctant to give up the insistent background throb. The guitar loon was guzzling from a bottle. The singer shouted something that Fletcher couldn't understand, but the audience cheered. He took a mouthful of beer. It was cold. He wiped his mouth and then stared in surprise.

A thin dark haired figure had appeared on stage. The singer handed her the mike and turned to count in the band. They began to play. The spotlight followed the girl. She sang.

Mags had said Sorcha had an amazing voice, but he was still unprepared for the seductive energy of it. The band was blasting along behind her, but her raucous singing rose above them. Fletcher knew the song, but he was hopeless at remembering the words. The crowd were singing with her, but she was way above them as well. He watched and listened. Spellbound. She was awesome.

She did three numbers and then tried to leave the stage. But she had to do another two before they let her go. With a final wave she disappeared from view and Fletcher wondered how he was going to find her.

He grabbed her drink and set off through the heaving throng. It took him a good few minutes until he was anywhere near the stage where he last saw her. She was nowhere in sight. He fought his way to the side again and found a chair to stand on.

There she was.

Next to a young guy with long blonde hair and a black shirt, and as Fletcher watched, the guy grabbed her and kissed her. She put her arms around him and kissed him back. When they stopped, they laughed, but still held each other. The man pointed over to his right. She nodded. They walked to the doorway. Another big bear listened to what the young man said into his ear and then pulled back the curtain. Sorcha went first and they both disappeared. Fletcher could feel his face burning with embarrassment and his head raged with jealousy. He looked at the vodka in his hand and drank it in one go. Without thinking he pushed his way back towards the entrance, upsetting numerous people on the way. He ignored the curses and cries of outrage and reached the door.

He was out and up the steps before the doorman or anyone else could stop him. It was dark in the alley, but there were plenty of bodies milling about. Couples leaning against walls and the red glow of cigarettes like fireflies.

He strode between them, ignored, and ignoring them.

Out on the promenade there was a strong breeze off the sea. The smell was intense. He crossed the road and went to the railing. She was right. No waves in sight.

His head was bursting. Mortification vying with rage. He wanted to do something violent. How stupid had he been? Thinking a young woman like her would give him a second glance. What a pathetic, foolish idiot! He swung round and began to walk.

The walk eventually calmed him down. The voices in his head changed from stingingly sarcastic taunts to suggestions that he'd had a lucky escape and that she was a tramp and not worth it.

It got him back to the hotel. He went up to his room and stood by the window. Would she come back? He doubted it. He went back downstairs and found the bar. It was quiet, three couples, and a handful of businessmen. He took his drink to a window seat and stared out into the night. The voices continued, even though he tried to ignore them. When he looked back to the bar, he noticed that a woman had appeared and was now sitting on a stool on her own. She was looking across at him. She had blonde hair. A short skirt. Probably his age or older. As he looked she smiled.

He nearly smiled back, but shook his head in disbelief. How much worse did he want it to be? He looked away.

The perfume killed it. She stood at the far side of the table.

'You on your own?' she asked.

He steeled himself to smile.

'Sorry, love. The wife's upstairs. Nice try though. Thanks.'

She shrugged her shoulders.

'Lucky woman,' she said and walked away.

When he looked again she'd gone. He sighed in relief, finished his drink, and went to his room.

He stood a long time looking out of the window. The promenade was still busy even though it was gone eleven. Groups of men and women, couples and dog walkers. The dockside was in darkness, only a big red lamp glimmering on the mud beyond. Further out there were other red lights, and in the far distance a row of tiny lights on some distant shore. He couldn't imagine where.

Eventually he took off his shoes, lay on the bed, and closed his eyes. He didn't expect to sleep and couldn't stop the images from replaying over and over in his head. But he did sleep.

* * * * *

He could hear a voice. Feel a hand on his face. In the dream he couldn't see who it was.

But the hand was real.

'Are you angry?' she asked.

He pushed her hand away and sat up. Sorcha stood up and backed away.

285

'Why did you go?' she asked.

He rubbed his hand across his face. Mouth and eyes all gummed up.

She tried to sit next to him, but he moved away.

In the darkness he could make out her silhouette and the glint of her eyes.

He couldn't think of what to do or say. She didn't help him out. He could hear her breathing.

She stood up and he felt her move away towards the door. She stopped.

'What did you think?' she asked.

He couldn't speak.

'I'm no good for you, you know,' she said.

Fear fought with yearning. He put his head in his hands.

'You're lucky. Go back to your woman. Forget me. I'm not worth it.'

He heard the door click as she opened it and a sliver of light crept along the floor.

He looked over towards her. Her silhouette was now trimmed with a golden edge. She stepped into the light, through into the corridor and was gone.

He sat there on the bed for a long time, until exhausted he fell onto his side, and cried himself to sleep.

* * * * *

He wasn't the only person to cry that night.

But well before dawn, Sorcha slipped down the back stairs and out into the cold wet street. She walked quickly across to the dockyard, which was now a hive of noisy activity, men working and machines busy. On the dockside cranes lifted the containers like toys and deposited them neatly on board the throbbing ship. At the back, the maw of the cavernous loading bay yawned wide and a stream of lorries slowly wound their way back to the dock gates. The girl flitted through the shadows until she found the one she was looking for. She clambered up on the step and the door quickly opened and she was inside. Ciaran gave her a kiss, before she scrambled into the bunk, and covered herself with the blankets.

She was asleep when the Customs Officers gave Ciaran the nod and he drove the lorry down the gangway into the ship.

An hour later it was battling the current in the channel and then out and free onto the open sea. They were half way to Ireland by the time Fletcher woke up in his clothes and stared at the ceiling.

* * * * *

She'd gone.

Her bed was rumpled, but there was nothing else to show she'd been there. For no reason he looked in the bathroom. Nothing. No sign she'd even been in there.

He stood by the bed and reached down to touch the thrown back sheet. Before he could stop himself he lay down and put his cheek on the pillow. It was cold, but there was the faint hint of her scent. He closed his eyes. Her face appeared in front of him with that enigmatic, nonchalant half smile. She swept her hair in slow motion across her forehead and looked at him with that dark gaze.

He opened his eyes and there in the doorway stood a girl.

Not her, but with the same dark hair, tied loosely in a ponytail behind her head. By her side were a hoover and a trolley heaped high with clean bedding. She was staring at him with an open mouth.

'S-s-sorry,' she said.

He got up and with all the dignity he could dredge up walked

287

towards her.

'No, I'm just going. My daughter thought her earring might be here...'

The girl shuffled out of his way.

'Er ... alright...' she said. 'I'll look out for it.'

He set off along the corridor.

'Thanks,' he said. 'Thank you.'

He hurried to the stairs, down to reception, refused the breakfast and paid.

He threw his bag in the car and got in. He stared through the windscreen at the dockside. There was little sign of activity apart from a few lorries already lined up, waiting for the next high tide.

He felt alone, desolate, and empty. Hollowed out like an emptied hoover.

He didn't know how long he sat there, but with a shrug he put the key in the ignition and started the engine. The wiper blade had decided to do a mouse impression and squeaked with every sweep across the glass.

It was only as he started to leave the promenade behind that he realised he'd no idea of the route. There was no map in the car, so he stopped in the first village and went into a corner shop post office.

After listening to a long-winded set of directions he set off again. He had to stop another couple of times before he found himself on the A6 heading north. Including the stop for breakfast to make up for the one he'd paid for but missed, it was nearly midday before he pulled up outside the vicarage.

There were several vehicles parked in the courtyard and on the grass verge outside. He sat in his car and wondered whether he could face all these people. He told himself that he'd have to deal with them at some point, so he might as well get on with it.

As he opened the door he was expecting to hear a chatter of voices from the kitchen, but was surprised to find that there was only the muffled sound of a piano. He peered into the kitchen, but it was empty, although the table, the Aga, and the sink were littered with the debris of a large party's breakfast endeavours. He went in search of the music, dreading a hushed auditorium. He realised that he'd not been in these other rooms as he passed through the main entrance hall, glimpsing ceiling high bookshelves in a room to the left. The pianist had upped the tempo and was now heading for a final crescendo. He opened the door.

The player had his back to him. He'd not thought who it might be, but he'd not have guessed the small figure now turning to look at him. He was young, perhaps thirteen, or fourteen. Blue eyes stared at the intruder from beneath a blonde fringe. The music stopped, but his hands rested on the keys, as though unwilling to give up the playing completely.

'I'm sorry,' said Fletcher. 'Please don't stop. I was enjoying it.'

The boy didn't move or stop staring.

Fletcher took a step into the room.

'I'm looking for Mags,' he said. 'Any idea where she might be?'

The boy continued to stare. Fletcher smiled.

'My name's Fletcher,' he said.

The boy didn't return the smile, but swung round on his seat and put his hands in his lap. They were thin and delicate.

'You're the detective,' he said.

Fletcher nodded.

'That's right. So who are you?'

The boy's face was stern.

'Are you going to find out who killed my parents and Aunt

289

Sybil?' he asked.

At least Fletcher now knew who he was talking to, but he was still disconcerted by this.

'Er ... well ... it's not so easy, I'm afraid,' he replied.

The boy frowned.

'Aunt Maggie said you were very determined.'

Fletcher couldn't stop himself from smiling.

'Ah, well,' he said, 'that may be true, but sometimes it's difficult when there's so little evidence to go on.'

He risked going further into the room, but the boy seemed unperturbed.

'Evidence,' repeated the boy. 'You mean fingerprints and lipstick on cigarette butts.'

Fletcher smiled again.

'Very good. But a witness or two would be more helpful.'

The boy was thoughtful.

'I fancy a drink. How about you?' asked Fletcher.

The boy shook his head and turned back to the piano. He paused and without looking at Fletcher again, took a breath and set his fingers to the keys. He began to play, something slow and repetitive. His eyes were closed and he moved with the rhythm of the music, his hands rising and falling like two gentle wings.

Fletcher watched and listened for a few moments, before quietly withdrawing.

He walked slowly back to the kitchen, found the kettle and put it on the Aga.

He was still sitting there waiting for the kettle to boil when the door opened and the breakfast party returned.

Fletcher survived.

He was introduced to those he hadn't met: the Wallace's relatives, including the boy's older sister, Helen, her uncle and aunt and grandmother, three or four ex-colleagues from Bristol, whose names he instantly forgot, and was reacquainted with Roger and Mark and the attendant coterie of Sybil's family, who were even harder to remember. The room was overflowing and people were all talking at once. Mags whispered in his ear that his things had been moved to a smaller room, which she'd show him to later. He allowed himself to be interrogated and asked the predictable questions, although none of them were as direct as the young boy. He realised after a time that he could no longer hear the piano and wondered where the boy was.

The throng eventually reassembled itself under the command of Mags and followed her and Mark to go to Sybil's house. Fletcher declined the invitation saying he'd things to do, although when they'd all gone, he just sat down at the table and sighed into the quiet emptiness.

He'd learnt that they'd all been round at the church organising things for tomorrow's service. He felt numb at the prospect, but knew his main reason for staying was that Sorcha was unlikely to miss it. He was determined that would be the end of all this and yet found himself wondering what he would say.

'Sorry', or, 'forgive me', or what? That sounded soppy, he wouldn't do that. So what was he going to do, or say?

He was still there racking his tired brain, when the door opened and the boy's sister stood looking at him, with the same blue eyes under the same blonde fringe as her brother. Like a couple of Midwich Cuckoos he thought.

She held out a folded newspaper towards him.

'I think you'd better look at this,' she said.

She came over to him and unfolded it on the table to reveal a crossword. He glanced at the top of the page. It was the Guardian. The crossword was the bigger, cryptic version and it was completed. Small, neat, old-fashioned handwriting.

'Sybil's writing?' he asked.

'Definitely,' she nodded.

He looked again. He wasn't a regular crossword doer, so he couldn't easily see why she was so animated about it.

'Look at fifteen down,' she said.

He glanced at her face. It was stern, but the gaze was fierce. He looked at the crossword.

'Exclusion,' he read out.

'Look at the clue,' she ordered.

'Religious leader from Australia raised on a hot day,' he said slowly.

He looked up at the young woman and frowned,

'Zoroaster,' she said.

He looked from her to the paper and back again.

'That's the correct answer, not 'exclusion',' she said

He was still puzzled.

'Why Zoroaster?' he asked.

She shook her head.

''Oz' upwards, and 'roaster',' she explained, her exasperation beginning to show.

He was still baffled.

'Try seven down.'

'Belgrano,' he read out. He looked at her again. He looked at the clue.

'Colleague's pain over collapse of market,' he murmured.

'Workmate,' she said.

He didn't get the clue, but the name clicked.

'If you check out all the incorrect answers, it's a message,' she said.

'Saying?'

She turned the paper over and pointed to what she'd written.

'Belgrano heading away from Exclusion Zone. Thatcher ignored Peruvian Peace Plan.'

He looked at her wondering if this meant any more to her than him. He'd not heard of any Peruvian Peace plan.

Mags was now standing behind Helen. Her face was equally serious.

He looked from one to the other.

'So what can we do with this,' he asked.

'I'm not sure,' said Mags. 'It's only what some people have been saying anyway. Thatcher denies it, of course, and most of the papers are dismissing it.'

Fletcher looked from one to the other.

Other people began to filter back in.

In the end they were all sat round the kitchen table. The arguments swayed this way and that, but eventually it was decided there was little they could do. An erroneously filled in crossword making an unsubstantiated claim wasn't much use. It could be just what Sybil was thinking.

Fletcher was quiet. He was thinking of what the woman with the red nails had said. Was Sorcha hanging on to some real evidence about this?

The group disintegrated into desultory alternative discussions and the subject was dropped. It was getting late in the afternoon and most of them, seeing the bright sunshine outside, decided to go for a walk.

Fletcher declined and went to find the new room he'd been assigned.

He lay on the bed and stared at a hole in the cornice.

What should he do?

No answer came. He could only wait to see if she turned up and ask her again.

His thoughts turned to Laura and so he went back downstairs to use the phone.

As he descended he could hear the piano again. He wandered

along and opened the door. The boy glanced over at him, but continued to play. Without a word he looked away. Fletcher could think of nothing to say either, so he quietly closed the door and headed for the kitchen.

✳ ✳ ✳ ✳ ✳

The vein in his neck was throbbing painfully, but his rage was subsiding. Ferris tried to brush aside the memory of the butchered body in the derelict house, but at the same time he was drawn to it. On the one hand it wouldn't have been so bad if she hadn't fought so hard, but on the other the sheer thrill of the fight had taken him to realms of ecstasy that he hadn't experienced for a long time.

He knew that she'd been energised by the strong drugs he'd provided. He needed to be careful about that. There were a few moments when he knew she'd got the upper hand and nearly turned the tables. She'd found a piece of wood from nowhere and chased him up the stairs thrashing at the steps only inches behind his heels. The floors up there had missing boards and the roof had holes gaping open to the stars. He'd hidden behind a door and listened to her creeping about, calling his name, or rather the name he'd given her, and yelling what she was going to do to him when she got hold of him.

Instead he'd beaten her with her own weapon and then strangled her slowly with her own bra. He loved to watch the dying of light as it flickered in their eyes. The anger turning to terror changing to recognition and acceptance as her struggles lessened. He held her tight long after she'd expired, feeling her body relax with its final stuttering exhalation, and yet keep its warmth, the sweat glistening on her breasts and shoulders.

He'd dragged her battered body under one of the beams hanging precariously from one side of an upstairs room and without much effort persuaded it to fall on top of her, crushing what was left and pile driving its way down through the rotten floor boards into the old kitchen beneath.

Finally he poured a full can of diesel onto where she lay hidden amongst the rubble and he now stood by the side of his car as the flames took hold and the whole building began to collapse.

One final explosion and he eased down into the car. Ten minutes later he was on the motorway heading south. He wasn't looking forward to the meeting later that afternoon and suspected the worst, but at least he'd be calm now and be able to deal with whatever they threw at him.

* * * * *

It was worse than he'd expected.

They were sending him away. To Berlin, for God's sake!

He'd had to listen to that pathetic excuse for a human being, Worsley, canting on about 'reliability' and 'seeing a job through', without the slightest understanding of what he was talking about. He would make him pay for it and blanked out his drawling voice with images of him screaming for mercy as he cut off every finger, ear, and toe, before he moved onto his tongue and his dick.

But worse than that was the laboured whinging of the PPS, how he felt let down and embarrassed.

He had stopped listening.

The charges were listed. The failures enumerated. The nigh on complete elimination of all possible awkwardness as a result of other people's failings ignored. Instead he was to take the rap for their grotesque incompetence.

They tried to put a gloss on the exile calling it his 'behind the wall adventure' and, 'a much envied promotion', which was all so much arrant tosh. He could see the evil glint in the eyes of his enemies. They couldn't wait to see his back. But they would all regret it, one way or another.

In the midst of it all he found himself talking to Stephane. How could that have happened? The man had seemed invincible. It had taken all his nerve to hire those two thugs, who would have made Burke and Hare look like a couple of camp hairdressers, and persuade, or rather bribe, them to recover his body. God what a mess. He'd had to pay them extra afterwards and to be fair they'd earned it. At least now there was no evidence. He'd seen to Stephane's avowed wish. The flames destroying the body of the screaming harpy would add her ashes to his in that derelict house. United in death, although he doubted she was sort of limp little girl he seemed to have preferred.

The orders were clear, Heathrow tomorrow morning, and Berlin by dinnertime. At least the whores were plentiful according to his friend Gorton. So he'd be able to assuage the anger and he could wait. If the shopkeeper's daughter kept on like this who knows what might happen. The wheels of fortune would turn. James Torquil Ferris would rise again.

His final thoughts as the plane taxied down the runway was to think of Fletcher and his dalliance with the terrorist minx. That was 'one job' he was 'seeing through', even without being there. He'd like to see Worsley manage something like that. Hurk and Bear as he'd decided to re-christen them, had reluctantly accepted the follow-up task of shutting the stable door after the horses had cantered off into the woods. It wasn't entirely necessary, but it would be neater.

* * * * *

By the time the fire engines arrived the fire was past its best. It had tried to extend its range into the nearby woods but the foliage was green and wet. The derelict building had stood little chance and feebly collapsed into a shrunken hulk, burying its sad secrets.

The following morning the remains were shrouded in mist and then pummelled by heavy rain. So that by the time the weather improved in the late afternoon, the investigating officers were not overly keen to spend much time poking about in the sodden collage of burnt timbers and crumbled stone. Even if they'd found the charred remains of her body, there would have been nothing to help them. Her bag was in a canal miles away and by the time Ferris had finished her clothes had been shredded to rags. If they'd dug deep enough they might have found her badly damaged teeth, but she hadn't been to a dentist since she was a child and had moved a hundred times since. She'd been lost long before she died.

Stephane was merely dust by this time. Ashes re-burnt and refined like the sand he'd wanted to be. Not drifting in the Saharan wind, but the odd mote was carried away by the little streams, which now trickled towards the valley below. The wood and the dereliction were soon buried and forgotten in the fresh greenery of early summer.

CHAPTER 14

Wednesday 2nd June

To be honest Mick Fletcher preferred funerals to weddings. At least you didn't have to pretend to be happy. Having said that, he hadn't been to many funerals or weddings, so he wasn't brimming with enthusiasm for the day ahead, and if everything went to plan, he'd be home by the middle of the afternoon. His telephone call last night to Laura had been guarded, to say the least, so he was less than sure of his reception when he got there.

The weather was doing its best, a huge downpour for breakfast and then steady rain ever since. The cortège was timed to leave the funeral director's emporium at nine forty five and arrive at the church for ten thirty. Fletcher had agreed to accompany Mark and Roger in the car behind the hearse, although he wasn't sure why. The rest of the party, and other guests, would wait at the church. It was because of this arrangement that he was able to witness the sullen power of the Cumberland resentment of off-comers at its most witheringly stubborn best.

The men in black had covered all eventualities. There was a car already stationed outside the church by seven o'clock. Four men, all armed, in contact with back-up by radio, although the signal wasn't good. The back-up included another four man landrover, which was detailed to follow the hearse, as well as the communication van and a minibus filled to the gunnels with a gang of bored-to-the-teeth, utterly sober uniforms from Southend-on-Sea, known to themselves as SOS. Their explicit instructions were to make sure that nothing untoward or anti-British occurred or be allowed to pass unchallenged, but more importantly to be on the look-out for a number of activists, who they were assured would not be able to resist attending such an important event, and if possible apprehend those who were wanted for questioning, and particularly to arrest a rather elusive lady with the trade mark red nails.

This was all well and good.

The first hint that Fletcher had that things might not go as planned was the sound of the escort as they pulled away from the funeral parlour. He didn't need to turn and look, but he couldn't resist. Sure enough there were over thirty bikes grumbling alongside before they even got to the first corner. He couldn't be sure, as they were all goggled and helmeted up, but he just knew that Hilda was somewhere amongst them. They formed a solid mass of metal and leather, which was as impenetrable as any Roman phalanx. He watched as they kept coming and then spotted the police landrover trying to edge out from the kerb. They were flashing their lights and even tried the siren, but for some reason it died almost as soon as it started.

As it was they were unable to get out until well after the cortège had disappeared. There were a few agitated calls between the four police vehicles, but the inspector in charge at the church, who believed he was noted for his sang-froid, calmed everyone down and told them to stick to their plan.

Fletcher watched as the hearse turned down towards Wath Bridge over the Ehen, where the bogus road works had blocked people getting to the inquest last Tuesday. He began to smile. He didn't know how or when it was going to happen, but he could sense a dose of their own medicine coming up. He wasn't wrong.

The bridge is narrow and the turning on the east side awkward at the best of times.

'Watch out,' he whispered to the young man driving the funeral car, but the man just smiled into the mirror, and Fletcher knew he was in on it.

The hearse slowed across the bridge and took the corner at a stately pace. The second car followed and then the bikes. They had been four abreast, but now they had to go two by two. This slowed down the whole business and the following police landrover was now hopelessly way behind.

Gradually they edged towards the bridge, but by the time they were crossing it, the hearse was out of sight. They radioed to let their superior know. He reassured them again.

It was a good fifteen minutes before they were across the other side, and now other vehicles had joined the slow moving line of traffic. The police driver was good, but he was better at high-speed chases. Not this snail trail. He tried the siren and edging out to try to pass the vehicles in front, but there was nowhere for them to go. It wasn't helped when a tractor and a trailer was allowed out into the line ahead, rendering him apoplectic with frustration.

By now the hearse and the following car had arrived at the village. But back at the bridge the police landrover had come to a stop. First one and then another of the heavily built officers got out and looked at the back tyres. Anyone could see they were flat. Not surprising given the huge slashes in both tyre walls.

The sergeant passed on this information to the communication van, but they were having a different sort of trouble. From out of nowhere a gang of youths surrounded the vehicle and within

300

seconds had spray-painted all the windows through the protective grills. Apart from the two civilian technical officers in the back, the only other officers were the driver and his young companion. The two of them were so astonished that all their training went out of the window as the windows went dark. They both opened their doors and stepped out onto the road. Where they were also spray-painted. They staggered about like Keystone cops, and in the classic manner bumped into each other and fell to the ground. Before they'd managed to do this, a lithe figure had leapt into the driving seat, fired up the engine, and driven the vehicle away. By the time the two officers had removed their paint smothered goggles their vehicle was gone.

The two radio men inside the van let out cries of alarm as the vehicle rocked and rolled. Anything unattached ended up on the floor, including the two men. By the time they'd understood they'd been hi-jacked the vehicle came to a sudden jerking stop. The back doors were wrenched open and the two men were pulled outside. Before they had time to defend themselves their attackers had gone, and, with a screeching of tyres, so had their vehicle and all its expensive equipment. The last thing they heard was a series of shouted calls from their colleagues elsewhere.

The Southend-on-Sea gang knew nothing of this. Their sergeant, who was from Enfield, was in a nasty mood.

'You cheating bastards,' he was saying, as he threw his cards down. 'I don't know how you're doing it, but I know you can't be that damn lucky.'

There was a squawking on the radio.

'Answer the bloody thing, will you?' he shouted.

'I have done, Sarge,' came the answer. 'But they've gone dead.'

'How d'you mean? Gone dead?' he demanded.

'As in 'not answering', Sarge,' came the reply.

The man from Enfield stood up and banged his head on the roof. Cursing, he got out of the back of the van and walked round to the front. He reached in and took hold of the radio and started pressing the buttons. He only got static. He looked at the machine and then threw it back into the cab.

'Something's gone wrong,' he said. 'Let's get out to the church.'

It was a good idea, but he could see it wasn't going to happen with his own eyes as he set off to the back of the van. Both tyres were flat ... and the rest.

'What the fuck!' he exclaimed.

The SOS gang got out and individually confirmed his first impression. He glared at them.

'Before you ask, Sergeant, I'd like to say walking to the church is not an option,' said the lanky, laconic git with the short quiff.

'We need a phone and pronto,' growled the sergeant.

And what do you know? On that particular day in that particular part of West Cumbria there was no one at home, except those people who claimed not to have a phone. Not only that, every pub's phone was out of order and all the public phones had been vandalised and spray-painted. So it was well over forty minutes before they found a phone, by which time the funeral was nearly over.

Back at HQ in Carlisle, ACC Gough was playing it by the book. If this was a Special Branch operation, which they'd decided not to inform him about, then how was he supposed to know what they were trying to do? He was unable to contact any of their vehicles and so had little idea where they might have been stationed. He got through to the local station and gave them orders to search for the afore-said vehicles and spent the rest of the afternoon on the golf course.

The desk sergeant at Whitehaven was not in a good mood. DS Crake had been granted the day off as she was going to the funeral. The phone was hot with calls from people complaining about a traffic jam out at Wath Bridge, which was now backed up onto the main road. He'd sent all his available officers out to see what they could do, but then that meant he was on his own. His mood didn't improve.

* * * * *

Meanwhile back at the church the hearse had arrived and the coffin had been carried in. The singing had started.

In the car outside the church there was consternation. The inspector in charge with the reputation for the 'cold blood' was in danger of having a heart attack. Not only had he lost contact with all the rest of his team, the signal had been poor anyway, but his vehicle had been demobilized. How had that happened? All four tyres were punctured and they hadn't seen or heard a thing. They'd neither heard nor seen the lad with the high-powered air rifle, nor taken any notice as he'd strolled past after he'd completed his task, and they certainly hadn't understood the reason for his wide grinning face. He reckoned five shots and four hits was pretty good going.

The Inspector gave his men some clear tasks.

'Ross and Kennedy. You get yourselves inside the church and keep your eyes skinned. I need to know if there's anyone in there we need to speak to.'

With a smirk at the other officer they set off.

'Dawkins. You come with me. We need to find a phone.'

How was he to know that the village public phone was always being vandalised or that everyone who lived in the village was at the funeral and had locked their doors. Even the hotel door was closed and no amount of banging could raise a response.

At this point his advance training took over. He decided to commandeer another car.

As he was standing outside the vicarage at this moment, his choice was considerable. His mistake was in choosing the best looking car. He wasn't to know it was the pride and joy of the Professor of History at Bristol University. Using the skills he'd learnt on a recent course, he gained access to the car and while Dawkins watched in astonishment, successfully 'hot-wired' the vehicle.

'Alright Dawkins, Don't tell me you've never seen that done before. Get in and drive the damn thing. We need reinforcements.'

Without another word the younger man got in and, with his superior beside him, set off back towards the bridge.

Perhaps the power of the vehicle had excited him, but it meant that he had little chance, even with his advance driving skills, of avoiding the tractor that pulled out in front of him. He knew the car was a write-off before he'd extricated himself from the driving seat. The inspector was a little dazed and so was not fully aware that, when the owner of the van who stopped to help, suggested he'd take them back to Whitehaven, that there was a glint in his eye, the young driver didn't see it either. Equally, how could Dawkins know turning left at the bridge was not the way to Whitehaven? He'd only arrived in the area yesterday.

However, even he began to have his doubts as the van driver, who obviously knew his way, the speed he was driving at in these narrow lanes, drove them up steeper and steeper lanes, until they could see the sea and the power station way below.

Just as Dawkins was about to ask whether this was the right way, the driver stopped and leaving the engine on, opened the door and disappeared over the nearest dry-stone wall like a goat. Dawkins got out of the car and surveyed the scene.

It was beautiful. The sun had broken through the clouds and

it had turned into a warm sunny day. Lambs gambolled in the fields and blossom glimmered on the bough.

His vernal dream was broken by a yelp from the van. He turned to see what was happening to find that the van had disappeared. He looked to his left to see it gathering speed as it rolled back down the steep slope. Fortunately for the injured inspector inside, it went into the deep ditch before it had gone very far and Dawkins rushed down to help his superior out of the van. Remembering his accident training, he dragged the poor man as far away as he could. The two of them looked at each other and the inspector passed out.

* * * * *

Back at the church the service was a huge success.

'All things bright and beautiful' wasn't perhaps a traditional funeral song, but it was Sybil's favourite and even Fletcher knew the words.

He was sitting at the back having persuaded Mark that he didn't want to be on the front pew.

The church was heaving, maybe two hundred people or more, most of whom, obviously, Fletcher had never met before.

But, to his surprise, there was Elizabeth Kirby and her man, Gregor, down at the front. She was wearing a huge black hat, but the hand that had steadied it as they came in was scarlet nailed and when she turned to speak to Mags on the way past, her lips were the same startling red.

The rest of the service was unforgettable. Instead of the usual hymn and prayer routine, various people went to the front and either told a story about something Sybil had done or read some wise words she had written or shared. These people were from a wide spectrum of backgrounds: professors and delinquents, hippies and politicians, artists and gardeners, climbers and beekeepers, teachers and engineers. All with a tale to tell. In between an array of musicians and singers played and sang a huge variety of songs, ranging from classical to the latest New Romantic stuff that Grace liked.

Fletcher couldn't help regretting he'd never met the woman whilst she was alive. All the stories were about her intellectual prowess and her storytelling, her cooking and her parties, her lovers and her unfortunate enemies. She'd caused trouble and resolved arguments. She'd made amazing discoveries in her research and motivated hundreds of students onto higher things. What an amazing life.

He knew that the service was coming to an end and was beginning to think Sorcha wasn't coming, when he saw Mags approach the lectern at the front.

She first thanked everyone for coming and then told them there was to be one final song, but that the singer was very upset, and although she knew Sybil would have wanted her to sing, she could only do it if they didn't turn to look. She was waiting at the back and was ready to start. The audience obeyed Mags and steadfastly faced the altar. From the organ a note was sounded. The church created its own venerable hush.

From only a few feet behind Fletcher the note was repeated. He shivered.

He knew instantly it was Sorcha. Even though this was nothing like the raucous, deep throated bellowing that he'd heard in the cellar bar in Blackpool.

This was clear. The song was slow, operatic, building in volume as she sang.

He didn't know it. Could hardly understand the words, even though they were unmistakeably English, but the repeated phrases were clear enough.

'When I am laid, am laid in earth … No trouble, no trouble in thy *breast ...*

Remember me ... remember me ... but never forget my fate

Remember me ... but never forget my fate ...'

Her voice and the words were piercing. Tears streamed down his face. He heard her sob behind him and the softest swish of cloth as she departed.

He wasn't the only one.

All the pent-up anguish for the loss of this amazing person was released in those moments of pure beauty. The whole church rang with the sound of weeping ... and no one tried to stem it.

It must have lasted for a good five minutes before Mags felt she could exert some control, she led them in a gathering rendition of the 'We shall overcome' as the coffin was carried out.

And that was it. No final words from Godfrey. She was gone.

People turned to each other and there was multiple hugging and kissing and all talking at once. Fletcher turned round and followed the coffin.

Outside Sorcha was standing next to the hearse. He wanted to walk over to her, but she saw him and shook her head. He watched as the coffin was placed in the hearse and Mark, Helen and Sorcha got in the accompanying car, no one else, not even Mags, to accompany her on her final journey to the crematorium.

He watched them drive away and then realised he was not alone. Many of the congregation had come out to stand with him. Gradually the talking began again. Some people still needed a hug, but soon Mags ordered them all to get themselves to the hotel.

* * * * *

Back in the church Ross and Kennedy had given up banging on the door of the storeroom or trying to force it open. There were

307

windows, but they were high up and neither of them could have squeezed through even if they'd been able to get up to them. They'd been unceremoniously pushed in there by some local rugby lads, who'd been stationed at the main door awaiting just such an opportunity, having been granted immunity by a prominent local magistrate.

In the hotel the wake was in full swing. The crowd had spread out all over the ground floor, although the majority were still crammed into the bar. Some people who couldn't put up with the melee and noise had retired to the dining room and a further overspill had retreated to the residents' lounge.

Fletcher was ill at ease with most of these people. Many of them knew each other and old acquaintances were recalling tales and adventures, not all of which included Sybil. He found himself in the hotel porch watching the rain splattering in the numerous puddles beginning to take over the entire car park. Whatever he might say, he knew he was only waiting to see if Sorcha came back from the crematorium.

As he stared out into the drizzle, he reflected on the last couple of weeks. What was happening to him? He knew he was in danger of being suspended or even sacked the way things were going. How could he let a mere girl take over his life so completely? Was she his Delilah? He grinned to himself at an image of himself standing in the portico of the police headquarters in Carlisle and bringing the whole lot down about their ears.

He was still there nearly an hour later, when the funeral car reappeared, gaily splashing muddy water in its wake. Mark helped Helen out of the back seat and Sorcha's head rose out of the other side of the car. Their eyes met. Her face was stern. She followed the two men into the hotel.

Fletcher held his ground. She came abreast of him and hesitated.

'My room. It's on the third floor, last door on the right.'

Before he could respond she carried on and turned into the bar. Did she mean now? Who else ordered him about like this?

Without answering the second question he obeyed the instruction, glad to be out of the heaving mass of increasingly raucous revellers.

He walked slowly upstairs like a condemned man. Uncertain of his fate, but helpless, even resigned, to whatever was decided.

It was only a minute after he'd disappeared that three police vehicles pulled up in the drive and disgorged a flurry of grim faced officers, headed by a disgruntled ACC Gough, failing to hide a startlingly pink and yellow V-necked jumper under his raincoat.

As he headed for the front door, another officer directed his men to whatever external doors they could find. They had been informed who they were to look out for, but as they were local men who'd been off duty and drafted in from family and various leisure pursuits, they were sullen, reluctant, and bordering on the rebellious. Failure to achieve the results Gough had been charged with was inevitable.

Upstairs Fletcher was unaware of their arrival and in fact would have been indifferent. He surveyed the room he'd just entered.

He couldn't stop himself comparing it with Grace's. They couldn't be more different. Here was austerity. Poverty. No pictures on the walls. No mirror. No clothes strewn across the furniture. Hardly any furniture at all, a neat and tidy bed, an old wardrobe against the wall, a small table and a single wooden chair. Like Van Gough's room without the colour. He knew none of it was Sorcha's. There were no clothes or a hairbrush or shoes. He began to wonder whether he'd come the wrong room.

Without thinking he went to the wardrobe and opened

the door as if he was investigating a disappearance. There was the blue dress and a few others. Jeans on a shelf, and a drawer of underwear. Shoes parked neatly in rows on the floor. He wondered if she'd ever been in prison. There was an institutional order here. He closed the door.

In the corner of the room was another door. Inside was a small bathroom, inside a mirror with a crack crossing at an angle from the bottom corner. A hairbrush and a toothpaste tube squeezed to death, and a small irregular piece of yellow soap.

How could anyone live like this?

He went to look out the window. A large chimneystack restricted the view. Only the hills in the distance told him which way it faced. He could see the clouds clearing the tops and weak sunlight fluttered on the wet roof tiles.

He sat on the edge of the bed and waited.

* * * * *

Downstairs ACC Gough had managed to attract the attention of the landlady who pointed him in the direction of a tall woman whose booming voice he'd heard as he came in.

With evident distaste he made his way through the throng towards her.

'Excuse me, madam,' he began.

Mags took in the sweater peering out from behind the black raincoat and smothered a giggle.

'Yes, Mr Gough? What can I do for you?'

Startled to find that the woman knew who he was, Gough was momentarily at a loss.

'I'm Margaret Cavendish,' she announced and held out her hand.

He winced as he felt the strong, warm hand grip his and recalled that he had met her before or rather been humiliated by her in a court case a few years back. Something to do with a pack of hounds savaging some ramblers; the local huntsmen had been less than pleased with her pronouncements and her finding against them.

'Er ... I need to speak to these people urgently,' he said. 'We have reason to believe there are certain ... er ... individuals we need to speak to regarding on-going investigations.'

Mags gave him a shrewd look.

'I hope this is a serious request, Mr Gough. Most of the people in this room are my friends and many of them are in positions of authority and of high reputation.'

Gough controlled his mounting anger.

'I assure you, madam, this matter is of the utmost importance – a matter of state security no less.'

Mags couldn't resist the opportunity. She laughed.

'Well you couldn't wish for a more interested audience, Mr Gough. This room is full of people who know plenty about 'state security' and how it is maintained.'

ACC Gough was then subjected to the most torrid experience of his entire career. He was jeered, provoked, and harassed, whilst his questions and warnings were ignored and unheeded. After half an hour he stormed out, fuming with exasperation. There was nothing more he could do other than to carry out his threat to stop and search every car that left the hotel. This was made even more difficult as most of them didn't leave until the following day and none of the people he had been told to look for were apprehended.

* * * * *

Sorcha had slipped out the staff door into the back corridor as the police arrived. She went up the service staircase and quickly to her room.

Inside Fletcher was still sitting on her bed. She closed the door.

For a long moment neither of them spoke. She brushed the hair from her face and gave him a weak smile.

She crossed the room and sat on the chair.

'The police have arrived,' she said.

He shrugged his shoulders.

'Do you think they're looking for me? Us?' she asked.

'I doubt it.'

She looked away.

'You have an amazing voice, you know,' he said.

She looked back at him, her face stern.

'What do you want?'

It was his turn to look stern.

'Why did you trick me?'

'Trick you?'

'Leading me on. Teasing me?'

She shook her head.

'I'm not teasing you. You can fuck me any time you like.'

He stared at her.

She stood up and pulled her jumper over her head. Underneath she was wearing that thin green T-shirt she'd been wearing when he gave her a lift. Her hair fell down across her face and she pushed it to one side.

'Well?' she asked hooking her fingers in the belt of her jeans.

He shook his head.

She stayed where she was, her eyes burning into his.

'Where are the papers?'

She continued to stare.

'I've got them.'

'Where?'

'Not here.'

'So? Are you going to give them to me?'

'How do I know I can trust you?'

'You don't.'

She came towards him and sat on the bed. He moved away to give her space, but was still near enough to smell the warmth of her. He wanted to reach out and caress her hair, but her eyes were hard. Black pearls.

'And why should you trust me either,' she said and leaned back against the headboard and closed her eyes.

They stayed like that for a long time. Fletcher could feel his body seizing up.

'You don't know anything, do you?' she said.

'That's how it feels,' he murmured.

She opened her eyes.

'I shot the sheriff,' she sang softly.

He stared at her.

'You?'

'Yeh.'

He stared at her. Somewhere deep in his brain, he'd suspected it, feared it, but hadn't let it speak. Didn't want it to be true.

'In the cave. I followed you and Gavin.'

He looked at her with a mixture of disbelief and fearfulness.

'Well, not followed exactly. I was already up there. I came down the Ghyll from the top.'

He waited, still couldn't fully accept it. Was she really capable of that? Heroine or monster? Cold blooded killer?

'You found the treasure,' she continued, a slight smile playing on her lips.

Again he shook his head, although he couldn't take his eyes of her. 'You took it away?' he breathed.

She nodded.

'I was the one who put it there,' she said. 'Me and Alice.'

'You … and Alice. Why?'

She hesitated.

'It's a long story … all of it is genuine stuff. Stolen from other collections. Alice thought it would help us continue the deception. The story's well-documented and he could have ended up there.'

'What deception?'

'It was Alice's cover story. It allowed her to get around from one lot of activists to another. It's surprising how many university people are involved … or maybe it's not.'

Fletcher stared at her, trying to make sense of what she was saying.

She crossed her legs and leant towards him. She reached out and put her hand on his.

'The thing is they may be intelligent, but a lot of them are so naïve,' she whispered.

'Like me?' he asked.

She made a face.

'No, not you. Apart from sex, of course.'

His turn to make a face. He pulled his hand away and stood up.

'So what other deceptions?'

She sighed and leant back against the wall with her hands behind her head, making the shape of her breasts more prominent behind the thin green material.

'Where did I go when I left you in that hotel?'

'Larne.'

'Which is where?'

'Ireland.'

'You need to be more precise?'

'Northern Ireland.'

She nodded and folded her arms across her chest.

314

'And … so?'

He felt the pieces slotting into place. The jigsaw is easy when someone shows you the picture on the box.

'IRA?'

She nodded and sat staring at him.

'So what do you know?' she asked.

He shook his head.

'Not much. Although I think I was partly responsible for preventing an assassination attempt by them about a year ago. I didn't actually meet any of them. They were paying others to do their dirty work.'

'Dirty work?'

'A turn of phrase,' he answered.

She stared him out, her eyes blacker than ever.

When he glanced back she was on her feet.

'You want a drink?' she asked as she opened the wardrobe door.

The bottle was in her underwear drawer. She fetched him the glass from the bathroom and pulled a mug out from under the bed. So much for his scene of crime detection skills.

It was Black Bushmills. Fletcher had heard of it but never tasted it. It was certainly different.

He could see that she was weighing up what else to tell him.

'The less you know the better,' she eventually decided to say. 'For me and you.'

He nodded his agreement.

'But what has that got to do with the documents? I thought they were something to do with the Falklands?'

'Ay, right enough. Just think what the IRA would do with something that would make the British Government look bad. Show them to be the bunch of lying bastards that they are.'

There was a gleam in her eyes. The adrenaline rush of the

impassioned idealist? He'd seen it in Grace's eyes as well, be it for a different cause. Did he ever feel it? He didn't think so. Why not?

'So what's stopping you?' he asked.

'Ach,' she spat. 'They're no more honest or true themselves.'

She took a big swig of whiskey and coughed herself hoarse. He waited, taking little sips so as to avoid the same punishment. It was fiery all right.

'What about Elizabeth Kirby?'

Sorcha was still gathering her breath, but shook her head.

'I can't bring myself to trust someone who paints her nails red ... can you?'

Fletcher couldn't prevent himself from smiling. He couldn't disagree, although he knew it wasn't logical.

'And that man of hers, Gregor, gives me the creeps,' she added.

He agreed with that as well.

'So how come you're involved with the IRA?' he asked.

She gave him a sharp look.

'I didn't say I was, did I?'

Fletcher waited, impassive.

'Hilda would tell you why, but she'd be wrong.'

He took a sip of the firewater, trying to keep as still as possible.

'She thinks my dad was one of them, but it's not true. He drank himself to death after the British killed my brother. It's true he hated them, but he never did anything.'

'Your brother?'

'Yeh. He was in the IRA. He was a murdering bastard and a vicious thug.'

'No love lost there then?'

'Never was or ever will be,' she said and took another big

gulp. This time she didn't cough; she just closed her eyes and shuddered.

'But you know some of them?'

She looked him in the eyes.

'Ay I do.'

Her eyes told him more than she said.

'He's called Ciaran and he drives a big truck. He doesn't do much, just ferrying stuff and delivering messages.'

'I see,' said Fletcher.

She looked at him long and hard over the top of her glass holding it with both hands. 'But the offer is still there,' she said. 'It won't stop me loving him or him me.'

It was Fletcher's turn to cough.

'It's not your loyalty I'm bothered about,' he said.

'Ah, the lovely Laura.'

He gave her a fierce look.

She shrugged her shoulders and leant back again.

He stood up and placed the glass on the window ledge.

'To be honest with you,' he said. 'I've had enough of all this. If you decide to give the documents to me that's fine, but you need to do what you think is right. What would Sybil have wanted?'

She looked away.

'What would you do with it?' she asked without looking.

He sighed.

'I've no idea. Depends what it says.'

'I'll tell you now if you like?'

He waited.

'It's a transcript of a conversation between Thatcher and her advisors.'

He reached for the bottle and poured himself another dram.

'It was her. Thatcher insisted that they should sink the Belgrano.'

'So what? She's the Prime Minister? She's entitled to make that sort of decision.'

'Against the advice of her advisors and behind the back of her Foreign Secretary? Ignoring the efforts of other governments trying to broker a peace deal?'

Fletcher pulled a face.

'I've no idea. I don't trust any of them. I think they're all two-faced liars without any thought for anyone but themselves, whatever they claim.'

Where did that come from?

He looked up and Sorcha was smiling at him.

'How can I contact you ... indirectly, via another person you trust?'

'Sergeant Irene Garner at Penrith nick,' he said without hesitation and immediately regretted it.

She stood up and came towards him.

'That doesn't mean I've made my mind up, but I can't keep on like this ...'

She was up close now. She reached out and pulled his head towards her until his face was against her breasts. He could hear her heart beating and the warmth of her body pressed against his. He pulled away and stood up. He embraced her and they kissed. He felt her leg push against his and force its way through so that her pelvis rubbed against his crotch. He put his hand into her hair and held her close. She bit his lip. He kissed her hard. They both came up for air. He pushed her away and staggered back.

She stood swaying, her eyes glistening. He picked up the glass and placed it on the chair. Without another word, he walked past her and opened the door. In the doorway he weakened, but when he turned to look she had her back to him, her head on one side. He walked.

He drove home in a daze, couldn't recall any of the journey.

When Laura came home and saw him sitting in the armchair with a glass in his hand, she took him straight to bed. Few words were spoken. Enough for her to understand the nightmare he was living through. Eventually exhaustion defeated his over wrought brain.

She wrapped him in her arms, and held him until the shaking stopped and the next day crept up into the leaden sky.

CHAPTER15

Ferris had been to Berlin many times before and so already knew a few people, the sort of people who he could now call on for help. He didn't kid himself that they would do things for him for nothing. He had money. His mother had left him a sad collection of Hebridean estates, which he'd never visited, but which contributed a steady flow of funds. He'd invested cleverly, using inside information extracted from an old school friend with unsavoury habits. In another five years or so his brother's disappearance would be accepted and he would inherit his father's grander and much more lucrative estates in the Borders and beyond. He knew their worth, as he'd been appointed guardian of them in his brother's absence. He knew very well what had happened to the arrogant bastard and had ensured that his wife and child had suffered the same fate. All he needed was patience, which he sorely lacked.

But the idea of Fletcher and that wretched girl escaping his clutches rankled with him even more and so he assembled, instructed, and dispatched a quartet of hard-bitten East German army deserters, whose day job included protecting Berlin black market gangsters. In his official position it was easy to arrange false passports and visas to enable their passage back and forth.

He'd showed them pictures of the two targets and hinted that they didn't need to dispose of the girl without enjoying themselves first. This didn't even bring a smile to their leader's face, but Ferris knew it added spice to the action.

They disembarked from different European ports and only met up again as the leader walked out of the foot passenger exit at Hull and joined his compatriots in the van waiting for him.

Later that day they met up with Hurk and Bear, who had been trailing the two targets and had been informed by Ferris of the latest planned meeting. As it was they knew where and when before Fletcher.

* * * * *

Tuesday 8th June dawned early. The sun came up as a burning orb suffusing the purple with red and gold. It was going to be hot. The rain had stopped six days ago and already the authorities were warning of hosepipe bans.

Fletcher had been told to have two week's leave. So far he'd spent most of it walking; mostly alone, but Laura had taken a couple of days off as well, and they'd revisited some of their favourite fells. Despite all that had happened they had slipped back into an easy closeness, which Fletcher still didn't think he deserved. He hadn't suggested the walk up Ennerdale he'd promised himself to take her. It was too early for that yet.

In fact he'd not thought about Sorcha for the last couple of days and if he'd been asked he'd have said he'd assumed she had decided not to contact him again. He half expected to see the IRA on the TV making damaging comments about the government, but at the moment it was still gung-ho stuff about Bluff Cove and other battles.

So he was surprised to pick up the phone and hear Irene's voice.

'I've got a message for you, sir,' she said. 'Agricultural Arms?'

* * * * *

Ten minutes later they were both sitting towards the back of the pub, whilst the farmers' voices filled the room with their friendly banter. Fletcher had only a few moments to reflect that it was here last autumn that the wild goose trail in Saltburn had kicked off, before Irene arrived. The Goth look was long gone and he suspected her absence from recent drinking sessions and the sharp suit and short back and sides she had adopted might all be heading towards the promotion she hankered after. He didn't object to this, merely reflected on his own lack of ambition ... and he knew he would miss her.

'It's the girl,' she said, when they'd taken a couple of mouthfuls each. Hers was a coke, which added further confirmation to his theory.

'What girl?' he asked.

'You know, the barmaid,' she said, trying hard not to smirk.

Fletcher made a face. He knew he had disappointed her.

'You mean my Irish contact?' he asked with as straight a face as he could manage.

Irene shrugged away her immediate response and merely nodded.

'What does she want?' he asked.

Again she had to almost bite her lip.

'Another secret rendezvous,' she said, 'although it doesn't sound terribly secret.'

Fletcher wondered just how much Irene knew. He doubted Hilda would tell tales about her sister, but he suspected the rest of her colleagues would be less parsimonious with their gossip.

'Oxenholme Station. Ten thirty tomorrow morning. Wear your walking boots.'

322

Fletcher frowned.

'Where's that?' he asked.

'It's the Kendal mainline station.'

His frown remained.

'There's also the little train which goes to and from Windermere,' added Irene. 'It's the same platform. Sounds full of possibilities to me.'

'And why the boots?' murmured Fletcher.

Irene and he could both invent a whole range of scenarios, but they didn't share them. He could feel their relationship disintegrating like sand through an egg timer.

'How's the homework going?' he asked.

'Just fine thanks,' she said raising her eyebrows. 'Who told you?'

Fletcher grinned.

'No one, you daft tart, I'm a detective remember. Dallas suit plus army haircut, plus non-alcoholic drink equals promotion hunter at work. Even the ploddest of your colleagues must have figured it out by now.'

Irene nearly blushed and stared into her drink.

'It's in Manchester,' she offered.

'Good luck to you,' said Fletcher, although his heart sank further as his suspicions were confirmed.

'I should have told you,' she said.

'Why should you? I'm not your dad.'

She gave him a fierce glare.

'No you bloody well aren't.'

'Turn of phrase, Irene … now get me another drink and fuck off.'

He didn't get the drink and regretted his tone the minute he'd spoken. He watched as she pushed her way roughly through the farmers and their lads. No mean feat considering the crush of muscle and weight. By the time they realised who was knocking their elbows and spilling their drinks she was gone. A quick brown fox slinking between the bulls' fat thighs, he thought, and allowed himself a wan smile.

He bought himself another pint and wallowed in the din of Westmoreland gossip not understanding a quarter of it. Was he going to stay here? Laura seemed happy. Especially when they were out on the fells. DCI Aske had been fairly sure that he'd have to go, but no word yet.

He thought about the rendezvous. What if he didn't go? But he knew he would. Would he tell Laura? He went for another pint

Later, lounging in a chair in front of the television with the sound down, he still hadn't made his mind up and fell into a drunken sleep. Laura read the signs when she came home and left him there, until she'd made something to eat and roused him roughly from his hangover. No comfort or sympathy from her. He went like a lamb and was in bed by nine, still uncertain whether he'd go or not.

* * * * *

Fletcher woke with a start. He didn't realise it, but it was Laura banging the door as she set off for work. He staggered to the bathroom and washed his face. It was red and bloated. Not a pretty sight. What was the time? Was he going to go? One last time?

Without really knowing what he was doing he drove to Kendal and found his way to the station up the hill. Difficult to believe it was on the main line, but as he reached the top of the steps he could see the sign that said the Glasgow train was due at 10.34 and on time. He'd time for a brew.

Armed with the mug of tea and a bar of chocolate he

wandered along out into the sunshine. Was she going to turn up? Was she going to give him the secret documents? What would he do with them? The war didn't seem to be going to plan. This morning's headlines were full of gloomy prognosis. Bluff Cove had been a disaster. Maybe people were having second thoughts about Maggie and her South Atlantic adventure. What would revelations of dubious decisions do to her?

The platform was gradually filling up and then behind him he heard the squealing of brakes. A short two-carriage diesel train nosed into the side bay. The gaggle of walkers and tourists on the platform noisily changed places with those on the train. The destination indicator changed to Windermere. Glasgow bound passengers eyed them with a mixture of disdain and envy. Was Sorcha amongst them? The arrival of the mainline train was announced on the tannoy. He looked down the track and saw it in the distance. He searched the departing Windermere passengers as they headed for the underpass. The Glasgow passengers waited expectantly as the train came rushing into the station, its engine roaring and the brakes complaining. It came to a screeching stop.

He was surprised at how many people were queuing to get off even though the carriages still seemed full of people staring out with glazed expressions. The passengers on the platform waited patiently. Was he supposed to get on? He hadn't bought a ticket, but knew he could show his warrant card if necessary. The waiting passengers were now climbing aboard. An elderly stationmaster strode past with his red flag in hand and a whistle already in his lips. Fletcher looked this way and that. A large man with a square head and military crew cut stood looking at him. His eyes were small, but a vivid blue. He looked away.

Fletcher looked once more towards the front of the train. The platform was nearly empty. He heard the station-master blow his whistle. He looked back the other way. The big man had disappeared. Had he got on the train?

The train made a grinding noise and began to move. Right in front of Fletcher a door opened and looking up he saw Sorcha's face. Her hand reached out to him. He grasped it and she pulled him up the step. He heard the whistle again being blown angrily and followed by a shout of exasperation. As he gathered himself and felt his grazed shin, he saw a man running along the platform, gesticulating at someone further down the train. He wasn't wearing station uniform and his coat didn't seem to fit him. But most incongruous of all was the glimpse of a gun hidden inside it. Not a handgun, but a sub machine gun. The sort soldiers use.

Before Fletcher could take all this in, he felt Sorcha tug at his arm.

'Quick! This way,' she urged and set off through the interconnecting door to her left.

He could feel the carriages dislocating as they went over a junction and the train snaked onto another line. Ahead of him he could see Sorcha as she hurried down the corridor. It was one of those carriages with compartments at right angles to the train. In the first compartment there were people still stuffing their bags onto the overhead rails. In the next one people were already seated reading papers and books.

Sorcha was nearly at the other end, but stopped to shout back at him.

'Come on, down here,' she yelled.

Before he could catch up with her he saw a man appear behind her. Fletcher recognised the coat. It was the man who had been running along the platform.

'Look out!' he yelled, his instincts confirmed as Sorcha turned to face the man, he was only a few steps away. He raised his gun and an ugly smile gathered itself on his face like a spider was crushing it. Fletcher saw Sorcha's arm move. There was a faint sound and the man's spider face exploded into pulp and brains. He collapsed like a stricken buffalo. Sorcha retreated, gun in hand, nearly falling backwards.

Fletcher was frozen in his tracks. He couldn't take it in. She'd done it again.

Sorcha ran back to him and pushed him towards the way they'd come.

'There'll be more of them,' she said in a hoarse voice like she'd downed a couple of Bushmills. Her dark eyes were red rimmed and her face was taut. Her hair was tied back into a single plait.

He allowed himself to be pulled along.

The next carriage was open plan, with seats facing forwards and back, some facing each other. The carriage was full. Some people were still standing, sorting themselves out. Sorcha brushed past them, ignoring their complaints. Voices were raised. She'd put the gun away. Fletcher found himself apologising, wondering whether he should show his card. The man's exploding head repeated itself in his blurred brain, reprising the terrible moment in the cave. How could she do that?

The next carriage was the buffet car. There was a queue. Sorcha pushed past them as well. He followed.

In the interconnecting section she waited for him.

'Here, the documents,' she said and pulled them out from her coat.

Fletcher's eyes went big as he focussed on the man who had materialised behind her. He wasn't as big as the one she had shot but he looked just as unpleasant. Before he could do anything he felt someone tap him on the shoulder. He turned to see a third man. The same smile and the same gun, but smaller. Ratface. White teeth. As if to confirm his credentials there was a neat scar down his left cheek.

Fletcher would never know why he did the next thing. Foolhardy doesn't begin to cover it. He took one step and head butted the man in the face. To their mutual astonishment it worked. The man staggered back, blood streaming from his nose. Fletcher kicked him hard in the crotch and he was down. Behind him he heard Sorcha's muffled scream.

He turned to see the man behind her with his arm round her face and the gun pointing at him.

He dodged to his left behind the bulwark of the interconnecting doors. The gun made a terrifying noise and splinters flew this way and that. The man he'd knocked down made the terminal mistake of trying to get up at this point and turned into a blood splattered punch bag.

The noise stopped and the man writhed to the floor and lay still.

Fletcher could hear screams coming from the next corridor.

He took a quick peep through the gap. Sorcha and the gunman had gone.

Without thinking too much, he followed them.

The next compartment was first class and it was mayhem. People were down between the seats whilst one or two were lying still on the floor. At the far end the gunman was still dragging Sorcha, waving his gun in the air. Seeing Fletcher appear he let off a volley in his direction, but Sorcha managed to push him backwards so most of it went into the ceiling. A light bulb exploded. A woman was screaming and screaming. Fletcher knelt behind the first seat. A young woman stared up at him from the foot well across from him, a mask of terror frozen onto her carefully made up face. He took a look down the carriage. The man and Sorcha had disappeared.

He stood up. The woman further up the carriage was still screaming. To his left he could hear whimpering. But before he could do anything he felt a sharp pain in his back and turned to see a fourth man. He was pale skinned with close-cropped white blonde hair. He wasn't smiling. He pushed Fletcher with his gun. Not a machine gun.

'Keep going, Mr Policeman,' he said.

He did as he was told. He guessed that the man wanted him in front of him when they got to the next carriage. He stared to calculate what chance he had in the next interconnecting section. Very little.

They got level with the woman who was still screaming. They'd passed four or five people huddled to the floor, terrified eyes looking their way.

Fletcher turned to look at the man. He pushed him on. Fletcher held onto a seat to stop himself from falling.

The man looked down at the woman and pointed his gun.

'Shut the fuck up, lady,' he said. The phrase was American, but the accent was German.

She stopped. The blonde gunman gave a quiet laugh and shot her. Twice.

Fletcher took his chance and launched himself at the man.

They went down in the aisle. The gun was between them. It went off. Fletcher expected the pain but the blood that gushed all over him wasn't his. The man screamed like the woman he'd shot, a high pitched wail right into Fletcher's ear, but then his mouth filled with pink froth and the screams died into bubbles. His back arched and collapsed. He shuddered a few times and lay still.

Fletcher extracted himself from the bloody corpse and stared at it before backing away towards where Sorcha had disappeared.

Before he got there the train jolted and the brakes cried out. There was a hissing and further jolting. The train came to a shuddering halt. Someone must have pulled the emergency cord. Fletcher staggered on and hurried to the door. There were no other carriages. He was at the front. The outside door hung open. He cautiously looked out. There were trees dropping down to a road. He could see cars driving past. Hills in the distance. She'd disappeared. Further back down the track he could see a man in a peaked cap running towards him. He stepped back inside.

At the other side of the aisle there was a toilet.

The door was ajar.

He took a step towards it, his heart in his mouth. Even as he looked a thin river of red dribbled through the gap. He pushed at the door. It didn't budge.

He managed to force it open far enough so he could look inside.

It was the man who had dragged Sorcha away. He was slumped down beside the bowl. His face and neck were covered in blood. His hand dangled into the water. Something was blocking the toilet and the man's body was pressed against the flush. Water was coming over the top of the toilet and mixing with his blood.

Fletcher backed out into the door space and slumped down onto the floor.

Where was she?

He couldn't remember much of what happened next. There was a lot of rushing about. More police than he expected and men in black if he wasn't much mistaken.

He was helped off the train and down to an ambulance on the road below. There was a woman on the other bed, but it wasn't Sorcha.

* * * * *

In the hospital he was examined and put in a private room.

Nurses and doctors came and went, until eventually Laura

arrived.

She hugged him until it hurt.

He was glad she didn't interrogate him. He'd not tried to order it himself yet. He had only one question.

Laura shook her head.

'I've no idea. I'm sorry,' she said.

He sighed and looked away.

She held his hand.

He cried.

Before either of them could speak again the door opened and Anthony Adversane breezed in.

'Afternoon, Inspector,' he said and smiled at Laura.

'Well, the medics say you're a bloody miracle. None of the copious amounts of spilt blood was yours apparently. Nothing broken. Be on your way home within the hour.'

Fletcher stared at him.

Adversane turned to Laura.

'Laura, my dear, I'd appreciate a few minutes with the hero, if you don't mind. I'll be glad to give him back. Just need to check a few details.'

This was all said as he ushered her gently but firmly through the door.

After she'd gone, Adversane pulled up a chair and placed it close to Fletcher's bed.

He was so close Fletcher could smell his aftershave ... or maybe it was perfume.

His eyes were a luminous grey green that matched his beautifully cut suit. He didn't speak straight away but stared resolutely into Fletcher's face.

At last, having apparently seen enough, he leant back in his chair, produced a cigarette and lit it with a gold-plated lighter. He blew the smoke up into the air and uttered a long sigh.

'The thing is, Fletcher old thing, you bloody well are a damn hero … again, for God's sake.'

Fletcher shook his head.

'Not me,' he whispered.

'Ah yes, your mysterious assistant. Barmaid and part-time Bond girl.'

'Is she alive?'

'Disappeared into the ether, dear boy.'

Fletcher waited.

'Not a clue. I'm afraid. You any ideas?'

Fletcher shook his head. There was a headache coming, he could tell.

Adversane leant forward.

'Did you see the documents?'

Fletcher shook his head again.

Adversane looked at him hard.

'Read them?'

Fletcher said nothing.

'Do you know what they were about?'

'Maybe,' said Fletcher.

Adversane gave him another stern look.

'Well it won't do you any good. They will be destroyed. They're piss wet through anyway. Literally.'

Fletcher nodded.

'Who were the men?'

'You don't need to know really. German professionals.'

'So you knew they were coming?'

Adversane looked away.

'Generally we know most things, but we can't take into account maniacs like you, even when we know you're involved.'

Fletcher shook his head.

'Not me, I assure you.'

'Never-the-less it'll be you picking up the commendation, but if you hear from her ... you will let us know, won't you?'

Fletcher stared at him.

'How many dead?' he asked.

'Better than we usually do,' replied Adversane with a grim face. 'Four – one.'

'A woman in first class?' asked Fletcher

Adversane nodded.

'May I also remind you of those papers you signed in Todmorden,' he said. 'One word astray and you'll be sleeping with the enemy: the absinthe dorms, dear boy ... Wormwood. Plenty of old acquaintances with open arms, eh?'

He stood up and went to the door where he paused, looked like he was going to say something else, but changed his mind and was gone without another word, smoke and scent lingering in the air.

Fletcher closed his eyes.

* * * * *

June 15th. 5.30 pm. Berlin.

Ferris lay naked on the bed beside the woman. Both covered in blood and sweat, but only her blood. Her eyes and mouth were still open. The gaping wound had stopped bleeding.

After a few minutes when his breathing regained its normal pace, he rolled over and stood up. Without looking at the woman he picked up the phone and made a brief call.

He took a leisurely shower and got dressed for his evening engagement. The woman's body would be removed while he was out and the room cleaned.

In the car on the way to the party he stared at his reflection in the window. Not as heroically handsome as his brother, but what use was that to him now, mouldering in his cell.

Where his brother had been lion-maned, with typical Scots baronial flaming hair, he was dark like his diminutive mother. Probably the only thing he ever thanked her for.

He hated parties with their forced bonhomie and adolescent sexual shadow boxing, but tonight he was relaxed and open to more mundane opportunities than last night's excesses. It hadn't finished until mid-afternoon, when he'd come back to put her out of her misery, after inflicting yet more excruciating and exciting pain.

As the car slowly cruised towards the hotel, he saw a thick-set man striding along on the pavement. The sort of confident gait that he imagined Fletcher would have. The car passed the man, and Ferris caught a glimpse of his face. He doubted the detective would have such a ridiculous moustache and shook his head. He'd told himself to forget him. The moment had passed. There were plenty more opportunities for him to explore in this cesspit of a city. The Wall wouldn't last forever and there were fortunes to be made if you had the right connections and were unafraid to use them.

The car pulled up outside the brightly lit portico and he stepped out into the warm night air. At the same moment a tall blonde woman appeared in the entrance and held her hand out towards him. They smiled at each other and he took her hand. They made a striking couple. The doors opened and they disappeared inside.

* * * * *

Wednesday 16th June 9.30 am Penrith

Fletcher heard the post drop onto the floor in the hall. He didn't go straight away. Laura was at work and he'd been reading the paper, which was full of the surrender of the Argentine forces in Stanley. Fletcher had ignored most of it and gone straight to the sports pages where England's chances against France were being hyped up, now that the government had decided to let the team play in the World Cup. There was little chance of them meeting the Argentines until the final, which neither team was likely to manage.

He'd still not heard any news from DCI Aske and it was now well into the second week of his enforced absence. It was beginning to feel like a suspended sentence. The nightmares had started to recede, but looking in the mirror he knew he still looked like a zombie.

He put the kettle on and looked out of the window. It was difficult to believe that most of the investigation in Ennerdale had been conducted in the pouring rain. The sun was stuck up there in a blinding blue sky like in a child's painting.

As the kettle began to grumble, he went to fetch the post.

Lots of rubbish and a few bills.

And a post card.

From Ireland.

On the front a wooded scene with hills in the distance and a lake.

On the back a few words written in an awkward hand.

"We shall overcome. Some day."

He closed his eyes.

Her face swam before him.

Her hand came up …

… and swept her ruby shining hair to one side.

The phone rang.

He picked it up.

'Fletcher?'

'Yes.'

'DCI Aske. How are you?'

'Fine … and you, sir?'

'Okay…'

Fletcher heard him hesitate and feared the worst.

'Look I won't beat about the bush,' said Aske.

Fletcher held his breath.

'First thing, your commendation will be awarded this Thursday at the station. You, Superintendent Conroy, and me. No guests … or press, obviously.'

Fletcher made no response. He couldn't think of any.

'You still there?'

'Yes, sir,' he replied

Aske hesitated again and then said what he'd been told to say.

Fletcher listened, but didn't understand.

'What?'

Aske repeated what he'd said.

'Where's that?'

Aske told him.

Fletcher put the phone down.

The postcard fell to the floor.

About the Author

Rick Lee was born in North Yorkshire in 1948, went to study History in London in the late 60's, but spent most of his time going to Jimi Hendrix and Cream concerts, whilst squatting in a series of elegant but condemned Edwardian mansions.

He became a drama teacher in 1974 and later studied for a MEd in Education through Drama with Dorothy Heathcote. He worked in a variety of secondary schools, colleges, special needs departments and residential homes – including a 4 year spell as Senior Advisory Teacher with Leicestershire LEA – after which he returned up north to be a Head of an Expressive Arts Department in Barrow-in-Furness, followed by 5 years working for the Barrow Educational Action Zone and as an education consultant. As well as classroom drama, he was also writing and directing plays with students including several successful Edinburgh Fringe productions.

He has an MA in Writing Studies from Lancaster University and written many short stories and has already published two volumes of poems. His involvement in outdoor education, taking city kids into the wilds of Snowdonia, the Lake District and the mountains and islands of Scotland, have provided the backdrop for his London cop's adventures.

He moved to France in 2006 to enjoy retirement – although serious bouts of DIY and gardening have kept him busy!

He began writing the Mick Fletcher suspense thrillers two years ago and has not been able to stop since!

Other titles by Rick Lee

DAUGHTER OF THE ROSE   ISBN 9781908098474

(Extract)

Fern Robinson didn't become a serial killer until after her mother had died.

She'd not lingered, slipping away unaccompanied in her sleep as the sun set on her eightieth birthday Sunday February 29th 1976. Fern had been the previous evening. Her mother was asleep most of the time when she visited. Fern knew that it wasn't the drugs. She wasn't ill, didn't complain of any pain, but the nurses did it as a matter of course. Afterwards Fern found a stash of them in a hidden pocket of her handbag. She showed the staff nurse, who pulled a face. Fern had smiled at her. She'd enjoyed that – stuck-up cow.

Her mother had only opened her eyes the once that last visit. Fern was reading and had looked up instinctively to find the clear blue eyes gazing straight at her.

'One white rose, my dear. Only the one.'

Fern was about to speak, but her mother gave her a contented smile and closed her eyes. She knew then that her mother was going to die the next day. She knew why and the anger began to ferment.

Ursula Robinson was buried in the Shap graveyard on the third of March 1976, alongside her mother Annie. She'd outlived many of the folk who'd been evacuated from Mardale, but there was nearly twenty people at the funeral – many of whom Fern didn't know. Folk like them didn't say much, but Annie's niece

Elizabeth was there. She didn't walk so well and was helped to the graveside by her son, John. She looked down at the single white rose which Fern had obediently placed on the coffin.

'Ay, well,' the old lady said. 'There's a strange tale goes wi yon flower, lassie.'

Fern looked at the old lady, who she knew was just a bit older than her mother. She might be crippled with arthritis, but the hazel eyes beamed intelligently.

'I know,' said Fern quietly.

She could feel the gaze on her, but wouldn't meet it. Eventually she heard the old lady sigh.

'Some things are best forgotten. No point in digging up old bones, eh lass?'

Fern looked at her. Old bones? What did she know? She decided it was best not to ask.

'I'll not forget,' she said and turned away. She walked out of the graveyard without another word. She knew where she was going.

* * * *

A RIPPLE OF LIES   ISBN 9781908098771

(Extract)
Saturday June 20th 1981

Luca paid the entrance fee and accepted the guide pamphlet. He found the man sitting on a bench looking over a large stone walled pond. He nodded and sat the other end of the bench.

'One of the main breeding places of the great-crested newt,' said the man.

'So I understand,' replied Luca, having glanced at the pamphlet.

They sat in silence for a few minutes as a noisy family took over the arena for a while.

'Decapitation and hand severing,' said the man.

Luca nodded.

'Positively medieval,' he added.

'We try to make the punishment fit the crime as often as we can,' said Luca with a smile.

The man stood up and slowly made his way towards the outer wall. They passed through the gate and set off down towards the river.

'I'm afraid we don't have the luxury of such a close encounter for you this time.'

'Long range is possible.'

'We know that or otherwise you wouldn't be here.

Luca was silent. He didn't take rebukes easily.

'However, the contract is complicated. One kill to cover another.'

Luca waited. They were strolling through the trees alongside the meandering stream.

'The date is fixed. First of July. We're not sure of the time, but imagine it will be early afternoon. Trafalgar. A suitably iconic name. The second target is a moveable feast. You choose the when and how it coincides with the more high profile target, who will have the highest level of security the British government are capable of providing. The secondary target is no easy hit either, which is why we are hiring you as a team. We suspect your two sexually excessive companions might be a great help in this second enterprise, but beware – he is utterly ruthless. We suggest you also enlist the help of the local criminal fraternity led by a nice wee chap called Eric Nellis.'

They'd come back up to the car park.

'My two companions will drive you back to Appleby.

Goodbye.'

The man wandered off and disappeared round the corner. Before Luca could consider anything else, the woman appeared and guided him back to the car. Quarter of an hour later he was deposited by the bridge in town with an envelope in his inside pocket.

He walked into town, found his car and drove back to the hotel he'd selected in a smaller village not far from the garden he'd just visited. Back in his room he ordered a small lunch and sat down. From his pocket he took the envelope. Inside were two photographs: a man talking to another man in a suit at what looked like a private view with lots of people, pictures on the walls. The other was at night-time: the same man with his arm round a much younger woman. Tall with a short, cropped hairstyle. On the back was his name. Thomas Hadden.

Luca's lunch arrived. Afterwards he sat and looked out of the window at the garden. He waited for the phone call. He was still there when dusk began to fall.

****

SOME DANCE TO FORGET   ISBN 978-1-908098-94-81

(Extract)
Tuesday 17th October 1981

'Penny for them?' said a voice.

Fletcher found himself in a corner of the Agricultural Arms.

He looked at the person responsible for interrupting his daydream and recognised the landlady, Janice. The fact she was already all glammed up reminded him it must be Tuesday, market day in Penrith, and that soon the place would start to get busy. He looked down at his drink. He was relieved to see that it was

343

a coffee rather than a beer, as the old station clock on the wall declared it to be just before ten in the morning.

'Worth a lot more than that, Janice,' he said, as he picked up the cup.

'Oh, aye,' she asked with a smirk. 'Anyone I know?'

The coffee was cold. He rubbed his mouth.

'Wouldn't be seen dead in here, Janice. Far too posh.'

Janice smiled and leant over the table towards him, so that the mixed scents of musky perfume and acrid hairspray assailed him. He managed not to back away, but felt his nostrils betray him.

'Aye well, that's as maybe, but the offer's still open.'

He leant back into the leather seat. Was she serious? At this time in the morning? He shuddered at the thought, and as Laura was about to arrive any minute for her midmorning break, he thought it best to give Janice the cold shoulder.

'I'm no use before lunch, Janice, and in any case I've only had the one coffee so far, so be a love and get us a refill.'

Janice gave him a wink and weaved her way back to the bar. He sighed with relief as the sun burst through the window and caught the motes of dust she had disturbed. This instantly took him back to his daydream. How old was he? Ten or eleven? He couldn't be certain. He was in a farmyard with those German boys. Couldn't remember their names. It was round the corner from his Aunty Emily's house in the Rutland countryside: Rupert Bear land, green woods and fields snuggling amongst rolling hillsides into a misty distance. They'd made bows and arrows and were trying to hit one of the swallows, which dived and swooped in the hot air catching the flies that had swarmed around the baking walls of the echoing hay barns. They'd never hit one, but it didn't stop them from trying until they were sweating and coughing in the dust they'd kicked up, and the boys' English mother brought them some juice. Even as he recalled that moment, the farmer's daughter smiled her way into his memory, bringing with her that evanescent sense of lost desire. She must have been ten or twelve years older than him, but that hadn't mattered. He had lusted after her in the sultry summer nights and recalled the time she'd taken them in her car to a nearby village, the smell of her brown wavy hair still lingering just out of reach.

He opened his eyes and realised he couldn't remember her name. He sighed again, but before he could question why he was thinking of that time, the door swung open and DS Irene Garner stood silhouetted in the doorway. She quickly focussed on her superior and made her way towards him.

'She's started again,' she said.

Before he could he question this, she confirmed his immediate fear.

'Woman's body found yesterday afternoon in the woods near Alnwick. It's Rose. Her signature all over it, apparently. DI Nixon has asked for you to go over straight away.'

He sighed a third time. His girlfriend Laura had followed Irene through the door. One glance told her that their rendezvous had just been hi-jacked. Fletcher explained what he'd just learnt, but that didn't improve her mood. He told Irene to go and make the necessary arrangements and delayed the inevitable as long as he could. One moment he was dreaming about one woman and within the space of a few moments four others turned up to confuse and complicate his life: Janice, Irene, Laura and 'Rose White'…and now another victim. He didn't know her name yet, but Janice's interruption had been unknowingly prescient. The victim's name was Barbara 'Penny'. His old friend Cassie – another woman! – would have merely raised an eyebrow. Everything is connected, she would say.

'He's your son.'

'What?'

'He's called Christian – although he prefers Chris.'

There was a pause. She could hear his breathing.

'What do you want?'

She bit back the sob.

'I don't want anything. I owe you my life. I don't know why I didn't . . . tell you before.'

There was another long pause. She could hear voices in the background, laughter ... it sounded like a pub.

'I'm sorry. Who are you again?'

'Roz.'

'Roz?'

She began to think this was a bad idea. He didn't sound like the man she remembered; although to be fair it was thirty years ago. No. More than that, Chris was thirty-one two weeks ago.

'Todmorden. February 1980. Michael Quirke,' she said.

Someone was speaking to him. He must have put his hand over the phone because she could only here muffled sounds. She thought of putting the phone down.

'Okay. Listen, I'll ring you back,' he said.

'I hope you do,' she said.

She listened. He was still there.

'I will. I promise ... just give me an hour or so.'

She couldn't think of anything to say, but couldn't cut the connection. Neither did he.

'I do remember you. In the Bear. Blonde spiky hair.'

She laughed.

'Not any more.' She paused. 'It's good to hear your voice, Mick. Ring me back. I've lots to tell you.'

She pressed the red button.

* * * * *

It was lunchtime and the bar was full. A group of walkers had just come in out of the rain, leaving muddy boot-marks all over the place and pile of waterproofs dripping in the entrance hall. Laura and Freddy were at full stretch in the kitchen and Julie was struggling with the variety of drinks this crowd was asking for, behaving as if they were a gang of CAMRA spies. Laura had asked him to get some more hotpots out of the cellar freezer and been disconcerted with his faraway look.

'Who was that?' she asked.

'I'll tell you later,' he replied and opened the door to the cellar.

Two minutes later he was stood at the bottom of the stairs wondering what he'd come down for. He knew it was something urgent, but all he could think of was getting into a battered old multi-coloured VW Beetle right outside this pub – although of course, he didn't own it then – the pub that is.

'Are you alright, Mick,' shouted Laura from the top of the stairs.

He jolted into action. More hotpots! He opened the freezer door and pulled out a plastic crate.

The rest of the lunchtime passed in a blur of past and present like a revolving film set. When Laura had gone upstairs for her afternoon nap, he sat with a cup of tea looking out across the valley. Back then there'd been one of the heaviest snow falls he'd ever seen. Grace had been just fourteen and he'd been on the brink of one of the most terrifying rollercoaster events of his life. He and Laura had only been together for a few weeks and it nearly didn't last. Roz had slipped in and out of his life in those dark days when Laura kicked him out. But it was Roz who'd given them the vital information that had helped them stop Michael Quirke from carrying out his insane mission.

He'd not thought about her for years. He knew she'd been provided with a fresh identity and a new start, but he'd not been told any of that and had assumed that's how she'd wanted it. Now this? A son? He couldn't take it in. What was he going to say to Laura? Was it true? What did Roz want? A thousand questions crowded into his head. He picked up the phone.